ESSENCE OF STONE

ALSO BY HALEY RYLANDER

LIFESTONE TRILOGY

Essence of Stone

Ashes of Stone

Shaping of Stone

LIFESTONE TRILOGY BOOK 1

ESSENCE OF STONE

HALEY RYLANDER

Aspen Leaf
Press

Aspen Leaf
Press

CONTENTS

Prologue   1

PART I

1. A Request   9
2. Electricity   23
3. Feast Interrupted   33
4. Earthquakes and Vierstone   47
5. The Kindom Council   59
6. To Run a City   77
7. The Hunt Begins   87
8. Heat Rising   97
9. Shadows of Mind and Past   113
10. Invisible Links   121
11. Crafting and Councils   137
12. A Meeting for Mutiny   153
13. Shadows in the Mist   163
14. A Vision Obscured   173

PART II

15. Tradira   181
16. The Politics of Mansions   193
17. The Black Stain   201
18. Into the Void   209
19. The Dacian Ball   215
20. Outside the Walls   227
21. Spreading Stains   241
22. The Alliance   253
23. The Fall   267
24. Monsters Among Us   273
25. Walls of White   287
26. An Audience of Men   299

PART III

27. Knife in the Night — 313
28. A Spar of Two — 327
29. Writhing River — 333
30. A Pillar of Stone — 343
31. Through the Gates — 361
32. Under the Hood — 367
33. Nescari — 379
34. A Thirsty Ride — 387
35. Restring Pass — 391
36. Soldiers Hidden — 399
37. The Horn — 403
38. Swords on All Sides — 409
39. To Save a City — 413
40. Shadows of the Past — 419
41. A Fleet of Ships — 425

Epilogue — 429

Character List — 433
Ashes of Stone Preview — 439
Acknowledgments — 451
About the Author — 453

For David and Pamela

TERULIAN MOUNTAINS
CIEL
MORCANAN
RIVERSEEP FOREST
YAVRAN
THE WILDWOOD
LAY HILLS
REMSGRAEN
LAKE ORHIRION
MARAMOR
ARD GAEL
RONE
BRAIDED RIVER
THE GRASSLANDS
ORHIRI RIVER
TELEM FIER
CALAFOR
TURA
SEMESTRIAL SEA
FAERAN

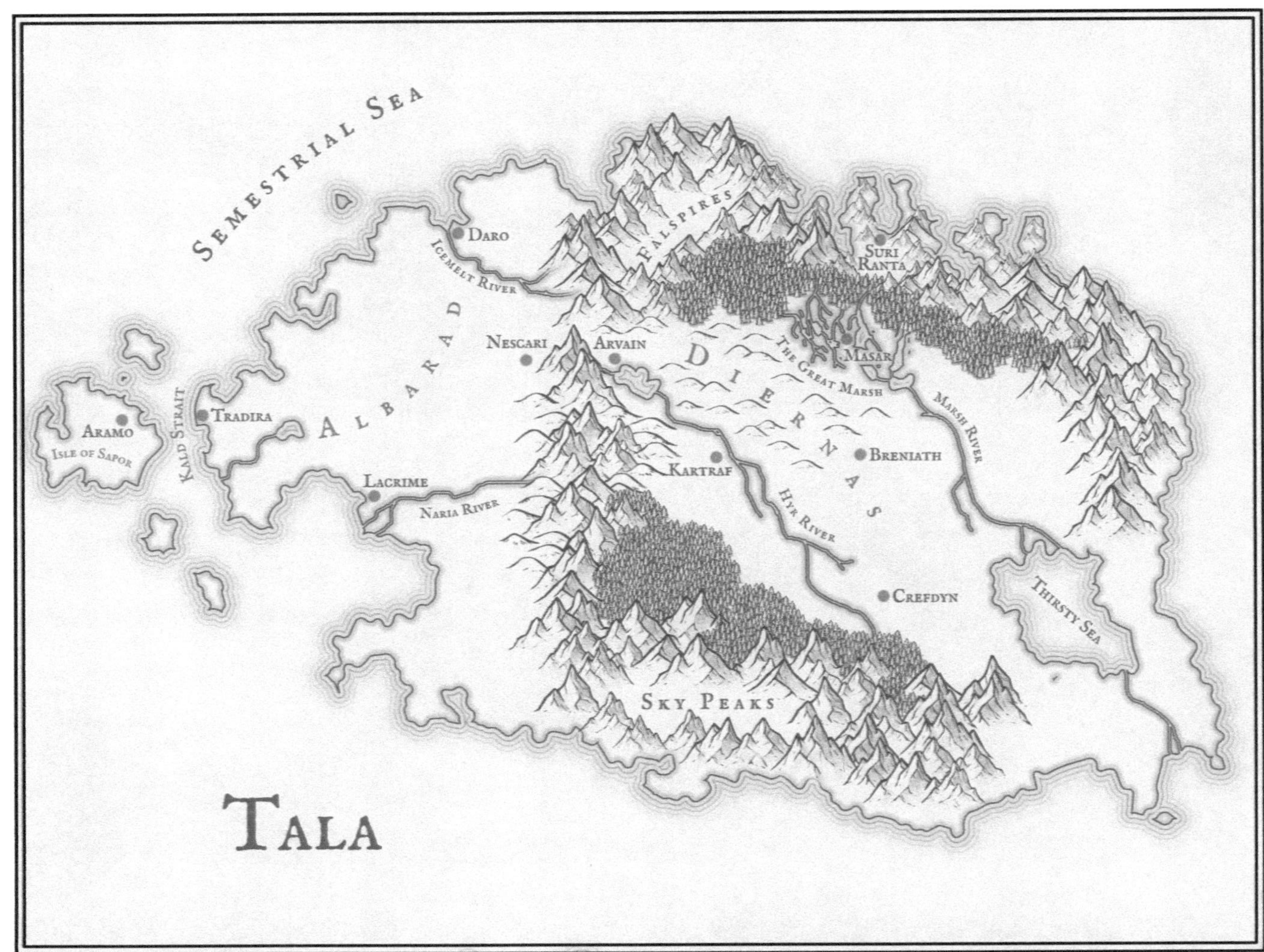

SEMESTRIAL SEA
DARO
ICEMELT RIVER
FALSPIRES
SURI RANTA
NESCARI
ARVAIN
DIERNAS
THE GREAT MARSH
MASAR
MARSH RIVER
ARAMO
ISLE OF SAPOR
KALD STRAIT
TRADIRA
ALBARAD
KARTRAF
BRENIATH
LACRIME
NARIA RIVER
HYR RIVER
CREFDYN
THIRSTY SEA
SKY PEAKS
TALA

PROLOGUE

Eldian's breath came hot in his throat. Adrenaline was crackling through his nerves, and he had hardly slept in days. His fists clenched around a spear as another chunk of stone hurtled past him to shatter on the steps below. He kept running.

Where was it? The beast had flown past minutes before, then disappeared amid the tiered buildings.

He had to get higher.

Eldian's eyes locked on the nearest lift. Was there still power in the city? He ran onto the metal platform and kicked the lever with more force than he intended. For a moment he thought the magnets would not activate, but then a low hum sounded, and the platform rose into the air with a buoyant cadence. The lift rose faster and more smoothly as it gained height and stopped level with a street four stories above.

Eldian made to step off the lift, then stiffened. Cold rippled over his skin.

A panther had stepped around a pile of rubble to the right of the lift. It bared black teeth and yowled. Eldian shuddered at the unearthly sound and raised his spear. His eyes darted along the rooftops. He didn't have time for this. Some of the army had already slipped into the city. The panther was evidence of that.

The cat lunged at him with a hair-raising hiss. Its eyes were crimson and held a light far more sentient than any cat should possess. A corrupted terra spirit, or maybe a flame spirit? It didn't matter. They were all corrupted now. Eldian dodged to the side and speared the beast in the ribs, then jumped off the lift and kept running.

The elves had held the army at bay for two days, but they were running out of strength. Riu above, they had been fighting for two centuries. The strength of the elves had run dry long before today. Now every Kindom was here, hoping to accomplish in one last united force what they had failed to do for two hundred years.

But Eldian knew what the rest did not. This force of elves was imperative to the phoenix's defeat, but without Eldian, it would never succeed. There was a reason neither elf nor weapon had killed the phoenix in all this time, but knowing the answer held as much danger as salvation. Eldian braced himself against the sucking fear in his chest. The answer would die with him. It was for the best.

Around him, the roar of flames mingled with the distant screaming of beasts and elves. A crack of splintering stone sounded in the air. Eldian paused. He listened. Neither common beast nor wight could have broken stone like that, possessed by spirits or not.

The sound had come from the western tower.

Eldian leaped over strewn rubble and made his way across one of the floating platforms of Maramor. The platforms were legendary in Faeran —the pride and joy of the city, and of Eldian.

Legendary and laborious.

He would have to cross three more to get to the western tower. The phoenix must be there. Eldian squinted at the backlit spire, trying to make out any signs of the beast.

When Eldian had seen the phoenix fly over Maramor, he had known the end was in sight. It meant the elven wall had failed at last; the great bird was a herald to its army. This was Eldian's only chance.

A group of elves ran past, coming from the direction Eldian pursued.

"Get to the river!" one of them shouted. "The Fieri have regrouped on the lake."

Eldian recognized the elf, but could not place his name. The man's hair was dusted with ash, his face sprinkled with blood.

Eldian nodded. He watched the elves disappear down a spiraling stair, then continued his ascent to the west.

He could not defend Maramor; Eldian had always known that. If the Great Cities could not stand against the phoenix, Maramor did not stand a chance. Yet Eldian had agreed to lead this last defense. He had remained here with his people. He had waited, and the phoenix had come.

He gripped his spear harder. He ran faster.

Another lift. Another platform.

Eldian's chest was burning. He crossed a bridge and slashed the throat of a ragged wolf. Would he have to face a wight before the end?

One more platform.

A shriek emitted from the western tower, and Eldian saw the outline of wings rise above its spire; they flamed against the dying sun.

Yes.

He crossed the platform in bounding strides, then slid to a stop.

"Father!"

Eldian stared in horror. Tornac stood at the base of the tower, a sword in his hand. Surrounding him was the Council of Maramor—four of Eldian's most trusted advisors. His friends. They weren't supposed to be here.

"What are you doing here?" Eldian's voice was hoarse. A new kind of fear gripped his insides as he looked at his eldest son. "Where are your brothers?"

"Heading off the army in the mountains." A wild fire burned in Tornac's eyes. "I came alone, followed the phoenix when it left the armies." His eyes flicked to the top of the tower, then to the elves around him. "Come with us. We will end this."

Pity and grief twisted Eldian's stomach at the look on Tornac's face. He knew the look of one ready to face his death—eager to face his death. Eldian should have known Tornac would try something like this. It had only been a few weeks since Vyra's death.

Eldian's Council looked at him with guilt.

As they should. They should have turned Tornac away at the gates.

"Go to your brothers."

Tornac stared at Eldian. "What?"

"Go. Now! They need you more than I."

Anger flashed in Tornac's eyes, but whatever he would have said died in his throat as another shriek rent the air and a fiery tail lashed down from the top of the tower. Stone exploded to their right, and Eldian shielded his head with his arms. The phoenix had seen them.

"Go now!" Eldian's desperation mounted. Tornac could not be here. He could not go into the tower.

"I'm not leaving you." The wild look had returned to Tornac's face.

Eldian ran a hand through his hair in frustration, then looked his son in the eyes. "Listen to me. I can kill it. I can kill the phoenix. I know how." He held up a hand. "There is no time to explain. You must trust me."

The phoenix's tail lashed again. Eldian could feel the bird's liquid eyes boring into him.

He ran to the side of the tower. The other elves flattened themselves against the stone beside him.

He knew Tornac would not leave. None of them could escape now, anyway. Eldian tried to think, but there was too much happening around him. Ash was raining from the sky. Fire licked the sides of the tower. Elves shouted far below, toward the river.

The phoenix would collapse the tower. It would flatten them against the walls with its tail. It would land on the platform and ruin everything. Eldian turned to his son.

"There is something you can do. Distract it. Keep its focus downward while I go up the tower. It must stay where it is. Can you do this for me?"

Tornac hesitated, clearly loath to remain outside while his father entered the tower, but then resolve settled on his face and he nodded.

"All of you, help him," Eldian said.

Tornac and the others leapt out from the shelter of the wall and turned their faces to the sky, weapons lifted in challenge.

Eldian took one last look at his son's face before moving along the side of the tower to the entrance. Fear made his limbs go rigid. The terror of the beast above froze the air in his lungs. His hand reached automatically for the vierstone pierced through his ear, but this last comfort was denied him. He had taken the earring out before the battle. He would not be able to complete his task with the stone against his skin.

Eldian held his spear to his chest and pulled a dagger from his hip. He shivered as the cold surface of the hilt-less blade met his skin.

Riu save us all.

He entered the tower.

PART I

1

A REQUEST

The first earthquake came thirty-six hours after the human's arrival. It was difficult for Gellion to determine which of the two events would mean more strife for Daro. Both were unexpected. Both were unwelcome. The coincidence of the circumstances made Gellion's skin burn. It made his planning obsolete, his sleepless nights for nothing, his centuries of building and perfecting somehow diminished. Gellion couldn't allow it. The schemes of an emissary and a geological upheaval would not sink him. Not again.

That it all happened in the space of two days was unsettling enough, but to happen the first two days of the Kindom Council? It wasn't fair. If Gellion could have gotten past his anxiety enough to consider it, it was even suspicious. But even before his plans had the chance to shatter in his hands, Gellion had been a writhing mess of nerves. For days, thoughts slipped through his mind, pens slipped through his fingers, and any attempt at sleep was as evasive and pointless as trying to shape wood with lifestone.

Thus it was that on the day of the ship's arrival, before any humans or earthquakes had come to truly disrupt his life, Gellion rose early and frayed and set his feet toward a place where he would not be able to see the advent of his pride and his doom. He went where he always went to occupy his mind, to escape the obligation of society and the emotions it necessitated—to do something.

The arena was unnaturally silent, and cleaner than it had a right to be. Glancing around to ensure he was alone, Gellion stepped from stone onto sand and looked up at the sky, barely touched by the first light of dawn. Rows of benches framed the star-salted orb and fell in circling ranks to the edges of the arena. Their emptiness was unnerving—far more unnerving than Gellion had anticipated. Solitude he had sought, but not this sterility. The air was laden with the oppressive weight of a space prepared and preserved. Waiting.

Gellion ground his teeth and dragged his feet through the too-pristine sand as he crossed the arena to a rack of staves. He knocked several of the weapons over as he reached for one but assured himself that the action was out of further spite, not due to his unsteady hands. Ignoring the dislodged staves, Gellion slid his fingers around the tallest staff still standing.

The effect was instantaneous. The lifestone stud pierced through the cartilage in Gellion's ear warmed, and a gentle heat rippled over his skin until it reached the tips of his fingers and transferred into the staff. The metal of the weapon seemed to awaken against his skin. A lattice of atoms. Structured. Simple, yet beautifully complex.

Any shaking of Gellion's muscles stilled. He took a slow breath, and his mind settled as readily as his body. Grasping the staff with both hands, Gellion focused on its solid, unchanging physicality.

The bones of metal were derived from stone, and "stone was the living essence that bound the world." Thus were the words of Gellion's mentor. It seemed lifetimes rather than centuries since Gellion had last heard the dramatic phrase uttered, yet the memory was still sharp as shattered glass, and far more cutting.

Gellion's hands tightened around his staff.

Do not think of him. Not now.

Loath as Gellion ever was to dwell upon reminiscences of his past mentor, it was even more vital to suppress them in light of the company sailing to his shore in mere hours—a company that shared those memories.

Just a few hours.

Were the elves from Faeran only hours away? Were they still hours away?

If Gellion knew a given day would bring his death, he would pray to Riu for the minutes to double their speed so he could meet it faster. To wait was to think, to feel, to dwell. Always better to be doing, to busy the mind and hands until the past and the future could take no space in the present.

That was why he was here.

Giving his head a firm shake, Gellion re-centered his attention to the metal in his hands and slid his feet over gritting sand into the first steps of the A'vaeri. The muscles in his arms follow suit with smooth and thoughtless fluidity.

Focus. Center. Balance.

Some of the tension in Gellion's muscles evaporated through his skin into the unnatural silence of the arena. His released emotions seemed to disperse the sterility pressing upon him. Taking a breath, Gellion closed his eyes and moved his body through the next motions. Then the next.

It was only when a voice ripped him back to the arena that Gellion realized he had finally achieved a true sense of calm. Scrubbing the glower from his face with the back of his hand, he turned toward the voice to see an elf striding toward him—a familiar woman, but not one Gellion knew personally. Strands of dark hair floated around her head in a frizzed halo, and a sheen of sweat slicked her skin. Gellion could feel the cool damp of his own skin and noticed with a start that the sun had nearly cleared the arena's walls. A thrill of adrenaline lit up his nerves. Had the ship arrived? Conflicted as he was about greeting the Council's arrival, Gellion knew his absence would be both noted and frowned upon, even by ever-grinning Dulon. The woman before him now was certainly not grinning.

"This is where you've been all morning?" The woman threw a hand into the air and glared at the empty arena as though accusing it of concealing the object of her pursuit. "Nearly an hour I've been searching this city for you, fighting crowds for space on the lifts. The Rale paths aren't even usable in this mess!" The woman flattened her palms over her flyaway hair, but the strands stood up again as soon as she dropped her hands. "Dulon sent for you."

Gellion's stomach twisted. "At the wharf—"

"No, not the wharf!" the woman said. "The Domes. There's an emissary. Just arrived. Urgent." The intensity of her glare intensified on the last word.

Gellion's brows pulled together. "An emissary? From where?"

The woman shrugged. "He's human," she said, as though this negated the question. With that, she spun on a heel to leave the arena, clearly of the opinion that her job was done.

Gellion stared after her. By the time his shock dispelled and more questions rose to his tongue, the messenger was already lost to the streets of Daro. Gellion's nails sank deep into the skin of his palms. All the heat he had dispelled through his work gathered anew in his chest, hotter than ever.

A human? Humans rarely conducted trade with the elves in person, and never without forewarning. Of all the days for one to show up on a whim. Gellion would have to deal with the emissary before the Council arrived. Dulon was doubtless entertaining the man already. Gellion ran a hand through his hair and tried to smooth his damp shirt. He would be as late to the unplanned meeting as he was disheveled.

Cursing, Gellion dropped his staff in the sand and hurried toward the Court of Daro.

The air in the Domes of Rhelyon was a cold shock against the sweat Gellion had accumulated in his rush. He tried to wipe the moisture from his face as he made his way to the building's main meeting room. The negligent messenger had not even specified where Gellion was supposed to meet Dulon, but knowing the Lord of Daro, he would take any human emissary to the most impressive room in the city. A hint of a grin broke through Gellion's frustration when the dregs of voices began to float down the hall. His instincts had been correct. Even muffled by metal and stone, Dulon's familiar voice rose and fell with unmistakable grandeur. No doubt the human was at least being thoroughly entertained as he waited.

Gellion paused outside the doors and took his second deep breath of the day. He could allow no remnants of his ill-suppressed nerves to enter this room. Fortunately, a diplomat's practiced charm came nearly as easily to Gellion as the flow of the A'vaeri.

With a final tug on his shirt and a barely forced smile, he dropped his hand to the door handle.

The voices within the room trailed off at once, and two figures stood and turned to face him.

Gellion assessed the human in a glance. The man had the look of one who spends his life studying other men—influencing other men. The gaze he passed over Gellion was hungry and intelligent. He had to tilt back his head to meet Gellion's eyes, but did so with a confidence that somehow suggested Gellion was in the wrong for being tall.

"Ah! You are Gellion?" The man's accent bounced over the words. He spoke Albaren.

"Yes." Gellion eyed the emissary's olive skin and dark hair. Albaren, certainly, but his features were unfamiliar. Gellion preferred to be more informed of his political relations before meeting with them. Annoyed by his own ignorance, he said, "And you are?"

"Amadeo Benta." The answer came not from the Albaren man, but from a fair-haired elf standing behind him. Dulon, the Lord of Daro, stepped forward with a half-hearted grin. "An Earl from Tradira." He gave Gellion a meaningful look.

Tradira was the capital of Albarad. Gellion paused in surprise, then nodded his understanding. Any messenger from the city was likely sent by the Albaren king. This was an even more unusual occurrence than Gellion had first thought. He gathered himself and flashed a smile at Amadeo.

"An honor to make your acquaintance, Earl Benta. I apologize for the wait—it is a busy day in Daro, and Dulon's messenger had trouble finding me. I hope I have not inconvenienced you."

"Oh not at all, not at all!" Amadeo returned Gellion's smile with interest. His teeth were very white. "I have been admiring your city." He swept an arm toward the windows that stretched from the ceiling to the floor. "An incredible sight indeed. I hardly believed the stories, but even they do not do it justice."

Gellion accepted the compliment without comment. "Please, sit." He motioned to the chairs Amadeo and Dulon had vacated upon his arrival. Taking a pitcher from a nearby table, he tilted it into a glass.

"I did not know we were expecting a visit from Tradira. What brings you so far north?" Gellion watched Amadeo over the rim of his glass. The man's countenance betrayed no hint of his purpose.

"I had business in the north. Dull matters—taxes, complaints—I am sure you know how it is." Amadeo tried to draw the elves in with his eyes like they were a secret club. Gellion watched him with some fascination. The man's eyes were like pools of rich mud. Gellion had always found humans' eyes disconcerting—unfeeling and inexpressive compared with the shining green irises of the elves.

Gellion did not, in fact, know what Amadeo was talking about. The politics and economics of the humans had always perplexed him. The elves did not have taxes; they did not have coins with which to pay them.

"Of course," said Gellion, joining Amadeo and Dulon around the low table. "Daro is only a stop of interest for you then?"

"Oh, of interest, and of other matters." Amadeo waved a dismissive hand. "I did bring the season's trade propositions, along with some small tokens of our continued friendship."

Gellion and Dulon exchanged a glance.

"Oh?" said Dulon. He turned his face to the side as though checking on the pitcher of tea but slipped a wink at Gellion. Gellion had to wrestle his grin into a polite smile. While he was aware of no palpable hostility between their two races, he would hardly call them 'friends.'

"Certainly," said Amadeo. "The elves of Daro have always been most gracious to our king and to our people. It is the least we can do to show our thanks with what humble gifts we can afford: soft wool from our finest herds, pearls from the shores of Tradira, specialty spices from the Isle of Sapor. I left them with your servants."

Dulon's eyes flashed at the last word, a break in his usual cheery composure, but he did not dispute the term. "You are generous, Earl Benta," he said in a measured tone. "We will, of course, look over your trade documents and respond in kind."

Amadeo bowed his head. There was a moment of silence. Amadeo turned his face to the windows. Several stories below, the city descended in giant steps to the foot of the sea. Ribbons, swaths of cloth, and stringed lights shimmered in the sunlight through the Court and the streets. The mass of movement of the city's inhabitants toward the wharf was evident from this height. Gellion glanced toward the water, but saw no sign of a ship.

"You are having festivities?" Amadeo said. "Or is your city always so?"

"We are expecting visitors." Gellion hoped the man would take the hint and get on with his intentions.

"Ah, I am sorry to intrude upon your celebration, but I admit I am not sorry to see it—an amazing sight!"

Gellion watched Amadeo shrewdly. The man was prattling now.

"Are there any other matters you wish to discuss?" Gellion asked.

Amadeo looked between Gellion and Dulon, then a corner of his mouth drew up in a smile, his sleek mustache stretching.

"Yes," he said at last. "I was in the north on other business, but it is true I did not come to Daro merely to discuss trade, nor to see your great city. King Naval has sent me with a message—a request if you will."

Dulon and Gellion kept their impassive gazes on Amadeo, waiting. When the silence of the elves did not break, Amadeo continued.

"The King seeks to expand the friendship between the Albaren and the elves, to form an alliance between himself and the Lords of Daro." He fixed his eyes on each of them in turn. "An alliance of war."

Gellion kept his face carefully composed against the shock of heat that had spread from his chest. His eyes roved Amadeo's face, but he could read nothing. It had always been so. The connection that flowed between elves like a current hit an abrupt wall at humans. The humans had a phrase: "unreadable as stone." Well, Gellion could read stone. He could understand it, see its parts, its behavior, but the inner workings of humans were entirely withheld from him.

"We are not interested," Dulon said.

Gellion let out his breath, grateful Dulon had broken the silence.

He clenched his fist and tried to regain the control he had assumed before entering the room.

"My lord—" Amadeo began

"We are not," Dulon repeated, "interested."

Amadeo took a breath. His serene smile had strained, but not dissipated. "May I explain?"

Dulon stared at the little man, scrutinizing him, then met Gellion's eye. There was nothing the man could say to change Dulon's mind. Gellion knew that. The elves had endured enough war for an eternity and would never enter another voluntarily. This knowledge calmed Gellion, yet his curiosity betrayed him. What could possibly drive the Albaren Empire to seek martial aid from the elves?

Gellion nodded once.

Amadeo began to speak.

"You are aware of the region of Diernas that shares our eastern border?"

Gellion had heard the name, but only in passing from his contact with the Albaren. He nodded.

"The Dierna are a savage people, a cruel people," Amadeo said. "Nonetheless we have harbored trade relations with them for centuries. We have tried to bring civilization to them repeatedly, to bring order and peace to their cities. They rebuke us. They cheat us in trade, encroach upon our borders, and raid our towns—towns of women and children! We have battled the Dierna for hundreds of years, but now their unrest and violence have escalated beyond precedence."

Amadeo paused for effect before continuing. "If we could but secure our border beyond the gap: drive back the Dierna from our lands, stop the senseless slaughter of our herds and our people ..." His eyes burned with emotion. "That is what we ask of you—the elves whom we have always respected, always treated fairly and with friendship, and from whom we have received nothing less. We do not have the men nor the power to make a quick end of this, but with your help, we may succeed." He entreated them with a look of earnest solemnity. "Will you help us bring peace to our people?"

The speech was so obviously rehearsed, Gellion would not have been surprised to find a hidden script in the man's sleeves, complete with acting cues. Gellion and Dulon exchanged no glance this time. They did not need to. Gellion leaned forward.

"I regret the pain of your people, Earl Benta. Well do we understand the suffering of war. But the elves will never agree to such an alliance. I am sorry."

Dulon's silence confirmed his assent, but Amadeo's smile did not falter.

"Is there anything else?" Dulon asked flatly.

Amadeo raised his eyebrows, clearly unperturbed. Gellion felt the heat of anger begin to rise within him at the man's patronizing smile.

"I do not think you understand—" Amadeo began.

"Oh, on the contrary," Dulon said. "I think we understand perfectly. And we are refusing."

The Earl's smile faded at last. "We could end this war within the month with the might of Daro behind us—in a single battle. Without your aid, the fighting could last years, with needless suffering and death. There would be almost no sacrifice on your part!"

"There is no battle without sacrifice," said Dulon. "And it is a sacrifice I am not willing to make."

"It would not be without reward."

"Reward?" Dulon scoffed. "Bribe, you mean. What would you offer us? Wool? Pearls? Spices? Or are you referring to jewels, or gold? The elves have no use for any of it. We need nothing." Dulon began to stand. "I am sorry, Earl Benta, but our answer is no."

"Not jewels," said Amadeo, a shadow of his smile returning. "Stone. A green stone, smooth as glass."

Gellion's insides turned to ice. Dulon froze as though struck.

The Lord of Daro stared at the ground for a moment, then slowly lowered himself back into his chair.

By the time Gellion reached the water's edge, the sun had ascended beyond the peak of the sky and begun to sink back to the west. The meeting with Amadeo had not gone on long after the man's jarring revelation, but Gellion and Dulon had sat in stunned silence for some time after his departure. Gellion's head was still reeling. As if hosting a month long Kindom Council in his own city wasn't enough to deal with. This changed everything.

Gellion shook his head, trying to control the measure of his breath.

The ship was still not here. He squinted at the horizon, searching for any sign of storms hanging over the water. Surely the ship had not been caught in any weather? The stone in Gellion's hand discounted the possibility. He had picked up the rock on his way to the wharf—something solid to occupy his hands while he waited. The stone was warm. Warm as life. Warmer than Gellion's own blood. Though he could still taste the last dregs of winter on the breeze, the heat of the rock and his sweat from the day was evidence that the sun had regained its strength for the spring. The hostility of the Semestrial Sea would have drained away with the cool winds of winter. No, the ship was simply running late.

This should have brought Gellion relief. The human's untimely arrival had not affected the start of the Kindom Council. Yet Gellion would have gladly missed half the Council itself if it meant he could forget the Albaren Earl's words.

Don't think about it now. You agreed to wait.

"There!"

Gellion dropped the stone in his hand. His brother had stepped up beside him and was pointing to the horizon, where the smudge of a ship now marred the seascape. Gellion's awareness came back to the present with as much grace as the stone, now cracked in two at his feet. He heard the docks creaking with the rise and fall of the water, accented by the cry of gulls. Underneath these sharp sounds ran a current of voices. Most of the elves of Daro stood at Gellion's back, their attention now pointed beyond him toward the crux of their anticipation.

"Don't look so thrilled," Valder's voice dripped with sarcasm, but the smile behind his tone was evident.

Gellion turned an irritated glance on his brother, but said nothing. He took a breath, trying to relieve the clenching of his diaphragm, and squinted against the sun to watch the ship progress toward the wharf. Its sides gleamed silver in the slanting sunlight. She was a narrow craft—all sloping lines and sharp points. A wrapped sail bulged against ropes on an aluminum mast, and Gellion could hear the gentle hum of the ship's motor above the slap of the surf.

A dozen coils of chains leapt from behind the ship's railing and into the hands of the elves waiting along the wharf. Metal met the wood of the docks with a resonant clap.

Silence fell.

First to step onto the gangplank of the ship was a straight-spined woman with a hairstyle as severe as the angles of her face. Liera, the Lady of Tura. Gellion had known she would be coming, but the knowledge did not prepare him for the shock her appearance dealt him. It was not that the woman had changed, it was that she was precisely the same. The same shrewd eyes, the same flat mouth always turned down at the corners—every bit the same woman who had been present in nearly every memory Gellion had spent the last two centuries failing to forget. Of course she would be the one to lead the Council off the ship.

Gellion dragged his eyes from Liera's face before she could return his stare and forced his attention to the other Council Members filing off the ship behind her. Each was a representative of one of the four elven Kindoms: the Fieri, the Morcani, the Remsgri, and the Turi. Liera was a Turi Council Member, as was Gellion's mother. Gellion ground his teeth against the fresh surge of his pulse. He did not yet see her among the bobbing heads.

"Come on," said Valder, moving away from the crowd to join the group of elves welcoming the new arrivals. Gellion stepped up behind him with markedly less enthusiasm.

Other elves from the ship, mostly traders and craftsmen, were joining the Council Members. The diversity was staggering in such a modest number—cropped hair, long braids, flowing locks, and bobbed ponytails. Skin of every shade showed beneath clothing that ranged from scant linen to flowing silk. Some of the Morcani had even worn their furs.

Gellion's eyes darted from face to face. Many of the countenances were familiar to him, but he had yet to identify those most welcome and dreaded to him when a voice split through the milling crowd.

"Welcome!" A grinning Dulon stepped up onto a beam of the docks, a ringmaster looking down upon his audience with arms spread wide. "We are thrilled to open the gates of our Great City to so many honored guests, friends, and kin." He paused, letting his words ring in the silence. Gellion hid a smile. "There will be a time for formalities, but it is not now. You have journeyed far, the evening approaches, and I can smell food all the way from the Court. Enjoy what remains of the day and leave your responsibilities for tomorrow!"

Dulon's speech was met with smiles and laughter from all but the Morcani and Liera, who narrowed their eyes in confusion. Dulon himself was Morcani by blood, but differed from his stoic kin as starkly as a parrot among a flock of falcons. It was not difficult to see why the man had left the severe mountains to make his home in Daro.

The crowds dispersed slowly and in all directions. Some elves moved to greet those coming off the ship while others left the water's edge to make their way to the third and highest tier of Daro, where food, music, and a night of celebration awaited.

Gellion watched those elves climbing away from the docks, then turned his boots back toward the ship. He huffed in annoyance at his pounding heart.

Riu, take this cursed cowardice.

A frantic motion caught his eye, and Gellion sucked in a breath. Valder had found their youngest brother, Veldon. He was waving at Gellion wildly over Veldon's back while they laughed and embraced. The two could have been twins with their black hair and matching smiles.

"Gellion!" Veldon had seen Gellion and was upon him before Gellion could reply. Gellion laughed and clasped one arm around his brother's back, surprised by the force of his joy at their reunion. For all that had happened in Faeran, Gellion had never feared rebuke or coldness from Veldon. His youngest brother was a testament to joy, with no capacity for resentment. His presence, however, meant that their mother must be close by.

No sooner had Gellion thought this, his hopes and fears became flesh. Over Veldon's shoulder stood their mother. Gellion's smile became more strained, but he forced it to keep its position. He pulled away from Veldon and straightened.

Tenille's auburn hair mirrored Gellion's own to the strand and swayed in the breeze. Every other part of her was still. Her eyes were fixed upon him, expressionless.

"Gellion," she said.

Valder and Veldon looked between Gellion and their mother, their smiles turning as strained as his own.

It had been over two hundred years since Gellion had seen his mother. Her letters during that time had been frequent enough, but always formal. He had brushed aside the finely structured accounts of Maramor and carefully worded inquiries after his work as the impartial objectivity of pen and paper—Tenille had never been a warm and gushing woman—but in the weeks leading to her arrival, Gellion had managed to convince himself that each letter's polite facade masked hostility and pain. This would not have bothered him as much if he did not feel he thoroughly deserved it.

Tenille raised an eyebrow.

Gellion knew he should say something, do anything other than stare at his mother with something between a grimace and the fearful eyes of a child caught in his transgressions, but all the anxiety he had felt leading to this moment seemed to have settled in his throat and was making a valiant effort to choke him.

For a moment longer, Tenille retained her frozen features, then her face melted into a smile. Eyes suddenly full of joy, she closed the distance between herself and her son in a single stride.

Gellion stiffened as her arms wrapped around him.

"I have missed you." She let out a breath against his shoulder that could have been a laugh or a suppressed sob. Gellion did not know which would be worse. He returned his mother's embrace as though she were made of spun glass, as afraid to return her emotions as he was to believe them.

Tenille squeezed him tighter. "All of us have missed you."

Gellion's tentative relief tempered at this. His mother's implication was obvious, but Gellion would give it no response.

To Gellion's substantial relief, his eldest brother had not accompanied the Kindom Council to Daro, but Tornac's absence made his mother's claim all the more unbelievable. Gellion would bet that Tornac missed him about as much as he missed the Great War.

"I missed you, too." Gellion backed the words with a more forceful hug. Whatever his misgivings about their reunion, he truly had missed his family. Most of them anyway. If Tenille chose to hold as little resentment as Veldon over his absence—or abandonment as Tornac would call it—Gellion should be grateful and move on. Pasting a smile on his face, Gellion stepped back from his mother so Valder could receive his own greeting.

"Ah, Tenille, I am glad you made the journey here at last!"

Gellion turned to see Dulon disengaging himself from the milling crowd. The Lord of Daro sauntered forward and bestowed an elaborate bow upon Gellion's mother as she slipped her arms from around Valder.

It was by conscious effort that Gellion did not roll his eyes. Dulon was an apt leader, and his knowledge of city infrastructure was as impressive as his political prowess, but his conduct generally seemed more suited to a stage than to a social gathering.

Dulon straightened, swinging his head to keep his hair from falling over his eyes. It was a practiced motion.

Tenille's eyebrow rose again, this time in obvious appraisal.

Dulon responded to her regard with a still more beaming smile. "A few of us are going on a turn about the city on the way to the Performance Hall," he said. "Would you care to join us?"

Tenille glanced at her sons. Gellion waved her on.

"Go," he said. "We will find you later."

Tenille eyed him for a moment, then nodded to Dulon.

"Very well," she said, and strode past him, ignoring his outstretched arm. Dulon gave Gellion a knowing look and a wink, dropped his arm, and followed her.

It was not until Gellion had watched them disappear up the nearest stairs that he noticed another elf standing still among the constant motion of the wharf. Liera stood near the ship, where elves were beginning to unload raw materials from Faeran. Her gaze was pointed not at the traders, however, but straight at Gellion. A muscle worked in her jaw, and Gellion could read the same caution and tangle of emotions upon her face as was burning beneath his own skin. She gave him a slow and stiff nod, then turned and followed the rest of the Council Members toward the city.

2

ELECTRICITY

Gellion walked with his brothers up Master's Street. The path was choked with elves, a stark contrast to the strips of closed shops bordering the street. Down the center of the road, a smooth path of metal followed the curvature of the street, lined on either side by discrete rails. Few elves were using the Rale path today. With crowds this thick, levit boards would hardly be faster than walking.

Veldon's eyes darted in all directions, shining with interest. Gellion felt a personal pride seeing his city through the eyes of one who never had. Before Daro existed, Gellion had been a part of the expeditions to find new sites of vierstone—lifestone. He had not been on the ship that had at last found deposits of the precious mineral along the sea cliffs of what was now Daro, but had immediately joined the elves sent to build the quarry and the city that stood beside it. Now Daro was at least as impressive as any of the Great Cities of Faeran.

"It's beautiful." Veldon's eyes were so big he looked as though he were trying to fit the whole city into them. "A city built upon the technology and craftsmanship of all the Kindoms."

"The fifth Great City indeed," said Valder, grinning at Gellion over their brother's enthusiasm.

Though the shops along the street were dark and empty in light of the evening's festivities, each bore the symbol of its purpose: metal smiths, stone workers, glass blowers, chemists, engineers—craftsmen and scientists of every vocation practiced their art on this street that wound its way through the second tier of the city.

At the end of the street, the brothers ascended a tall stair that rose between the city Archives and the Performance Hall. Each building soared upward from the curving cliff face like extensions of the white stone, with shining metal supports and filigree adorning their sides and windows.

Gellion took a deep breath. The scents of food were stronger now, and the resonant notes of a flute rode the breeze.

"The performance won't start for a while," said Gellion. He led the way to the Court, which stretched in front of the towering Domes of Rhelyon like a great carpet, with strips of grass, shrubs, and fountains weaving through the platform of stone. The Court was transformed for the festival. Translucent silks in every shade of blue hung from poles and trees, laced with strings of pearly lights that sent dancing reflections across the paved stones—reflected stars in shifting water.

Gellion's mouth watered at the rich smells around him. Within a quarter of an hour, the brothers were gathered at the edge of a fountain, each carrying his chosen delicacy.

"Was the sea cooperative?" Gellion asked Veldon, sinking his teeth into a thick skewer of fish.

"Cooperative enough. Rain, some nasty wind, but nothing unmanageable."

Gellion nodded. The Semestrial Sea was so named for its cyclical nature. Six months of the year, the waters presented a smooth expanse of easy sailing between Daro and Tura, the Great City on the southeast tip of Faeran. The other six months of the year, it was a heaving, violent beast that prevented all travel between the two continents. This first week of spring marked the sea's taming for the coming seasons, and the Sea Festival celebrated the resumption of travel and trade between the sundered populations. The festival was twice as big this year as it was preceding the elves' centennial Kindom Council that circulated between the cities of the Kindoms. This would be the first Council held in Daro—the first held outside of Faeran.

Veldon leaned back and sighed. "I can't tell you how wonderful it is to be traveling again, to be doing something interesting. I haven't left Maramor for ages. We took the river to Tura and stayed there for months before departing for Daro." His emerald eyes glinted in the lights of the courtyard. "Perhaps I will not return."

"That would go well." Gellion scoffed. "Tornac would drag you back by the hair along the ocean floor if he had to—though Farra may beat him to it."

Color crept up Veldon's face, but a corner of his mouth twitched upward. "Farra could come here too. I think she would like it." He dropped his eyes, fingering the sweetbread in his hands. "And Tornac holds no power over my decisions."

Valder looked at Gellion, who avoided his eyes and changed the subject, wishing he hadn't mentioned their eldest brother. "Farra is well?"

Veldon lifted his head, his face softening into a smile. "She is a force of nature."

"One that has clearly overpowered you, body and soul," Gellion said with a smirk.

Veldon narrowed his eyes. "Just because you value your own company above that of any other ..."

"Hey now." Gellion chuckled, holding up his hands in surrender. "It was only a joke. Truly Veldon, Valder and I deeply respect and revere your wife and all those who choose such a bond."

Valder winked at him over the top of a still steaming flatbread.

Veldon's lips thinned, but he rolled his eyes with a good natured quirk of an eyebrow.

They ate in silence for several minutes before Veldon spoke again, this time with his gaze lowered to his hands. "You haven't written to Tornac."

Gellion nearly broke his empty skewer in half. "No," he muttered.

Veldon paused. "Have you spoken to him at all since—"

"I have no grievance with Tornac," said Gellion, twisting against the twinge in his stomach. "He may speak to me whenever he wishes, and I will respond in kind."

"You are as headstrong as he is. He misses you, both of you, and if—"

"If we want good seats for the performance, we should go." Gellion stood and ran a hand through the loose waves of his hair. "Have you ever seen a show of Sira, little brother?"

<hr>

The Performance Hall was cavernous. Columns, narrow at the base, thickened and branched as they reached toward the ceiling, crossing and entwining with one another to form a silver canopy above. Gellion and his brothers filed into the tiered seats that encircled a stage of lacquered cherry wood.

The hall was filling rapidly with elves. The light of lamps and glass spheres cast an ethereal glow about the room, flickering rapidly between the moving bodies like sunlight through the windows of a Rale car. Gellion scanned the room. Many of these elves he had known long and well. Even most of the newcomers were familiar to him from ages past, if only by their faces. He raised hands of greeting as the last seats filled.

The lamps winked out all at once, leaving only the blue gleam of the orbs. The crowd grew silent, and a coil of crimson rope dropped from the ceiling to suspend just above the center of the stage. A lone figure moved from within the audience and strode gracefully toward the stage. Paint shimmered about her eyes and lips, and her hair was swept back in a braided knot.

She paused at the base of the rope, then climbed the apparatus with the startling speed and grace of a panther. When she was twenty feet above the ground, she wrapped the thick cord around herself with a flourish, flipping backward in one fluid movement. She hung motionless, face to the ground, and smiled.

The silence was broken by the music of a stringed instrument, notes cascading over one another as the woman began to twist and spin in the rope, wrapping it further around herself and revolving faster and faster. Suddenly she pulled her hands free and spun in a dizzying, tumbling dive toward the stage, stopping a handspan from the ground suspended by one ankle.

The music stopped and the hall echoed with cheers.

Act after act brought gasps of shock, cries of joy, and oohs of wonder from the audience. Gellion had seen Sira shows before, but this one had been designed to shock, to move, to impress an audience beyond its normal scope—an audience of lords and ladies. It succeeded.

Gellion felt himself sucked into the world of the stage—a trio of elves swinging and flipping about a single airborne hoop like dolphins, dozens of luminescent rings flying through the air in an impossible pattern between three pairs of slender hands. His ears rang with a myriad of notes and melodies, swelling and shrinking with the cadence of the performance.

After what could have been minutes or hours, the lamps of the hall slowly illuminated, and a mass of chattering elves began to make its way to the foyer of the Performance Hall. Gellion excused himself from his brothers, leaving Veldon professing his amazement to Valder with exaggerated hand gestures, and stepped into a corridor outside the entrance hall.

He took a breath and felt the stillness around him, a cushion between himself and the tumult of the crowds. After walking down a corridor and into the familiar labyrinth of passages backstage, he emerged into a large room milling with costumed elves and the burr of excited conversation. He strode to the back of the room.

"You are not allowed here," Renyra said, carefully unraveling a string of delicate lights from her hair in front of a mirror. Tattoos laced her fingers, and thin silver earrings pierced her ear in a curved line from tip to lobe, ending in a diamond-shaped cut of vierstone.

Gellion shrugged and fell back into a chair.

"I do believe you have outdone yourself this time," he said, helping himself to a glass of wine from the table next to him.

"Mmm?" Renyra's lips twitched upward. "Did you hear that, Firas? Gellion is giving out compliments."

A chuckle came from the other side of a dressing wall. "A successful show indeed!"

Gellion snorted. Firas, a lanky elf with kind eyes, came out from behind the wall, tugging his shirt straight. He began to help Renyra with her hair. Gellion watched them. Their hands worked together as though they belonged to the same body.

"You saw the ship come in?" asked Firas. "I wish we could have been there. How many came?"

"The six Council Members, maybe forty others."

"Will there be a competition this year?" Renyra asked eagerly. "I hope it's good. I went to Telem Fier for the last Council and the contest was incredible—A'vaeri, targets, caesir." Renyra smoothed her ebony hair and straightened her braids, each falling just above her shoulders.

"Dulon will make his announcements about the Council tomorrow at the feast," Gellion said.

Renyra rolled her eyes, clearly not fooled by his skirting of her question. She stood up, a head shorter than Firas, and turned to face Gellion. Her green eyes shone against the chocolate of her skin. "Auralia came? And Cuvan?"

Gellion nodded. The Fieri Council Members had been easy to make out, their skin as dark as Renyra's. "Cuvan and Auralia for the Fieri, Miyela for the Morcani, Rhosti for the Remsgri, and Liera and my mother for the Turi."

Firas, who had been pulling his hair into a stubby tail atop the cropped fuzz of blonde beneath, paused for a moment before lowering his hands. He turned his big eyes on Gellion. "Did you speak with her? Your mother?"

Gellion felt the beginnings of heat rise under his skin. The sympathy in Firas's doleful look grated on him. He smiled.

"Yes. Veldon came with her. He's with Valder now. Seeing them together, it is a wonder they were ever separated. I had almost forgotten how close they used to be."

Firas nodded. "I look forward to meeting him." His eyes stayed on Gellion. He looked like he was going to say more. Gellion bit the back of his tongue behind his smile, which he was careful to ensure reached his eyes. As Firas took a breath to reply, Renyra grasped his hand.

"Come on, help me change so we don't miss the fireworks."

Firas glanced back at Gellion, who waved his hand dismissively. "Please. Go. I should find my brothers." He stood to leave, but caught Firas's eye again.

"Well done tonight." He meant it.

Firas blushed as he nodded. Renyra flashed a smile at Gellion before leading her husband away behind the dressing wall.

Outside the Performance Hall, Gellion stood off the road, looking for Valder and Veldon. He raised his glass of wine to his lips. It tasted of cherries ripe to burst, of applewood and sunlight and the heat of summer. As he watched the passing elves, he absently twisted the vierstone earring pierced through the cartilage of his ear. He shuddered at the thrill of awareness that passed through him and dropped his hand.

A pleasant fog hovered about his mind from the wine, and the night was cool.

Elves filed past him, adorned in their best garb for the evening. The clothing largely identified each elf by his or her Kindom. Some wore soft leathers in black, grey, or white, others flowing silk in rich colors. These fashions, along with the patterned wraps and sashes of the Fieri, were familiar to Gellion, but though Daro was home to elves of all Kindoms, few of the Remsgri had chosen to leave their towering jungle for the dry coastline of Daro. Tonight, however, even the paneled skirts and barely covered torsos of that secluded Kindom interspersed the crowd, visitors for the Council.

Gellion quickly gave up any hope of finding his brothers in the crowds and joined the elves moving into the Court. Everyone was facing north, toward the tall viaduct that ran along the cliffside. On the other side of the viaduct was Quarry Bay, a U-shaped inlet lined on one side with the vierstone quarry of Daro. Music was floating through the Court, seeming to emanate from the air itself. Gellion set down his empty wine glass on an unoccupied bench and found his hand immediately supplied with another. He sipped the liquid absently as the firework show began over the bay.

As with the Sira performance, the elves of Daro had outdone themselves. The best chemists in the city—mostly Fieri—had worked at this task for months, and the result was spectacular. Explosions of sparks in reds, blues, greens, and yellows ate through the dark sky in circles, stars, cylinders, and diamonds. Each thunderous boom and searing flash of light was met with exclamations from the gathered crowd until the show ended in a display that seemed to split the air apart in its intensity. The hair on the back of Gellion's neck stood on end with the snapping energy of the air.

When the lights faded, leaving a hazy darkness in their wake, Gellion applauded with the others, then set down his second wine glass, politely refusing another. It was growing late, and he really should find his brothers. Veldon would be staying the month in the home that Gellion shared with Valder, but Veldon would have little hope of finding the place on his own in the twisting neighborhoods of the city. Gellion hoped he was with Valder.

As he turned back toward the Performance Hall, a dark shape suddenly materialized before him. His right hand raised up automatically to stop himself running into the shadow, and by reflex grabbed the arm of an elf. A shock passed between their bare skin with a visible snap of light and clap of sound that seemed as loud as the fireworks. A queer rippling sensation passed along Gellion's skin, and he stepped back with a sharp intake of breath; his motion was mirrored by the woman. They stood staring at one another in surprise, eyes locked in the smokey confusion around them.

Then Gellion laughed, and the tension dissipated.

"Sorry," Gellion said.

The woman looked at him a moment longer, then let out her breath in a snigger. "The atmosphere is rather charged at the moment. No harm done."

Her pale face seemed to hover in a sea of darkness, her hair blacker than the surrounding night. Gellion felt something strange about the woman. She seemed ... apart. Different somehow from the faceless elves pushing against him from three sides. His hand strayed to his earring again, but he caught himself and passed the motion off by running his hand through his hair. He realized he was staring and dropped his eyes.

"Did you come with the elves from Faeran?" he asked, but when he raised his head again, the woman had already dissolved into the passing crowds.

Gellion stood, perplexed by the woman he had not recognized and by the tingling that still seemed to linger in his fingers. Then he shook himself. He was giddy with wine, and the air was laden with electricity and excitement.

He joined the flow of elves and turned his feet toward home. He had more important things to worry about. Tomorrow was the first day of the Kindom Council, the first Council in which Daro would be represented by its own two Council Members. Gellion smirked. He and Dulon would make quite the pair.

His smirk fell. For the first time in hours, Amadeo Benta's face swam in Gellion's foggy mind. He shook his head, and his steps landed with more force. A worry that had not existed this morning was now forcing Gellion to reevaluate the entire Kindom Council, but he and Dulon had agreed that Amadeo's purpose was best left concealed until the first full meeting of the Council. Gellion must simply put the memory and the knowledge behind him until then.

It was not a simple task.

Once remembered, Gellion could not help but agonize over the decision before them. Before today, the humans had never indicated any knowledge of vierstone. It struck Gellion as suspicious that the Albaren now revealed not only an understanding of the stone's importance to the elves, but knowledge of a vierstone quarry in their own lands, right when they needed help from the elves. Gellion's suspicions, however, were overpowered by the cold dread that snaked through his veins each time he considered the possibility of returning to battle. He blinked against visions of blood and ash, raking claws, and glowing eyes. At least a battle with the Albaren would not be against the demons he had faced in the Great War, but was it any better? Worse than the memories of horrifying creatures were the memories of elven eyes. Blank. Staring into a distance beyond the essence of the world. Could anything be worth that? Even vierstone?

As Gellion turned onto the path leading to his house, he took a shuddering breath and paused outside the door. It was several minutes before he had regained enough composure to walk through the door.

3

FEAST INTERRUPTED

Three hours before the earthquake, Gellion bent over a bar of hot metal, eyes shimmering in its reflection. His hands were steady, his hair bound back from his face. All of his concentration was on the glowing bar as he slowly stretched it, hammering with firm, precise blows. Beads of sweat formed curving tracks down his forearms, merging with one another and gaining speed until they reached the linen strips tied around his wrists and absorbed into the damp fabric. Each time the color of the metal bar faded, Gellion bathed it in the fire again before resuming his work.

It was not exciting work, but it was necessary. The rusted grates on several of Daro's ships needed replacing. Gellion did not mind. He enjoyed working with the metal for its own sake, and it was providing a distraction for his cluttered mind.

Gellion had been in his workshop most of the day. He needed time to think—time to distance himself from the Council and the Albaren Earl's request before the feast tonight. It was not a distance easily maintained.

As Gellion turned to submerge the metal in the furnace again, he heard the scuff of boots on the marble behind him.

"There you are," said Valder. "We thought you must be with the

Council Members after so much time, but then we found mother, and she said she hadn't seen you." He looked appraisingly at the iron bar in Gellion's hand. "Urgent work that could not wait?"

Gellion shrugged and sank the metal in the fire. He watched the dull grey infuse with light and imagined flame spirits grabbing frantically at the metal, fighting over the right to imbue it with heat.

Valder did not press the matter. This was not unusual behavior for Gellion. The charismatic charm he brought to his position in the city required frequent recharging, and the sweltering metal shop was his favorite place to do it.

"What's with the human?" Valder said.

Gellion went rigid. "What?"

"Oh come on, if I know about him, you must. Everyone is talking about the human man staying in the Domes of Rhelyon. What's he here for?"

Gellion let out a breath. He thought quickly. "He was traveling in the north on business for his king and brought trade propositions from Tradira." He set down his tools. "He is leaving tomorrow. We will review the documents and send our response later."

It was not a lie.

Valder nodded. "Will he be at the feast?"

"I expect so. We invited him."

It would have been an insult not to. Gellion hoped the man did not make a scene or hint at the more nefarious purpose of his visit.

"Mmm. Veldon will be delighted." Valder smiled.

Gellion forced a chuckle. He could understand Veldon's fascination with humans. When the elves first came to these shores, they had no idea humans existed, let alone that the continent was inhabited by at least as many humans as Faeran was by elves. It had taken half a century for the Albaren to stumble upon Daro, and their appearance had been an equal shock to both races. Gellion had been intrigued by the humans, learning their language and acting as an emissary of Daro. He had been both enthralled and dismayed by the Albaren cities. It was a different world to anything he had ever known. The darker realities of the humans had tempered his fascination with their race over the centuries, but many of the elves recently arrived in Daro would have never seen humans, Veldon among them.

"Speaking of the feast," said Valder, "you would do well to start getting ready." He looked over Gellion foot to head with a wry smile.

Gellion glanced down at his thick leather apron and the wrinkled shirt sleeves pushed past his elbows.

"What time is it?" he asked.

"An hour or so until sunset."

Gellion had lost track of time. He would be pressed to clean up his workspace and make himself presentable for the feast. He unbound his wrists and untied the apron from around his waist. He had been looking forward to this feast for weeks, but now met it with a grim reluctance. To be forced to a table with Amadeo, Dulon, Liera, and his mother ...

At least the food will be good.

"Welcome!" Dulon's voice echoed in the cavernous Dining Hall. "I am afraid the time for formalities has come at last, but I will keep them as concise and entertaining as I am able." The Lord of Daro beamed over the long tables before him, his shimmering tunic catching the light from the crystal chandeliers.

"We, the elves of Daro, are honored to host this fourth Kindom Council held since the end of the Great War. We are proud to share what this city has become and celebrate the reunion of our friends, our families, and our people as a whole. I trust you all enjoyed the entertainment last night?"

An acclamation from the audience rang out.

Dulon's grin broadened. "May we continue them tonight! Now, I am sure many of you are aware of how a Kindom Council operates, but for those of you who have never been in a Great City for the duration of one, allow me to enlighten you. The eight elected members of the Kindom Council—yes eight now." He flashed a smile at Gellion. "Will meet over the course of the next month to discuss trade, news, relations, and all manner of other boring necessities between the four Kindoms. In addition to these important but mundane and exclusive meetings, recent Councils have included a way to bring together all elves of the host city and visitors alike—to hone their skills off of one another in the way of friendly," he tilted his head and raised his eyebrows conspiratorially, "competition."

A murmur of excitement rose in the room.

"And so," Dulon resumed, "the tradition will continue at this first Kindom Council of Daro. The Council Members will be both congressmen and judges this month—judges of the typical tournament, yes—there will be A'vaeri in all its forms, plus javelins, knives, and caesir." He waved a hand dismissively, as though this was all old news and not the most sought after demonstration of physical feats the elves held each century. "But also judges of a different contest—a contest of craftsmanship."

He let the last word bounce off the walls before continuing. "Each competitor will create one item. You may use whatever you wish—stone, metal, glass, jewels, liquids, solids, or anything in between! But your final product must be remarkable. Unique. A piece of exceptional, extraordinary, unprecedented artistry and erudition. The Council Members will judge every entry from Kindoms not their own—yes, that means we may also participate—and the winner will receive the incredible, the rare, the ever sought after prize of ..." He scanned his audience slowly. "—prestige." He said the word with a droll cock of the eyebrows, eliciting a low laugh from the room.

"The tournament of sports will begin next week and continue until the end of the Council. Entrants are to speak with Coren, the Master of Sport from Tura, who has graciously joined us for this Council. The craftsman competition will be judged in four weeks. For this, we limit three entries per Kindom, so discuss among yourselves, or sign up quickly while the others are discussing. Now, let the feast begin!"

The tables in the Dining Hall were already laden with food, and everyone began to fill their plates. Dulon strolled down from the head of the room and sat across from Gellion. He pulled in his chair and exchanged looks with many of the Council Members. Most looked on him as one would a fond nephew—with indulgent amusement. Miyela, the Morcani representative, looked at him like he had just lead a merry chorus at a funeral. Amadeo, sitting between the Council Members, just looked entirely out of his element and bent to the food heaped in front of him.

Gellion sliced off a leg of roasted seabird, its skin cracking under his knife and giving off the pungent aroma of herbs. He arranged shining red currants, olives, a slice of goat cheese, and warm bread next to the leg on his plate.

The Council Members split into conversations among themselves. Liera was discussing Rale line developments with Miyela and her assistant, Lythin, who kept glancing over at Gellion with hints of a blush. Gellion turned a determined gaze on Auralia.

The Fieri Council Member was a striking elf. Muscles shaped her bare arms and shoulders, and cropped hair swept forward toward her face. Along the skin of her arms, black and red tattoos formed intricate patterns and pictures, most likely denoting Auralia's Kindom, occupations, and faith. Gellion himself bore several tattoos, but the Turi were more subtle than other Kindoms in their physical expression, and tended toward artistic markings rather than practical ones.

Auralia was discussing boat travel between Rone and Maramor with Gellion's mother. Gellion listened, willing Tenille to turn the discussion to Maramor itself, but when the conversation threatened to move to another topic, he interjected.

"The elves of Maramor are well?" He kept his tone as casual as he could. He could feel his mother's gaze, but centered his concentration on an olive as he carefully cut it in half.

"Maramor and its people are much the same," Tenille said. "Though in truth I do not know why I am still named Lady of Maramor—Tornac sees to most of the running of the city these days."

Gellion looked up before he could stop himself. Tenille's face softened.

"We are all well," she said, "and the city has grown in size and beauty."

Gellion nodded. "I am glad." And he was. Maramor had been his home for most of his life in Faeran. When he was a little over two hundred years old, he had moved there with his mother, his elder brother, and his father, Eldian. His father had been Lord of Maramor, and Gellion had remained in the city for three hundred years—through the Great War, through the birth of his younger brothers—until the last battle of the war in Maramor itself. After the horrors of that battle, including the death of his father, Gellion had left and never returned. Barely a month later, Valder had followed him.

Well did Gellion remember the domed buildings, the platforms that seemed to hover over the rushing gorge, and the redbud trees. They haunted him in both dreams and nightmares, but still he cared about the elves that walked in the city by day, and missed them.

Amadeo's singsong voice drew Gellion's attention. The earl was talking to Cuvan, the other Fieri Council Member, about the state of affairs in Albarad. Next to them, Dulon translated, wearing a polite expression, but his knuckles were white around his fork.

"King Naval is trying to strengthen our trade with the Kayda in the Falspires," said Amadeo. "They are a strange people, the Kayda, but honest enough. We have begun to expand our maritime trade due to some conflict on our borders." Amadeo smiled at Dulon and Gellion as though sharing an inside joke.

A muscle in Dulon's jaw twitched.

The little man went on to brag about Tradira's steam and coal industry and the latest intrigue in the courts.

Cuvan was watching Amadeo like one suddenly confronted by his horse discussing the business of herd life. Despite himself, Gellion fought back a smile. He and Dulon were the only two at the table who were accustomed to humans.

As plates cleared and wine glasses emptied and refilled, music started to fill the hall, and the assigned seating loosened. Amadeo seemed to be behaving himself reasonably well, and Gellion had spoken to all the Council Members except Liera, who seemed as content as he was to limit their interactions to polite nods and averted gazes. Political duty thus fulfilled, Gellion slipped away to find his own company.

His brothers were sitting with Firas, who looked remarkably normal in his soft leathers after last seeing him in Sira costume.

"Ah!" said Valder upon Gellion's arrival. "To the great Council Member among us!" The others toasted their glasses. Gellion rolled his eyes and sat down.

"Riveting conversations among the wise?" said Valder.

"Not exactly." Gellion took a filled glass from Firas. "Where's Renyra?"

"With some friends." Firas nodded toward a group of Fieri gathered around the musicians. "Valder said you spoke with that Albaren man earlier. It is strange to see him at the festival. Did you know he was coming to Daro?"

"No," said Gellion. "He just showed up yesterday."

"But what did he say?" asked Veldon. "What has he been talking about? Are all humans like that?" He looked like a boy presented with a new toy.

"Well, he is rather short for his people, but otherwise a typical Albaren, I suppose," Gellion said.

"The hair on his face?"

Gellion chuckled. "Yes, most of the males have that in some fashion."

Veldon's eyes lit up, and he stared over at the table of Council Members.

"Go sit with mother and you can speak to him yourself," said Gellion. "Maybe he will even let you touch his mustache." He motioned to his upper lip.

Veldon narrowed his eyes at Gellion's grin and turned around, though he kept glancing back at the Council's table.

"So, did you know about this craftsman competition?" asked Firas. "Have you been keeping it secret all this time?"

Gellion smiled.

"You devious blaggard," said Valder.

"I was not at liberty to say," said Gellion.

"Like that has ever stopped you."

Gellion shrugged. "Well, now that you know, do any of you plan to enter?"

"Unless I am to build a ship within the month and drag it through the streets of Daro for judgment, I think my talents are ill-suited to the task," said Valder.

"You could make a very small ship," said Firas.

"Ah yes!" said Valder, "The smallest ship ever seen. That would be—what was it?—remarkable, unique, exceptional, extraordinary?" He snorted. "I suppose I don't need to ask if you're entering?" he said to Gellion.

"Of course."

"I daresay the competition was your idea." The warmth of Valder's smile belied his mocking words.

Gellion took a breath to reply, but stopped with his mouth half open.

A current ran through the room—no, through the floor, or was it through himself? He was not even sure if 'current' was the right word to describe the peculiar feeling, except that it had seemed to flow somehow. It was more similar to vertigo—like the material world around him had for a moment existed less firmly, its lines and very essence blurred. The music and conversation in the room faltered. Then the sensation passed as suddenly as it had begun.

Gellion stared at his brothers and Firas. They looked as bewildered as he felt. So it had not been him alone.

"What ..."

"You felt it too?"

"What happened?"

The music in the room was replaced by excited muttering. Gellion turned toward the Council table to see Dulon looking straight at him. He looked confused and worried. Next to him, Amadeo was asking, "What is it? Why did the music stop?"

"Gellion," Veldon said. "That wasn't ... planned, was it? Whatever that was?"

Gellion shook his head, his brows knit.

"Could it have been something in the wine?" asked Veldon. "Or a ... a storm beginning outside?"

Firas frowned. "That was no storm, nor do I think we all simultaneously lost our heads to drink—" he trailed off, eyes going distant.

Gellion felt a chill at the look on Firas's face. It was the look of one thinking of something half-remembered, something familiar but indefinable, and it mirrored exactly what Gellion felt. Certainly he had never before experienced whatever current just passed through the Dining Hall, but nor had it been entirely unfamiliar to him. It was like a smell he knew but could not name.

"I am going to find Renyra," said Firas, pushing back his chair.

Gellion and his brothers watched Firas go, then sat in silence.

"Well," said Valder, glancing at Veldon. "It could have been some atmospheric drop in pressure." He shook his head and took a gulp of wine.

"Maybe." Gellion did his best to look unperturbed.

The conversation in the room was gradually returning to normal as the elves passed the episode off, unable to explain its source. The music began again, and the festivities resumed, if a little more subdued.

Veldon started telling Gellion more about his journey to Daro. Gellion listened with one ear, while tuned to the elves moving around him, to anything out of place. But there was nothing. He began to relax again, even to enjoy himself. Elves were getting up to dance now. He could see Renyra leading Firas away from the tables. Firas twirled her gracefully as they walked. Veldon was interrupted by a woman asking him to dance. He accepted and bowed—a motion made more comical than chivalrous by the deep color creeping up his face.

"That one has more shades of red in him than the sea has blue," said Valder, watching their brother fondly.

"I missed him," said Gellion.

"So did I."

As the night wore on, the atmosphere returned to normal. Gellion assented to a dance with Lythin, then stepped away, insisting on a dance with his mother. Some elves had begun to leave for the night when a woman appeared at Gellion's shoulder. He started and looked down into a face outlined in familiarity. It was a moment before recognition dawned on him.

"I do not think we officially met," the woman said, her mouth curving into a crooked smile.

Gellion stared. Her presence had caught him nearly as off guard as the night before, though he could not explain why. "No, I suppose not," he said, regaining a measure of formality. "I am Gellion."

"You are on the Council?"

"Yes."

Her smile curved further up her face.

Gellion paused. "And you are?"

"Kyna."

"You came from Tura?"

"Most recently."

Gellion smiled. "And before that?"

Kyna shrugged. "Near Ard Gael and the southern Wildwood mostly."

Both were Turi lands, the former the region in which Maramor lay. Gellion was not surprised. She looked Turi—familiar even. He wondered if she was a relative of someone he knew in Tura or Maramor.

"Have you lived in Daro long?" she asked.

"Since it was built," he said. "Before it was built, actually. But I was born in Tura."

Kyna nodded slowly, not taking her eyes off Gellion. He felt flustered. There was still something inexplicable about Kyna. Granted, he was once again mildly intoxicated and surrounded by an atmosphere far from calm, but he couldn't help feeling unsettled by her. Unsettled, but intrigued. He searched frantically for something to say.

"Are you entering the craftsman competition?"

"No."

Gellion nodded as though he found the fact highly interesting.

Kyna smiled. "Are you?"

"Naturally." He tried to summon an ingratiating smile and was relieved when it came. "You should see the metal guild on Market Street. We have some of the finest metalworkers in all the Kindoms."

"Yourself included?"

Gellion chuckled. "I aspire."

Kyna gave him an appraising look. "You'll have to show me."

Gellion lifted a hand to tuck a lock of hair behind his ear, his fingertips brushing his earring. He felt momentarily warmed, but the usual sense of awareness fell flat. He looked at Kyna in consternation, his hand falling slowly back to his side.

"Is something wrong?" she asked.

He broke his stare. "No. No, I was just—"

The air shimmered again. Gellion's skin—the very makeup of his body—seemed to vibrate with an ethereal force that moved the *wrong* way, like a comb pulled against a beast's fur.

Then a deep rumble echoed from within the ground.

A moment later, the stone floor shuddered, then pitched. Gellion staggered and nearly fell on top of Kyna. From the corner of his eyes, he saw elves all around him stumble and fall and heard a chorus of cries amid the rattling of tables, chairs, and sconces. He blinked and shook his head, trying to find Dulon in the intensifying chaos.

"I have to go." Gellion spun away from Kyna and hurried across the hall. His progress was halting, arrested by staggering bodies and the tremors that shook the ground with increasing force, though the shimmering air seemed to have stilled after the initial onset of the earthquake.

"Everyone outside!" Gellion shouted over the tumult.

Dulon. Where was Dulon?

A hand fell against Gellion's shoulder, then pulled him backward as another shuddering lurch ripped through the ground. Gellion saw a flash of Dulon's flaxen hair before a high-pitched snap rent the air and diverted his attention to one of the towering windows of the Dining Hall. A thick crack ran through its middle. Spider webs of smaller fissures were rapidly spreading from its center, emitting more crackling sounds as they grew.

Gellion stared open-mouthed. His mind was spinning with the flickering light of swinging chandeliers and the torrent of voices around him.

"Evacuate the building!" he said. The words were meant for Dulon, but the Lord of Daro was already shouting formal orders above the cries of dismay and incessant rumbling of the building. Elves flooded through the doors of the Dining Hall, holding their arms over their heads. Dulon had hold of Gellion's shirt sleeve and was half dragging him along behind the rapidly retreating crowd.

"I don't understand." Dulon's eyes darted around the room.

Another window cracked.

Dulon shook his head as though trying to dispel dizziness. "We have never had an earthquake here. And before ... what *was* that?"

Gellion did not respond. He had no more suggestions than Dulon.

The light of the chandeliers cast unsettling shadows around the room. The rumbles of the ground rose in pitch and a deafening crack sounded closer and louder than any of the others. Gellion leapt sideways into Dulon, moving them both away from the fissure that had just opened in the stone floor between the center tables.

"Out!" he shouted.

No elf needed his encouragement. Within the space of ten heartbeats, the last heels of the crowd disappeared through the swinging doors of the Dining Hall, and just in time. Gellion threw his arms over his head as a final shattering crash rang against his ears, and the air filled with shards of glass.

"Get down!" The voice sounded like Dulon's, but Gellion could not be sure. He obeyed the nameless voice and dropped to his knees as sharp points of pain scattered over his hands and shoulders. The noise seemed to last an eternity.

When the last tinkle of glass on stone finally ceased, the ground stilled.

Slowly, Gellion lowered his arms. His clothes had protected him from the worst of the glass, but his hands were covered in beads of blood and thin slivers of glass. A breeze blew through the Dining Hall, scattering the finer bits of debris across the floor.

Gellion looked up.

Every window in the hall was now a gaping archway to stone and stars, ragged bits of glass clinging to their frames.

"Is it over?"

Gellion turned to see Dulon sitting on his heels, looking at Gellion with wide eyes partially obscured by errant strands of hair.

Gellion listened. Waited. "I think so."

Lights flashed against the strewn glass. Overturned cups and discarded food littered the tables, which were turned at odd angles. A cold stillness settled over the hall; a silence somehow louder than the previous merriment clung to every particle of the space.

Gellion took a breath and allowed his thoughts to catch up to his body.

All the elves had gotten out of the Dining Hall. The building still stood. The damages were repairable. But still ... An earthquake. An *earthquake*? Only once in his life had Gellion ever felt one, and the memory still sent stabs of dread through his core. This earthquake wasn't related. It couldn't be. The elves had only been in Daro two hundred years. Maybe earthquakes were a rare but natural occurrence here. His eyes strayed to the jagged crack in the stone that ran through the center of the hall to his feet. The elves may not have built Daro with earthquakes in mind, but the city's foundations were imbued with vier-stone. Surely the floor should not have broken like this?

A tendril of cold snaked down Gellion's spine.

Stop being ridiculous. It's only a crack in the floor.

"We should make sure no one is hurt," Dulon said in a dreamlike voice. His eyes were roaming around the Dining Hall, lingering on each sign of damage and fallen glassware. "And check the rest of the city," he added.

They exchanged a long look and a nod. Dulon smoothed the hair from his face, then stood and offered Gellion a hand. Together, they walked out of the Dining Hall to their panicked guests. The lights were still flickering when they closed the doors behind them.

4

EARTHQUAKES AND VIERSTONE

Water ran in rushing sheets down the sides of the dome above Renyra's head. It was raining. Hard. She could almost see the water spirits of Riu reveling in the chaos, though she knew they also rejoiced in the life the rain brought the earth. Radiant lamps, strung below the glass ceiling, reflected in rainbows off the flowing torrent. Fifty feet below, Renyra sank her bare feet into a sponge of earth and moss. She was dry and warm, the greenhouses a bubble of peace amid a raging storm. She took a deep breath, relishing the smells of earth and fresh water.

In the two days since the feast, life had gone more or less back to normal, the excitement of the earthquake passing into story as the Builders repaired the damages to the Dining Hall. No elves had been injured. No other parts of the city had been damaged. The earthquake itself was easier to forget than the reality altering waves that had preceded it, but while Renyra found the experience strange, she was not concerned over it. Not like Firas.

Renyra frowned. Firas seemed deeply affected by the earthquake, but then he had not been himself since the Council Members and their company came to Daro. He was spending a lot of time with the newly arrived Morcani elves. She expected he was just feeling nostalgic. He had spent most of his life in northern Faeran among his Kindom, just as Renyra had in the grasslands of the Fieri with hers, but Firas had lived many more winters with the Morcani than Renyra had with the Fieri.

Visitors or no, there was plenty of work to do. Plants did not pause their growth for festivals or disasters. Early spring in the greenhouses was a time of planning and planting. She needed to fertilize the sprouting greens in the smaller chambers, check that the fruit shrubs were properly pruned, and sow seeds for the summer gourds and tomatoes.

Renyra bent over a series of metal pipes above a spout in the ground. She pulled several levers and heard the hiss of liquid rushing through the twists and turns, eager to escape through the sprinklers suspended over each crop bed. A fishy smell assaulted Renyra's nose as the fertilized water soaked the soil of the greenhouse. Tiny leaves stretched out of the earth as though reaching for the sustenance. At least they were enjoying it.

"Ah, the smell of fertility." A broad-shouldered elf not much taller than Renyra passed behind her. He scanned the rack of tools on the wall and selected a pair of shears. "Good day for it."

Renyra smiled. Soran, like Renyra, was from the grasslands in Faeran—a vast swath of land stretching east of Telem Fier. The Fieri by nature were gifted chemists and supported much of Faeran's agriculture through their crop formulations. Soran now applied that knowledge to a much smaller scale. He bent down for a closer look at the seedlings.

"They do not seem bothered by earthquakes."

"A notoriously stoic species," said Renyra.

Soran chuckled. He spun the shears in the air and caught them by the handle. A bolt of lightning forked across the sky, accompanied by a crack of thunder that shook the glass ceiling. Soran eyed the dome with some apprehension. "If I were superstitious, I would say this Council is not boding well for Daro."

Renyra watched another flash of silver light. Fog was forming on the glass, turning morning to night. Ever since the bizarre earthquake, she had felt something wrong about the city. She squared her shoulders against a shiver. Unconsciously, Renyra moved the fingers of her right hand to her forehead, shoulder, and heart in the triangle of the three-pointed star: mind, body, soul.

Riu protect us.

Soren had turned away, not noticing the discomfort his comment had caused.

"Ah well, work continues." He nodded to Renyra and passed through the tunnel into the next chamber. Renyra watched him for a moment, thoughtful, then turned back to her seedlings.

Outside the greenhouses, the streets were largely deserted. Renyra expected many elves were bustling about inside the Domes of Rhelyon, preparing for the Council meeting the next day, and the rest were simply avoiding the deluge. Renyra didn't mind the rain. A leather cloak shielded her orange and blue wraps, and boots kept water from soaking her feet. She found the raindrops on her face pleasant. Her hair, free of its braids today, hung in wet fangs above her shoulders.

She approached the gates of Daro on foot—the Rale only served to make one wetter on rainy days. The great slabs of marble that separated Daro from the outside world were as thick as three elves. Renyra had always thought they resembled tombstones. Firas said she was being morbid.

The stables stood next to the gates. There were not many horses—hardly a dozen for the whole city, and even those were only taken outside the walls for hunting and rare travel beyond the Icemelt River. Most of the elves ignored the animals' presence altogether; many did not know how to ride. Renyra opened the doors to the stable and was greeted by a wave of humid air smelling of straw and salt—quite a different salt from the ocean breeze outside. Several large heads swung out of stalls to see if breakfast had just entered through the door. A smile tugged at Renyra's lips.

Such strange beasts.

She pulled a lever near the door and a shower of grain pinged against the hollow raceways above. Metallic clicks sounded as hatchways opened and closed above each stall, neatly depositing a serving of oats into buckets for each horse.

Renyra reversed the lever's position and walked through the stable, trailing her fingers along the cool metal of the stalls. She stopped beside the stall of a black gelding. The animal raised his head from his feed and snorted in Renyra's face before returning to his grain.

"Hello, Nightjar." Renyra leaned against the stall door and watched the horse with a cocked head. Most of the time, Renyra hunted on her own two feet, but on the occasion she took a horse, she tried to stick to a single animal. The last decade it was always Nightjar. He was strong but silent with an elegant face. At times Renyra felt she could even understand something of his nature. Almost.

Walking back the way she had come, Renyra peered out the stable doors. She tried to estimate the time from the light, but it was hopeless.

Was Firas in the Archives? Surely he would not be working on the docks in weather like this?

Renyra jogged down the street to the Archives and did her best to wring the water from her hair and cloak before stepping onto the library's gleaming floors. Hanging lights glowed about the cavernous space, and stacks of books and scrolls lined the walls. Renyra passed through the aisles, cringing at the squeak of her boots, and scanned for her husband among the books.

She found him hunched over a table with a glowing sphere of glass hanging low to its surface. Several books were open before him. Firas turned toward Renyra upon hearing the squeals of her boots, eyebrows raised as he looked from her face to her shoes.

"How long have you been here?" Renyra asked, ignoring his amused expression.

"Not long. I have only skimmed through half a book." Firas turned his chair sideways and gestured at the titles before him. *Stones of the Sea Coast* lay discarded in a corner of the desk with a book on weather patterns stacked above it. Renyra stepped forward to close the cover of the book lying open in the center of the desk: *Physycs of the Earth*. Firas's eyes glittered.

"It took a while to find that one," he said. "It is not written for this region, but it has some mention of volcanoes." The slightest hint of unease passed behind his eyes at the word. The thought of volcanoes did not affect Renyra as it did most elves. She had not been born until after the end of the Great War—had never experienced the fiery explosion of the mountain that began it all.

"Anything on earthquakes?" she asked.

"Not much, only that they often accompany or precede volcanic eruptions." He knit his brows in frustration. "If we were in Morcanan there would be more information on this, I am sure of it. Precious few tomes were copied from those libraries for Daro. They did not seem relevant." He sighed. "Not at the time."

Renyra made a noncommittal, "Mmm." She suspected the primary reason Daro contained few Morcani books was not due to the laxity of Daro's scholars. The Morcani guarded their knowledge as closely as they guarded everything in their culture. Somehow she could not imagine them printing extra books to distribute across Kindoms.

Renyra flicked through the pages of *Physycs of the Earth*. It was old, bordering on ancient.

"What about geography? The climate of Daro is similar to the lands surrounding Tura. Surely elves have collected information on that?"

"They have, but only a single earthquake has ever occurred in Tura, and even that was an aftershock." He looked down. "Five centuries ago."

Renyra bit her lip. Firas never talked about the war. He was not alone in his reluctance. No elf talked about those centuries of pain and terror. To speak of the devil was to invite him in, and in this case 'devil' was all too real a word.

As far as any elf knew, it had been Olcon himself, the devil that defiled and corrupted Riu's creation, who had sent the demonic monster that tormented the elves for centuries. From a blanket of ash left by the volcanic eruption above Morcanan, Olcon had raised a phoenix—a great bird the size of a ship with a black heart and cunning mind. Though the creature could make itself understood, it had never graced the elves with its name, and so it had been known simply as 'the phoenix.' The creature had first tried to deal with the elves, offering power, prosperity, and new life through its authority. The elves had refused. Instead, it had brought brutal war, and through it achieved what its original offer had not—ambition and strife sown through the fabric of Faeran and its inhabitants.

Dread settled over Renyra's shoulders.

"You don't think something has happened in Faeran?" she said. "Another eruption, or—" She could not bring herself to finish the sentence.

"No," Firas said firmly. "I cannot imagine an earthquake could travel across the ocean. It is possible that there are volcanoes on this continent, though—that one of them erupted and caused the earthquake here."

Renyra frowned. It still didn't seem right. The Dining Hall was the only building in all of Daro that had shown any damage from the earthquake. She was no geological expert, but it seemed to her that the center of the thing must have been right below their feet, not in a distant mountain range.

"But you have experienced earthquakes before," Renyra said. "In Morcanan. None were like that? Not the ... the air, or whatever that was before the shaking?"

Firas's face darkened. "No."

"Have you felt anything like it?"

Firas hesitated, then shook his head. He was a terrible liar. Renyra stood, watching him with an eyebrow raised until he looked up and flushed. He turned back to his book.

"Firas."

His eyes stared at the words before him without seeing. Renyra laid a hand on his shoulder. Her vierstone earring warmed, and she could feel Firas's discomfort flow up her arm.

"What is it?" she asked, disconcerted.

"I have never felt anything exactly like that night," he said at last, "but the current that ran through the hall before the earthquake was ... familiar." He opened his mouth, then closed it.

"What do you mean?"

"Did you not find it so?"

Renyra thought back. "No, I don't think so. What did it remind you of?"

"I could not think of it at first, but now I think I have realized what it was. It was almost like," a line formed between his eyes, "vierstone."

Renyra stared at him. "Like—vierstone?"

"Like how it—how it feels," he added lamely. "Oh do not look at me like that, it is difficult to explain. Have you ever stood in the presence of a large quantity of vierstone? In a quarry for example?"

"No." Renyra had never gone to Daro's quarry, only seen it from the towering heights of the viaduct.

"It is powerful stuff. You can feel it, almost giving off a—" He cupped a hand in the air, palm facing up and fingers constricting in an attempt to describe the feeling. "I don't know." He dropped his hand in frustration. "But that undercurrent, or life, or whatever you want to call it, that vierstone gives off—those moments before the earthquake were similar, only that night it was stronger even than a vierstone quarry, and *wrong* somehow."

Renyra's hand strayed to the lobe of her ear, fingering the green stud. Could she detect something of what Firas was talking about? In truth, she never gave much thought to her earring, or to vierstone in general. It was simply a part of her—a part of life, like her skin or her voice. She had never had much interest in specializing in a craft that utilized the stone's direct influence.

A faraway look clouded Firas's eyes. Renyra could see worry in their depths. She placed her hand on his.

In a moment, focus returned to Firas's gaze, and his big eyes softened as he looked at Renyra.

"I am sure there is no reason to worry," he said with a soft smile. "It was probably a simple atmospheric phenomenon or strange effect of the earthquake itself."

Renyra could tell he did not fully believe his words, but she didn't press the matter. With a smirk, she said, "Well, doubtless if there is any written word to explain what happened that night, you will find it."

Firas chuckled and pulled his hand away from hers. Cold air washed over Renyra's skin where his warm embrace had been; goosebumps trailed up her arm. Firas's smile did not reach his eyes, and Renyra felt another wave of apprehension from him as he turned back to his books.

The rain let up over the afternoon, petering out to an intermittent drizzle. Renyra drew saturated air into her lungs and let it out in a heavy breath. She turned her face into the mist. Light was fading from the sky, but with the cloud cover it merely transitioned through shades of grey.

Her fears in the Archives seemed foolish in the free air, without the mark of history surrounding her on all sides. Elves passed by in small groups. The glow of string lights and street lamps became stronger in the dimming evening. Renyra walked toward the Rale path in the center of the street, her hand enveloped comfortably in Firas's. There was only one levit board nearby, but she could see others a short distance away. She made to walk toward them, but Firas's grip tightened, drawing her back to the lone board nearest them. He stepped onto its smooth surface, still not releasing Renyra's hand, then crouched, smiling at Renyra with a rare glint of mischief in his eyes.

"Come on then," he said.

Laughing, Renyra swung toward him, placed one foot on his thigh and nimbly perched herself onto his shoulders, her skirt draping to either side of his neck. Firas stood up straight as easily as if she wasn't there. A subtle click sounded as Firas activated the magnets in the board, and then they were gliding forward along the path. Several elves turned to watch their progress, curious smiles on their faces. Renyra held her head high, enjoying the elevated view down the sea cliffs to the north.

Firas only went as far as the stack of boards down the street. He slowed and stepped onto the path. Renyra leapt off his shoulders, still giggling, and turned back to grin at him.

Her gaze caught the eyes of an elf approaching Firas from behind. Silvery hair hung past the elf's chin on one side of his face; on the other, his hair was cropped short, a flowing geometric pattern shaved into it. His heavy brows drew together in a glare, and his glinting eyes passed over Renyra before glancing briefly at Firas.

"Tathé," he spat at Renyra as he passed.

Renyra's grin faded. She did not recognize the word, but its connotation could not have been clearer. She felt Firas stiffen next to her. His eyes followed the elf until he had disappeared down the lift to the second tier. Anger was etched on Firas's gentle face.

"Let's go," he said softly, squeezing Renyra's hand before releasing it and stepping back on the levit board.

Without speaking, Renyra activated her own board and followed Firas along the Rale path toward their home.

———

Renyra waited until Firas's silence was unbearable. "So, what did he say?"

She sat curled on a couch with a cup of nettle tea.

Firas sighed. "Nothing that matters. Nothing that one would be likely to hear outside Morcanan in this day and age."

"That's no definition."

Firas closed his book and lifted his eyes to meet Renyra's. "It means 'country,' 'rural.'"

Renyra raised an eyebrow and cocked her head. "And that is ... an insult?"

"Yes."

"Your loquaciousness constantly astounds me."

A smile tugged at Firas's lips. "It is a long story."

Renyra moved her head from side to side in an exaggerated search of the room for something more important to do. The smile broke through Firas's defenses.

"Alright then. How much prewar history are you familiar with?"

"Three thousand five hundred years before the discovery of vierstone, Riu created the elves from stone, at each of four lifestone deposits across the continent of Faeran—" Renyra laughed at Firas's look. "Ok then, I know the basics, what are you so cryptically referring to?"

"I'm referring to thousands of years later, when the elves started leaving those 'lifestone deposits' to disperse across Faeran. That was long before the Turi crafted vierstone earrings, long before elves used vierstone to build towns and roads. Those elves that left the Great Cities distanced themselves from vierstone's effects, and over centuries, they changed."

Renyra sat up on her knees, drawn into his story despite herself. "Changed how?"

"The elves distanced from the Great Cities could no longer build, nor carve, nor forge as their kin in the cities could, their skill slipping away even as the beauty and might of the city elves waxed. Country towns crumbled with time and likewise did their inhabitants' character."

"Their character?" Renyra said incredulously. "What do you mean?'"

"As the centuries wore on, those elves furthest from the cities bore little love for one another, living solitary and selfish lives. The elves of the cities began to distance themselves from their 'uncivilized' kin."

Understanding dawned on Renyra. "The rural elves. The Tathé."

Firas nodded. "The elves began to build vierstone into the towns and villages of the country, but though their towns increased in beauty and continuity, it was not enough to bring the elves that lived there back to themselves. That is why the earrings were made."

Renyra fingered the vierstone pierced through her skin again. She had never thought to take it off. She had never considered what would happen if she did. "And it worked?"

"Yes. I was barely of age when the earrings were distributed throughout Faeran. The change in the rural elves was incredible and fast. Within a few years, remote villages were rivaling the Great Cities in skill and ingenuity, and doing so with joy and humble grace. But it took much longer for the prejudice to wear away. All the same, the Great War brought elves together of all Kindoms and all backgrounds, and by its end, the word 'Tathé' was more or less a memory."

Renyra gritted her teeth. It had been a Morcani who had called her 'Tathé.' If any elves held fast to prejudices from the past, it was the Morcani.

"Yet the Morcani still use it?" She tried to keep any accusation out of her voice. Firas could not help the Kindom he was, and she knew he did not adhere to all of their beliefs.

"Some do. Not all, or most for that matter." His voice carried the slightest edge of defense.

Renyra did her best to soften her expression. She moved close to

Firas so their legs were pressed together. "I understand. Thank you for telling me."

"Pay it no heed. Any elf who knows you can see that the quality of your work and your heart rival that of any elf across Kindoms and regions."

"Flatterer." Renyra took one hand off her mug and squeezed his arm affectionately.

The Morcani elf's insult stung, but that was not foremost in Renyra's mind. Her head was spinning with the meaning of Firas's description of vierstone. All her life, she had thought the stone merely increased the skill of crafters, chemists, and engineers—lent strength to city foundations and roads. The elves' desperation to find more vierstone after its depletion in the war made more sense now. Daro was not just a city of beauty and prosperity, but of necessity and security. She thought of the earthquake, and of Firas's description of its effects, and suppressed a shiver, hoping that neither the shaking nor the sensation that preceded it presaged any threat to this Great City.

5

THE KINDOM COUNCIL

The room was large. Much too large for eight people. To Gellion, the disparity only emphasized the paradox that so few elves were expected to represent the interests and opinions of so many. How could Gellion know what every elf in Daro would feel or think when presented with the decisions discussed in this Council—elves from backgrounds and places he had never experienced? But he knew the elves of Daro. He spoke with them, lived with them, ate with them, celebrated and mourned with them. Surely that was enough to understand what experience had not taught?

Gellion had never been bothered by such thoughts while serving on the local Council of Daro. When faced with questions like 'should we build a new dock closer to the sea gate,' or 'are we farming too many fish from the south strip of coast,' it was easy to forget that one spoke with the voice of hundreds. Besides, these were the trivial decisions the elves of Daro had expected Gellion to make on their behalf. Would they have still chosen him to represent them if they had known a question of battle would arise? Would he have accepted the position?

"So begins the first meeting of the fourth Kindom Council!"

Gellion's head jerked up at Dulon's voice.

"We will have two more meetings before your time here is finished,"

Dulon continued, "but I suggest we bring up as much as we can in this first meeting so that we may discuss them throughout the month."

Gellion shifted his gaze to each elf around the table. Those representing the same Kindom or region sat across from each other: Dulon and Gellion, Tenille and Liera, Auralia and Cuvan. Furthest from Gellion sat Miyela, so upright she was almost bending backward. Miyela was the picturesque Morcani in her white leathers and utter lack of adornment or smile. She eyed Rhosti across from her, his caramel skin very much revealed and what seemed hundreds of long braids bound behind his back.

The beginning of the meeting was a dull litany of updates from each Kindom. Gellion and Dulon shared Daro's announcements in turn, skating over the subject of the recent earthquake with a confirmation that the city had sustained no damages from the occurrence apart from the Dining Hall, which would be as good as new by the end of the Council's visit.

The lack of citywide damage was a matter that had left Gellion and Dulon both relieved and confused. No other parts of the city showed any signs at all that an earthquake had hit. Gellion had pushed the speculation from his mind. The earthquake had been a freak occurrence on an unfortunate night. Best not to dwell on it, and certainly best not to prolong the discussion in a Council meeting. The next topic, however, was almost worse.

With some reluctance, Gellion reported that the vierstone quarry of Daro was three quarters depleted. Miyela skewered Gellion with her eyes at this news, then turned a considering look on Dulon, whose gaze was so intently fixed upon Gellion that the veins in his temples strained from the effort.

Heat rose to Gellion's face. Though no elf at the table was as obvious in his or her displeasure as Miyela, Gellion was sure the rest of the Council Members were shocked by the meager amount of raw vierstone remaining in Daro. The entire purpose of building Daro had been to mine its quarry—to resupply the elves with vierstone after the mineral's depletion during the war. The elves of Daro had not abandoned this purpose, but Dulon and his Builders had used far more vierstone in Daro's construction than many thought wise. The city was beautiful and modern, but it was also isolated, and small by comparison to the Great Cities of Faeran. Sometimes even Gellion questioned whether they had built too lavishly.

Before any words of question could break the stunned silence, Gellion cleared his throat and turned the Council's attention to the Turi representatives. Tenille's look told Gellion she knew exactly what he was doing, but she smiled and began her reports, Liera drumming her fingers impatiently until it was her turn. No one brought up the vierstone again, but the tension that its mention had sown in the air was slow to dissipate. Gellion listened to his mother's updates with frayed attention. On one hand, Daro's meager supply of vierstone would seem a trivial matter in the face of a proposed alliance of war, but then, that meager supply was also the only reason the elves might entertain the possibility of accepting the alliance.

A nudge to Gellion's foot and a subtle cough from Dulon's direction made Gellion jerk and look up. Dulon's pointed look told Gellion that his brooding was becoming noticeable. Sitting up, Gellion relaxed his face with some effort and turned to Liera as she began her report.

By the time the Lady of Tura had finished detailing what seemed every minor occurrence in Tura from the past century, Gellion's stomach was rumbling, and his attention was waning once more. The Fieri report that followed was even more of a struggle to sit through with Cuvan's slow, deep voice, but at least the Fieri had achieved some interesting developments over the past century.

"Telem Fier is fully rebuilt, and its laboratories grow faster even than its population," Cuvan said, with undisguised pride in his broad face. "We have just released a new type of solar panel that can increase power conversion by almost a third, and we are implementing the technology in all public spaces within the city, soon to expand across the grasslands."

"Have you brought any with you?" asked Dulon, eyes shining.

Gellion bit back a smile. Dulon was an engineer by trade and loved electricity. He had designed Daro's hydroelectric power plant himself, though solar power was a science generally left to the Fieri, its inventors.

"Prototypes only," said Cuvan. "But we can send more once we have expanded our production."

Dulon grinned. Across from Cuvan, however, Auralia did not seem to share in his excitement. On the contrary, her expression was grim.

"Telem Fier is advancing our technology admirably," she said. "But the city's growth does not come from new births. The populations of the grasslands are flocking to Telem Fier, even to Maramor across the lake. Entire communities are depleting and fading. We should focus on distributing our prosperity and innovations to towns and villages across our lands, not on the continued growth of our cities."

The resulting debate ate away the rest of the morning and drew no conclusions. Finally, Dulon was forced to move matters onward to the Remsgri.

Gellion glanced at the glass clock above the door and drummed the tips of his fingers against his palms. The Kindom Council met once every hundred years. That was too often in Gellion's opinion. Since the end of the Great War, little significant changes occurred among the elves beyond the local level. Each Kindom had its own Council that met to discuss internal affairs, and each major city had its own Lord or Lady to handle city-level concerns.

Gellion blinked hard and concentrated on Rhosti's soft voice. The Lord of Remsgraen was a concise and well-spoken man, his report almost poetic in its cadence. The Remsgri were a peaceful people, largely remaining concealed in the jungles of the west, yet their contributions to elven society were of no small significance. Rhosti outlined the success of the inter-Kindom Rale system, the full construction of which had concluded shortly before the last Kindom Council. Gellion had already been in Daro at the time and listened to the report with rapt attention, momentarily forgetting about the Albaren. Miyela's clipped tones quickly brought him back to reality a few minutes later.

The Morcani report was short, and contained nothing of any real importance or interest. Miyela stated mundane facts about Morcanan and the surrounding Morcani lands that Gellion could have learned from a trade document. He glanced at Dulon, who was watching Miyela with a carefully polite expression. Dulon's opinion of his Kindom had always been a mystery to Gellion. The man seemed to go out of his way to differentiate himself from his upbringing and he rarely spoke of Morcanan. Then again, few Morcani ever spoke of Morcanan.

Including their Council Member, it would seem.

A sudden silence took Gellion by surprise. He looked around in alarm, realizing that all the Council Members had finished their reports. After a delayed pause, Dulon glanced up, finally noticing the end of Miyela's speech himself. Gellion saw the briefest hint of panic flit across the man's eyes before he locked his gaze on Gellion. Resolve flowed down Dulon's face. He nodded and took a breath.

"I have told you before of our trade relationship with the humans of Albarad. At the feast, all of you met the man Amadeo, a trader—or rather an envoy—of their king."

Nods moved around the table, curiosity apparent in each face. Amadeo had left Daro the morning after the feast. The man had been visibly disturbed by the earthquake, calling it a bit of Kayda magic he had thought contained to their haunted mountains. This enigmatic description only increased Gellion's anxiety over the phenomenon. Clearly earthquakes were as unknown in Albarad as in most of Faeran.

"I told you he came to discuss matters of trade," Dulon said. "And he did. But that was not all." Dulon leaned forward onto the table. "Albarad is at war with Diernas—a region of humans southeast of here past the mountains. We of Daro have never had personal communication with these people, though we knew of their existence. The Albaren claim that the Dierna are a violent people—raiding and pillaging their lands, cheating their traders, attacking their crops, livestock, women, pride, etc." Dulon waved a hand and attempted a weak smile before moving on. "The Albaren fight to reclaim their border and security, but say they do not have the men to support such a war efficiently."

Gellion surveyed the Council Members. Most looked confused but wary. A few were exchanging glances. Liera's eyes bored into Dulon. Did she anticipate his next words?

"The Albaren ask for our aid," Dulon continued. "An alliance with the elves of Daro to help the Albaren in battle."

Gellion's breath stopped in his throat, suddenly too loud for the silence that had descended upon the room like a blanket. Every Council Member was gaping at Dulon.

Gellion sat still, waiting.

"You said no," Liera said.

"I did not answer," said Dulon.

"Didn't answer?" Auralia's brows drew down to shadow her eyes. "Why?"

"There is an ... offer, involved that warranted discussion."

"An offer?" Miyela said. Her voice was controlled, but her eyes blazed. "What could the humans offer us? What could justify entering a war voluntarily—a war that does not even concern our people?" Miyela's indignation spread around the table. Everyone was nodding, staring at Dulon as though he had lost his mind. Dulon avoided Miyela's gaze as he answered.

"The Albaren claim to have a deposit of vierstone on their coast."

Gellion counted to five in the silence.

"They are lying," said Liera at last.

"Amadeo could describe it," said Dulon.

"He has seen it in Daro, then."

"He has never been to Daro before now, and any Albaren that have been here over the centuries have never gone to the quarry."

"Then how do these humans know what vierstone is?" Miyela interjected. "If they have never seen it nor heard of it?"

Dulon shifted in his chair. "Amadeo said that his people had heard of the stone through elvish traders and emissaries, though neither Gellion nor myself recall speaking of vierstone with the humans. For all we know, some visiting Albaren trader saw the quarry from his ship a hundred years ago and asked about the stone from a passing elf on the docks. A decent number of our people can speak some Albaren." Dulon shook his head. "It doesn't matter how the humans know about vierstone, the fact remains that they clearly do, and they will cede the quarry to the elves if we help them. They say that with our aid, the 'war' may merely consist of one battle. It seems to me that it is increased intimidation more than skill they are after."

"It doesn't matter whether it is one battle or a hundred," Cuvan's smooth voice cut in. "Lifestone is ours by right. Who are these humans to use it as a bargaining chip? We could take it from them by force without batting an eye."

Gellion's hands squeezed into fists under the table. "You would attack a nation unprovoked for a piece of their own land, yet you bridle at the idea of attacking their enemy?"

"I did not suggest that we should attack these Albaren," Cuvan said. "I was merely pointing out a fact. The humans do not possess the right or the power to keep lifestone for themselves. It is therefore not a prize with which they can negotiate. The stone is ours by birth—by existence if you will. Rui created elves from stone—from vierstone itself."

"So legend says," Liera said.

"So evidence shows." Cuvan raised his voice so its deep tenor reached the corners of the room. "Vierstone is of no use to humans, but serves as our connection to the earth itself, to each other. The humans cannot barter such a thing as though it were diamonds."

"Do *you* plan to explain your reasoning to the humans, Cuvan?" Liera said. "Do you expect them to apologize and turn over control of their quarry simply because we explain the depth of our attachment to their only means of leverage over us?"

Muttering broke out around the table.

Dulon stood. "We will not," his voice carried across the muttering and smothered it, "attack the Albaren. It is out of the question. That is not why I brought this decision to the Council. It doesn't matter by what right the Albaren offer us vierstone. It is what they offer. The decision we face is whether or not we will accept it—whether we ally ourselves with Albarad in their fight."

"It is no decision," Miyela said softly.

Dulon moved his eyes to her with obvious reluctance.

"If you freely choose to send elves to battle once more, it is murder," Miyela said. "As clear as any in our past." Her gaze shifted to Liera, whose skin drained to the color of chalk. "The reasoning behind the choice makes no difference. Would you have your legacy as infamous as—"

"That is enough." Gellion stood.

At Miyela's words, a ripple of emotion had passed around the table, though none of it was as strong as that beneath Gellion's own skin. He took a slow breath through his nose and kept his gaze steady on Miyela, though he knew his face must be the same color as Liera's.

"We did not expect to make this decision today," he said. "We told

Amadeo that we would send our answer at the end of the month when our Council is concluded. We have presented you with the facts, so far as we know them, and expect you to consider them carefully until our next meeting." He kept his gaze on Miyela's narrowed eyes for a moment longer before turning his attention to the Council at large. "When we reconvene, we will discuss the matter further."

Dulon pushed his chair back and stood. His usual pomp was replaced with a solemnity that sat awkwardly on his shoulders. "Thank you all for your attention and input," he said. "I look forward to our next meeting."

Gellion could not distinguish any audible irony in Dulon's final words, but would bet Dulon was as thrilled for the next Council meeting as Gellion was—that is, as thrilled as a lined fish awaiting its beheading.

With a final inclination of his head, Dulon turned and left the room.

In the stillness that followed, Gellion made the mistake of looking at his mother, whose expression was lined with unease. Gellion turned his eyes down quickly, then followed Dulon out of the room before any of the Council could question him.

Well did Gellion know his own feelings about the impending decision, but he was not yet willing to share them in the setting of the Council. When one spoke with the voice of hundreds, each word carried a weight too heavy to let fall without consequence.

"That went well." Dulon fell back onto the couch.

Gellion sat next to him. "Did you expect any better?"

Dulon snorted and reached for a pitcher beside the couch. He poured two glasses of chilled tea. Gellion took one.

"No. The elves of Faeran do not understand humans."

"Do we?"

"Better than they! This should be Daro's decision, but as it affects elves from all four Kindoms—" He looked at Gellion. "Should we have waited until the Council left?"

Gellion shook his head. "It would have been worse. They are already annoyed with us for handling vierstone without their input. To decide on an alliance of battle without them?" He ran a hand through his hair. "No matter how magnificent our city, the Kindom leaders will always claim ownership of the elves that inhabit it. Little as either of us want to deal with them, this was the only way to do it."

Dulon let out a dramatic sigh. "Do you think they will ever agree to it?"

Gellion sat up straighter. "Agree?" A cold dread spread through his limbs. "You want to accept the alliance?"

Dulon stared at him. "Well of course I don't *want* to accept it, but I don't see how we can refuse. In fifty years of searching with a score of ships in all directions, this," he pointed at the ground, "was the only site of vierstone the elves ever encountered, and it was already half the size of the original deposits in the Great Cities. Now another source of vierstone presents itself to us? The Daro quarry is a quarter what it was not even two hundred years ago. We must consider the meaning of that."

"What meaning? We rebuilt our cities in Faeran and we built Daro. All have vierstone in their bones. Every elf living has an earring—" He paused for a fraction of a second, unease stealing over his mind unbidden.

All but one elf.

The panic that had tried to drag him down after Miyela's unnamed accusation rose to greet him once more.

Do not think of him.

Gellion shook himself and continued. "For what purpose do we need more vierstone?"

Dulon gazed into the depths of his glass, twirling its contents. "What if there is another war? Or a natural disaster, another eruption, or—" He shook his head. "We would have nothing, no more to rebuild with."

"And you think that justifies joining a war now?"

"This will not affect Daro or Faeran. It may not even be a *war*. What is a single battle compared to what we have lived through?"

"Even a single battle will risk the lives of elves, not to mention taking the lives of the humans we fight."

"I know!" Dulon slammed his glass on the arm of the couch. Liquid sloshed over the glass's edge and seeped into the fabric. "And then there are the Albaren themselves to consider. Do they honestly need our help?" He ran his hands over his face and shook his head from side to side. "It's been a long day. I'm going to take my own advice and think on this over the next week." He grimaced. "Though I am sure my thoughts will be interrupted by the helpful opinions of others."

With a sigh, Dulon pushed himself to his feet; Gellion rose to meet him.

"To leadership and the Lords of Daro." Dulon tipped his glass toward Gellion and drained it in a single gulp as though it were liquor.

Gellion tried to focus his mind on one thing at a time, to evaluate each subject in full before moving on to the next. His hands provided an example, melting bars of silver, copper, and aluminum in a crucible. With the excitement of the last few days, he was just now beginning his work for the craftsman competition. He refused to let the recent drama interfere with his ambitions to win.

In the last forty-eight hours, the news of what had transpired in the first Council meeting had spread to every elf in Daro. The emotion was palpable; a dominant emotion was not. The ambiguity of attitude exhibited by the elves as a whole shocked Gellion as much as Dulon's had. For every elf who would not hear of voluntary battle, there was another drawn by the pull of its reward and the security offered thereby. Some even argued in favor of the alliance for its noble cause. This shocked Gellion more than anything. Since when had the elves possessed any sense of duty or loyalty to the humans beyond trading olives and sheepskin? He suspected this particular rationale was mostly pretext.

A few elves, to his dismay, even seemed intrigued by the idea of battle itself. Most of these were elves born after the Great War. Gellion could not imagine anyone who had lived through those horrors would wish for more. The Great War had begun over five hundred years ago. Gellion remembered how all of Faeran had shook, remembered the black clouds that veiled the sun from Tura for three days when the volcano erupted. From the volcanic ash had risen a nightmare—one that had tormented the elves for two centuries.

It was a nightmare Gellion had left behind when he came to Daro; yet as all nightmares, it refused to be suppressed by distance and was likely to flare up again in the presence of certain circumstances and people.

Gellion's mother had found him the day after the Council meeting despite his best efforts to avoid all involved.

"You have known about this for days?" she had asked. Gellion had not needed to ask what she was referring to.

"Amadeo told us the morning the ship arrived."

Tenille nodded slowly. "You did not say much in the meeting."

"No."

She raised her eyebrows and sat next to him. "What are you thinking?"

The question made Gellion's lips twitch. It had once been a common question between them. He took a long time to respond. His fingers twisted his earring as he thought.

"It is wrong," he said at last, dropping his hand. "I believe that to accept would be a mistake."

"Why?"

Gellion looked up at her. He could feel the heat in his skin and tried to keep it out of his voice. "Why? Am I the only one who remembers war?" His mother's expression turned his eyes to the ground. "I'm sorry."

A hand touched his leg.

"You are not the only one to remember, no," Tenille said. "But perhaps not all remember it as you do."

The look of understanding in his mother's eyes shamed and sickened him. He stood quickly and turned his back to her, forcing down the anger welling up in his throat. She had witnessed everything he had. She had lost her husband. Yet she had not left Maramor. She had not fled Faeran like a frightened child.

The conversation ended there.

Gellion shook his head in disgust at the memory and tipped the crucible in his hands, watching molten alloy pour into his molds and forcing his mind to concentrate on the task at hand. He would not allow his competition entry to suffer from his distraction. The molds would set overnight. Tomorrow he would begin his work with the sheets of metal.

He smiled to himself. Though he had refrained from beginning his work before the competition officially began, he had not been able to stop his mind from planning it. Through the sheen of the flowing substance, he could see the finished product, but even as he imagined its beauty, his smile faltered. The idea was original, extraordinary even, but it was tarnished by the memory of the inspiration from whence it came. He had been taught this technique when he was not yet fully mature, as an apprentice metalworker in Tura. It was a crafting style that had disappeared for hundreds of years, and Gellion hoped none would remember it. Its creator had not made the technique widely known. He had not had time …

As Gellion's gaze turned inward, the crucible tipped sideways and he had to throw his arm around it to keep the metal inside from spilling. He rebuked himself. He could not allow his project's association to a ghost of the past to distract him. He would put it from his mind—it was a discipline he had practiced most of his life.

As Gellion began to clean his work space, he noticed a shadow in the doorway. A figure stepped into the room. Gellion's chest gave a strange leap. The stifling work room suddenly felt like a furnace.

Kyna smiled, her face lit by the glow of the forge. She said nothing, but stepped around Gellion to look at his molds, their contents still shimmering.

"What is this?" she asked.

"That," Gellion said, moving to stand beside her, "is metal."

"Mmm." She gave him a sardonic look. "And what will it be?"

"A secret." Gellion looked at her sideways and pulled up a corner of his mouth.

"Fair enough. What else do you have here?"

"Well, I have some of the most exquisite ship grates ever made—could be soaked in water and fire for half a century without a spot of rust. And here are some hooks to adorn and transform the most lowly of walls into a stunning display of apparel." He swept his hand dramatically at each object.

"The greatest metalworker in Daro indeed."

"Oh, not just Daro, all Riure."

Kyna snorted and wandered around the room. Gellion watched her, conscious of the sweat rolling down his ribs. This was not the first time Gellion had seen Kyna since the night of the earthquake, yet he still felt thoroughly unbalanced whenever she was in the same room as him. Odd and discomforting as the feeling was, it was not entirely unpleasant.

Kyna stopped at a rack of knives, ran a finger along their hilts, and pulled one out. It was a dagger made of a single piece of curved metal that twisted back from the blade and flowed into a smooth, shining handle. There were swirls of copper folded through the silver, and Gellion could see the reflection of Kyna's eyes on the surface as she held it in front of her. He suppressed a shiver.

She replaced the knife and drew out another, then moved on to a lyre. Gellion stood in the middle of the room and clasped his hands behind his back, then crossed his arms over his chest and shifted his feet. His presence in his own workshop suddenly seemed foreign and awkward. Kyna turned back toward him, and he gave what he hoped was a charming grin.

"They are impressive," she said.

Gellion's hold on his grin slipped into embarrassment. He turned away, suddenly concerned about the positioning of the upturned crucible on the table.

"So modest now?"

He could hear the smile in her voice and cursed the heat spreading through his face. He bent to put his tools away. When he straightened, she was still looking at him, amused.

"Come on," she said, jerking her head toward the door. "I've still seen little of Daro besides the docks and the Court." She glanced at the fire burning to embers. "And it is sweltering in here. Can't you cool it?"

"I find the heat bracing."

Kyna rolled her eyes. "Let's go." She turned her back on him.

Gellion stared at her for a moment before following, then paused at the door, aware of his shirt sticking to his sides. "I should change."

Kyna let out a derisive huff and swept past him. Gellion smiled and followed her into the sunlit street.

"Gellion."

Gellion, staring transfixed at a leaf of lettuce, looked up at Firas.

"Are you alright?" Firas asked.

"Just thinking."

A line formed between Firas's brows. "Have you spoken with any of the Council Members since the meeting?"

"What?" Gellion dragged his mind back to the present. For once, the Council had not been on his mind at all. "Oh, yes—I mean, no, I haven't spoken with any of them." He thought of the short exchange with his mother, but did not correct himself.

Valder was sitting next to him. Tables stretched to either side, smattered with small groups of elves eating dinner. Upon a lengthy inspection of the Dining Hall, Dulon had announced the structure safe to reopen, though elves had been slow to return. The filled crack in the floor drew eyes like a corpse, and the breeze that wafted about the space from the empty windows served as an eerie reminder of the night Gellion wished everyone would forget.

"Anyway," said Valder, "while you were sharing a moment with your salad, I asked if you could help me at the docks tomorrow."

"The docks?"

Valder sighed patiently. "Yes. I am working on *The Nore* and I want your opinion on the metalwork."

"I'll come down in the morning."

"Thanks." Valder turned back to Firas to continue their discussion of ships. Gellion's eyes slipped back out of focus. He had spent a sun soaked afternoon walking the streets of Daro with Kyna and was not quite ready to step out of the memory just yet.

After a cursory tour of Daro's more interesting sights, Gellion had taken Kyna to the Tower of Stars and walked across the viaduct.

"That is the vierstone quarry?" Kyna had leaned through an archway, squinting over the bay at the rocky shoreline glinting green. Dark chunks were missing from the cliffs where elves had mined vierstone.

"Yes."

"Who do you protect it from?" She turned to the great Sea Gate that spanned the length of the bay, its towers rising like stone watchers from the churning waters.

"Leviathans, war ships, regiments of stone-hoarding merpeople."

Kyna snorted. Gellion wondered if the woman ever truly laughed. He smiled and continued.

"We keep the gate closed through the autumn and winter when storms take the Semestrial Sea. It stops the worst of the waves from reaching the quarry. That way we can still access it in those months, and the cliffs are protected from erosion."

Kyna turned back to the quarry, her eyes distant and unreadable. Gellion leaned through the arch next to her and watched the breeze twist in her inky hair. In the sunlight, with his head clear of alcohol or forge smoke, she was much less mysterious. He chided himself for his foolish behavior. And yet ...

He moved his hand to his ear, deliberately this time, and touched the vierstone pierced through it with the tips of his fingers. No. That part he had not imagined under the influence of circumstance. Kyna was not the solid wall that humans presented—he could certainly sense *something* about her—but it was unclear and irregular. He wondered if the same enigma existed with other elves and he had never noticed.

Suddenly, the hairs on the back of Gellion's neck stood on end. His eye was caught by something at the end of the viaduct—a movement, a shadow, a trick of the light? He leaned back from the arch and peered toward the door of the tower, but there was nothing there. The queer feeling passed. He frowned.

"What is it?" Kyna said.

Gellion turned his head to her, his eyes following slowly. "Nothing." He opened his mouth to say more, but closed it again.

"Gellion!" Valder exclaimed.

Gellion blinked hard, the sounds of the Dining Hall shattering his reverie. Valder was staring at him.

"Sorry, what?"

"Have you seen Veldon?"

"No."

Valder frowned. "I've hardly seen him the last two days."

Gellion thought back. He had not seen Veldon since the night after the Council meeting. The absence did seem odd now, and evoked a twinge of guilt in his stomach. He had been distracted lately by his metalwork. And those who interrupted it.

"I saw him this morning," said Firas. "He was walking toward Master's Street."

"Alone?" asked Gellion.

"No, with his legion of adoring females," Valder said.

Firas ignored Valder. "Yes, he was alone. I did not see where he went after he turned onto Master's Street."

"Probably sending secret letters to Farra," said Valder.

Gellion frowned at his brother.

"What?" Valder laughed. "I'm only joking. I love our dear brother and his saccharine ways." He eyed Gellion. "You usually surpass even me at banter. Are you sure you're alright? You've hardly heard a word I've said all evening."

Gellion smirked. "And that is out of the norm how?"

Valder narrowed his eyes, but seemed satisfied with Gellion's return of personality.

That night, Gellion turned to bed with a heart light in defiance of the troubling thoughts that had been his constant companions for days. He turned on his side, carried toward sleep with thoughts of cooling metal, distant waves, and a pair of eyes reflected in a shining dagger. The Albaren alliance seemed a distant concern, the elves' agreement to join it a ludicrous impossibility.

He fell asleep.

He dreamed.

He was in Tura. He stood in a courtyard and watched an elf walk past him escorted by guards. The elf's eyes were burning embers, his back the edge of a sword; anger sat on his shoulders, grief in his eyes. The fiery gaze met Gellion's own, and the city burned away into the towers of Maramor. Gellion ran through chaos, looking frantically for his brothers, but the light of the fires seared his vision. Elves fell around him. He could not feel them. He could not feel anything. The vierstone in Gellion's hands melted.

Gellion woke gasping. The room swam around him, the air vibrated with a grating rhythm, and his belongings rattled against the floor and walls. Holding his head in his hands, he staggered to the door and descended the spiral stairs to the common room he shared with Valder. By the time he reached the bottom of the stairs, his head had stopped spinning and the room was still. Valder stood next to the table, his face pale.

"Another one?" Gellion asked.

Valder nodded.

6

TO RUN A CITY

Dulon turned off of Master's Street and strolled down an alley leading to the western neighborhoods of Daro. His shined boots clicked on the stones, and he cursed with every step. He cursed politics, he cursed earthquakes, but mostly he cursed Earl Amadeo Benta.

This Kindom Council was supposed to have been a courtly affair of food, drink, friendly relations, and competition, not to mention a chance to show how far Daro had come—to justify the building of the great city. That human louse had ruined everything. His visit had put a shadow over the month's festivities and Council meetings, but it was growing more serious than that. The dissension caused by the Albaren's proposal was starting to divide the elves into factions of opinion. The issue was growing into a question of more than vierstone, or even war; past grievances were being dragged into the open, as was wont to occur in times of dispute.

Even though it had now been days since the second Council meeting, Dulon's jaw still tightened every time he thought of it. He walked faster, his curses of Amadeo matching the tempo. If only he could blame the little man for the seismic and seemingly transcendental activity of Daro as well. He took a breath.

Riu give me reason.

The mustached weasel could have nothing to do with the structural damage Dulon had been alerted to this morning. There had not been another earthquake for over a week as far as Dulon knew—not since the midnight tremors reported in the neighborhoods two days after the first Council meeting—but elves were starting to report damages from scattered locations now. Were the damages a delayed effect caused by structural weakness? Had no one noticed the damages until now, or was it more earthquakes that had gone unnoticed?

An elf was waiting for Dulon ahead. Along one side of the road, domed houses backed up against the cliff of the top tier of the city. To the other side, they sat in clusters, stretching away to the orchards.

Dulon stopped three houses down from the waiting elf. He stared between his feet. A deep crack split the street and ran in a jerking line past the length of five buildings. The smooth metal of the Rale path bent at a shear angle with the crack, though fortunately it had not broken. Dulon walked along the edge of the fissure to the waiting Builder.

"The crack was not here yesterday," said Aryn, her voice bearing the formal cadence of a report. "I asked the residents of these houses. Only one was home this morning. He said he felt some shaking, then heard a kind of snap outside his window." She looked away from Dulon, discomfort coloring her expression.

"And?" Dulon prompted.

"He said—" She cleared her throat. "Well. He said he felt," she glanced at the crack, "queer for a moment, before it happened. Dizzy. And the air vibrated against his flesh."

Dulon's head was reeling. So it had been another earthquake, and just like the other with its inexplicable side effects. But what did it mean? Dulon had felt no shaking this morning on the third tier of the city.

Earthquakes were no novel occurrence for Dulon. He had spent much of his life in Morcanan—a Great City built on the face of a mountain. But never had a quake been accompanied by this mental vertigo, nor did any of the streets of Morcanan crack from shaking ground. The streets of Daro were built the same—better even. It did not make sense.

Aryn was watching him, waiting. He smiled.

"It is easily fixed. I will have the street flagged to alert passersby. Can you have a team of Builders working on it by this afternoon?"

"Of course, Lord Dulon."

The corner of Dulon's mouth quirked up at the title. He had known Aryn long before moving to Daro, but still she insisted on formalities, even in the absence of company.

"Thank you, *Lady* Aryn." He emphasized the honorific. "And do continue to alert me to any reports of damage. I want to see each one."

Straight-faced, Aryn bowed her head and swept past him toward Master's Street to carry out his instructions. Dulon watched her go with some amusement, then knelt beside the crack in the road. He ran his fingers along its edge and into the crevice. The cleavage in the stone was peculiar. It did not quite follow the patterns it should. Peering closer, Dulon saw tiny tendrils of black lacing through the stone surrounding the crack.

Stranger and stranger.

A door shut with a clap a few houses down, and Dulon jumped to his feet. He took a breath to slow the flutter of his heart. He was stretched thin between the Albaren, the Kindom Council, and the ongoing running of his city, and this simple geological activity had him jumping at shadows. It would not do to have the head of the Kindom Council losing his nerve.

Dulon stood, brushed off his hands, and stepped purposefully over the crack. It was midmorning, and he had far too many appointments to keep before lunch. He scanned the Rale path for a waiting levit board, eyes locking on one that was two houses down the road.

The board hummed and rose from the ground as he stepped onto it and activated its switch. Next on his list were the docks, where he would discuss the blessedly mundane subjects of ballast and sailcloth.

***

The day passed swiftly, carried from task to task in a way that made thinking impossible. Some of the windows of the Performance Hall showed signs of cracking, and despite last week's rain, the river that ran along the southern edge of Daro's walls was low for the season, causing no end of trouble for the city's electrical supply. Most houses had some form of solar power, but Dulon had refused to put any windmills on the picturesque sea cliffs. If the river ran low, he would have to be more conservative with power allocations.

Dulon had been pleased with the progress at the docks. Work on the newest ship, *The Nore,* was moving along nicely, and Dulon had been delighted to see the progress of the city's largest spirit house, The Silver Swan, making a new wine from figs. He even managed to get through the better part of the day without running into a single member of the Council or being questioned about the state of his decision on the alliance. Whenever the subject arose, he assumed a face of unfazed civility. He listened politely while giving away as little of his own mind as possible—not that he truly knew his own mind. He had hoped the second Council meeting would make things clearer, but if anything, it had put him at more of a loss.

The conversation had started out civil enough, but despite Dulon's best efforts, it had once more degraded into irrelevant arguments.

"In less than two hundred years," Liera had said, "the vierstone supply of Daro has dwindled to a quarter of its original size! The deposit was always smaller than the original deposits in Faeran and the likelihood of finding more is slim. Any chance at a new supply would be foolish to ignore."

"The vierstone would not have dwindled so quickly if we had not built a lavish city next to the quarry using the resource we were there to mine," Miyela said in a measured tone.

"Daro," said Gellion with ill concealed fire behind his words, "is as great a city as any in Faeran, and has developed innovations to improve all of them. It brings together elves of all the Kindoms and unites them."

"You call this united?" Miyela scoffed. "I have not seen division such as this since the Great War, but at least then we had a common enemy."

Dulon's stomach clenched. He gritted his teeth and avoided Miyela's eye as he addressed the rest of the Council.

"Enough. This is a grievance of the past—one that holds no bearing over our current decision, and one that cannot be changed."

Cuvan's rumbling voice broke the silence "If we refuse, what will happen?"

"The Albaren are a proud folk," Gellion said, "and a martial one. This is not their first war, though I know little about its predecessors. I believe if we refused an alliance, they would take it to heart—make more of it than perhaps we intend. I have no doubt it would cause hostility in our trade relations. If we refuse, we will not get the vierstone except through force or trickery. Still, I think refusal of the alliance would affect us little within our walls. We do not rely upon the Albaren for trade, and even if hostilities became open, the humans would be mad to attack the walls of Daro. So." He shrugged. "If we refuse, I expect life will continue, but with a grudge-holding neighbor and a few less sheepskins and spices."

Dulon's clasped fingers tightened. "And," he said softly, staring at his hands, "if misfortune were to strike us—here, or on Faeran? Say, an earthquake?" He looked up. A chill of unease ran through the room. "If we had no way to repair, or rebuild, and found ourselves surrounded by bitter neighbors and war?"

"You speculate," said Tenille. "You imagine scenarios that have not yet and may never happen and base your decisions upon them."

"What else am I to base my decisions upon?"

"If we do run out of vierstone and have true need of more, we will do what we must when the time comes. What good is it to worry over it now? Are we to hoard our treasure simply for the sake of its beauty and power? Guard it jealously, but never use it?"

"It is not beauty and power we seek!" snapped Liera. "It is the livelihood of our very race, the timelessness of our cities. We do not hoard, we prepare; we do not guard but preserve. We cannot see only the present with blind faith in the future."

"No faith in the future? What of faith in Riu?" asked Tenille.

Dulon stopped Liera's retort with a look.

Rhosti's calm voice responded.

"We cannot expect Riu to drop solutions to our problems from the sky." Rhosti lay his hands palm up on the table. "If one prays to bring a deer home for dinner, he must still aim his weapon, not expect a doe to wander into his home and lay her head down for slaughter. To be prepared is not to lose hope or faith, it is wisdom."

Dulon had made a valiant attempt to draw the conversation back to a more objective analysis of the situation, but again and again emotions and arguments snaked their way back to poison the atmosphere. The Council meeting had brought no conclusions, only outlined the convoluted morals and wisdom that laced the alliance like a web. Pluck one strand and the rest shook, drawing attention to the size of the thing.

Dulon shoved the Council out of his mind. It was no good letting one unfortunate aspect of the Kindom Council ruin all the rest.

Shouts and cheers caught Dulon's attention as he made his way back to the Domes of Rhelyon. He smiled. A little distraction before dinner was just what he needed.

The sport tournament had begun over a week ago and was going as smoothly as the Council meetings were not. A remarkable turnout in sign-ups had filled the arena nearly every day until the end of the Kindom Council.

Dulon walked through the arena entrance. It was a modest space, but as beautiful as anything in Daro. An oval court formed the base of a bowl, which rose in tiered seats on three sides. The court was originally built for caesir—a multiplayer sport of rackets and balls with hoops and targets—but served just as well for A'vaeri. Just now, two elves were sparring with wooden sticks as long as Dulon's arms.

It was a fascinating fight, though fight was not the right word. One elf was a Remsgri, his braids bound behind his head and the tattoos on his arms glinting in the sun. The other was a Morcani, dressed in form-fitting grey with her hair in a flaxen tail. The two elves moved in a kind of dance, with styles as contrasting as their appearances, but somehow each complemented the other.

Dulon recognized the smooth movements and well-timed attacks of the Morcani. He could have mimicked every movement by heart. The Remsgri moved quicker, with high strikes and leaps that made him look nearly weightless. A kernel of envy sparked in Dulon's chest.

A'vaeri was an art as diverse as the elves that practiced it. For the Morcani, it was an art of discipline, precision, and focus. Dulon had always found the other Kindoms' forms more intriguing. And more fun.

The Remsgri spun in the air and aimed a kick past the Morcani's defenses, dodging both of her sticks. His foot caught her in the chest and sent her sprawling on her back. With a whirling flourish of sticks, the Remsgri knocked away his opponent's weapons and stood over her, his own sticks pointed at the Morcani's head.

A whistle blew, and the Remsgri stepped away from his opponent, grinning broadly. He offered a hand to the woman, and she took it, grumbling, but with the ghost of a smile on her own face. It had been a good match. A'vaeri was more about the dance one put on than who defeated his or her opponent.

"Dulon."

Dulon stiffened at the familiar voice. He took a moment to compose himself, then spun on one heel. His hair swung over his eyes. Miyela was striding toward him from the street outside the arena. Dulon's mouth went dry.

"Miyela," he said, tossing his hair back with a flick of the head and putting on a grin. "What can I do for you?"

Miyela closed the distance between them with a step and held him with her steady gaze. She was almost of a height with Dulon, her hair the silver of aspen wood.

"I hoped we could talk over dinner," she said.

Dulon held his grin but felt as though a fist had clenched in his stomach. Maybe she merely wanted to reminisce about Morcanan—chat about the spring weather. Somehow he doubted it. Dulon had lived most of his life under Miyela's rule. It was difficult not to respect her prowess as a leader, especially during the war, but Dulon's admiration ended there.

This newly switched power status between them was gratifying, but also disconcerting. Still more disconcerting was the thought of sharing opinions of war and philosophy over dinner. Besides, Dulon had promised Maranyl. He was almost shamed by the relief he felt at the excuse.

"Ah. I am sorry, but I have promised myself to my wife for dinner tonight. She will be terribly upset if I cancel again. In fact, I was just headed home."

Miyela's expression did not soften. Annoyance flickered in her gaze as she glanced at the court behind him. Two other elves now faced each other, this time holding no weapons. They bowed and set their feet in wide stances.

"I was just checking on the progress of the tournament." Dulon fought the heat that threatened to suffuse his face. "Another time?"

"Soon."

"Certainly!" Dulon said.

Miyela watched him with a level expression, then turned back the way she had come. Dulon glanced at the sun's progress toward the horizon, then turned his feet toward the Domes of Rhelyon, his steps hastened by the prospect of steaming salmon and Maranyl.

The rich smell of food gushed out the door like water from a floodgate. The air simmered with the heat of the stove, and evening light spilled through the windows, leaching from the blackening sky. Dulon closed the door behind him and sauntered up behind the woman peeking through a slit in the oven to check on two sizzling slabs of fish. She brushed the pale waves of her hair back from the oven's heat.

"You came," she said in a tone of mock surprise, keeping her back to him.

"Not for lack of effort on the part of every elf in Daro."

"Naturally." Maranyl picked up a bottle of wine and sat it on a small table pushed against the windows set with plates and glasses. Past the windows, lights were beginning to twinkle in the Court and the buildings beyond. Dulon watched Maranyl, eyes glowing. He could feel the tension of the day dissipating from his shoulders.

He caught her by the arm as she made to pass him again. Her lips curved into a smile as she looked up at him. He bowed his head and kissed her on the mouth. She smelled of clean salt and tasted of wine. Maranyl leaned her forearms against his chest.

"Hello," she said, eyes sparkling as they met his.

"Already started without me have you?" said Dulon.

"I had to test the bottle."

"Of course." His grin widened.

"Finish with the vegetables, will you?" she said, pulling away from him and returning to the oven. Dulon picked up the knife lying next to a plate of half-chopped vegetables and set to work.

After a few minutes of companionable silence, Maranyl asked, "So, how many elves did you meet with today? A dozen? Two dozen?"

"Too many." Dulon mumbled. He tossed the vegetables into a bowl and poured oil and vinegar over them.

Within the space of a few minutes, Dulon summarized his more important points of conversation and observance over the last few days. He had not had time to talk at length with Maranyl for nearly a week. She listened, asking the occasional question and providing insight. Maranyl was an apt engineer herself and was often better even than Dulon at the nuances of politics. As they sat for their meal, Dulon mentioned his encounter with Miyela.

"How is it with her here?"

"Fine," Dulon said with a shrug. "Why shouldn't it be?"

Maranyl eyed him shrewdly. Dulon studied his food.

"Has she said anything about the city?" said Maranyl.

"Oh plenty," Dulon muttered.

The sympathy in Maranyl's face made his skin burn. What did it matter what Miyela thought of his city? When had he ever given heed to what the Lady of Morcanan thought of him?

"Is she against the alliance?" asked Maranyl.

"Without question, though I know little of the opinion of the rest of the Council. The arguments stray to half-relevant ramblings as soon as the subject is broached."

"Mmm," muttered Maranyl, considering as she chewed. "Well, you will have to meet with Miyela at some point. She is not one to be skirted for long. What about the elves of Daro?"

"What about them?"

Maranyl raised an eyebrow. "Well, it is them you would be asking to go to battle—not Miyela, or Liera, or any of the Council. Except Gellion—what does he think?"

"We haven't spoken of it much to be honest. Only after the first Council meeting. But I can tell he is against it."

One side of Maranyl's lips twitched upward. "It seems to me, my dear, that you are not talking to the right elves. You question yourself and those with the standing to judge you, but not those who are most affected by the decision itself, those who should be making the choice in the end."

Dulon looked at her with a mix of admiration and frustration. The truth of wisdom did not make it easier to hear. He took a long drink and sighed. He was tired of discussing the subjects he had hoped to escape tonight.

"There are much more pleasant things to talk about, love," he said. "Tell me of the Performance Hall."

Maranyl eyed him for a moment, then began to outline the latest plans for two new performance rooms. Maranyl's greatest skill lay in acoustical engineering. She was a musician and had helped design the Performance Hall of Daro. It seemed that every year she came up with another improvement to be installed in the theater. Dulon's mind wandered through her technical descriptions, his attention focused on the light in her face as she spoke.

That night, Dulon lay on his back staring at the reflection of the moon on the ceiling. Maranyl was stretched out next to him, an arm flung across his belly.

"Mari?" he whispered. She grumbled indistinctly into his shoulder. He was silent a while longer, then asked, "What do you think of going to battle with the humans?" Maranyl twisted her neck up and considered him, then smiled and propped herself up in the pillows.

7

THE HUNT BEGINS

Renyra crouched behind a thyme bush. The potent smell made her nose wrinkle as she peered around its dense foliage. Two brown lumps sat amid the scrubland, barely detectable but for the slight nodding movements of their grazing heads. Renyra took one step sideways away from the bush, then pulled the titanium shaft of her javelin back behind one ear.

She closed her eyes, trying to sense the terra spirits beneath her. A tweak of the right foot, a shift of weight, and she was grounded and balanced. She tried to sense the ether spirits suspended between herself and the hares. There was a breeze. She moved the javelin's tip a hair's breadth to the left. Then she focused on her own spirit, intertwined with that of Riu. Taking a breath, she opened her eyes and threw the javelin.

With a faint *whoosh*, the weapon soared toward its target and passed through the first hare and into the second one, embedding its tip into the ground beyond them both. Renyra let out her breath. She did not practice A'vaeri as Firas did, but her mother had instilled the art's principles into her from the time she was born, and Renyra owed much of her hunting skill to its methods.

She stood and walked forward. The hem of her skirt brushed the earth as she knelt down next to the hares and pulled her javelin free. She made the sign of the star. She did not know if animals had souls, but it didn't hurt. As she picked up the hares by their feet, Renyra felt a twinge in her chest at the warmth and softness the little animals still held. She dropped them gently into her bag. Their deaths had been swift and clean.

Much cleaner than any they were likely to meet in this harsh land.

She now had a dozen hares—enough to bring something more exotic to the Dining Hall tonight.

As Renyra turned her feet back toward the gates of Daro, she moved her eyes from stones to boulders to the occasional cliff face. She searched for fallen trees, cracks in the earth—any sign that the hills had shaken along with Daro in the earthquakes. If the origin of the earthquakes was across the scrubland, toward the Falspires, these hills would have been affected worse than Daro itself. Renyra had heard rumors of earthquakes in the city that she had never felt at times of day when she had been awake and alert. Was it possible that only certain edges of the city were in range of earthquakes that had occurred miles away? Maybe Renyra had been too deep within the city to have noticed. If this was the case, she was determined to find out.

Renyra knew the countryside surrounding Daro better than any elf in the city. She had sharp eyes and a good memory, and was sure she would recognize any inconsistency. Yet the land remained pristine.

She chided herself for her dramatic musings. What was the likelihood of her coming across a blatant sign of damage in all the miles of these hills? It could hardly prove or even suggest the scrubland had not experienced the same shaking as Daro.

By the time she entered through the city gates and brought her grisly bag to the Dining Hall, the sun had gained still more strength. Beneath her leather tunic, Renyra's shirt stuck to her back. Squirming in discomfort, she set off toward the housing district to put away her javelins and change clothes.

She was surprised to find Firas at home. "What are you doing here?" she asked.

Firas looked up from the book in his hands and raised his eyebrows.

Renyra let a puff of air out of her nose and smiled at his expression. "I mean—it is the middle of the afternoon. I expected you would be out."

"Harbor no expectations and you will never be disappointed." He turned his eyes back to his book.

Renyra rolled her eyes and walked over to him. Even sitting, he was her height, and she had to raise onto her toes to reach her arms around his neck from behind. She kissed the side of his smooth face. He smelled of sea brine and metal. Firas leaned his head back and twisted his neck until they were nose to nose. His eyes were the pale green of a shallow shore and revealed as much as the stillest waters. Renyra smiled.

"You have been at the docks," she said.

Firas arched an eyebrow and kissed her lips. "And you have been in the sun."

Renyra narrowed her eyes, unable to decide whether his words implied insult. Firas laughed. "You are very warm, my love."

"Oh."

She took a step away from him and began to unlace and pull off her tunic, but the damp leather stuck to her arms. Had the morning given any hint of the heat to come, she would have worn her wraps rather than this restrictive Turi garb, but the looser fabric of wraps tended to hang up on the prickly vegetation of the scrubland and offered little protection against the chill of a spring morning.

As she struggled to pull her arms out of their sticky confines, Renyra felt warm hands on her shoulders. Reluctantly, she stopped struggling. Firas took her elbows and gently raised them above her head. She stood with both hands extended to the ceiling, feeling foolish as Firas peeled her tunic inside out, up over her head and arms. She had to pull against him to free her wrists of the sleeves' imprisoning grasp. Her undershirt was wrinkled and damp.

"Thanks," she mumbled, sitting at the table.

Firas draped the sodden tunic over a chair, then resumed his seat.

"Good day?" he asked.

"A dozen hares. Nothing terribly exciting." She hardly thought her failed search for evidence of earthquakes worth mentioning. "Did you work on the ship all morning?"

"Most of it. Valder was still there when I left, but I was meeting a few elves for lunch." He suddenly looked uncomfortable.

"Who did you meet?" she asked.

"Just Lythin, Carvell, Lia, Miyela. A few others."

Renyra laughed. "You went from a few to half a dozen."

Firas's mouth turned upward, but his eyes remained troubled.

"The others were Morcani as well?" Renyra asked.

"Yes."

She considered him. Though Daro boasted of its diversity of Kindoms and culture, there were far more Turi and Fieri in the city than Remsgri or Morcani. Renyra knew the Remsgri simply did not like to travel and maintained close families, but the Morcani had other reasons for remaining with their own kind.

"You miss them."

"It is nice to see them."

"What did you talk about?"

Firas sighed. "With the final Council meeting approaching, is there anything else to talk about? The lunch started out with only a few of us. Lythin, Carvell, and me. But Miyela saw us and sat down, and others slowly flocked to us like moths to a flame. Miyela has that effect on people."

Renyra nodded. She had never seen the Lady of Morcanan before this visit, but could easily see how she had commanded armies through centuries of war. Renyra was not sure she liked the woman.

"It seems there have been other meetings," Firas said, "though I do not know if 'meetings' is the right word. There is little discussion, more like a listing of grievances and rallying around shared feelings."

"What do they say?" Renyra asked warily.

"Miyela fears the Council will vote to accept the alliance. She is attempting to take measures to ensure that does not happen and plan for if it does. She has been talking to the other Council Members, trying to make them see reason, recruiting other elves—elves of Daro—to speak out against the alliance, but in truth she has not found as many as she thought she would. Even those she does find opposed to the alliance do not feel passionate enough to take an active stand against it. Her attempts are only increasing tensions, causing arguments and spreading the idea of factions and whispers of scheming through the city."

"Are they all Morcani—the elves in this group?"

"Mostly. Miyela has a unique pull on her people," he paused, looking uncomfortable, "on us. The Morcani may hold the same Council structure as the rest of the elves, but Miyela is more a queen than a representative—well loved and respected. Revered even. Her ardent stand against this issue is spreading through that reverence."

"Including you?" Renyra watched his expressive eyes. They were weary, grieved, anxious.

"I do not know." He looked down. "Regardless of how I feel about Miyela, I think she is going about this the wrong way. I am afraid of what she has begun. Afraid of what it will become."

Renyra was silent for a while. She had been aware of the tense political climate of late, but she had no idea it had gone this far. She remembered Soran's words, spoken so casually weeks before. *'If I were superstitious, I would say this Council is not boding well for Daro.'* Her stomach twisted.

"You said she was planning for 'if the alliance is accepted.' What did you mean?"

"I do not know exactly. She was vague. But that worries me still more."

Renyra stared at her hands. Her own views on the matter were too conflicted and confused to sort through. She had avoided giving it too much thought. She had no say in the final decision, anyway.

Riu give us guidance and save us from ourselves.

Just now the humans seemed little threat.

In the afternoon, Renyra did something most unusual. She went to the Archives of her own accord, with full knowledge that Firas would not be there. The sun was even warmer now, and her shoulders glowed with heat as she stepped onto a levit board outside her house. Twisting her hair into a bun, she activated the board with a heel and soared along the road. She sighed in relief as the cool air blew past her bare arms and belly, the indigo fabric of her wrap streaming behind her.

Just before she reached the end of the neighborhoods, she slowed her board. Two thick lines snaked their way over the stone street. Looking down, Renyra scrutinized the repaired cracks. Before the Builders had repaired the fissures, Renyra had come to investigate the scene when no one was around. She had thrown a pebble into the depths of one and had been alarmed by how long the bouncing echoes lasted. Firas said deep cracks were a common side effect of earthquakes, but Renyra could not imagine any opening of the earth as 'common.' The sense of *wrongness* that accompanied the quakes was anything but common. Firas seemed reluctant to delve deeper into the matter. He had enough to deal with as it was; they all did. But still, curiosity battered at Renyra's mind like Nightjar's hungry head against her arm, and she had as little power to stop it.

Shaking her head in consternation, she urged her board forward again.

The Archives were not as deserted today as the last times Renyra had been here. She did not recognize most of the elves and assumed they were visitors, taking advantage of the more recent writings of Daro which were absent from their own libraries. She passed through shelves of books, fingers trailing along their bindings. Most of the tomes were of a practical nature: detailed accounts and manuals of ship building, cropping, and craftsmanship; titles on engineering, chemistry, hunting, trade, and city infrastructure. Then there were descriptive guides to natural rocks and minerals, native flora, and oceanography, all sorted by location.

Renyra was not much of a reader herself. She loved the Archives because Firas loved them. He most often haunted the shelves containing poetry and natural history. On the binding of these books, Renyra could see the reflection of her husband's eyes.

The desk where Firas had been collecting books on earthquakes and weather sat abandoned. Renyra sat down and picked up a sheet of parchment containing Firas's writing. One section was labeled "From Books:"

Earthquakes occur in mountainous regions—associated with their formation?

Cause breaking of the earth's surface and occasional landslides.

Only earthquake reported south of the Terulian Mountains was associated with the eruption of the volcano in 2340.

Following this was a section labeled "From Memory:"

Minor shaking in Morcanan every few years—no damage

Heavier shaking every few decades—no damage

Violent shaking every few centuries, or longer—little damage

Reported non-physical effects—none

Further down the page were some incomprehensible notes on weather patterns and pressure systems. The writing trailed away as Firas had lost interest. His pen was still lying on the desk. Renyra read the notes again and thought. There were mountains east of Daro, but those were smaller than the Terulian Mountains in Faeran, and Daro was further from them than the southern regions of Faeran were from the Terulians. Firas's personal notes on earthquakes drew her attention.

Even the most violent quakes in Morcanan caused little damage to the city, she thought. *The tremors here were shocking, but I would hardly call them violent, yet the streets have sustained damage.*

Then, of course, was Firas's last note. *'Reported non-physical effects —none.'*

Renyra frowned at the page for several minutes, tossing out every ridiculous explanation that entered her head. Then her eyes fixed on the date: "2340."

She leapt to her feet and went to the shelves containing histories. She scanned the titles—books on the history of each Kindom, city, and the elves as a whole; genealogies; written accounts of prophets from the early days of the elves … there. *The War of Fire*. Renyra pulled the book from the shelf and took it back to Firas's desk. She did not have to look further than the first few pages to find what she was looking for.

> *The Great War began in the year 2340, though it was not until many years later that the elves realized the significance of that date. The great peak above the city of Morcanan blew apart, shattering its summit and sending liquid fire and ash spewing into the air. The city sustained great damage, and the vierstone supply within the mountain was destroyed. Many elves died in the eruption. The first any elf outside of Morcanan knew of the catastrophic eruption was a deep trembling of the earth—felt for miles beyond the mountains, even so far as Tura. In the days following, a black cloud descended upon the land, raining ash and blocking the sun for weeks. Above Morcanan, the mountains were as tombstones so thickly did the ash lay upon their faces. Little did we know then that two centuries of war had already risen from those ashes.*

Renyra skimmed further down.

> *The Morcani elves claim that the eruption of the volcano was preceded by a pattern of signs, the most notable of which was increased earthquakes in the months leading up to the eruption.*

The rest of the chapter recounted the year following the eruption: the unnaturally cold summer and crop failures, the regular sightings of a swooping shadow in the sky—probably imagined in hindsight rather than true accounts. The book mentioned nothing else about earthquakes.

Renyra closed the book, a trickle of fear dripping down her spine. Firas had tried to assure her that the earthquakes could not be the result of a volcano in Faeran, but what if he was wrong? Or what if the volcano threatening to explode was not in Faeran, but in Tala? Still, there had been no mention in the book of metaphysical effects of earthquakes. Surely such reports would have been included? Renyra returned to the bookshelf and skimmed the beginnings of a few other books on the Great War, but found no further information. Frustrated, she put the books away and left the Archives.

Not for the first time, she wished she possessed her own memories of the Great War. She was sure Firas suspected more of this situation than he was telling her. If the Archives proved no help after a few more tries, Renyra was resolved that she would convince Firas to speak his mind to her one way or another.

8

HEAT RISING

Gellion's eyes kept moving of their own accord to the door. He chewed his bottom lip and slipped another thin link into his half-constructed tunic. Each night the last week, he had left the metal shop with cramped hands and crossed eyes, and had to shake himself out of half-dreams of endless chain links and woven wire to get any sleep. With just over a week before the craftsman competition—and the final Kindom Council, but Gellion didn't want to think about that—he knew the next week would be the same. Probably worse. Not all the painstaking hours were without company, however.

Gellion's ears pricked at an imagined scuff, and he darted another glance toward the door. It was dark and empty. He blinked and bowed his head back over his work.

Gellion had seen Kyna across the street when he had walked into the metal shop nearly an hour before. She had been deep in conversation with Miyela—a strange match—and he was sure she had caught his eye.

At last, he heard the unmistakable swing of the door and turned to see the form of a woman. As she stepped forward, however, the muddled light of the room caught the red glints in her hair and Gellion recognized his mother.

The lurch in his chest twisted into something quite different. His mother had yet to see his shop. How had she known where it was? He was seized by the ridiculous urge to fling his hands over his unfinished work, but tightened his grip on his tools instead.

"This is where you have been all this time?" Tenille asked, one eyebrow cocked.

Gellion found his voice. "A fair portion of it."

Tenille was surveying the room with practiced eyes. "A thorough set up. Clean. Efficient." She nodded in approval. "Is it yours alone?"

"Yes." He could not entirely keep the pride from his voice. All the same, he was surprised and a little dismayed by his mother's visit. They had hardly spoken alone since her arrival, and he had refrained from talking with her about metal work at all. He had been waiting for the right time to bring her to his shop, though he did not know what that moment would have been.

"Who told you?" he asked.

"Veldon," Tenille said with a half smile.

Of course.

Gellion tried to summon anger, or even annoyance at his brother, but it would not come. Tenille's eyes moved to his tunic lying on the table.

"May I?"

Gellion's heart beat faster. No one had seen his entry yet. No one except Kyna, but she didn't seem to count, and not even she knew what it would do. He nodded.

Tenille picked up the garment. It flowed like liquid in her hands, absorbing and reflecting the lights around it in a dizzying ripple. Tenille's eyes widened. She tilted the tunic in her hands to watch the effect again, then brought it close to her face to inspect.

Silvery red chain links as thin as a few hairs formed a mesh that was interlaced with wires of the same material. The result was almost as tightly woven as fabric and moved with as much flexibility. Tenille pressed the metal between her fingers.

"Silver, copper, and aluminum," she whispered. A corner of her mouth lifted. "Incredible." She was nodding now. "Yes—it acts almost as a mirror, but—" She looked at him, eyes gleaming. "It requires some movement to work I expect—but it will make its wearer almost unde-tectable?"

Gellion grinned.

"The student has surpassed the master indeed." Tenille chuckled, holding the shirt up by the shoulders. Then her brows drew together. "I remember this style of work," she said slowly. "I have not seen it for ..." Her eyes slid out of focus as she thought, then snapped back to Gellion. She lowered the tunic. "He taught you this, didn't he?" she asked quietly.

Gellion's smile faded, his silence an affirmation to her question. He had hoped she would not remember, or would at least not bring it up if she did.

Tenille seemed to be looking through Gellion—that uncanny way she had of reflecting his own emotions in her eyes. Gellion set his mouth in a hard line.

At last she broke the unnerving stare and watched the tunic flow through her fingers.

"This was his specialty. I had almost forgotten." She shook her head. "The things he could have made," she whispered. "The good he could have done."

Gellion could feel his pulse pick up again. Had he not thought the same thing nearly every day for centuries? It was a useless thought.

The sound of a thousand beads on stone tinkled in Gellion's ears as his mother laid the garment back on the table.

"It is beautiful," she said. "I look forward to seeing it presented. Perhaps by then the Council will have seen reason and we can celebrate in peace." She shook her head. "I will not disturb your progress any further. I only wanted to see your shop."

"I was going to show it to you."

"I'm sure you were. And here I have spoiled the surprise." Tenille smiled. "Good night, Gellion."

"Good night."

He stood alone and stared at the tunic lying on the table.

You have only yourself to blame, dredging up the past in the company of those who share it. Did you really expect she wouldn't remember some of his most skilled work?

There was no doubt that Liera would recognize the tunic as well, but Gellion had resigned himself to that. He would simply avoid the Lady of Tura throughout the competition and hope she retained her silence afterward. Gellion shook his head and sat back at his stool to continue his meticulous work.

"Did you show it to her?"

Gellion started and jerked his head toward the voice. He saw a flash of black hair and a gleam of metal, and the vision of an elf wearing a tunic of woven silver stepped out of the shadows. Gellion's blood turned to ice. He took a step backward before registering that it was Kyna standing before him. She was wearing a silver necklace.

Take these phantoms away.

He resisted the urge to sign the star on himself and took a breath to dispel the tightness in his chest.

"Must you always do that?" he grumbled.

Kyna strolled to a chair next to the work table and sat, looking distinctly unrepentant. Gellion relaxed his face into a strained smile, which Kyna returned in kind, but dripping with irony.

"Well, did you?" she asked.

"Did I what?"

"Show your mother?" she said, exasperated.

"Oh. Yes."

"And?"

Gellion shrugged, engrossing himself in his chain links again.

Kyna smirked. "She loved it."

Gellion couldn't stop his lips from curving upward.

Kyna snorted.

Gellion turned away from her smug expression. "What were you talking about with Miyela?"

"Spying on me were you?"

"Says the elf who just asked about a personal conversation behind closed doors."

Kyna's smirk deepened.

"I saw you in the street," Gellion said. "The public street outside my own workshop I might add. Do you know Miyela?"

"Not really. We just ran into each other."

"A common pastime of yours."

Amusement danced in Kyna's eyes. "What's her relationship to Dulon?"

"Miyela? She's the Lady of Morcanan. Dulon lived in Morcanan before he came to Daro. I'm sure they know each other from centuries' past."

"She doesn't like him."

"No. I don't think that she does. But to be fair, I don't think Dulon carries a particularly high regard of her either." Gellion narrowed his eyes. "Why? Did she say something?"

"Not in so many words."

"But in some?"

"Yes."

"Mmm." Gellion did not like that Miyela was letting her poor opinion of Dulon show to the city's inhabitants. Theirs was a grievance best kept private.

"Dulon wants to accept the alliance," Kyna said. It was not a question.

Gellion clenched his jaw. He turned back to his metalwork. "It seems that way."

Kyna nodded, her expression contemplative. She watched Gellion work for a few minutes, then said, "There was another earthquake today."

A chain link twisted out of shape. Gellion cursed. "What?"

"Just an hour ago. By the arena. There wasn't much damage, but it caused quite a stir with the tournament going on."

Gellion stared. "How do you know this?"

"I was there."

"You watch A'vaeri?" Somehow Gellion could not picture Kyna as an avid fan of martial arts. He himself had not visited the arena since the tournament began, but that was for other reasons.

"I was bored. Until the earthquake, that is. Much more exciting."

A line creased Gellion's brow. He had hoped the second earthquake a week ago had been nothing but an aftershock of the first, but Dulon had said there was another one yesterday. And now today? This was more concerning.

"Was anyone hurt?"

"No. If it had been during knife-throwing or archery that would have been more interesting." Kyna smiled with half her mouth. Gellion could not tell if she was being serious.

"Oh come on." She snorted at his grim expression. "They're just earthquakes, right?"

"You don't think there's … more to them?"

Kyna cocked her head. "More?"

"What happened at the feast. Whatever that was, it was not just an earthquake. And I felt the second one, in my house. It was the same … the same …" He felt ridiculous trying to describe the shimmering of reality and crawling of his skin that had accompanied each occurrence. "Current," he finished lamely. He straightened suddenly. "Did it happen again? Today? Did you feel the current when the ground shook?"

Kyna raised an eyebrow and nodded.

Shaking his head, Gellion started to pace. "But what is it? What could cause it? It's almost like …" He raised a hand, and his fingers brushed his earring.

Kyna was watching his progress across the floor. "Like?"

"I don't know!" Gellion dropped his hand and sighed. "I don't know. And I shouldn't be worrying about it with this alliance hanging over us, not to mention this." He indicated his craft competition entry still lying on the table.

"Then don't."

"Don't what?"

"Worry about it. Until after the Kindom Council is over."

Gellion's arms hung at his sides. He felt both frustrated and foolish. He wanted to shout at her that it wasn't that simple. But maybe it was. He had to set his priorities somewhere, and if the earthquakes were not causing serious damage to Daro or harm to its citizens, maybe it was a problem best addressed after more pressing issues had passed.

Kyna raised her eyebrows.

"Maybe you're right," Gellion said.

"It has been known to happen."

Gellion rolled his eyes, but felt his lips twitch in a smile. It was easy talking to Kyna. She matched him wit for wit, and she never pried, at least not seriously. He met her gaze and felt a not-unpleasant twisting in his gut.

Stop it. You are smarter than this.

Gellion tore his eyes away from Kyna and started linking chains again.

"Need any help?" Kyna said.

Gellion found himself agreeing before he could think better of it.

That evening, Valder came by the shop and convinced Gellion to walk among his own kind for a while and join him for dinner. Gellion did not put up much of a fight. Mealtimes provided an excellent excuse to eavesdrop and glean popular opinion on the alliance. He also felt obliged to spend time with his brothers while Veldon remained in Daro. Of late, however, Veldon had been missing from the social scene of the city almost as much as Gellion, and gave vague answers when asked about the disappearances. If it had been another elf, Gellion may have assumed he had indeed met a woman like Valder jested, but Veldon would never betray Farra.

"You don't think he knows something do you?" Gellion asked Valder. "Something about whatever is affecting Daro?" Unable to find Veldon, the two of them sat sipping a fiery drink made from peaches and olives in the Silver Swan. He twirled his glass on the table along the pattern of dappled evening light filtering through windows above.

"No," Valder said. "He wouldn't keep something like that to himself. I'm sure there's an innocent enough explanation. We will wrest it from him before he leaves."

"I suppose," Gellion said. He suddenly caught the word 'Albaren' behind him and tilted his head toward the conversation.

"Liera and her people were not possessed of such selfless heroism when our fields were steeped in oil and blood after the war," said a woman's voice. "It was fifty years at least before the soil recovered enough to support its previous yields, but all the Turi offered was condolence and some crates of salt fish."

"They had their own recoveries to tend to," another woman responded.

"It wasn't only the lack of productivity after the war," the first replied. "Neither the Turi nor the Morcani overstretched themselves battling the wildfires of the more recent decades, did they? Not even the Remsgri crossed the floodplain to aid us. I'm not," she added quickly, over what Gellion assumed was another retort from her friend, "blaming them for that. Auralia is too proud to have asked for aid anyway. I'm merely pointing out that undue gallantry has not been forthcoming between the Kindoms since the end of the war, but now that these humans plead their weakness, we claim to be the valiant saviors of Tala? It is either hypocrisy or excuse."

Gellion looked at Valder, who was listening as well. He wore a strange expression. A muscle was working in his jaw, and he stared at his drink with blank eyes.

With the third Council meeting looming ever nearer, Gellion still did not know his brother's stance on the impending decision. This was not from any thwarted attempts or reluctance on Valder's part, Gellion simply had not thought to ask Valder's opinion. Of his two youngest brothers, Veldon had always been the philosophical one—the most philosophical of any in his family. In what little time Gellion had managed to spend with him these past weeks, Veldon had made it clear that he leaned toward Gellion's negative opinion of the alliance, but said he did not think it his place to take sides when Daro was not his home. Valder had a much firmer stake in the outcome of the decision, but he had never been one for politics or sides of any kind. By the tension now evident in Valder's eyes, however, Gellion felt a thin uncertainty beginning to take form in his stomach.

"Valder?" Gellion let his voice rise in question.

Valder blinked and looked up at him.

"What is it?" Gellion said, when Valder only stared at him.

Valder hesitated, then shrugged and took a drink. His gaze darted toward the two Fieri elves still arguing, and Gellion was further disconcerted to see resentment on his brother's face.

"It seems petty, that's all," Valder muttered.

Gellion's brows drew together. "What does?"

Valder shrugged again. "Why should the woman be angry about the elves wanting to help the humans just because her people didn't receive the same? She would rather they conform to her opinion of them than do something better for someone else."

Gellion was taken aback by the seriousness in Valder's voice. It seemed to dampen the air and dim the lights somehow. Gellion shifted, then looked around in mock confusion. "I know you resemble Veldon more than I remembered, but I didn't think you could fool me with a full switch. Come now, where's the real Valder?"

Valder rolled his eyes and twitched his lips into a smile that barely held any humor. "I'm serious, Gellion." When this statement only raised Gellion's brows higher, Valder shot him an exasperated look. "Look, I just don't like what it's doing to Daro—the alliance, the arguments, the anger. And the conversations like that." He tossed his head toward the women behind him. "I thought the elves who came to live in Daro were better than Kindom rivalry and grudges."

"I think you misunderstood their argument," Gellion said slowly. "The woman isn't angry about elves wanting to help the humans, she just doesn't believe the authenticity of the claims some elves are making that righteous aid *is* their motivation to go to battle." Gellion paused, trying to watch his brother's reaction out the side of his eyes. "And nor do I for that matter."

Valder only looked down at his glass, spinning its contents in a rhythmic motion. He did not answer, but the set of his mouth revealed more than words. A creeping dread worked through Gellion's veins.

"You are in favor of the alliance," he said.

Valder slowly raised his eyes to meet Gellion's. There was apprehension in his look, but also a hint of defiance that confirmed Gellion's suspicion. Heat rose into his throat. He fought to push it down, but tendrils slipped through to color his next words.

"You're in favor of the alliance?" he said through his teeth.

Valder straightened at Gellion's tone. "A lot of elves are in favor of the alliance, Gellion."

"Other elves, yes, but not ... not *you*. Why didn't you say anything before now?"

Valder let out a derisive snort. "Because I knew how well you would take it."

The heat had spread, and was pressing against Gellion's chest now. Of course he had heard arguments in favor of the alliance in his eavesdropping. He knew many of the elves who made them. But this was Valder. Valder was supposed to be reasonable. Valder wasn't supposed to take anything seriously.

"And for what reason," said Gellion, "do you think we should go to battle? To help the less fortunate?"

Valder's eyes flashed. "Since when is that a shameful thing?"

"This is the Albaren. They are hardly helpless innocents. What do you know of the Albaren other than the basics of their language? A language *I* taught you after learning it from the humans over years of dealing with them?"

Valder stared at him.

Gellion went recklessly on. "And what do any of us know of the Dierna? You would help the 'less fortunate' by killing humans you've never seen, let alone interacted with, who have done nothing to provoke us?"

It took a moment for Valder to respond. He closed his hanging jaw. "What does it matter that they haven't provoked us? Does that make them innocent?" Color was beginning to stain his cheeks. "If someone were attacked by a man twice his size, would you let the man go because he hasn't harmed *you*?"

"The Albaren are no cowering innocents."

"You've only been to Tradira a handful of times and met with Albaren nobility—half of whom are probably generations dead by now. How can you truly know the Albaren as a people? You've told me yourself you don't understand the humans!"

"I understand enough to treat their words with caution."

"We are stronger than them. Daro alone could rival half of Albarad, but they ask for our help. Why should we deny them when it would only take a small sacrifice from us?"

"A small sacrifice?" Gellion's anger was threatening to boil over now. He was aware of the glances of other elves in their direction. The two women behind him were gone. "You call war a small sacrifice?"

Valder hesitated. "This one—yes. Do you think the Dierna pose any serious threat to us?"

"No—and that is still further reason not to blindly accept the word of the Albaren! This is not our fight. It is not our people. It is not even our continent."

Valder glared at him. "And that means we should leave it to squander at our feet?"

"This is not a war to end suffering!" Gellion shouted, heedless of the elves turning to stare at him. "It is not sharing our good fortune with those in sore need of it! More likely it will magnify the Albaren's existing power at the expense of those they hope to conquer—bringing only more strife. Nor," he continued, "is any of this the reason Dulon is considering accepting this offer. He had no interest at all until vierstone entered the matter. This is no heroic obligation to aid the oppressed, it is a desperate attempt to get more vierstone. If you believe anything otherwise, you are as naive and innocent as these humans you have invented."

Valder looked like he had been slapped. He regarded Gellion for a few moments, then stood and left without a word. Gellion sat, trying to control the trembling that had overtaken his muscles. His vierstone earring was burning against his skin. The elves at the surrounding tables were openly gaping at Gellion now and ducked their heads when he met their eyes.

After a time, the pulse throbbing in Gellion's temples began to settle, and he walked out into the darkening street. The cool sea breeze took some of the heat from his skin, and his head started to clear. Gellion chose a direction and walked. Shame was beginning to burn in his throat, accompanied by a twinge of fear. Gellion's temper was a demon he constantly faced, but he rarely lost control like that. He couldn't remember the last time it had happened—and never with Valder. He raked a hand through his hair. It was bad enough that the whole of the Kindom Council had been taken over by this cursed alliance, now it was poisoning his personal life?

Gellion found himself on Master's Street. The thought of another night spent with his chain links—monotonous hours in which to relive his argument with Valder—was past bearing. He turned his back on the metal shop and continued to the housing district, then stopped at the door of his house. Valder's house. He stared at the door handle, willing his hand to turn it, then clenched his fist and walked back into the night.

Gellion only caught fleeting glimpses of Valder over the next few days. The tension between them had one positive effect—Gellion felt even more disposed to remain shut up in his metal shop. The construction of his tunic was nearly finished; all that would remain after was to enhance its properties and seal them. This would take skill, but no great amount of time, which was fortunate.

As the final Council meeting drew nearer, Gellion found himself ferrying documents and messages between elves and reading through proposals and lists in most of his spare time. Any other moments he spent moving throughout the city listening, directly or indirectly, to the elves he was supposed to represent through his decisions at the Council meeting. He did not like what he heard. He managed to keep his temper in check, but he could occasionally feel it rising to his skin, boiling beneath the surface, seeking an opening.

As he hurried about the Domes of Rhelyon, he often caught sight of Dulon, and had the feeling the man was trying to get him alone. Gellion knew they would have to talk before the last meeting, but he did not look forward to the encounter.

The opportunity finally arose one evening as Gellion was returning a report on ship motors. He left the paperwork in a stack in the Council meeting room. On the way out, he almost ran into Dulon.

"Ah! Doing official business?" Dulon glanced at the stacks of paper. "Do you have a moment?"

Gellion hesitated. "Of course." He forced a smile.

"Marvelous." Dulon spun on his heel and strode across the hall. He swung a door inward and gestured with a broad grin. "After you."

Gellion entered a sitting room similar to the one in which he had met Amadeo.

"A beverage?" Dulon picked up two glasses from a table and tipped a pitcher of crimson liquid into each. Gellion took the glass and sat in a straight-backed chair. Dulon collapsed onto the couch next to it.

"Some business this." He looked directly at Gellion. Though his face gave no betrayal, Gellion could see the strain behind his sparkling eyes.

"Some business indeed," replied Gellion. He took a sip from his glass. Spiced apples from the previous autumn. "Have the Council Members been bombarding you?"

"Heavens yes. I don't know which is worse, the stern lectures from Liera or the philosophical musings of Rhosti. Auralia just gives me disapproving glances in passing, Cuvan is quiet as usual, and Tenille is quiet most unusually." He frowned. "But it is the elves of the city that cause me true concern. They are as split on the issue as the Council. I've heard arguments—lots of them. The division worries me."

Gellion nodded, all too familiar with the description. He changed the subject. "And Miyela? You didn't mention her."

Dulon nodded slowly, looking uncomfortable. "Yes. I did speak with her. Just yesterday actually." He considered the reflections of his glass in the evening light, then looked up at Gellion. "She is not pleased."

"Not pleased about what?"

"That this is even a question I brought before the Council, that either way we decide, it is only bringing about discord. It is not as though this alliance was my idea! Had I made the decision myself—to accept or decline—she would have been affronted by my not consulting her, I am sure. As it stands, she is adamantly against any thought of accepting the alliance."

Gellion kept his silence. Dulon looked at him with obvious frustration.

"She will not hear of it. She says no amount of vierstone is worth such a deal, and it would be senseless to interfere with a war between humans, choosing sides like a spectator at a caesir match."

There was another pause. "Gellion."

Gellion looked up. Dulon looked drained. "What do you think?"

Gellion took a while to respond. "I agree with her," he said at last.

Dulon stared at him hard, as though trying to see into his mind, then nodded and sighed. "I had a feeling you would." He took another drink. "Please explain."

Gellion took a breath, determined to remain rational and calm—diplomatic. "I've listened to the elves of Daro, Dulon. As you say, the city is divided, but a desire to accept the alliance seems dominant."

Dulon nodded. "Yes, that is the impression I have as well."

"I understand some of the concerns and the reasoning ..." Gellion paused, gathering his thoughts.

"But?" Dulon prompted.

Gellion shook his head. "There may one day be a need for more vierstone, but at present the prospect seems too speculative to act on. As for the righteous aid of an oppressed people ... I have gathered that honesty and equality are not held in high esteem among the powerful and wealthy of Albarad. I know nothing of the Dierna. It is possible that what Amadeo claims of them is true, but it is equally possible he spoke in half-truths and exaggeration to make their situation seem more desperate."

Dulon was listening with a carefully blank face. Gellion continued.

"Having experienced two centuries of devastating loss and destruction through one war, I can't justify entering another without ironclad reason, and the reasoning to enter this is spun glass."

Dulon did not speak for a while. Slowly, one corner of his mouth quirked upward in a grimace. "You always were good with words, Gellion. You could persuade a piece of sandstone to become a diamond if given the time." He ran a hand over his face. "And worse, you make sense. But still, I disagree. The reasons to accept this alliance may not be ironclad but neither are they glass. They are like the heavy stone used in a foundation—difficult, even of debatable necessity, but in most situations vital to a long-lasting base. A necessary evil."

Gellion did not speak. A flicker of apprehension appeared in Dulon's eyes. Gellion realized the intensity of his own gaze and forced himself to relax his rigid muscles. There was a flare of fear to his anger. To hear the Lord of Daro speak this way, even in a tone of reluctance, was more disconcerting than the proclamations of those citizens most adamant to go to battle.

"Necessary is a strong word," said Gellion, keeping his voice steady.

"Yes," Dulon murmured, his eyes drifting to the windows. There was a long silence. At last, Gellion cleared his throat and Dulon snapped back to the present. His face relaxed into a grin.

"Thank you for sharing your thoughts with me. I will consider them."

"Will the final decision be put to a vote?"

"Yes I think so—no better way to do it. We will never get a consensus. I think further debate during the meeting should be avoided. We've talked ourselves in circles over the last weeks. It will be what it will be." He sighed. "Most importantly, it will be over."

9

SHADOWS OF MIND AND PAST

Renyra was surprised by the sun's progress toward the horizon. She had spent another afternoon in the Archives with absolutely no startling new insights to show for it. How scholars stood the hours of fruitless eye strain and dashed hopes, Renyra would never understand. She took a deep breath, relishing the air's briny freshness compared with the heavy must of the Archives.

The main street running from the gates of Daro to the Court was scattered with elves walking toward evening destinations and dinner. She passed the Performance Hall and gazed at its doors wistfully. She missed the Sira rehearsals that had filled so many hours before the Sea Festival. The distraction now would have been welcome, but everyone was busy with the tournament.

She passed the doors and made her way into the Dining Hall. The hall itself was almost entirely back to normal. New glass shimmered between the window panes, the crack in the stone floor was barely noticeable with a neat and perfect filling, and the tables sat in orderly rows. Groups of elves huddled at the tables. Despite the pristine appearance of the Dining Hall, however, conversations sounded hushed, strained. A few elves eyed Renyra suspiciously, as though she were eavesdropping; others watched to see where she would sit. Renyra stopped, taken aback by the atmosphere. Had things changed so much? How had she not noticed?

A wave of motion from the side of the room caught Renyra's attention, and she saw Caerlyn beckoning to her. Renyra smiled and nodded, then passed through muttered discussions to the back of the hall. She took a glass bowl from a table and spooned a spiced root vegetable mash into it, followed by a slice of bread and hunk of cheese. The aroma of the food made her stomach rumble as she took a seat beside her friend.

Caerlyn was elegant and dark, with almond eyes. She wore a crimson wrap that shone like a ruby against her skin. Malo, a Turi elf, sat with her.

"Festive, eh?" Caerlyn nodded her head toward the room at large. Malo's mouth thinned to a flat line.

"How long has it been like this?" asked Renyra.

"No more than a few days, I would say," said Caerlyn. "Not to this extent at least. Just before you came there was an argument between three or four elves. Nothing extreme, but loud enough to notice. It ended with several elves storming out of the Dining Hall." Annoyance flickered in her eyes. "I think they were Morcani."

"The Morcani have been causing a lot of trouble," said Malo. "They should speak in the open, not through whispers."

Renyra made a noncommittal sound and took a bite of bread.

Malo continued, "I have not seen an atmosphere like this since Tura in the war, but then we were at least united in a single goal, even if opinions about our methods of handling it clashed."

Renyra perked up. She remembered hearing Malo talk about events in the early history of Tura before. Had he been born before the war began? Elves of such an age were certainly not rare—they probably made up more than half of the elves' population as a whole—but Daro tended to draw younger elves. Renyra herself was young for an elf, born fourteen years after the end of the war.

"Enough darkness," said Caerlyn. "It's all we've talked about the last half hour. How's your craftsman entry coming along, Malo?"

Renyra looked to Malo with interest. She would speak to him alone after dinner. "I didn't know you were making something," she said. "What is it?"

Malo's serious face relaxed somewhat. He almost smiled. "Everyone is being staunchly close-lipped about the whole affair, so I will follow suit. I am pleased with my progress, however."

"What about you, Renyra?" Caerlyn asked. "Weaving a masterpiece out of grass? Fur?"

Renyra rolled her eyes, but smiled. Caerlyn had never understood her eccentric interest in plants and animals. She, like Renyra, had lived most of her life in the grasslands of Faeran. Both had left their homes to pursue Sira as a profession. Along with Firas and a few others, they had travelled the continent together as a troupe, performing and teaching their art. Renyra loved her life in Daro, but part of her still longed to return to her days of travel and excitement and budding romance.

"You should know as much about grass as any," Renyra said with a grin.

"I may know of it, but it doesn't mean I take any joy in it." Caerlyn shook her head. "I don't know how you stand the drudgery of the greenhouses. It's like trying to understand paper."

"Just because you can't understand a thing with a touch doesn't make it less complex or valuable."

"Oh I'm not doubting the value of plants, merely the futility of trying to comprehend them."

Renyra shrugged. "It's more rewarding to learn with time and observation. You can know everything about a stone with a touch. You can grow that knowledge over time, but anything you learn is essentially told to you by the stone. I would rather be shown. See glimpses through the mystery over time. What's the fun of knowing all at once?"

Malo was watching her thoughtfully, Caerlyn like she was mad. Renyra laughed. "Fine, keep your order and knowledge."

Caerlyn smirked. They sat in silence for a while.

Renyra let her eyes roam over the Dining Hall, and her gaze was drawn to the silver hair of Miyela sitting at the next table. The Lady of Morcanan was sitting across from a dark haired woman with sharp features. The two were deep in conversation. A line creased Renyra's brow as she watched them.

Her stare was broken by the clatter of dishes around her. Caerlyn was stacking their bowls and plates to take to the kitchens. Renyra muttered her thanks and stood.

"Good evening to you, Renyra." Malo nodded and was about to leave when Renyra stopped him.

"Wait, could I ask you something?"

Malo looked slightly taken aback. "Of course."

"Were you born before the war?"

Malo's brows lowered over his eyes. "Yes."

"So you were in Tura when the volcano erupted?"

A shadow fell over Malo's face. He nodded.

"Was it—the earthquake I mean—similar to what has happened here?" Renyra asked.

Malo paused, then spoke slowly. "It was comparable, yes. Though the shaking was not as strong in Tura as in cities nearer the mountains. Why do you ask?"

She ignored the question. "Was there damage in Tura? Or other cities you know of?"

"Not that I remember. Certainly not in Tura."

"And," she paused, "the ... the other effects from these earthquakes?"

She could see the understanding click behind Malo's eyes. He took a breath. "No. I never felt those." He tucked a lock of dark hair behind his ear, looking uncomfortable, and glanced around. "I have no explanation for that. No one does that I know of. I have never heard of such a sensation caused by an earthquake or otherwise."

Renyra nodded, the small flame of hope in her chest extinguished.

"I assumed as much, I just thought I would ask." She could tell the conversation was making Malo uncomfortable, but she could not stop herself asking, "Why are the streets of Daro breaking if this earthquake was less powerful than those in Faeran?"

Malo paused with his lips parted, considering. "I do not know." He said at last, looking down in thought. "It is ... strange. I would think Daro was built with more strength than any of the Great Cities."

They stood in silence until Caerlyn's voice made both of them start.

"Have I missed something?" She was staring between them with a raised eyebrow.

"Oh nothing," said Renyra. "Just more dark talk."

Caerlyn snorted. "Leave your dark thoughts for the light of morning." She nodded goodbye and strode toward the doors of the Dining Hall. Renyra turned back to Malo.

"Thank you. I'm sorry to trouble you."

"The trouble is there with or without you bringing it up. Do not let it worry you too much—it will not stop the earth from shaking." A corner of his mouth curved up.

Renyra smiled. "Good luck with the competition."

Malo inclined his head and left her. Renyra stood for a moment longer, thinking, then turned to follow his lead. She paused. The piercing eyes of the woman sitting across from Miyela had been lingering on her. As their eyes met, the woman turned her gaze back to Miyela. Renyra looked away, skin prickling.

The unseasonal heat of the day was nearly extinguished. Renyra did not feel like returning home yet. Her feet took her through the Court and down the stairs next to the viaduct.

Too many unanswered questions, too much speculation.

And which question was more pressing? The possibility that Daro could be seriously damaged, the earthquakes a sign of a looming disaster? Or the nearer possibility of battle with the humans or even among the elves? How far would the rising conflict between the elves go? Surely there would not be violence? Open violence between elves was virtually unheard of. There were disagreements, loud arguments, sometimes even a slap, rarely a punch thrown—but never more than that, never blood. When one could live thousands of years, grudges and physical damage were no light matter. Renyra had never heard of a cold-blooded murder between elves. It was unthinkable.

But what would the Morcani do if the Council voted to accept the alliance? Would they rebel? Attempt to override the decision?

Dulon shouldn't have let it drag on this long. She shook her head. *The humans should never have proposed the bargain in the first place.*

An elf turned sharply onto the road a few buildings ahead of her. Renyra's heart jumped, but she chided herself when she recognized the gait of Gellion. She considered calling out to him, but a moment later, her eye caught another movement ahead of him. She froze. As Gellion crossed to a street leading to the housing district, a silhouette paced in the shadows of the trees, then stopped behind him. An ether spirit? Renyra strained her eyes into the darkness. No, it looked like an elf—tall with fluid movements. It stood motionless as Gellion passed it. Renyra didn't know what to do. Should she call out to Gellion? Draw attention to the shadow? Follow them? Her heart pounded.

"Gellion!" she called as casually as she could.

Gellion stiffened, then turned to look back at her. In the instant he turned, the shadow gave a sudden movement. Renyra thought she saw the glint of eyes, and a thrill of panic seized her chest. She shuddered, and goosebumps spread down her limbs as the shadow disappeared into the night.

Gellion was walking toward her. A line creased his brow when he saw her face. "What is it?" he asked, glancing toward the copse of trees she was staring at.

"I thought—" her eyes darted around. "I thought I saw something in the trees."

Gellion squinted toward the trees. "I don't see anything—an animal?"

Renyra paused, mouth agape, then nodded.

"Probably." She did not know why she didn't tell him what she thought she had seen.

He would think me mad—paranoid. I'm just tired and worked up from the day's events. It was probably just in my head.

Or maybe it had been an ether spirit. Most of the spirits were good, or at least harmless—they came from Riu after all—but she knew they could be corrupted ...

"Are you alright?" Gellion asked.

"Fine," Renyra said, trying to bring confidence back to her voice. "Just a strange night."

Gellion stared at her. She thought she saw a trace of fear in his eyes. This breach of Gellion's self-confidence caused a much more substantial fear in Renyra.

Gellion eyed the surrounding darkness. "Yes," he murmured, "they all seem to be these days."

Renyra suppressed another shudder. She did not ask what he meant.

10

INVISIBLE LINKS

Notes floated around Gellion like down feathers caught in a breeze —closer, further, louder, softer. He watched the musicians sway to their music, backlit by the reflection of the sun off the sea. One elf held a violin, the mirror of her bow dancing on its platinum surface as she played. The airy tones of a flute accompanied the strings, and a man's voice completed the trio, weaving between the two instruments like a sinuous fish through strands of ocean weed:

> *I sing to the East, as the sun crests its hill,*
> *Though light floods the land, my dark lingers still.*
> *Yet the wind in the leaves whispers your name,*
> *And so does your peace fill me the same.*

The three elves sat on a wall rising above the market and wharf. A small gathering of elves had assembled on the lawn behind them. Gellion twisted a blade of grass between his fingers. He took a deep breath and leaned back against the tree behind him. Kyna sat next to him, legs folded under her, watching the musicians. A line creased her brow; her head was tilted sideways like a crooked portrait with her eyes fixed on the singer.

"Do you sing?" Gellion asked.

"No," Kyna said absently. After a few moments, she seemed to realize this was not a satisfactory answer and turned to Gellion, her eyes trailing behind before meeting his. "I never learned an instrument and know few songs. I don't see the point."

"The point?" Gellion raised his eyebrows. "Must there be a point to everything?"

"Yes."

"A bland life that would be."

"A life of purpose. Are you a musician then?"

"I'm no virtuoso, but I can carry a pitch well enough."

Kyna nodded absently, her eyes wandering over the gathering. Gellion sighed. When Kyna slipped into this aloof state, conversation was pointless.

That explains it. If there is no point *she does not speak.*

"Do you want to do something more meaningful then?" Gellion said.

Kyna's mouth turned up in a wry smile. "Like what?"

"Well, I have to pick up some trade documents to review before the last Council meeting."

"Riveting."

Gellion smirked. "What would you like to do then?"

"I haven't seen the vierstone quarry."

Gellion's smirk fell. He shifted. "We did see it."

"Not up close."

"We don't go to the quarry without cause." The words came too fast and too sharp.

Kyna raised an eyebrow.

"You're a Council Member of Daro," she said. "Is it not cause enough that a visitor wishes to see the heart of Daro's might?"

Gellion glanced at her. As usual, he could sense little of her thoughts, not behind the ironic mask she never seemed to remove. He was sure Dulon would not approve of him taking a relative stranger into the quarry. But what harm would it do? The thought of being in such a secluded and charged atmosphere with Kyna set wings flapping in his stomach.

Swallowing his reservations, he gave her a lopsided smile.

"Alright. Come on." He rose to his feet and extended a hand to pull Kyna off the ground.

The two cut behind a string of artisan shops and turned down an alley leading to Master's Street. Veering left toward the viaduct, Gellion made for the lift at the end of the street, but had hardly paced the length of two shops when his feet came sliding to a stop on the cobbled stones. Kyna ran into his shoulder, exhaled in annoyance, then stepped back and followed his gaze.

A gaping crack twisted up the side of an exterior wall. Powdered stone coated the edges like sawdust, and shards of rock littered the street. A few elves were gathered near the base of the building, murmuring to each other. Gellion felt his skin prickling. He had been on Master's Street earlier in the day, and nothing had been amiss. When had this happened? Why hadn't he noticed?

He closed his eyes and shook his head. There had been a midday thunderstorm—violent, but quick as they always were on the coast. Had thunder masked the crack of stone? Had the heat of his metal shop inured him to the shimmering of the air and a spinning head?

Kyna walked up to the wall, stepping over broken stones. Gellion felt a flutter of unease. "You shouldn't stand so close—it isn't stable." Kyna ignored him and ran her hand along the edge of the jagged wall, white powder dusting her fingers. Gellion walked up behind her and looked over her shoulder at the slice of room revealed beyond.

"I should tell Dulon," he said.

"He may already know."

"Maybe." Gellion shook his head. "Come with me. He's probably at the Domes. We can go to the quarry after."

Kyna gave him a resigned look. "Alright."

They did not have to go to the Domes. As they stepped onto a lift and crested the expanse of the Court, Dulon came striding toward them, flaxen hair trailing behind him. He wore a black and silver tunic tailored to his form and an expression of grim determination. Gellion called his name.

Dulon had been about to pass them without so much as glance, but seemed to break out of his internal musings. He glanced from Gellion to

Kyna, and his expression melted into his characteristic grin, tainted by some amusement. Gellion felt heat rise to his skin.

"Ah, Gellion. And Lady Kyna." Dulon gave Kyna a slight bow.

Gellion considered Kyna with some curiosity. He rarely saw her about the city, but she seemed to know everyone.

Dulon beamed at Gellion. "Last we met I forgot to ask you about the craftsman competition. Prepared to bring glory to Daro?"

"I'm almost finished."

"Excellent. Though I shudder to think what increased renown will do to your humble nature." He turned to wink at Kyna.

"Mmm." Gellion rolled his eyes. "Have you seen the building on Master's Street?"

Dulon's smile became more strained. "I have. I was just going to talk to Aryn about it actually. There is a crack on the side of the Archives as well."

"From this afternoon?" Gellion said with alarm.

"I don't know."

Gellion knew he should accompany Dulon and see the damages himself, but Kyna pulled at him like static. There would be time enough to deal with structural issues of the city after the Kindom Council was over.

"Oh it's nothing to worry about, I'm sure," said Dulon. "That street in the housing district is entirely repaired, and these fixes will be just as quick." Gellion saw the slightest glint of unease behind his eyes. "Anyway, must be getting along. A good evening to you both." Dulon flashed a final grin and descended the stairs next to the lift at a trot.

"You know Dulon?" Gellion asked Kyna.

Kyna shrugged. "He's spoken with all the visitors since we arrived."

"Oh." Gellion frowned. He had not bothered much with any of the visitors besides the Council Members and Kyna—and his brother of course. Dulon was always surprising him by all that he did without Gellion's knowledge. How did the man have enough hours in the day?

He doesn't spend half of them shut away in a metal shop.

Gellion grimaced. For all Dulon's showmanship, the Lord of Daro was undeniably good at his job, and put far more of himself into his city than Gellion felt inclined to spare.

The flash of a staff at the edge of Gellion's vision made him snap his head up and step backward.

The elf holding the weapon smirked at Gellion and moved his staff closer to his side.

"Sorry," he said. Looking quite unapologetic, he sauntered on his way, elbowing the elf beside him and muttering something.

Gellion ground his teeth, but a touch of longing brushed against his conscience as he watched the two make their way toward the arena. He had not set foot in the space since the sports competition had begun. This was probably another mark against his leadership, but the oversight had not been due to lack of time. Gellion had made a point to avoid the sparring matches.

He loved the A'vaeri and he hated it. The flowing style of fighting had saved his life more times than he could count through the war. So too had the art's calming and focusing effects kept him sane in his darkest moments. The patterns still calmed him, but they also drew his mind inexorably to the A'vaeri's original purpose—survival and spiritual centering in an era of fear and death.

The art had become so entrenched in elven culture during the war that it had remained in some form in every Kindom after the war's end. Even elves born after the war often took up A'vaeri as a spiritual discipline and physical exercise. But Gellion had always felt there was another reason A'vaeri remained an active part of elven life. The beginning of the Great War had been disastrous for the elves, who had only ever used weapons to hunt before. It had taken decades to build the skills to defend themselves. With the A'vaeri in constant practice, the elves would never be caught so vulnerable again.

Gellion had hoped the moment would never come when A'vaeri's original purpose became relevant once more. He had certainly never imagined the moment would be under circumstances within his power to affect. Could this tournament be training for a true fight only months away? He closed his eyes and turned away from the arena.

Kyna was watching him with her head cocked. "So? Are we going? Or would you rather watch those two bash each other with sticks?"

Gellion flinched, not just because Kyna had caught his stare, but because she spoke of A'vaeri so harshly. Whatever misgivings the tournament brought to Gellion's mind, A'vaeri was so much more than 'bashing each other with sticks.'

"No." Gellion blinked himself back to the present and turned to face the viaduct. "This way."

They crossed the Court and passed through a set of iron doors to the Tower of Stars. A spiral staircase led up to the viaduct above, but behind the stairs was a bolted iron door. Gellion pulled a key from his pocket and fit it into a thin slot in the center of the door. A number of levers clicked into place, and the door shifted open with a creak.

They were greeted by a rush of salty air and sunlight. Quarry Bay lay glittering before them, the tall Sea Gate in the distance. Gellion led Kyna down a set of stairs cut into the cliffside and along a narrow path running above the lapping tide.

The air snapped with energy as they neared the vierstone. Gellion could feel his awareness of the rocks around him enhance; his earring seemed almost to vibrate. Yet Kyna remained apart beside him, a block of wood amid an electric current. He watched her, perplexed, but either she did not notice his gaze, or ignored it. Some distance from the stretch of green in the cliffside, Gellion stopped. The expanse of vierstone only ran the length of a small ship and did not stretch far up the cliff. This was all that remained of natural, raw vierstone.

All that remains under our control.

"Let's stop here for now," Gellion said. "Standing next to this much vierstone takes getting used to." Even now he was acutely aware of his anxiety at taking Kyna to the quarry, his delight at the beauty of the glittering bay, the squirming in his stomach from standing so close to Kyna.

Kyna stared at the vierstone like it was some strange creature she had never encountered face to face. Gellion, watching her, suddenly realized something.

"You don't wear a vierstone earring?"

"What?" Kyna turned to him, pulling her eyes away from the cliff with obvious reluctance.

Gellion repeated the question.

Kyna cocked her head. "Maybe it's just not in my ear."

Gellion raised his eyebrows.

She snorted at his reaction and turned back to the vierstone. "So this is what entices the elves into a human war?"

A lurch of anxiety radiated from Gellion's chest and rippled to his fingertips. Thus far, he had kept a stark separation between his political life and Kyna. Until now, she had seemed happy to oblige. Why would she bring this up now? Here of all places? Gellion's nails bit into his palms as he tried to calm his rioting emotions.

"Part of it," he said.

Kyna looked at him sideways when he did not elaborate. "No opinion?"

Gellion took a breath. "I have my thoughts."

Kyna gave him a searching look, then turned to face the bay. "Strange isn't it? That the decision will be made by only a handful of elves, most of whom won't even play a part in the consequences."

Gellion swallowed the unease welling in his throat. "Each of them has a stake in the outcome. All elves do."

"Yet all elves do not have a stake in the choice." Kyna cocked a brow. A corner of her mouth quirked up.

Heat was rising up Gellion's body now. Was Kyna standing closer to him than she had been? He shook his head and tried to focus his thoughts. "That would be impossible. We would never reach a decision."

"Mmm. And so each must trust that their choice of spokesperson is enough."

Gellion could feel his heartbeat in his ears. Kyna was definitely closer. Almost touching him. Suddenly the vierstone's airborne presence seemed to converge upon him. His blood was saturated with emotions, pressing against his mind, threatening to overwhelm him. Pressure. Inadequacy. Anger. Guilt. His head spun in confusion. Grasping at thoughts and reason like wisps of smoke, Gellion tried to break through the onslaught.

"The Council Members decide their input and votes in light of the views of the elves they represent," he said.

Kyna smirked. "Do they? From what I've seen, each 'representative,'" the word dripped with irony, "merely argues for their own opinions."

Heat stained Gellion's face and spread through his body. He ground his teeth and tried to stop the shaking in his hands. What was wrong with him? Was this just vierstone getting in his head? He had never reacted to it so strongly before.

Kyna was silent for a time, watching him, then turned back toward the vierstone. Gellion started, suddenly aware that their hands had been touching. Gellion's eyes drew to a leather cuff wrapped around her wrist. He had noticed the accessory before, but had never seen the intricate patterns cut into the material, nor the smoothness of the skin on either side of it. He shivered.

"There is nothing to be done for it now, I suppose," Kyna said. "Are you sure you don't want to go closer?" She looked back toward the cliffs.

Gellion stared at her with his mouth open. What in Riu's name had that conversation been about?

Kyna flashed him a lopsided grin and started to walk down the ledge.

"I—" Gellion shook his head back and forth. "Maybe we should ..." He was just regaining some measure of control over himself. The last thing he needed was to go closer to the vierstone, but what would Kyna think of him, a master crafter and leader of this city, if he let her know he was afraid to go nearer? Muttering a silent curse, Gellion followed her.

Kyna stopped a pace back from the vierstone. Gellion moved beside her. The hair on the back of his neck stood on end, and he grimaced against the new flare of his emotions. He didn't know how the vierstone masters managed it. He wasn't even touching the stone and he could barely stomach its effects. Gellion's father had spent most of his life studying the strange and powerful substance. Gellion had never possessed the inclination to follow in his footsteps.

After a moment of silence, Gellion looked at Kyna. There was no ironic smile on her face now. A hundred expressions chased each other behind her eyes as she stared at the green wall. She took a step back.

"Are you alright?" Gellion asked, unsettled by the sudden change in her demeanor. She did not answer. She did not even turn to look at him.

Unsure what else to do, Gellion raised an unsteady hand and reached it toward her arm.

Kyna looked up, startled by his touch, then the world split apart.

Gellion was not conscious of the ground shaking, but he later assumed that it must have, because he fell against the wall of vierstone. In that instant, he was perfectly, painfully aware of the stone of the cliff surrounding him—every metal, every particle, every atom. It was all wrong, all moving and behaving in ways that should not be possible, that went against the rules of nature, against the rules of Riu. The very identity of the world around him seemed to change. His vision blurred, burst with color, and went black. Then it was over.

He saw a face over him, a look of alarm written across it. He narrowed his eyes and blinked in confusion.

How was she above him? He was taller than her.

His thoughts were muddled and confused by the stillness around him.

"Gellion!"

The name registered something in his mind, and he came back to himself as though crawling through molasses. The jagged ground was beneath him; he saw the sky beyond Kyna, who he now realized was kneeling over him. She leaned back on her heels as Gellion sat up and looked around wildly.

Everything appeared to be normal. The water rose and fell below him; the viaduct stood along the cliff; the sun shone.

"What—"

"Are you ok?" Kyna looked uncertain.

"I—what happened?"

"There was an earthquake. You fell."

Gellion's wits were slowly returning. "You didn't ... you didn't fall?"

Kyna shook her head, looking at him as though fearing for his sanity. He tried to calm himself, but with the wall of vierstone next to him it was like trying to still the sea with his bare hands. He rose to his feet, careful not to touch the stone.

His eyes were immediately drawn to a patch of vierstone just beyond Kyna. A deep crack ran from the base of the cliff to the top of the vierstone deposit. The edges of the crack were black. A stain of ink in a sea of green.

The dread that seized Gellion was strong and sudden. Never in all his life had he seen vierstone so much as fade in color, let alone *lose* its color. Nor had he ever seen the stone break without control. He knew little of vierstone crafting, but every elf knew that vierstone's structure could only be influenced by an elf of deep knowledge and skill. If Gellion had taken an axe to the wall of vierstone in a fit of rage, he had no doubt the stone would have proven harder than diamond, impossible to cut. Yet a single, brief earthquake had done this ...

Gellion looked from the crack to Kyna. The apprehension in her eyes was nearly as frightening as the damaged cliffside.

The earthquake had been a small one, barely felt by those in the Court and entirely unknown to those in the lower tiers. It was strange, this localized shaking, yet no one else in Daro showed any great concern over the phenomenon beyond there having been two earthquakes in one day.

Against his better judgment, Gellion kept the incident in the quarry to himself. He knew he should tell Dulon about the crack in the cliffside —certainly about the edges of black now marring the otherwise pristine sheet of vierstone—but then he would have to explain why he had been in the quarry in the first place. That, and he hardly wanted to add yet another worry to their growing layers of misfortune and anxiety. Besides, what could any of them do about the cliffside? Take all the vierstone out of the quarry? Find a way to stop the earthquakes?

The sudden and shocking end to Gellion's venture to the quarry was upsetting, but what had happened before the earthquake was downright mortifying. Why in Riure had he agreed to take Kyna to a *wall of vierstone*? Had he truly forgotten how potent the atmosphere was next to such a large quantity of the stuff? Now that he could think clearly, his reactions in the quarry seemed completely irrational. It was as though the vierstone had imparted emotions upon him without his knowing or consent. The memory was strangely muddled in his mind, but it still filled him with both shame and confusion. Vierstone was known to affect and respond to the emotions of those that touched it, but Gellion had never felt anything like this before. Had it felt wrong somehow, or was Gellion now making up shadows and excuses to explain away his own lack of control?

Over the days following the disastrous outing, Gellion slept poorly and found his concentration slipping. By day, he spent as much time in his workshop as he could, and by night, he walked whenever rest evaded him. The walks did not calm his mind, but gave him an opportunity to think. He thought about the Albaren and battles and death, he thought about the rift still wedged between himself and Valder, and he thought about Kyna's words regarding the Kindom Council.

A clearer head did not change that conversation. Everything Kyna had said walked far too closely with Gellion's own thoughts.

Each representative argues for his own opinion.

Gellion opposed this alliance. Of that there was no doubt. But that was just it: *he* opposed it. As sure as he was of his own opinion, so too was he sure much of Daro held a different one. Did he know so much better than these elves—the elves who had chosen him to choose for them—that he could refute their opinion for their own good? But could he vote for something so against his own values—vote as the elves of Daro, not as Gellion?

If they are wrong, is it my duty to use my power to stand against them? Or is this only selfish pride tempting me to refute, to betray even, those elves who placed their trust in me?

But some elves in the city were as strongly opposed as he was.

Such thoughts were his constant companions. The day before the craftsman competition, Gellion was exhausted from the struggle.

His tunic hung on a rack. Gellion paced around the work of art, scrutinizing it from every angle until he was satisfied it was as perfect as he could make it, then he took a breath and placed both of his hands on the garment.

Up to this point, any metalworker could have made this tunic, but only the most skilled could hope to accomplish what Gellion was about to do. He closed his eyes, feeling the latticework structure within each link and wire of the garment as he ran his fingers across them. He knew the metal. He had created it—gently coaxed it through every step of the process. Now he drew on that understanding, and the training he had imbued in the metal, and began to subtly pull at the structure. Heat spread from his earring and washed over his skin, enhancing his reach into the metal further still.

He persuaded the crystal lattice to release its hold on the negative charges hovering at its edges, to cause them instead to move in preordained patterns when hit by light. He smiled as he felt the metal slowly comply with his coaxing. The reaction rippled out from his fingers until every exposed surface of metal held the property. Finally, he sealed the outer surface from corrosion and tarnish, then stepped back.

The reddish silver color of the metal was gone. It no longer held any color of its own; instead it took on the colors surrounding it and bent them in mesmerizing patterns across the surface of the tunic. It didn't quite *blend* with its surroundings, but shaped them into something else. Gellion extended a finger and tapped the stand. The tunic all but disappeared as it shimmered and reflected shifting light in every direction.

Gellion beamed.

A hood hung from the back of the tunic, and the long sleeves could be pulled over hands. When moving, all that would be visible of the elf wearing it were their lower legs, but in a crouch, the tails of the tunic could cover even those. Gellion pulled his shirt off, took the tunic off of its stand, and let it drop over his head. As the metal flowed over his bare skin, it conformed to his body temperature almost immediately. It felt like the smooth scales of a reptile. Gellion began to walk and watched himself take on the coloring and contours of the surrounding stone floor and table. He could hardly feel the weight of the garment on his shoulders.

Reluctantly, he took the tunic off and hung it back on its rack. One last hungry look and he pushed it into a corner and covered it with a cloth.

If this didn't win the craftsman competition, he truly looked forward to seeing the creation that did.

Gellion spent the early evening taking care of last minute business for the Kindom Council. There would be little time tomorrow to do anything official with the festivities. There was a spring to his step that had not been present for weeks. Finally, something that was entirely in his control, and a gathering where no mention of wars or earthquakes would mar the atmosphere.

Still, a tendril of apprehension squirmed in his belly at the thought of Kyna's likely presence at the competition. He had been rather short with her after their trip to the quarry. He knew it was petty to blame her for what had happened, but truly, they would not have been there if it weren't for her. His bruised pride warred with his guilt. That was two elves he could hardly look in the eye now.

The sky had turned an inky blue by the time Gellion walked in the door of his house. Valder was sitting hunched over a table, four colorful cards spread in his hands. Veldon sat across from him, grinning as he watched a line crease Valder's brow in deep concentration. Several polished stones—crimson, teal, amber, and emerald—lay between them. At last, Valder selected two of his cards and laid them face up on the table, then slid one of the amber stones along a pattern of lines toward Veldon. Veldon studied the move, then looked up at Gellion.

"Our brother is clever, but too reserved." He slapped down his three remaining cards. "And too trusting!" He laughed as Valder stared open-mouthed at the hand. Veldon moved his teal stone in the shape of a scythe across the board to the other side. Gellion smiled despite himself.

"I didn't know you were an accomplished player of spyre."

"My skill has vastly improved by being whetted against the iron prowess of Farra," Veldon said.

Gellion's eyes drifted to Valder's. His brother's expression was reserved, but not hostile. Gellion dropped his gaze.

Veldon looked between them. "Do you want to have a game?" he asked Gellion. "I was just about to leave."

"Where are you going at this hour?"

"Just going to check on a few things," Veldon said casually, betrayed by his reddening face.

Gellion raised an eyebrow. "What things are those?"

"Nothing important."

"Can I come?"

Valder hid his snort with a cough and for a moment shared a smile with Gellion.

Veldon seemed to be frantically trying to come up with an excuse to refuse. Finally, he closed his hanging jaw. "No." He reddened further and slipped out the door.

Gellion and Valder stared after him. "Should we follow him?" asked Gellion.

"Nah, let the lad have his secret." Valder's face was soft with fondness. Valder was only five years older than Veldon—practically twins for elves—but Valder always spoke of Veldon with the air and protection of an older brother.

A heavy silence fell over the room; neither brother seemed able to push through its weight. Finally, Valder started putting away the spyre game. Gellion helped, sorting the cards back into a stack. He could feel unease radiating from Valder. As Valder tipped the stones into a copper tube, Gellion stared at the deck in his hands, running his thumb down a corner; it made a satisfying sound—dozens of rapid snaps in a rush of air. He took a deep breath.

"I'm sorry," he said into the silence. The words were barely audible. He couldn't bring himself to utter them louder, or to look up from the cards. A hand extended into his field of vision, and he placed the deck of cards into it. As their hands touched, he looked up and saw Valder's crooked smile. Gellion returned it, relief flooding through his body.

"You're finished with your masterpiece then?" Valder asked, as though the last days had never happened.

Gellion grinned.

Valder laughed. "I'll take that as a yes. Should have known, of course. You wouldn't be here if you still had work to do. Do you know who else will be in the competition?"

"No."

"But you're a judge!"

"Dulon is the only one who knows all the entries. He's being very secretive about it—thinks it will be more fun as a surprise." Gellion turned his eyes to the ceiling.

"Ah—pity the elf who tries to cheat Dulon out of his fun."

Gellion chuckled.

"Can I see it?" Valder's eyes sparkled.

Gellion hesitated, but the renewed friendship of his brother was more than he could resist. He sighed.

"Alright then." He couldn't pretend he did not want to see the tunic again himself, and secretly relished the thought of seeing his brother's reaction.

The streets were sparse. Gellion looked up at the sky as he walked with Valder. The soft glow of lights from the surrounding buildings did not obscure an impressive display of stars scattered across the sky. The breeze was cool, but held an aftertaste of warmth from the day.

"I think we will be able to finish *The Nore* before the Council leaves next week," said Valder as they walked. "I would like mother and Veldon to see it before they leave."

Gellion felt a twinge in his chest. Preoccupied with other thoughts, he had nearly forgotten his family would be leaving so soon.

"I'll miss them." Valder echoed Gellion's thoughts.

"Yes." Gellion steeled himself before his next words. "You plan to remain in Daro?"

A line creased Valder's brow. "Of course. I miss them, but my life's here. You know that."

Gellion nodded. "And you will remain no matter what is ..." he paused, "decided?

Gellion sensed a flicker of understanding and apprehension from his brother.

"Yes," said Valder. "Of course I will stay. Will you?"

Gellion nodded.

Valder's face relaxed. "You don't think others will leave, do you?"

"I don't know," said Gellion. He had heard no blatant talk of elves threatening to leave the city, but the possibility had occurred to him. Dulon's worry over the city's atmosphere was not unfounded. If anything, the tension had increased since their last meeting.

"Gellion?"

Gellion realized Valder was no longer walking beside him and turned to see his brother standing several steps behind him at the entrance to his metal shop, an arched eyebrow and a smile on his face. Gellion had walked right past his own shop.

"Right." He strode back and pushed the door open. With the flip of a switch, warm light suffused the room. His chest fluttered as he walked toward the cloth-covered stand. He grabbed the top of the stand and pulled it out of the corner.

His brows knit.

The stand had moved forward quicker than he had expected and nearly ran over his foot. Shaking his head, he flashed a grin at Valder before turning back to the stand and whipping the cloth back.

Gellion's heart turned to ice. Cold spread outward to every limb—every nerve in his body—and solidified.

The stand was empty.

11

CRAFTING AND COUNCILS

Dulon swept from one room to another as though carried on a continuous current. He had been up since dawn preparing for the craftsman competition, but the early morning and hectic atmosphere fueled his energy—he was brimming with it.

"Seven of the entrants are here, and half the judges," he told Maranyl. "Have we opened the doors? Where is Gellion? And I haven't seen Tenille or Miyela all morning. I have each of the entrants in separate rooms by their order of presentation." He was still walking, bright eyes darting in every direction as he talked. He felt a hand close around his elbow and stopped, spinning around to face Maranyl.

"Take a breath between words or you will collapse before the competition begins." She smiled. "You have told me most of this already, darling, you are rambling."

Dulon took a breath, his shoulders starting to relax, then his eyes snapped back up.

"Gellion! There you are!" He beamed and strode past Maranyl, who rolled her eyes and sighed. "Where is your entry? Have you seen the presentation room? The other judges? I haven't seen your mother or—" He trailed off, looking more closely at Gellion. He was pale, and his eyes were bloodshot—the usual fire in them gone to coals. Dulon arched an eyebrow. "Stay up all night finishing?"

Gellion just looked at him. "No."

The smile faded from Dulon's face. "Is something wrong?" he asked warily. He had never seen Gellion so devoid of emotion, so drained of confidence.

"I do not have it."

"Have what?"

"My entry."

Dulon stared at him. "What?"

"It is gone."

"What do you mean gone?"

A tongue of flame flashed behind Gellion's eyes, but was quickly swallowed by their cold depths. "It—is—not—there." He spoke as though trying to explain the rules of spyre to a child.

"Not where?"

Annoyance flared in Gellion's face again. "My workshop. Where I left it. I spent half the night looking for it and the other half staring at the ceiling thinking of where I had not looked. Then I looked there. It is gone."

"Someone—stole it?"

Gellion shrugged. "I can't think of another explanation. Can you?"

Dulon felt suddenly cold. He shook his head. "But who? Why? Just to increase their chances in a competition?"

Gellion did not answer. His eyes slid to the entrance of the room, filling with spectators. "I'll go take my place," he mumbled, and walked away.

Dulon's excited energy had hit a wall. He stood dumbfounded for half a minute, then saw Tenille coming toward him.

No good sacrificing the rest of the competition for Gellion's misfortune. Must move on.

With a slight hesitation of guilt, he slapped a grin back on his face, tossed a stray lock of hair out of his eyes, and strode toward Tenille.

Many conversations and a few miles of walking later, Dulon stood behind a high-backed chair at the center of a table. The Council Members sat on either side of him and faced a stage stretching in an arc before a two-story window. Behind the judge's table, ranks of chairs filed to the far wall. This was Dulon's favorite room in the Performance Hall, possibly in all of Daro. Through the window, one could see Master's Street, the domed roofs of the housing districts, the towers of the Sea Gate, and the glittering water beyond.

The rumble of conversation vibrated through the air at Dulon's back. His eyes ran along the judge's table. Liera stared stoically at the stage, looking as thrilled as if she had been asked to inspect the sewer systems of the city. Tenille sat next to her at the end of the table, equally delighted by her seating arrangement. Rhosti was talking with Auralia and Cuvan, a rare display of excitement and vocal ability, and to Dulon's left sat Gellion, staring out the window with blank eyes.

He looks like he is mourning the death a friend.

Dulon's throat tightened. He knew Gellion had worked night and day the last month for this competition. Gellion had been instrumental in its instigation in the first place.

Gellion broke his stare and turned to Dulon. The green of his eyes brightened slightly, and a corner of his mouth curled up in a grimace.

"Do not mourn for me Dulon, it is a matter of no permanent consequence. Only my pride has been wounded, and as you say yourself, it could probably do with some crippling."

Dulon snorted and gave Gellion a sad smile. "All the same, I would not have it this way." He knit his brows in sympathy. "I am sorry."

Gellion shifted uncomfortably and nodded, dropping his eyes, then stared back out the window.

Never have I met an elf who feels so strongly yet fights so adamantly against acknowledging it.

Dulon had known Gellion as long as Daro had existed. The two had practically built the city together, and had been on more than one notorious adventure to Tradira. Yet Gellion had never told Dulon of his life before Daro, nor confided in him anything more personal than his current metalworking projects. Dulon had been shocked to learn just a week before the Council Members' arrival that one of them was Gellion's own mother.

Dulon sighed and turned toward the back doors, but paused when he saw Miyela watching him with shrewd eyes. He attempted a grin, but she turned away. A prickle of unease and annoyance snaked up Dulon's spine. Even in Morcanan he had never gotten along with Miyela, but he had hoped she would show a little civility, if not respect, to the host of the Kindom Council. Clearly he had set his expectations too high. He only hoped her attitude did not turn the other Council Members against him.

Outside, the bell tower rang, signifying midmorning, and Dulon faced the crowd. Their myriad of voices trickled away as he held up his hands for silence. He took a breath, cleared his mind of everything but the moment, and smiled.

"Here we are at last!" His voice rang through the room, clear and full of joy. "Eight judges and a host of superb craftsmen exhibiting the most sensational, unparalleled, extraordinary works of talent and prowess we have ever encountered in one room." He paused, chest glowing and eyes alight. "Each participant will display his or her achievement to the judges and the audience, and a winner will be chosen based upon technical skill, uniqueness, beauty, and innovation. I will announce the winner at the parting feast in three days' time. Now, we begin!"

Cheers filled the room like gushing water. Dulon turned his back to the crowd and sat, and the noise died down as an elf stepped before the glass windows. Dulon could not keep the broad grin from his face as he watched her. He had no need to show impartiality; he was not allowed to judge other Morcani entrants.

Maranyl, carrying a small bag, stepped onto the stage. From the bag she drew what appeared at first to be a pair of horns, but upon closer inspection proved to be a double flute. Two slender mouthpieces twisted around each other and flowed into metal tubes lined with finger holes. Maranyl placed both mouthpieces in her mouth and began to play.

It was a haunting sound, like two elven voices twining around one another. She played a melody and harmony simultaneously so that it was impossible to tell from which flute either part came, or even at times to tell it was an instrument at all. When she finished, there was an awed silence, then applause.

Maranyl strode to the judge's table with her flute. Dulon took the instrument and ran his fingers along its length. The body was made of titanium and platinum, and an intricate lace of rose gold connected the two prongs of the flute at either end. He could not tell what she had done to produce such a unique tone. It was a feat of true engineering, and one she had achieved through a very personal touch. Few elves could do such a thing. It required a depth of understanding and a skill with the channel created through vierstone that was incredibly difficult to learn. Dulon cocked an eyebrow over the instrument and winked at Maranyl before passing the flute to the next judge.

The second craftsman was one of the visitors from Morcanan. He presented an opal the size of Dulon's head, polished and carved to depict waves crashing against a beach. In the center of the stone, color swirled and billowed outward like sea-foam to a granular amber. It was an impressive piece, but Dulon knew the patterns had existed within the stone already. The elf had needed skill to reveal the beauty within the opal, but the creation did not show the same depth of base prowess and knowledge as Maranyl's. Dulon smiled.

The three Fieri entrants were next. Dulon drew his score sheet closer, now able to give points freely. The first elf demonstrated a dark ink that did not bleed from paper or blur a single written word when she dipped it in a basin of water. Impressive and useful. Dulon scribbled his marks. The next entrant had encased a chemical slurry inside a sealed leather pouch that generated and retained heat for hours. Dulon fantasized about the glories of this product in the winters of Morcanan. He laughed aloud as he held the hot pouch in his hands, enjoying the warmth even in the controlled climate of the auditorium.

When the second Fieri entrant had taken his seat, Auralia pushed her chair back and strode to the stage. From a leather belt slung around her waist, she drew a small vial of clear liquid and a handful of twigs. Dulon leaned forward in his seat, eyes sparkling with interest. Placing her twigs on the table, Auralia pulled the stopper from the glass vial with a *pop* and tipped the vial over the twigs until the liquid balanced on its rim. She paused for dramatic effect, of which Dulon approved mightily, then twitched her fingers so a single drop of liquid fell onto the twigs.

Upon impact, the drop caught fire instantly, sending up a bright flame for a moment, then shrinking down to a simmering burn that slowly spread over the twigs.

The crowd gasped, oohed, and applauded. Auralia bowed and brought her vial to the judges for inspection. Dulon never would have taken Auralia to be a chemist given her aversion to Telem Fier and its innovations, but he had to admit he was impressed. His partiality was still for his wife, but she would have stiff competition for the prize.

Next was a Turi elf named Malo, who had made a goblet of fluorite. It was as thin as glass and curved in the shape of a flame, with opalescent rings of purples, blues, greens, and every shade in between, twisting and rising from the base to the brim like layers in a stack of paper. It was beautiful, but like the Morcani's opal, it had little value beyond aesthetics and bore no properties apart from its separate components.

The judges commented and took notes, then sat waiting for the next competitor.

A stout Remsgri bounced onto the stage, a metal chest in his arms and a broad grin on his face. Dulon returned the smile. He knew Aiken well. The man was one of the few Remsgri that had lived in Daro for nearly a century.

Aiken placed the chest on the table, which now bore scorch marks from Auralia's fire, and removed a curved basin of metal with three thin prongs extending from the bowl in a triangle around its rim. Reaching into the chest again, he pulled out a gem. It was mostly clear, but was flecked with bits of color on the inside. Aiken placed a hand on the basin, then pulled back with a hard movement so the basin spun at a dizzying speed. The prongs moved so quickly, it looked like a solid wall had arisen along the rim of the bowl.

Aiken held the gem over the top of the spinning contraption, then dropped it. The gem fell, then stopped in midair, perfectly centered above the bowl and prongs, and began to spin, tumbling over itself faster and faster. The colors within the stone blurred and seemed to expand until all Dulon's eyes could see was an ephemeral body of color and light spinning and morphing into every shade of the rainbow so quickly he could not name a single one of them before they disappeared and reappeared again. The bowl eventually slowed to a stop, and the gem dropped into it.

The crowd cheered their pleasure. Aiken smiled and bowed, his heavy plaits of hair flopping over one shoulder.

Dulon stepped up to the table and inspected the bowl and the gem. The corners of his mouth quirked upward. The bowl was made of iron, cobalt, and several rare earth metals that the elf had oriented north to south. He had somehow imbued the gem itself with nickel and iron. The result was a powerful and well-balanced magnetic system. Dulon nodded his approval to Aiken, who beamed all the brighter, and allowed the other judges to approach the table for a closer look.

The judges recorded their scores and comments and returned to their seats for the last presentation.

Veldon walked across the stage.

Dulon glanced sideways and saw Gellion's mouth hanging open. His eyes followed his brother as though he had never seen him before. Down the table, Tenille smiled knowingly.

It would appear there have been some family secrets the last few weeks.

Dulon fought the urge to laugh.

Veldon stopped in the middle of the stage.

He was holding a lamp. It was small, with a triangular handle and smooth, curving bars to either side that attached to a rounded base. Suspended between the silvery metal was a glass bulb, blown into an elegant shape that swelled at the base, tapering and spiraling upward to join the metal handle. It looked as though the bulb had dripped from the top of the lamp. The glass itself was an iridescent green, just thin enough to allow light through, like stained glass.

Behind Veldon, a thick curtain began to move across the window. No other lights were on, and darkness moved through the room like ink spreading across cloth. When the darkness had fully descended, Dulon heard a faint click, and the lamp in Veldon's hands illuminated instantly, filling every corner of the room in its intensity. Curiously, the light was a clean white. Had Dulon not seen the lamp in the light, he would have guessed its glass was clear.

Every eye in the room was fixed upon the light as though it were about to speak a prophecy from Riu.

Veldon's voice broke the silence.

"It will take scores of years to burn out," Veldon said. "If ever it does burn out. The bulb will not break by any impact, and the lamp requires no recharging."

Dulon looked at the little lamp incredulously. The bulb seemed so delicate he would fear to touch it, and the lamp itself was laughably small to hold power for years. Veldon saw Dulon's look, but did not seem daunted. With a sheepish smile, he approached the judge's table and sat his lamp before Dulon.

It was even more intricate up close. The glass contained infinite seams that swooped and swirled in patterns across its surface. Dulon reached his fingers toward the bulb, wary that it would burn him, but the lamp emitted no heat. Still more perplexed, Dulon touched the glass.

His gasp was audible throughout the room. The bulb was cool, and it was not glass.

It was vierstone.

A chill spread over Dulon's skin. He had never seen vierstone worked like this. Though all elves crafted through vierstone, to craft vierstone itself was altogether different. Vierstone masters were rare. They were the ones who crafted vierstone earrings and melted vierstone into the foundations of cities. Often, there were only one or two of them in any given Great City, or even a Kindom. Aryn was one such elf. Dulon had been lucky to bring her to Daro to aid in the city's construction.

At the look on Dulon's face, Gellion reached for the lamp. His eyes widened as he touched it.

"Vierstone," he whispered.

Every judge leaned toward the lamp, extending hands to see it next.

Dulon turned his eyes to Veldon, who looked profoundly uncomfortable.

"How?" Dulon said.

"The vierstone continually excites the electrons, perpetuating a steady electric current through the diodes, which sit in the base of the bulb. The striations on the vierstone spread the light through the bulb, and its green pigment completes the spectrum within, so the light emitted appears white."

Dulon stared. Veldon spoke as though it were the simplest thing in the world. Dulon reached for the lamp again, holding the bulb in his hands and trying to concentrate on what was happening within. His arm hair stood on end, and he shivered and released his hands. How had Veldon worked with this? Dulon could not get past the vierstone to feel anything beyond, yet he believed what Veldon said was true.

The curtain began to move back across the window, flooding the room with sunlight.

"And you are *sure* it will not break?"

Veldon nodded, but Dulon could not bring himself to risk the miraculous thing by testing the claim. With a smile, Veldon reached for the lamp. He clicked it off, then to the astonishment of every elf in the room, threw it onto the judge's table with the bulb facing its surface.

Dulon flinched backward, but other than a loud *clank*, the lamp simply lay on its side, unharmed.

Dulon turned to the audience and held the lamp aloft.

"An unbreakable lamp of vierstone that keeps its power indefinitely." He almost laughed at the description.

There was a moment of silence as the room decided whether Dulon was serious, then someone began to clap. Thunderous applause followed. A flush crept up Veldon's neck until his face was crimson. He was looking not at the audience, but at Gellion, who still sat in stunned silence.

The two brothers stood face to face. Apart from their hair, the resemblance was striking, which made the difference in their current expressions all the more amusing. Veldon's flush was draining from his face, and his big eyes almost quivered with anticipation of his brother's reaction.

Gellion held his expression carefully neutral. Then his mouth curved into a grin.

"You conniving slink." He shook his head and laughed, then extended a hand to clasp his brother's. Relief and color suffused

Veldon's face. Gellion sat back down in his chair, and Veldon took his lamp and left the stage.

Dulon turned back to Gellion, whose mouth was still curved upward, but more in a grimace than a smile. A muscle worked in his jaw as the shadow in his eyes returned.

—

Sleep came to Dulon that night with a rapidity that surprised him. Despite the looming Council meeting, his spirits were higher than they had been in days. He was pleased to see that the tense atmosphere that had permeated the city during the last week had lessened with the festivities. The last of the tournament competitions had ended shortly after the craftsman competition, and of the craftsman competition itself, he was even more pleased. So many of the entries had been astounding in their craftsmanship and innovation.

A grain of worry still lay within Dulon's satisfaction, however. He could only imagine Gellion's devastation at his ruined chances, but was even more concerned by the act of theft itself. He could not envisage a single one of the other entrants sabotaging a fellow competitor in such a way. Even the identities of those competing had been relatively secret. Had a friend of one of the entrants committed the crime without his or her knowledge? Or had the intentions been more sinister still? An act of political rebellion against a Council Member? Dulon had tried to pull more details of the disappearance out of Gellion, but met little cooperation.

"It doesn't matter now," Gellion had said with a flat voice.

"It does matter. Was your shop locked?"

"No. It's never locked. Do you lock your office? This is Daro, not Tradira."

Dulon sighed. "How long was your shop unoccupied that day?"

"From midafternoon to night."

"Do you have any idea who would have done it? Who could have done it?"

"No."

"Who knew you were entering the contest? I could ask around, look—"

"It does not matter!" Gellion snapped. His eyes blazed.

Dulon took a step back. Gellion swallowed with obvious effort and took a breath. "It is too late."

Dulon wanted to say more, but thought better of it. He nodded slowly.

Gellion had regained control of his temper, but his teeth were clenched, and his hand shook as he raked it through his hair.

"What was it by the way?" Dulon asked. "Your entry?"

Gellion's eyes fixed on a reality beyond Dulon's vision. "Something better left in the past," he muttered.

Dulon still had no idea what Gellion had meant by the enigmatic comment. He wanted to ask around about the missing whatever-it-was despite Gellion's reaction, but would make little progress without knowing what he was looking for, and Gellion seemed in no mind to tell him.

Dulon let out a long breath and felt Maranyl move in the bed beside him.

"Sleep well?" she said.

Dulon let his head fall to the side on his pillow. Maranyl lay facing him.

"I dreamt I was spinning between three magnets held by Liera, Auralia, and Miyela," he said.

Maranyl raised her eyebrows. "Did you?"

"No. But that would have been a perfect dream."

Maranyl snorted, and Dulon smiled. Maranyl's hair was pulled away from her face, but stuck out in odd places from sleep. Her eyes danced with laughter. Dulon raised a hand to smooth her hair back from her face, and his fingers trailed over the vierstone pierced through her ear. He shivered as her eyes seemed to deepen. He could feel a shadow of her amusement, of her love. Behind it, there was concern.

She smiled sadly.

"I fear you have built a tower too high to safely climb, that whatever happens today you will hurt yourself, if only by your own expectations."

Dulon withdrew his hand and turned his head back to the ceiling.

The final Kindom Council meeting was today. He had been doing his damndest to forget. He sighed.

"It is too early for philosophy, Mari."

"You cannot please them all."

"I know that."

"You cannot try to please them all."

Dulon didn't respond.

"You are a good leader, Dulon. You care for your people. But that care of each individual can be your downfall. When difficult decisions come, you cannot be everyone's friend. Leadership is lonely."

"Leadership is lonely," Dulon muttered with a half-hearted chuckle. "To be surrounded by more people than you can please and take solace in none of them."

Maranyl slid across the sheets and lay her head on his chest. "More alone still when they each want something different of you."

Dulon groaned. "Mari, please. Can I have just one morning to pretend my problems don't exist rather than contemplate their meaning?"

She wrapped an arm around his ribs and nestled her nose against his throat. "I suppose so."

Dulon hugged her to him with both arms. She tilted her head up and kissed him long and hard. When she pulled away, Dulon could hardly draw a breath through the hammering of the pulse in his throat. Mari giggled and rolled sideways, pulling him with her.

When I walk back out of these doors, it will be done.

Every nerve in Dulon's body was burning in anticipation. Gellion stood beside him. They exchanged a glance. Gellion looked more himself this morning, but with an air of resigned determination. He nodded, and Dulon opened the doors.

The Council sat around the same table as the last two meetings, and in the same order. The two seats at the nearest end sat vacant. Dulon's boots clicked on the floor and echoed around the silent hall. He lowered himself into his chair and surveyed the elves surrounding him. Some faces were impassive, some weary, some burning with emotion.

"I need hardly announce this meeting, or its purpose," Dulon said. "We will address all other matters that still need attention first, then come to a decision on the alliance at the end. Agreed?"

No one challenged him. He moved on.

It took less than an hour for Dulon to finish his list of subject matter. He could tell the Council wanted this meeting over and done with as much as he did. It had been an exhausting month.

"Very well," he said at last, his heart lurching to a faster pace. "We have talked ourselves to death about this cursed alliance, and any more debate today will make no progress toward a decision. Each member will vote. No interrupting, no arguing. Understood?" He eyed each elf. A few nodded, most just looked at him.

"I will begin," he said.

Dulon tried to swallow the lump threatening to burst through his windpipe. "The security of a second vierstone supply is essential, especially in light of recent events. The Albaren have been trustworthy trading partners, and I believe they ask for our help in good faith. I vote yes to the alliance." He was careful not to look too long into any one face, but he could feel the heat of Miyela's eyes. He nodded to his left.

Liera sat board straight, her sharp features serious. "The alliance makes political sense. The Dierna cannot hope to be a threat to the elves, and we further our trade relations in addition to a secured supply of vierstone. I vote yes."

The tension around the table doubled. All eyes turned to Tenille. Dulon could see a trace of Gellion's fire in her eyes.

"We fight an unknown enemy who has done us no wrong," she said. "We hoard vierstone against need and risk our lives to do so. No."

Auralia was spinning a pen in her fingers. Her eyes did not move from it as she spoke. "We used half of Daro's vierstone to build this city. Its people may as well do all they can to secure another source." She grimaced. "I do not like it, but I vote yes."

Cuvan looked at her gravely, then turned his hooded eyes to the Council. "The elves of Telem Fier are no strangers to hardship. I do not blame those who seek vierstone as insurance against future uncertainty. But, I believe there must be a better way. I vote no."

Dulon had been holding his breath. It turned to ice in his chest as all eyes fixed on Miyela. Her eyes were molten. They burned with a light separate from the surrounding room, and her face was unyielding. She locked her gaze on Dulon. It was an effort to sit still, to hold his head up, to not run. Yet Dulon felt his jaw clench in anger at the sight of Miyela's accusing stare. He was not the only one who had voted yes. Would they all blame him?

At last, Miyela blinked once and said, "No." Her tone was explanation enough. Dulon sat helplessly trapped by her stare for a few more moments before she looked to Rhosti. Dulon let out a shuddering breath.

Rhosti sat silent for several moments. His eyes were solemn, and his bearing straight. "I will not condone violence for any reason where there is a possible alternative. I vote no."

Silence fell. Dulon thought quickly.

Three yes's, four no's. If Gellion votes no, it is decided. If not ...

But he knew Gellion's opinion of the alliance. He would vote no, and it would be over. Dulon could not decide if he was relieved or devastated.

Gellion took a deep breath and let it out through his nose. At last he looked up, ran his eyes around the table, then turned slowly to Dulon. He looked almost sorrowful, pained. Did he see this as a betrayal of their friendship? Dulon inclined his head.

Go ahead.

"Yes."

The silence before Gellion's answer was dwarfed by the stillness that permeated the room after it. Even the air stood still, afraid to disturb so much as a hair of the gathered company.

Dulon's eyebrows shot up. He stared in shock at Gellion before wrestling his expression back into proper inscrutability. Gellion had dropped his eyes to the table, but held his chin up. He gave no explanation. Tenille looked as shocked as Dulon, Miyela furious.

Tied. The vote was tied. Dulon's heart hammered against his chest.

We cannot re-vote. We must come to a decision. No. I *must come to a decision.*

He clenched his fists under the table.

Riu what do I do? What do I decide?

He squared his shoulders and steeled his eyes.

"I thank each of you for your input. I am sorry this decision ever came to us and hope it has not caused animosity between us or the elves we represent." There was a barely audible scoff from his right. Dulon ignored it. "I value all of your opinions, but as we are evenly split on the issue, I think it right that Daro makes the final decision. Gellion and myself represent the elves of Daro. We both," he glanced at Gellion, trying to hide the incredulity in his voice, "voted yes today."

Dulon scanned the faces before him once more, then forced himself to look at Miyela. "We will accept the alliance with Albarad."

He put the last of his confidence in the words. The rest seemed to drain into Miyela's eyes.

1 2

A MEETING FOR MUTINY

"She's beautiful!" Renyra ran a hand along metal, smooth as glass. She looked through a sea of beams and ropes toward the bow of the ship. Firas was gazing fondly at the gleaming craft.

"Yes," he said.

Firas had taken Renyra into the belly of the ship—through the store rooms, the kitchens, and the passenger quarters lined with silken hammocks in every color beneath the sun. Every doorframe, railing, and beam seemed to be etched with patterns. The ship itself curved like the base of a swan's neck from stern to bow.

The sound of boots on metal made Renyra turn around.

Corron, a fair-haired elf, marched up the gangplank. Renyra felt a flutter in her chest. His eyes were angry and urgent. Renyra, like most of the elves of Daro, had been doing her best to put the final Council meeting out of her mind throughout the morning, but it seemed the results of the meeting had come to them. Corron turned on his heel and made for Firas, who held a mild expression with just enough strain to show the wariness beneath.

"Corron." Firas nodded. "What can I do for you?"

"It is decided. We are meeting in half an hour in the central storehouse." His face was set with an intensity that left no question as to what the Council had decided.

A muscle in Firas's jaw twitched. His eyes slid to Renyra and back. Corron glanced at her, annoyance evident in his face. He opened his mouth as though to protest, then closed it. "She can come. But hurry."

Firas watched Corron stride away until he was back on the docks, then turned to Renyra. His eyes reflected the worry she felt. The alliance would be accepted. There would be battle. What was Miyela planning?

The storehouse was dimly lit, lined with shelves of sacks, jars, and tools. A nutty smell of dry grains and disuse permeated the air. At the back of the room was an expanse of bare ground surrounded by aluminum barrels of fresh water and wine. Elves stood across the open space and sat on any open surface.

Renyra examined the crowd. She estimated almost fifty elves present, and more were trickling in. Most were pale with the light shades of hair indicative of Morcani. She saw no Fieri or Remsgri and could identify only a handful of possible Turi. Lythin stood toward the front, facing the crowd and leaning against a shelf.

"Where is Miyela?" Renyra whispered to Firas.

He was scanning the crowd, a line between his brows.

"Not here."

They slipped in behind some elves off to the side. After about ten minutes of tense muttering, silence fell over the room. Renyra felt Firas's hand on her shoulder and turned to see Miyela walking through the gathered elves. They parted before her like water before the bow of a ship. Miyela stopped at the back of the room and stood. She seemed to absorb all the sound in the room. Renyra leaned against Firas, feeling smothered by the silence and the palpable hum of agitation.

Miyela stood with her shoulders back and head lifted, expressionless, yet exuding intensity like heat from coals. She moved her eyes over the crowd to ensure every gaze was fixed on her, then spoke.

"Daro will ally with Albarad."

Renyra had been expecting it, but still felt a stab of adrenaline in her chest. She made the sign of the star over herself. Firas's hand tightened on her shoulder.

"An alliance with the humans," Miyela continued. "An alliance in war." She let the slightest hint of fury show on her face before masking it again. "Do you remember war?" she asked. "Do you remember death?"

Mutters rippled around the room, some angry, some fearful.

"Do you remember the permanence of that death? A permanence we still live with today? Kin, friends, wives, husbands, brothers, sisters— gone. Gone to Riu, yes, but beyond our reach for the stretching centuries and millennia we are fated to live on Riure. Some say *this* war bears little sacrifice to our people, that we have nothing to fear of these Dierna with their inferior strength and wisdom. But is the sacrifice of a single elven life not greater than that of any mortal for whom we fight? In a handful of years, these humans will rejoin those they have lost for eternity. Can we say the same?"

Heads were nodding, eyes burning. Renyra had never seen a single elf draw this kind of attention, this reverence.

Firas didn't exaggerate. She holds the hearts of these elves like a queen.

"This alliance is a partnership of greed. We further the greed of the humans in pursuit of our own greed. We plan to kill other beings on the word of a nation we merely share a border with! As of now, how many elves have deliberately taken the life of another elf or human?" A tension laced with emotion permeated the room. Most of the elves were incensed, shaking their heads, but a few exchanged glances or looked to the floor. Renyra frowned. As far as she knew, no elf had ever deliberately taken the life of another.

"In the Great War, we killed, yes," said Miyela. "But we killed monsters—ungodly demon spawn raised by Olcon himself. Do we now take it upon ourselves to determine which mortal beings should live or die?" She let her words echo in their minds before continuing. "If this war were a just cause, would Daro be pervaded by such dissension?"

Dissension you have brought about.

Renyra's unease was mounting. She did not want to go to battle, but Miyela was stretching the truth beyond her comfort.

She separates grey into black and white, twists truths into ultimatums blasphemous to deny.

"The question of this alliance should have been extinguished the moment it was uttered. Instead it has been allowed to flow through the hearts and minds of our people and pull us apart, to tempt us to greater things when we were content with our lot before. And now it has been accepted."

Renyra flinched. Despite the unplaced blame in Miyela's words, she left little room to question where that blame should be directed. Renyra had not failed to notice the tension between Miyela and Dulon over the weeks. At first she had thought it strange that two of the same Kindom were so at odds, but the more she learned about Miyela, the more she understood the disparity between the two leaders.

"I do not propose we can stop this alliance from happening. I will not see bloodshed among our own people. We can, however, make a statement. Tomorrow, those of us who sailed to Daro from Faeran will depart, leaving the city to its fate. We will not leave silently, and we will not leave alone. The Morcani are not murderers, of humans or elves. For those of you who reside in this city, I cannot force you to leave this home, but remember your first home still waits as ever before. I urge you to leave this place. Refuse to accept a decision made against your will. Show the leaders of this city that they alone do not decide the fate of any race."

The stern mask of Miyela's face had been eroding throughout the speech, and now she let naked passion show for all to see. "Will you join me?"

A zealous assent met her words. Fear snaked down Renyra's spine. She looked to Firas. He was staring at Miyela with eyes narrowed in thought. Renyra reached for his hand, which had dropped from her shoulder mid-speech. His gaze did not leave Miyela.

Renyra felt his uncertainty, but also his respect. She looked back at Miyela, whose eyes burned fiery orange in the flickering torchlight. The Lady of Morcanan stood before her people, the epicenter of an earthquake Renyra feared would reach far beyond the walls of the storehouse, beyond even the walls of Daro.

"Say something," Renyra said.

Firas broke his fixed stare at the comb in his hand and looked up. Renyra stood beside him, wearing wraps the color of oak leaves over her dress. Her hair was swept into a twisted knot at the back of her head.

"I left you here all afternoon to think, as you asked," she continued, "but there is little time. The feast is in less than an hour. We have to discuss this."

Renyra had spent the sun's brightest hours tending to the plants in the greenhouse. Firas had said next to nothing since she returned, only stared morosely at alternating objects around the house.

He sighed.

"What can I say to you when I cannot order the thoughts in my own head?"

"Speak them out loud, and maybe order will come to them."

"Miyela is a strong leader," he said at last.

"I gathered as much," Renyra mumbled.

"She cares about her people. She believes in the righteousness of her words and actions. And," he sighed, "she has some fair points."

"You agree with her?" Renyra tensed.

"Not all of what she says. Not the way she says it always, but on most accounts, on the principle of it ... yes."

"You think it is truly greed that we pursue?"

"Greed is a strong word. Vierstone brings good to our people, there is no denying that, but perhaps our need for it has crossed the line into a desire closer to lust—to obsession."

Renyra wrinkled her brow as she considered his words. "But you told me yourself how it was without vierstone. Surely that is a fate worth some sacrifice to prevent?"

"Yes. But it would take much more than a few earthquakes to reach that point again." Firas shook his head. "But if Miyela exaggerates anything, her description of war is not one of them. She strikes the heart when she talks about sacrifice and what it means for us."

"But to condemn killing humans as Riu's creatures and then portray elves' sacrifice as so far above humans' as to not be worth it? She contradicts her own values, but does so with a conviction that makes it seem reasonable."

Firas snorted. "Miyela could make tearing a city down a stone at a time seem reasonable. But she is not just talk and fervor, Renyra. She led more elves through the Great War than any other leader. She is a headstrong and fierce woman, but a good one, with significant skill and knowledge." He smiled sadly. "Do not look at me like that. I know you think me as brainwashed as the others. I do not accept Miyela's words blindly, nor do I think she is right to oppose Dulon in such an underhanded way."

"Will you go?"

Uncertainty flickered behind Firas's eyes at her choice of pronoun. He looked away. There was a long silence. "Daro is our home."

"You miss Morcanan."

"Yes, but that does not make it more my home than Daro. I would miss Daro as much or more if I left. Sometimes I feel I can never have a true home again."

Renyra nodded. She felt the same about the grasslands. "You will stay then?"

Firas hesitated. "I do not want to fight in another war," he whispered.

"I know."

"And what she said about murder ..."

Renyra tensed. "She went too far. Not all killing is murder."

Firas drew his brows together.

"Is killing a hare for food murder? I think death is necessary sometimes—to feed, to protect. So long as you don't commit the act with hate or find joy in death, I can't call it murder."

Firas said nothing. He sat in contemplative silence for a long time, then sighed wearily. "What should I do?"

"I can't answer that."

"If I did leave ... would you," he seemed afraid to finish the question, "go with me?"

Renyra stared at her hands. She couldn't imagine being separated from Firas, especially with battle, political conflict, and earthquakes threatening from all sides. But how could she leave Daro? Her friends, her work, the city itself, she would miss, but more than that, it would mean abandoning the elves with whom she had built this city and community. It would be a betrayal to Gellion, to Dulon. And then there was the thought of living in Morcanan itself. Could she bear being seen as a *tathé* the rest of her life?

There is no right decision here. Either way, one of us betrays someone. Either way, one of us sacrifices the other.

She squeezed Firas's hand and put her head on his shoulder.

***

The atmosphere of the parting feast was as like to the welcome feast as a sickroom to a wedding. There was an air of waiting. Smiles were tense, laughter fell short, conversation was low. No one had officially announced the decision of the Council, but clearly word had spread.

Renyra sat across from Caerlyn, who sat up straight with a somber expression. Renyra looked down the table, past Veldon and Valder on the other side of Firas, to the head table where the Council sat together. Auralia and Cuvan were talking quietly, and Dulon occasionally exchanged a comment with Gellion, but otherwise no one spoke.

As the bells of the Tower of Stars echoed in the distance, Dulon stood. He wore a cobalt jacket with black trim that split at the waist and extended in tails to his calves. A shirt of cream silk showed beneath his collar. He tossed his hair out of his face and, with seemingly little effort, split his face into a grin.

How he manages to remain so composed I will never know.

"Before we begin this celebration of the end, we have an important decision to announce." Dulon grinned at the shocked hush that fell over the room. "The winner of the craftsman competition!"

Valder chuckled and rolled his eyes, nudging Veldon, who blanched. At the head table, Miyela looked murderous. Either Dulon was incredibly brave, or incredibly foolish. Renyra would never have stood with a smile on her face while the Lady of Morcanan skewered her with those eyes.

"We judges have analyzed the entries in depth over the last day and a half. Let me first extend my thanks to every worthy craftsman who participated. The results of this competition were truly astounding." He bowed his head in respect. "But! Only one can be extraordinary, phenomenal, *revolutionary* enough to hold the place of glory. And the skilled, talented elf to hold that place is ..." He let his eyes travel to every entrant.

"Veldon!"

Dulon's eyes fixed on the elf. Veldon turned so scarlet Renyra almost feared he had choked on something.

The tension in the room broke as elves applauded. Valder leaned across the table and clapped his brother on the back. At the head table, one side of Gellion's mouth curled up as he clapped his hands.

When the noise died down, Dulon continued.

"Well done Veldon, well done Veldon." He grinned broadly and bowed. "I grant you the prestige and glory of an accomplishment well achieved."

Veldon's mouth turned up as he dropped his eyes.

"Now!" said Dulon. "Today marked the last meeting of this fourth Kindom Council of the elves. The end of four weeks of hard work, difficult decisions ..." His pause was barely noticeable, but seemed to reinfect the room with tension. "And fellowship among friends and family." Dulon's smile was almost gone now, the sparks of his eyes petered into solemnity. He scanned the crowded room.

"I thank all of you for your presence here in this city—for your input, for the dedication and work you have put into this Kindom Council and all we have here in Daro. I am honored to serve all of you, and honored to have played host to our kin from Faeran. Enjoy this final evening of food and fellowship. The morning is soon enough for worry and far from now!"

He smiled again and reached behind him for a glass of wine. "To the evening! To Veldon, to kinship, to food and wine!" He toasted the room, and a chorus of clinking glasses met his proclamation.

"Bit of a strange speech." Caerlyn frowned at Renyra as the murmur of conversation padded the room once more. Renyra watched Dulon lower himself into a chair, looking distinctly subdued.

"A strange speech for a strange night," Renyra mumbled with a knitted brow. She looked at Firas as he laughed with Valder and Veldon.

She noticed his left thumbnail working its way across each of his finger-tips in a repetitive arc.

Dulon is not the only elf putting on a show tonight.

Renyra let her eyes hunt through the faces surrounding her, trying to gauge the true sentiment behind the scores of shining eyes, but through the sea of green that met her gaze, she could read no truth, neither fear nor reassurance. Renyra moved her food in winding tracks around her plate. If tomorrow was soon enough for worry, it was certainly not far enough from now.

13

SHADOWS IN THE MIST

Gellion could hear voices, but they echoed from without—a distant noise of words and mingling that could not touch him here. There were no lights on in the arena, but the glow of the surrounding streets and buildings infiltrated the steep walls to cast cool colors into the shadows.

The best time to find solitude in a space was immediately after its purpose was served. The A'vaeri tournament had ended days before, and the court lay barren, but the activity of the last month seemed to linger as a ghost in every surface, brought to existence by the very stillness.

Gellion took a breath and moved his staff between both hands in a soundless cascade. The weapon spun faster and faster, creating a wind that began to hum, then Gellion dropped one hand. The staff turned over his wrist twice before halting in his palm, and he spread his feet in a lunge, moving the staff's tip to the side so its other end crossed his back.

He paused for a moment, taking another breath.

Shifting his feet again, he brought the staff up to his collarbone, then twisted his wrist and let go, turning on the spot so the staff spun against the back of his neck and shoulders before coming across his chest, where he wrapped his hand around it once more.

He took a breath. His pulse slowed.

After the parting feast, so many sensations had roiled in Gellion's body, he had not been able to separate or discern any of them. He felt he was clinging to a log in the middle of the sea, unsure when his tie to safety would roll and become his downfall. Everything was becoming too unpredictable. All evening, he had feared some unexpected outburst or disaster to disrupt the parting feast. Though nothing nefarious had occurred, the atmosphere had never relaxed.

He feared the morning, the parting of the ship. He feared the consequences of his decision at the Council meeting. He feared the volatile nature of the humans with whom he was about to entreat.

Already it seemed days since the Council meeting. Had it been only this morning that his vote had decided the fate of Daro? Even now, he doubted the wisdom of his decision.

No doubt. No anxiety. Breathe and feel.

Wind whistled past his ears as he moved the staff in rapid figure eights in front of him. He stepped forward and sideways as he spun, picking up more speed, more force, until he channeled it all into a swing that linked arm to staff in a powerful arc. The staff smashed into the dummy so hard it sent shockwaves up Gellion's arm that reverberated through his body. The stuffed figure let out a cloud of dust and vibrated against its iron bearings.

Gellion let the tip of the staff fall to the ground. He stared at the dummy. Could he strike a Dierna soldier as easily when a blade tipped the end of his weapon?

The waves of panic came again. Gellion gritted his teeth and picked up the staff, matching his breath to its movements.

The distant voices slowly faded as elves retreated to their homes, some for their last night in Daro. By the time Gellion left the arena, arms shaking from his efforts, he was nearly alone on the streets. He needed to go home. He needed to pack.

You need to talk to your mother.

Gellion shied away from the thought. After tomorrow, it could be centuries more before he saw his mother again, and though their relationship was clearly more stable than Gellion had dared hope before her arrival, he had never brought up the reason for its strain in the first place.

Coward.

It was late. His mother could be in bed for all he knew. He would talk to her tomorrow.

The windows were dark when he arrived home. Were his brothers asleep, or out celebrating their last evening together? Guilt stiffened Gellion's spine, and he pushed through the door.

In his room, he stepped in front of the wardrobe. There was no point in sleep just now. He may as well start preparing for his journey.

Gellion barely managed to slip a finger through the strap of the pack on the top shelf of his wardrobe. As he pulled it down, a puff of dust sounded its protestations at being disturbed after so many years of peace. Gellion brushed the smooth leather of the pack clean and placed it, mouth agape, in the center of his bed.

Setting out a pair of pants, a jacket, and a traveling coat, he began to carefully roll several sets of attire in varying degrees of courtly fashion. He would need an outfit for any occasion, to dazzle or to calm, to stand out or blend in. Gellion held a hat in his hands. Was this still in fashion in Tradira? The humans changed customs, fashions, and values faster than a gull switched prey over a school of fish. Gellion did not have much concern for fitting in with human ways for his own sake, but if the two races were to forge an alliance, political offense should be avoided.

Gellion tensed as a soft tap echoed through the door to his room. He turned to see the door open a crack. His mother's head slipped through. Gellion's breath caught in his throat.

Tenille gave the clothes and pack on his bed a considering look, then walked into the room and sat down beside them.

"Must you go in person?" she asked.

"There are too many negotiations and too much planning to accomplish by letter. Even to send a letter, we would have to send a messenger. We have no birds from Tradira to send by air, and there is no Rale system here."

"Can you not wait until another human comes to Daro?"

"That is a much rarer occurrence than this month has given suggestion to. Besides, Dulon told the man Amadeo that we would send our answer."

"What of the villages nearer to Daro? Surely you could send a human messenger from one of them?"

Gellion snorted. "Even if I could get one of their country folk to talk with me, I would never trust them with a message so important. No mother, I will go. I have dealt with the humans in Tradira before." He rolled a crimson tunic and tucked it into his bag.

"Will Dulon accompany you?"

"He can't leave Daro, not in this state."

"What about Valder? He can speak Albaren, yes?"

Gellion nodded reluctantly. Valder had learned some of the human language when Gellion had, but he had never accompanied Gellion on any trips to Albarad. Valder just did not seem the diplomatic type.

"Yes, he can," Gellion said. "But his presence would only complicate matters."

"Or make them safer."

"Or make our presence more intimidating."

"Is that a bad thing?"

Gellion sighed. "I don't know."

Tenille grew silent. When Gellion looked up, she had him fixed with a troubled stare. "You were so against this alliance."

He nodded.

"You still are?"

He nodded.

"Why did you do it?"

Gellion clenched his jaw, trying and failing to form words to explain himself, to describe his conflict, his reasoning. Doubts flickered in his mind again.

No. Riu grant my decision was the right one, but I cannot go back now.

"Why should I allow my personal feelings to negate those of the elves I was chosen to represent?" Gellion said.

"Elves do not always pursue what is in their best interest."

"Elves? You set yourself apart from them? Would they say the same of you if your positions were switched?" He shook his head and sat on the bed. "It doesn't matter now. It is done, and I must follow through."

After a prolonged silence, Tenille stood. Her eyes were full of sorrow, an expression Gellion had not seen so prominent in her face for centuries.

"Be careful," she said, an uncharacteristic pleading in her voice. "Do what you think to be right, but ..." She closed her mouth, unable to summon sufficient words. She leaned over and kissed him on the cheek. Nearing eight centuries old, Gellion felt a child again, enveloped in the loving regard of a woman infinitely stronger, wiser, perfect ... able to solve all things. Then she stood back, and again Gellion saw the cracks. Behind his mother's eyes was sadness, fear, even a flicker of anger. Her unlined face somehow showed its years in the very pigment of her skin.

As she turned to leave, Gellion's stomach twisted with the guilt he had been suppressing for a month; his throat choked on the unspoken words.

"I'm sorry," Gellion blurted as his mother reached the door. She paused with her hand outstretched to the handle and looked back.

"I'm ... I'm sorry." Gellion's voice cracked. He sat on the bed with slack hands. No other words came.

The sadness in Tenille's eyes deepened as she walked back across the room. "Son." She sat next to him.

Gellion clenched his fists at the burning in his throat. "I couldn't ... I didn't want to leave. I just couldn't stay there."

"I know."

"Tornac ..."

"You and your brother are very different. Do not compare yourself to him."

"But ..."

Tenille pushed his shoulder back so he was facing her. "Do not take Tornac's opinions to heart. He judges you based upon his own understanding of the world, just as we all do. He was in a dark place at the end of the war. Your father's death pained him, but losing Vyra left him shattered. He does not understand why you left, but he misses you."

Gellion shook his head.

"I miss you," she continued, "but I understand." She squeezed his shoulder.

"I did not ask Valder to come with me when I left. I wasn't trying to split our family."

Tenille dropped her hand and smiled. "Valder was born during the war. He had never known a safe and free world beyond the walls of Maramor. If you had not left first, I have no doubt he would have. Our family is not split Gellion. It is just living in different places for the time being. Maramor, Daro—" a shadow crossed her face, "and beyond. It is through no fault of your own, and it is temporary—as is anything else in this life."

"Centuries do not seem temporary."

Tenille sighed. "I know."

Gellion closed his eyes, but instantly opened them again at the visions of staring, blank faces painted against his eyelids. He did not want to talk about this. He stood.

"When does the ship leave tomorrow?" Gellion knew the answer, but could think of no better question to change the subject.

Tenille watched him for a moment longer before answering.

"Midmorning," she said. A line creased her brow. "Have you spoken with Veldon?"

"About what?"

"He has been acting strangely."

"He was making his secret invention wasn't he?" Gellion tried to keep bitterness out of his voice. He still flitted between amused pride in his brother's achievement and the twisted pain in his chest every time he thought of his sabotaged chances. Next to this pride and pain dwelt a sliver of jealousy, that Veldon should prove to possess their father's skill with vierstone.

"No, I knew about that."

"You did?" Gellion's head jerked up.

"I was the only one who did, I think." Tenille's lips twisted upward. "You know how he is embarrassed by attention. And how highly he values the regard of his brothers." She raised an eyebrow. "But that is just it. He usually speaks openly with me about these things. I think the events of the past weeks have deeply troubled him, but he keeps to himself. He has not mentioned anything to you? Or Valder?"

"Not at all." Gellion felt a twinge in his chest. He had not spent much time with Veldon the past week and had hardly had a chance to speak with him since the craftsman competition. Amid the anxiety and excitement, it had been all too easy to pretend his mother and brother were not leaving the next morning. At least the ship would take Miyela with it too.

The twinge in Gellion's chest turned to an icy stab. He stiffened. Was Kyna going with them? She seemed so separate from those she had accompanied from Faeran. Gellion had come to consider her more as a mystery raised from the sea itself, not an elf from Faeran, bound to return at the end of the month.

"I need to go to the Domes," he said, trying to keep his words controlled. "I'm sorry, I've forgotten ..." he searched for an excuse. "I need to talk to Dulon before the morning."

Tenille eyed him, but nodded. He could feel her gaze on his back as he descended the stairs and hurried into the night.

Mist was beginning to curl across the Court, scattering in frantic swirls as Gellion's feet pushed through it. He knew that Kyna was staying at the Domes of Rhelyon—all the visitors without immediate family in the city were—but he had never been to her rooms.

The city was mostly deserted, save the few stragglers trickling home from the parting feast. The emptiness seemed heavy with apprehension, the mist a sentence of judgment come to pass through the streets.

Gellion stepped through the doors into the entrance hall of the Domes. Orb-like lamps glowed along the walls. Gellion could hear the distant echo of feet on marble, but saw no elves. He ascended the stairs to the third floor, where guest rooms stretched north to south in a curved hallway. He looked side to side, at a loss of what to do next. There were dozens of rooms. How was he supposed to find Kyna's? He could hardly knock on every door. Gellion squeezed his eyes closed. Why hadn't he just talked to her at the parting feast? Gellion drew his brows together. He had not seen Kyna at the feast. Surely she had been there, but Gellion had not been in a particularly social mood and had remained at the Council table the whole time.

Ah let me find her! Gellion projected the thought heavenward, hoping such a meager request might still catch the attention, or at least the amusement, of Riu. But no doors swung open.

Gellion began to pace the hallway, hoping someone would exit their chambers so he could ask if they knew which room belonged to the raven-haired woman with sharp eyes. He had almost decided to knock on a random door when he heard a familiar clack of boots on the stairs.

Gellion froze, unsure whether he wanted to involve Dulon in this foolish undertaking, then retraced his steps. He intercepted Dulon as the man was turning to climb the next flight of stairs. Dulon stepped back in surprise. He was still wearing his jacket from the feast, his hair hanging forward over tired eyes. It took a long moment before Dulon registered who was standing before him. His eyes brightened in recognition, and he swung his hair back from his face.

"I thought you went home," Dulon said. He looked past Gellion at the hall of guest chambers and his brows knit. "Were you looking for me?"

Gellion glanced backward to give himself more time to think what to say.

"No," he said slowly, "I was looking for ..." He took a breath. There was no other way. "Kyna. You know her, right?"

Dulon arched an eyebrow. "Yes."

"Do you know where her rooms are?"

Dulon's brow climbed higher up his forehead.

"I need to ask her something," Gellion added quickly.

Dulon did not change his expression for several seconds, then blinked. "No."

Gellion's heart sank. He could feel warmth starting to spread up his neck. Then Dulon's face split in a grin. He slapped Gellion on the shoulder.

"Ah, I'm joking, I know where everyone's rooms are. What kind of Lord of the City do you think I am?" He swept past Gellion and down the left side of the hallway. Gellion turned to follow him, grinding his teeth.

Dulon stopped in front of a door and gestured to it with his hand.

"Lady Kyna's chambers," he said in a low voice, an all too knowing look on his face.

Gellion clenched his hands, trying to make his face as neutral as possible. "Thank you."

Dulon winked and strode back down the hall. Gellion took a deep breath, humiliated, and waited until the clicks of Dulon's boots were well up the stairs before knocking on the door in front of him.

He waited.

He knocked again.

Was she asleep? Was she still out in the city? After an unanswered third knock, Gellion dropped his hand to the door handle. No good could come from what he was considering. The door was probably locked, and if it wasn't, he would either be intruding upon her empty living space like a thief, or worse, find her inside, asleep or hostile to uninvited company.

He pressed weight into his hand. The handle resisted his grip. He tightened his fist in frustration until his knuckles were white, but the handle stoically retained its position. Gellion turned back toward the stairs, heart hammering. Should he look for her? It would be absurd to try to find her in the city, especially so late. She was probably asleep just on the other side of the door, just beyond his reach.

A blast of wet air met Gellion when he stepped into the Court. The mist was thicker now and tasted of brine. He glanced longingly at the Rale path, but it was dangerous to use levit boards in low visibility like this. With a sigh, Gellion descended the stairs to the second tier, flitting a glance into the Silver Swan.

With each step, his resolve weakened. He would simply have to wait until the morning to talk to Kyna. Gellion turned his back to the sea and began to wade through the mist up Master's Street. The veiled light of the moon and the glow of Daro's lights dissipated through the water droplets, giving his surroundings an eerie illumination. Gellion watched the condensation shift with his movement.

A shadow moved to his left. His head snapped sideways.

Gellion's eyes fixed on swirls of disturbed mist. Mist he himself had not disturbed. A shadow couldn't cause that.

He took a step forward, then another. Nothing else moved. Through the blue haze, however, Gellion thought he could see an outline. A water spirit? Suspended in the mist?

"Hello?" Gellion's voice was muffled, falling flat in the thick air. No one answered.

Gellion began to walk toward the outline, his pulse mounting in his ears. He ran a hand through his damp hair and shivered as his thumb brushed vierstone. Goosebumps crawled down his arms. As he got closer, the outline seemed to become more hazy, almost a shimmer. The mist surrounding it danced. When Gellion was a few paces away, he raised a hand, sending a billow of mist into the shimmering light.

He heard it before he felt it.

A crack resounded, echoing all around him despite the dense haze. He felt the ground lurch beneath his feet, then he no longer felt the ground at all. He threw his arms forward as he dropped and gasped in pain as his foot wedged between two jagged pieces of rock. His hands slapped the ground, which was now almost chest-high. Reality careened around him in a sickening, now familiar way, and he screwed his eyes shut, trying to hold on to some form of sense in a world now devoid of any.

Clawing at the damp stone, Gellion managed to drag himself out of the fissure. He tried to stand, but sucked in a breath as pain shot up his leg, and the ground gave another tremble, pitching him back to his knees. Gellion shook his head and wiped the condensation from his eyes, trying to see through the mist, but the lights of the nearby buildings were dancing and shivering through the suspended water. A horse could have galloped past him, and Gellion would not have noticed.

Two more rumbles rolled through the street, then the world stilled.

Wincing, Gellion pulled himself to his feet and looked around wildly, but the backlit mist had gone as still as the ground.

14

A VISION OBSCURED

Sweat beaded on Dulon's brow. He swiped at it with his sleeve. Heat had always annoyed him. It was simply not conducive to productivity or enjoyment of any kind.

Nor can one look faintly appealing with saltwater trailing down his face.

He thought of the cool mountain air of Morcanan, the swirling snows of a winter he had not seen for centuries. Then he thought of the rules, the sickening practicality, the simple leathers and furs. No. He would take the heat.

Dulon stood on the wharf, watching elves file past with crates of stone, produce, and wine. The ship would depart within half an hour, and most of her stores were filled. A small gathering of the returning elves lingered near the bow of the ship, and some locals were lined up several paces back to watch the send-off. Dulon's eyes swept the docks. Where were the rest?

His stomach had been in knots all morning. He longed for the Kindom Council to be officially over. He hoped the discord sewn by the Council Members would accompany them across the sea, leaving Daro as it had been before. It was a dangerous thing, having so many leaders in one place. The coming months would be difficult enough.

Dulon's head jerked up as several figures descended the stairs from the second tier. Tenille walked toward the gathered crowd, her expression unreadable and her three sons flanking her like wolf pups. Veldon looked positively miserable, and Gellion stepped in an uneven gait. The muscles in Dulon's jaw tensed.

Now if I could only bargain with the earth to settle its internal conflicts elsewhere.

Last night's earthquake had not been any worse than the others recently afflicting the city, but it was the first to cause any harm to an elf. Gellion had suffered no more than a bruised ankle, but the likelihood of the earth opening exactly where he had been standing was more than Dulon could hope to explain. Gellion had seemed understandably shaken, but Dulon got the impression he was still holding something back from his story.

Dulon frowned at the limping elf. The Gellion Dulon had known all these years had brimmed with self-confidence, been sharp of tongue and wit and easy to laugh. Now he bore the look of one hunted, either deep in troubled thoughts or roving his surroundings with his eyes, though Dulon could not guess what he looked for. Dulon was reluctant to send Gellion away while his temper and fortunes seemed so unpredictable, but no other elf knew both the humans and the politics of Daro as well as Gellion. Dulon would trust no other with this task save himself, but his place was here.

Dulon tossed his hair back and fiddled with his sleeves as more elves trickled down to the docks. Auralia, Cuvan, Rhosti, and Liera came one by one, until all but the Morcani seemed to be present. Dulon's discomfort grew.

Friends bent their heads together, speaking in low voices. Brothers and sisters embraced and passed letters to return to Faeran. Dulon's throat constricted by the minute. As each moment passed, his surety that something was wrong increased. His unease was paralleled in the waiting elves. All were glancing backward at regular intervals, and conversations were hushed.

Just when Dulon was about to begin the boarding of the ship, a hush of voices from the docks turned his attention to the water. The mist of the night had not entirely dissipated, and it took a moment before Dulon realized what he was looking at. Three anchored ships bobbed on the water to the left of the vessel waiting to sail, but through their masts Dulon could see the bowsprit of a fourth ship moving behind them. Dulon's nostrils flared. No other ship was supposed to arrive or set sail this morning.

The ship turned and floated to the other side of the wharf. A lone figure appeared on its deck and strode to the railing.

Miyela stood tall and stern, looking down her nose at the elves below her as though their very presence offended her. Behind Miyela, the deck began to fill with more elves. Dulon recognized Lythin and most of the Morcani visitors, but the deck continued to fill. Dulon's breath caught in his throat. There were at least fifty elves on board the ship. Over half of them were from Daro. Dulon drew himself up and glared at Miyela. Silence fell.

"Dulon." Miyela did not shout, but her voice carried on the still air. Dulon could feel a concentration of gazes turn to him, awaiting his response.

"Miyela." He refused to look away from her. At last, Miyela blinked and looked out at the elves behind Dulon before putting a hand on the ship's railing and vaulting over it to land lightly on the dock below. She strode forward and stopped an arm's length away from Dulon, eyes level with his. Every muscle in Dulon's body was taught as a harp string.

"These elves," Miyela let her eyes wander to the ship and back, "want no part of your war—of your benefaction." The latter word was laden with sarcasm. "You have chosen for your people to lead them into senseless, unjustified destruction—to make murderers of them all and victims of some—all for the sake of a security that never would have been compromised, and greed that never would have come to be if not for the building of your city."

Heat was suffusing Dulon's face like water moving up a rag. He remained perfectly still, jaw clenched and eyes flat. Miyela opened her mouth to continue, but a voice spoke up from Dulon's right.

"You had your say in this, Miyela," Liera said. "Everyone had their say in this. No one is being forced to fight. Nothing beyond an offer of help has been decided."

"Oh no?" Miyela scoffed. "Tell me then—who of the elves gathered here will voluntarily fight, and who will remain behind to watch their city crumble?" She smiled at the charged silence her words evoked.

Her eyes moved back to Dulon. He did his best to swallow the fear rising in his chest, to keep his face a mask of indifference.

"Riu himself is showing his hand against your folly," Miyela continued. "Your great city is breaking even as the unity of the elves it contains does."

"Any broken unity between elves came from your hand, Miyela, not Riu's." Liera's eyes were blazing now. Dulon clenched his fists. Liera's retorts were making him seem weak, a silent spectator in an attack against himself and his city. He shot her a silencing look, but she was not paying attention to him. Miyela looked at Liera with something little short of loathing.

"My hand?" Her voice was soft as silk and burning as acid. "In a matter of four weeks, Dulon has managed to turn the Council Members and all the elves in Daro against each other in a way I have never seen before." Her eyes lit with malice. "Unless of course, you count the strife following the breaking of the Siege of Mathtier."

A hush followed her words. Dulon dug his nails into his palms. How dare she use that as an insult, as leverage for whatever point she was trying to make? Over half of the elven army had been killed in that battle—an army of all four Kindoms—an army led by Liera.

Liera's expression did not change, but the color drained from her face.

"I should not be surprised that you support this alliance, Liera," Miyela said. "Beyond even the battle at Mathtier, your family has shown its disregard for elven life."

Liera stepped back as though slapped. It was the first true break in composure Dulon had seen of her since her arrival in Daro.

"You go too far." Dulon said to Miyela. It took every ounce of his self control to keep his voice steady, though it still did not carry as far as he wished. "These past grievances have no place here. They are petty and cruel."

"They are necessary," Miyela spat at him. "What can be more relevant here than the only time in our history that an elf has purposefully taken the life of another—of two for that matter! You all fear unpleasant memories like the dark—pushing them deeper and deeper and pretending they do not exist. To forget is to risk repeating. Kaelo was Liera's son—I doubt she has forgotten."

Liera flinched at the name. She was not the only one. A hiss of muttering spread through the crowds.

"That is enough, Miyela." Cuvan's voice rumbled above the mutters. "You have said your piece. You have made your point."

Miyela considered Cuvan for a long moment before turning her eyes back to Dulon. "You are right, Cuvan. I have."

Sweat was running down Dulon's sides now. He could not tell how much of the crushing heat around him came from without or within. He looked into the smoldering emerald of Miyela's eyes. Try as he did to summon a response, no words would form on his lips.

Miyela smirked.

"This is who you would follow into battle?" she asked the elves. "How will he protect you when he cannot even defend himself? An upstart 'lord' more interested in his own glory than the lives of the elves he governs."

Dulon blanched. His sweat seemed to freeze on his skin. Even his anger cooled, to be replaced by a cold hand of fear pulling him downward. He tried to form a retort, a defense of any kind, but his mouth seemed glued shut, his mind blank.

Miyela turned away, disgust in her eyes. An elf from the unanchored ship tossed a rope down to her and she climbed it.

From the deck, she called back, "There is empty space in the other ship for anyone who should come to their senses." She disappeared into the ranks of her subjects as the ship began to drift away from the wharf, turning toward the open sea.

Dulon slowly turned to face the silent elves on the docks. He wrenched his eyes up to meet them.

"You may go gather your possessions if you wish to leave," he said in a flat voice. All energy had left him. He kept his face devoid of expression. No elves moved. After a painful silence, Dulon nodded. "Those returning home may board the ship now."

It took several seconds for the first elves to start moving, then a subdued procession started toward the gangplank of the anchored ship.

Cuvan and Auralia nodded to Dulon before disappearing below deck. Liera looked at no one. Dulon watched her dark hair bobbing along the deck and realized he had not seen Kyna board the ship. He scanned the docks and spotted her standing behind the remaining elves, shrewd eyes watching the scene before her. She carried no bags.

Dulon's eyes found Maranyl's in the crowd. She was looking at him with a sort of scared sympathy. He looked away, biting the back of his tongue. Next to her stood Veldon, who seemed to be experiencing an internal crisis. His eyes were darting between the ship and the elves around him. Attention caught, Dulon watched Gellion's family.

Gellion himself looked fit to burst into flames, his eyes glinting red. Tenille squeezed one of his clenched fists with her hand and kissed him on the cheek. His eyes softened only slightly, but he nodded as she turned to board the ship. She was almost up the gangplank before she realized Veldon was not with her. She looked back.

"I am staying," Veldon said.

Tenille looked at him a long time. Her eyes moved to Gellion and Valder standing behind him, then fixed on her youngest son. She looked grieved, but unsurprised. She inclined her head once, then continued onto the ship without a word. The gangplank slid back behind her.

Dulon stood facing the sea, arms limp at his sides. His hair hung in his eyes as he watched the ship disappear into the distant mist.

PART II

15

TRADIRA

Gellion sighed. The wind had changed direction again. He leaned forward and gathered the mainsheet of the sail in his hands, pulling the supple fabric until the sail snapped taut again, and moved himself to the port side of the small craft. The Semestrial Sea was in its tame season, but only by a few weeks. Weather could still be unpredictable this time of year, and navigating the coastline could prove tricky. Gellion had not sailed in years, but the movements were still practiced in his hands and body. He relaxed again as the little boat sliced through the waves. Despite the fickle wind, it was a beautiful day. Gellion looked up to watch tendrils of clouds racing each other across a blue dome of sky. He imagined time speeding past as the world spun under him, a solid point in the immovable sea.

Movement caught Gellion's eye, and he glanced toward the coastline. The scrubby cliffs were still. Probably a bird. Strange how the sea was a world for creatures of the air. The two seeming opposites melded in a way that was ironic and beautiful. Water and air always seemed to possess a level of grace unknown to land. Perhaps ether and water spirits were simply more graceful inherently and had morphed their elements and the animals that inhabited them to their own nature. Gellion ran a hand along the smooth metal of the railing behind him. Only in boats did creatures of the land taste that grace, venture into a part of the world they were not created for. Such ventures were dangerous, but surreal and freeing in a way that made the soul long for more. Some more than others.

Gellion remembered the first time Valder had sailed, accompanying Gellion on a vierstone expedition before the founding of Daro. His brother's eyes had shone in wonder, glistening with unabashed moisture as the ship rose and fell and wet wind twisted his hair behind him into tangles. Gellion's eyes glassed over in memory. He could see the jagged coast of Faeran, the golden rise and fall of the grasslands, the Orhiri River coursing joyously through the gorges of Ard Gael as it threw itself against rock walls and plunged over cliffs. He did miss it. He missed traveling and being in a land well known by his people and inhabited by his kin.

But Gellion's longing was for a Faeran of centuries past. The coast, the grasslands, and the gorges were still there, but the life to which he longed to return was not. Would never be again. He knew he romanticized his recollections. Even his life before the Great War had been touched with pain, and the years of the war were certainly no paradise, but still, there had been times of peace and joy. The end of the war should have been the epitome of joy, but it had been bittersweet at best, and for Gellion it had been the end of much more than the war.

Memory pulled Gellion deeper toward Maramor, coaxing and dragging him with that mesmerizing attraction all elves seem to have to reliving pain. He saw his older brother's face, so like their father's, accusing eyes boring into Gellion's back as he walked out of Maramor. By then the paths and stairways of the city had been cleared of rubble and ash, but gaping holes remained in the towers, and scorch marks stained every stone, lending an almost artful illusion of marble to the city. Gellion knew he should have stayed to help rebuild Maramor. He should have stayed with his family as they mourned the loss of his father.

His father's death had been a blow not just to his own family, but to the elves as a whole. The loss of any vierstone master was a tragedy, and Eldian had made powerful contributions to elven society with his knowledge and skill. Those contributions, at least, had not been lost with his death, but none would ever know what more he could have discovered had his life not been cut short.

No one knew how the Lord of Maramor had killed the terror of the phoenix, when no other elf had succeeded. He had perished in the fiery explosion that resulted from the phoenix's death. Tornac had obsessed over the matter in his grief, but Gellion had seen little point in staying in Maramor when bigger things were happening in the Great Cities. Why walk the haunted halls of his home, dwelling on pain and reliving the memories that assaulted him at every corner, when he could move on and be a part of rebuilding the lives of all the elves? So he had gone to Tura, the city of his birth and upbringing. Over the years, he had witnessed the formation of the Kindom Council, overseen the building of a fleet of ships, and sailed until the fateful day elves had seen green glinting in what was now Quarry Bay.

He did not regret his decisions. He had enjoyed his time in Tura, on the vierstone expeditions, and building Daro. He had made a difference, a bigger difference to more elves than Tornac ever had shut away in Maramor ...

Gellion blinked. His sails were slack, and the little boat bobbed in the water. The wind, capricious as ever, seemed to have grown tired of its play and stopped altogether. Gellion let out the sail further in an attempt to catch what little breeze may pass, then moved to switch on the boat's motor. He had no doubt the wind would be back soon, but why waste time drifting? As long as he used the motor sparingly, its power would last the trip.

The warmth of the day was apparent in the momentary stillness. Gentle waves of heat lay on Gellion's skin like a quilt. He sighed in relief as the low hum of the motor joined the chorus of the sea, and wind blew through his clothes again. Sunlight skimmed off the water. The dazzling reflections made him think of his tunic, and he scowled.

How had everything gone downhill so quickly? The craft competition ruined, Daro assaulted by earthquakes and who knew what else, the elves going to battle, and now Miyela splitting the Kindoms from within. Gellion shifted against his anxiety. The specter in the mist still haunted his waking thoughts. Had Gellion seen the cause of the earthquakes just feet before him? What had it been? A terra spirit? The spirits had once held power to shape the fabric of the world, but now their power seemed limited to the daily running of natural processes. Corrupted spirits may cause trouble, but to create continuous earthquakes in such a short period of time? Gellion had never heard of a targeted attack like this. He raked a hand through his hair. As if all of this were not enough to worry about, he had never found Kyna to say goodbye.

He gritted his teeth against the lurch in his stomach.

Don't think about her.

It had been difficult to leave Daro so soon after Miyela's departure. Gellion warred over worry and anger at Dulon. The man was clearly shaken by the past few weeks and did not seem to be handling the pressure well, but then he was the Lord of Daro, after all. Shouldn't he be able to handle disagreement and resentment from those he served and those he opposed? Where had his sharp wit and easy smile gone when they were most needed?

All Gellion wanted was to empty his mind. His head ached with thoughts that darted and circled and morphed in never-ending motion.

For all Gellion's love of sailing, just now he hated how it left the mind to wander and dwell on matters best left alone. He longed to be in his workshop, working with his hands and concentrating his mind, but the distraction of Daro lay leagues behind him, and the distraction of Tradira leagues ahead.

Three days after departing Daro, Gellion brought his boat around a curve of coastline into the Kald Straight that lay between Tradira to the east and the Isle of Sapor to the west. Gellion knew the area well and had even been to the island once. The massive piece of land was dry as a piece of toast, but supported much of Albarad's spice industry through deep freshwater springs that littered the interior of the island. A constant stream of ships sailed between Aramo, the port city of the island, and Tradira. Gellion had no wish to go anywhere near it with his tiny vessel. There was a cove just north of Tradira, and he steered his boat toward its shore.

He anchored the boat at low tide and waded to shore with his boots held above his head and his pack strapped to his back. So far as he knew, no one ever came to this cove, and he had little fear for the welfare of his boat.

Across the beach, the land sloped gently and then rose into craggy hills rooted in shrubs and grasses. Vegetation crunched under Gellion's feet as he climbed. An incessant buzzing rose and fell around him as insects flew in drunken circles, and the smell of honey permeated the air. Gellion jumped back when a dove sprang out from beneath a particularly gnarled shrub, beating her wings and hooting in protest at his rude interruption.

Gellion was sweating by the time he reached the top of the hill. He tied his hair at the base of his neck and pulled a canteen of water from his pack, then stood back and absorbed the view. The hills in which he was standing circled in an arc to the east and merged back with the coastline in the distance. A flat bowl of land lay encircled by the hills with the coast stretching down one side and a thick wall encasing the rest. Every bit of land within the walls was covered in streets, buildings, and humans. Tradira was at least five times larger than Daro and extended into the hills through scattered settlements that eventually broadened into farmland. Tall, spiked buildings rose among paved streets in the center of the city, but slowly shrank and sprawled outward into twisting dirt roads and slanting homes.

The coastline followed the same trend. Proud trading ships docked at the central wharf, flanked by ever diminishing boats to either side that trailed away into one-man fishing vessels bobbing and pitching in the tide. Billows of black smoke rose from the city, choking out of pipes and chimneys as far as the eye could see.

Gellion grimaced. He had not been to Tradira in decades and could not say that he had missed it. He took a deep breath of fresh air, resigned that it may be his last for a while.

Riu let me navigate this nest of vipers.

With a final sigh, he began the long descent into the city.

The nearest city gates were a fair walk from the deserted hills. By the time Gellion reached Tradira's main entrance, long shadows stretched to the east, slashed with slivers of buttery sunlight. Two city guards watched his approach, eyes widening as his features came into relief. The two men exchanged glances. One stepped forward.

"What business have you in Tradira, sir?" The man's young voice belied his confidence, and his eyes showed a shadow of fear. Gellion smiled.

"I am an emissary of the elves of Daro, expected at the Courts by request of King Naval."

The guard stared at him. Gellion could see the muscles of his jaw working as his mind flitted through possible responses to this introduction. The poor man finally decided to ignore the unorthodox content of Gellion's claim and continued with what seemed a practiced routine.

"Do you carry any weapons?"

Gellion shrugged. "A utility knife." He pulled a curved dagger from a strap around his waist and offered it to the guard hilt first.

"That will not be necessary," the guard said, eyeing the weapon warily. Gellion's mouth twitched as he sheathed the blade. The knife may be simple, but it was sharp as a razor.

"You may pass, but know we allow no violence or disorderly conduct in this city."

Gellion inclined his head, concealing a scoff of derision at what he knew to be an entirely false claim. If violence, scheming, and any other manner of 'disorderly conduct' were forbidden in Tradira, it was a law enforced upon few.

Gellion strode between the two guards and into the city. He could feel the men's stares follow him down the street as he merged with the steady flow of humas converging toward the distant center of the city. Carriages interspersed the crowds, lacquered and pristine. Anyone wealthy enough to afford a carriage could afford to make it beautiful.

The main road from the gates to the courts was well paved and wide with gas street lamps spaced at regular intervals. The buildings flanking the street rose in straight lines with thin wooden beams arching between the windows—a fence encased in glass. Some of the buildings had coats, hats, walking sticks, and clocks displayed in wide windows. Others showed signs of habitation, with linen lines and chimneys. From one home, a pair of dark eyes peered over the sill of a window.

Several things about the eyes gave Gellion pause. They were too round, they were so dark the pupils blended into the irises, and they inhabited a face both small and oddly proportioned. A button nose joined the pair of eyes as the child rose on his toes to see Gellion better. Gellion raised an eyebrow at the child, whose eyes expanded to saucers before disappearing below the window.

A chorus of cries and giggles sounded behind Gellion. He turned to see a group of children running down the road, exciting curses and swats as they heedlessly ran into legs and carts.

So many children ... and so loud.

Yet Gellion felt a moment's envy at their joy. He had grown up in a large city, but even so there had been only a handful of children in Tura throughout his childhood, and none quite his age. Keeping the sole company of adults centuries or millennia old as a child certainly influenced one's behavior and ideas of entertainment.

The main road began to branch in different directions. To either side, streets snaked toward the outer districts of the city, growing narrower as they fled the bustle of the central paths. As the streets lost their girth, the buildings surrounding them grew taller and narrower, yet somehow less substantial.

Gellion had walked those streets to the edges of the city. As one neared the outskirts, wood began to splinter and buckle, ranks of windows turned to planked walls, and the handsome buildings of the public melted to little more than huts.

The whole city resembled a river confluence, tributaries from the outskirts pouring money and resources into rivers that converged toward the city center: the valley of wealth.

More like a mountain of wealth.

Gellion squinted against the setting sun. The horizon of the city center spiked toward the sky like giant stalagmites. Manors, each the size of Daro's Performance Hall, rose in ranks around the courts of Tradira. The manors belonged to the Marchons of Albarad—wealthy and powerful families favored by the king. Some families gained their status through military prowess, some through trading and industry, some through cropland holdings. At least a few, Gellion was sure, gained their status through corruption and deceit. The politics of Albarad were layered and complex, with mazes of titles, rules, and status. Gellion hoped he remembered enough to navigate unharmed.

As he neared the Central District surrounding the courts, he noticed a subtle shift in the company surrounding him. The crowd was thinning as tradesmen and workers disappeared down branching streets. Limp caps turned to top hats, coarse wool to supple silk.

Gellion had been the object of many stares and furtive glances since his entrance into the city, but now the stares bore a confidence, almost an arrogance, lacking in the former onlookers. The poorer citizens of Tradira may reside in the city, but the crowds striding about the Central District owned it, and Gellion was an intruder upon their court. He did his best to assume a casual bearing, allowing his shoulders to fall forward and keeping his gaze below the horizon.

All at once, the path spread into a wide expanse of flagged stones, buildings falling away to either side. Gellion stood still and looked on the center of all of Albarad. Even the mansions were dwarfed by the size of the buildings before him.

To one side was the bank. Arching windows soared the full height of the building, each only a handspan wide. Dark wood, sanded and lacquered to a shine, interspersed the windows, converging at the top to form a series of intertwining circles before joining in pointed pinnacles. To the other side stood the State Cathedral, its spires reaching away from the city at its feet, pointing to heaven. A fountain marked the center of the court, and through its dancing water Gellion saw his destination.

Two buildings stretched in staggered arcs, parallel to each other like overlapping lenses. They were joined by two bridges high above the streets. One was the Dom Creda, the center of the Albaren Church, the other the Dom Regirium, the house of government. The latter was Gellion's focus.

Gellion chided himself at the fluttering in his chest.

You have dealt with the Albaren countless times before. If you cannot hold your own in a foreign court, what kind of emissary are you?

But each time Gellion came to Tradira, a new generation held power. He had dealt with kings, but not King Naval, and he had discussed trade and territory, not battle alliances. The fluttering in his chest quickened.

<hr>

Gellion's reception in the Dom Regirium was nothing new. The resonant din of the entrance hall dimmed to whispers that ceased as Gellion neared. He finally managed to corner a servant who promised with much bowing and stuttering to find someone who could relay Gellion's message to the king. Gellion did not expect the message would reach the ears of anyone beyond the servant's friends, but he decided to wait a while before trying someone else. He was sure if he waited long enough, the news of an elf in the building would spread to the king anyway.

Gellion used the time to observe the humans around him. Fashions had changed dramatically since his last visit. He shook his head. Humans were obsessed with change. With lives so fleeting, did they feel a constant need to move on? A restlessness born from their imminent mortality to experience as many different things as possible? Or was it a function of the constant change of the people themselves, a continuous influx of new personalities? He looked in the faces of each person, trying to ascertain their age. He judged that most people in the room had been born not forty years ago.

There were almost no women. Gellion could count his past interactions with Albaren women on a hand. Women were barred from government business, and as far as Gellion could tell, served a mostly ornamental purpose in society.

One woman sat on a bench outside a set of double doors.

Probably waiting on her husband.

But if the woman was ornamental, she at least excelled at her purpose. She was possessed of a dark beauty and wore ebony skirts that accentuated her curves. Her hair fell in a sheet to her waist and shimmered glossy black as she turned to look at him. For a moment, it was Kyna Gellion saw sitting across from him.

He clenched his fists and turned away. He still didn't understand the

tangle of feelings Kyna had aroused in him. She was confident and fascinating, but she elicited a measure of discomfort and fear in him as well.
There was no room for either emotion in his life. Not that it mattered
now. Kyna had gone back to Faeran, and Gellion may not see her for
centuries, or ever again for all he knew. The twisting in his gut only
worsened at the thought.

The Albaren woman was still staring at him, one eyebrow arched.
Gellion inclined his head to her then looked pointedly away. He could
still feel her eyes on him, but a different set of eyes met his as he turned.

Amadeo Benta bounced toward him with a broad grin on his face.

"You have come!" The man clapped his hands together, squeezing
them as though trying to contain his excitement. "I was sure you
would." He released his hands and held one toward Gellion. Gellion
took it and tried not to grimace.

"Oh but the stories in the halls! I overheard a servant asking after the
king—most unusual. And then tales of a pale foreigner. I knew immediately of course and told them not to worry, I knew the man personally
and he was precisely who he said he was. I hope you have not been
waiting long?"

Amadeo had hardly taken a breath throughout his speech and now
looked expectantly at Gellion. Even through the man's enthusiasm,
Gellion sensed something less than genuine, but he could read nothing
in those dark eyes.

"It is good to see you again, Earl Benta. I am glad to see you made it
safely back to Tradira."

"Oh but of course! An easy journey really. But exhausting. I am sure
you are exhausted. There are rooms here you may stay in. Have you been
to the Dom Regirium before?"

"I have. And I have had a long journey, but I hoped to meet with
King Naval immediately."

Amadeo's face slipped into a placating grin and he shook his head.
"Ah, the king is most busy and was not expecting the arrival of any
guests tonight. Even one as important as yourself! No, I am afraid you
will have to wait to meet with the king, but I will set the appointment as
soon as he is able."

"And when will that be?"

"Oh not too long, not too long. Perhaps even tomorrow! I will do my best. Please, let me take you to a room for the night. There are many people you must meet, but it grows late. I can have a servant bring dinner for you."

Amadeo was already walking away before Gellion could answer. There seemed nothing more to do at the present. Gellion sighed, picked up his bag, and followed Amadeo into what he felt was the beginning of a divine game of spyre—one in which the Albaren held the cards and Gellion could only guess at what moves would maneuver him safely across the board.

And if I succeed, I bring myself and all of Daro toward greater danger.

16

THE POLITICS OF MANSIONS

By the progress of the shadows on the floor, Gellion guessed he'd been waiting for King Naval for an hour. He had spent half the morning waiting on word from Amadeo, and now it was past lunch and he was losing confidence that the king would show for their appointment. The bench outside the throne room was hard and backless, and Gellion was growing restless.

At last, a sharp tap on the doors announced the arrival of a thin man with a pointed beard. Gellion stood, assuming this was a servant sent to bring him to the king. The man cocked his head forward at an angle and straightened it again in a bird-like jerk, then watched Gellion. After a few silent moments, Gellion assumed the gesture had been a bow and returned the greeting. The man seemed satisfied.

"The king had an unexpected engagement. He will be unable to see you today, but sends his sincerest apologies and bade me ensure you have an introduction to the city. I am Solan Vespa, the king's financial advisor. You may call me Marchon Vespa." His voice was high, and he kept his chin raised as he spoke.

Gellion swallowed his annoyance. "Marchon Vespa," he repeated the name. "Thank you for your generosity, but I have visited Tradira before. A tour is really not necessary, and I would hate to distract you from your duties."

Vespa frowned and looked Gellion up and down. "You have been here before? The king made no mention of that."

Gellion smiled. "It was many years ago. Before King Naval was king."

Vespa's mouth gaped like a fish. He closed it with a snap, eyeing Gellion suspiciously, and drew his shoulders back. "Be that as it may, there are many important people you should meet, and I am confident the city has undergone vast improvements since your last visit."

Somehow Gellion doubted this, but he could think of no better use of his time if Naval was busy for the day.

"Will you come?" said Vespa.

"Very well."

"Good." Vespa bit off the word and set out at a brisk walk without a backward glance.

Gellion expected Vespa to take him through the Dom Regirium to meet the 'important people' of the current Albaren government, but the man led him straight through the hallways and out into the central court. Gellion walked through the doors into a sticky cloud of heat. The sun shone, yet a grey haze hung over the tops of the tall buildings, muting its light. Pedestrians milled through the streets in laughing groups, most of them resplendent in finery. The women waved fans and brushed hair back from their necks. Gellion saw few children in this part of the city, and those there followed on the heels of parents or servants.

Vespa strode through the passing citizens as though they were not there.

"There is the Dom Creda, of course." Vespa waved a hand toward the building connected to the Dom Regirium. "There is no need to go inside. The High Prophet is in the State Cathedral for noonmass and the rest of the building only houses clerics and their servants." He waved his hand again in an indistinct direction without turning his head. "There in the distance is the Academy. It has doubled in size since King Naval's rule. You would not have seen it."

Gellion shaded his eyes to look past the Dom Creda and saw a huge structure outlined against the horizon. Sunlight glinted off its domed surface.

"What is an academy?" he asked.

Vespa had clearly moved on, however, and was making a beeline for the imposing building of spires further down the court. Gellion lengthened his stride to catch up. Vespa stopped in front of the building.

"I trust you have seen the bank before?" He did not pause for a confirmation but launched into a lecture on how the bank was the true center of Albarad—what separated their civilized society from those societies in Diernas and in the mountains. "Only when the worth and works of a man can be measured does man have the motivation to improve himself and society; only through the sacrifice and contribution of the masses can structure and prosperity reign."

Gellion wondered if Vespa believed half of what he was saying.

As Vespa explained the Albaren system of currency, taxes, and loans, Gellion's eyes wandered through the court. Across from the bank, crowds of people choked the entrance to the cathedral. He supposed that was where the High Prophet was. Gellion had seen many cathedrals in Tradira, even in the lower districts, but none were as grand as this one. He expected it was funded by the ruling family.

Gellion realized Vespa had stopped talking. The man was looking at him expectantly with one eyebrow arched.

"I'm sorry," Gellion said. "What did you say?"

"Do you have a similar system of currency?" Vespa asked, annoyance clear in his tone.

"Ah." Gellion ran a hand through his hair and watched the passersby. He did not want to pursue this topic. Comparison of cultures was not why he was here and was probably the fastest way to cause insult.

"No," he said. "Not very similar." He began to turn away from the bank, hoping Vespa would let the matter drop.

"What is your currency system, then?" Vespa asked.

Gellion paused. "We do not have currency."

Vespa stared, looking Gellion up and down as though unable to believe one who appeared so civilized could in fact be such a barbarian. "None at all?"

"No."

A disapproving line formed between Vespa's eyes. Gellion didn't care what Vespa thought of his people, but he did not want to be the cause of any misconception or ill will between the races.

"Currency does not make sense for elves," he said.

"Sense? However can currency not make sense? What then, do you barter goods?"

"Yes and no."

"If you barter then you use currency, just in a highly inefficient way."

Gellion sighed. "The elves have very ... long lives. We value different things than humans on basic principle. You and your people assign value based on scarcity, time, and skill, the latter typically a result of the first two. We value goods based on inherent properties and usefulness, not scarcity, and time is not a precious commodity to one whose years stretch beyond centuries."

Vespa looked scandalized. "No value on scarcity? You tell me a diamond is worth the same as a stone to you?"

"The same? No. One may be more valuable than the other depending upon the situation." Gellion twisted his earring, thinking. "A diamond is no use to one building a wall, but of great use to one forging a knife that must be hard and sharp enough to cut stone. But then to pay in diamonds would make as much sense as paying in stones, or hand tools. No elf would want to be paid in diamonds because few other elves would value them as a form of payment."

Vespa was shaking his head in disbelief. He attacked from a new angle. "This entirely disregards the need for currency! The Albaren do not trade in diamonds but in coin. Even if you place a different value on objects," he looked skeptical, "you still must assign them some value, and a standard monetary unit is the only way to do so impartially."

"As I said, the value of an object is different for each elf. What is essential to one may be useless to another. You can more or less ignore this in your own system because of the time and skill value, but as I said, time means something very different to an elf, and skill is a function of time."

"What of beauty then? Do you see no difference between a jewel and a rock? A skillfully carved sculpture and a child's play toy?"

"Of course. To gift something beautiful, especially the work of one's own hands, is not something we take lightly. The giver may request a verbal or written agreement of some compensation of service or exchange of other goods, but many elves merely enjoy seeing the object of their labor valued and used by another."

Vespa appeared so baffled and outraged at this point, Gellion feared the man would shout, or send him away. Instead he opened his mouth, closed it, then finally sputtered, "Work! What of work? Is there no pay? Who does unpleasant jobs and for what motivation? Who toils the fields and prepares the food?"

Gellion was growing weary of the conversation and feared Vespa's growing temper. He somehow couldn't see this man appreciating the enjoyment and accomplishment that tending fields and baking bread brought some elves, nor the sense of pride and respect that kept their cities repaired and clean. He shrugged. "We take turns."

Gellion smiled at Vespa's expression and began to walk away. "Perhaps we should start meeting your important people now, Marchon. Time may be different for an elf, but we are still constrained by the same hours of the day."

The hours dragged. By late afternoon, Gellion had given up memorizing the names of every man and woman he met and instead struggled to remember titles, addressing people as "Marchon," "Lady," or "Earl." Vespa had taken him to the mansions of the Central District, tracking down the heads of the families—traders, plantation owners, and factory magnates. Some were haughty and eager to impress, but most were suspicious or even fearful of him. Gellion did not see the point of any of it. He was not here to make social connections; he was here to collaborate with the military and set plans with the king. He said as much to Vespa after a long visit with Marchon Sartor, who humbly outlined his family's near monopoly on steam engines.

To Gellion's complaint, Vespa replied tartly, "The king is busy, and you are to meet with no military personnel until you have spoken with him." Then he proceeded to drag Gellion to the Dacian Mansion.

Most of the mansions Gellion had seen stood unadorned, with clean windows and simple exteriors that drew the eye to the intricacy of the architecture. The Dacian Mansion exhibited no such constraint. Statues and carvings clung to, balanced on, or stood poised ready to fly from every surface. Gellion followed Vespa up a cobblestoned path that wove back and forth across the hill leading to the mansion, ensuring any visitor saw each and every piece of art before arriving at the front doors.

Gellion's shirt clung to his back with sweat by the time Vespa pounded on the thick wood. The doors swung inward to reveal an upright man dressed in red.

"Yes?" he asked.

"Is Marchon Dacian in? I am Solan Vespa, financial advisor to the king."

"One moment, Marchon." The doors closed again.

Vespa tapped his foot, clearly annoyed at being asked to wait outside in the heat. Within a few minutes, the servant came back.

"Please, follow me."

Gellion could see his reflection in the floor of the entryway. In the center of the room, a staircase climbed and split in two, sweeping upward in symmetric arcs to the floors above. The servant led them to the side of the staircase and into a room with high ceilings and a fireplace. Statues stared at Gellion from the walls, and he almost jumped when a living man rose from a desk in the back corner.

"Marchon Dacian." The servant announced.

Dacian was young for a head-of-family Marchon. His hair showed no silver, and only a few lines marred his face. His clothes would have shamed Dulon in their extravagance. Every inch of fabric was embroidered, with tails, ruffles, and buttons, transforming him into an exotic bird. He froze when he saw Gellion. His servant must not have elaborated on the nature of his guests. Dacian looked to Vespa and raised an eyebrow.

"Good evening Marchon Dacian," said Vespa. "I am here on orders of the king introducing our foreign guest—an emissary from the elves in the north."

Dacian turned back to Gellion, his surprise shifting to wariness.

"Gellion." Gellion inclined his head.

"Gellion," Dacian repeated. The caution in his eyes was slowly turning to a calculating interest. "I don't think we have ever had an elf visitor in Tradira. What's the occasion?"

"He is here to speak with the king on matters of relation and security," Vespa said before Gellion could open his mouth. "King Naval wants him to become acquainted with those in his council."

Realization was beginning to dawn on Gellion.

Of course, he thought. The Marchons were essentially the Council Members of the Albaren. Social standing was equivalent to power in Albarad, and to traverse the social circles was to meet the heads of government.

Dacian nodded, now looking Gellion up and down with a look that was almost hungry.

"I am a wine merchant," he said. "My family owns vineyards across the northern territory of Albarad. Have you had Albaren wine?"

"No," said Gellion.

Dacian made a tutting sound. "You must try it. The best wine you'll ever taste, though I have had the pleasure of sampling a rare bottle of elven wine." A conspiratorial grin stretched across his face, and he winked. "Good, very good, but not enough *spice* if you know what I mean. It lacks the fire and smoke."

Gellion smiled. "I will make a point of trying an Albaren vintage before I leave."

"I would offer you some now, but I have half my personal stock decanting as we speak. I am holding a ball tonight, you see, and my guests expect the very best for obvious reasons. Have you heard of the Marchon balls?"

"I can't say that I have."

"Ah, a splendid tradition. We must put these mansions to some use, yes? You can find a ball almost any night, and all proceeds go to the cathedrals and for relief of the poor." Dacian assumed a somber expression. "We do all we can for the good of the masses, you see. The Dacian Cathedral puts my humble mansion to shame. You will have to see it while you are here."

Gellion assured him he would like nothing better. He could not imagine what the Dacian Cathedral must look like if the family mansion and sense of fashion were any indicators.

While Marchon balls were a new tradition since Gellion's last visit to Tradira, the family cathedrals were not. Any wealthy family who was worth their name sponsored a cathedral in the city—a public display of their generosity and piety.

And their wealth.

"But you must come tonight! There is no better way to meet every Marchon and Earl in the city than to attend the balls. And you can taste my wine." His smile was oily, the hunger in his eyes alight with excitement.

"Oh, I—" Gellion searched for a polite refusal, but could think of no excuse. Vespa was watching him.

"I think that is a good idea, Dacian," Vespa said. "I am sure the king will have no time for an audience until tomorrow, and Gellion still has many people to meet."

Gellion was silent for a few moments, his eyes lingering on Vespa as he turned to Dacian. He swallowed his annoyance and plastered a flattering smile on his face.

"I would be happy to attend."

17

THE BLACK STAIN

Renyra did not know what to do with herself. In the five days since the Kindom Council ended, Daro had been a quiet place. Elves walked with their eyes averted, afraid to break the tenuous peace left behind after the disastrous ship parting. Renyra went about her business in the greenhouse and stables. She had even returned to Sira training in the Performance Hall, but could still not seem to find enough pursuits to occupy her time with the city so somber and no performances ahead.

Her research on earthquakes had turned up nothing, and her interest was waning, though she did often find herself thinking about Gellion's accident. She wished she had gotten a chance to speak with him before he left for Albarad, but he had left so soon after the Council, and the opportunity never came up. The coincidence of his accident nagged at her, adding to the list of irregular characteristics the plague of earthquakes carried. What had Gellion been doing when the ground opened beneath him? Had he seen anything?

It was useless to wonder.

Renyra raked her palms over her eyes and sighed, leaning her elbows on the countertop of her kitchen and glancing toward Firas, who was sitting at the table pouring over ship blueprints. Always an elf of few words, he had been almost silent since the other Morcani left. She paused and studied his features—calm eyes skimming the page in front of him through blonde lashes, a slight crease between his eyes as his mind interpreted and contemplated the diagrams. A strand of hair hung in front of his face, but he paid it no heed. Renyra's heart clenched.

Riu, but he is lovely.

Relief at Firas's staying in Daro warred with anxiety over his unhappiness. Renyra had always found it infinitely easier to live with her own worry and pain than with Firas's. She would rather suffer a week than watch him suffer an hour. Helplessness gnawed at her. She stood, restless.

"Do you want to go for a walk?" she asked.

Firas lifted a finger from his pages to indicate he had heard her, but did not look up for half a minute. Renyra fidgeted. At last he looked up.

"A walk to where?"

"I don't know, just a walk."

Firas's eyes drifted to a window showing blue sky. He took one last look at his papers, then sat them down and stood.

"Alright." He smiled, though Renyra could tell he was loath to part from his prior occupation.

The neighborhood streets were nearly deserted despite the clear day. Renyra walked with a purpose. Firas ambled after her on his long legs, his fingers entwined in hers. She wanted him to talk, but feared serious conversation, so compromised by saying nothing at all.

As they neared the Courts, Firas broke the silence.

"You seem quite determined for one with no destination."

Renyra shrugged and slowed her pace.

"We can run through the streets for all I care." Firas chuckled. "But it seems something is bothering you."

"Bothering me?" Renyra stared at him. "What could be bothering me? Except maybe the battle we've just agreed to fight, the earthquakes threatening to break the city, and your silence the last week?" She didn't raise her voice, but the words came faster and faster. Concern filled Firas's eyes.

"I meant nothing by my silence. I had not realized ..."

Renyra squeezed his hand and shook her head. Now she had him apologizing to her, as though he didn't have enough worries.

"I just wish I knew what you were thinking," said Renyra. "I wish I could help."

Firas turned her to face him, raising her chin with the tip of a finger until their eyes met. "Do you fear that I regret my decision to stay? That I resent Daro?" He shook his head. "I do not. Any regrets I harbored for my decision were dashed by Miyela when she confronted Dulon and Liera. I do not wish to fight, but nor do I wish to return to Morcanan out of spite or pride."

Renyra nodded. "I understand."

But something else Firas brought up had been bothering her. Miyela's confrontation with Dulon was expected, but her vehemence toward Liera had caught Renyra off guard. She had heard about the tragedy at the Battle of Mathtier, but the accusation against Liera's family had been unexpected.

And yet almost every elf in the harbor reacted to the insult as though Miyela had physically assaulted Liera.

"Who is Kaelo?" she asked tentatively.

A shadow passed behind Firas's eyes. His finger dropped from her chin and he looked down.

"Firas?"

He spoke in a soft voice. "You have not heard of him?"

"No." Anxiety was building in Renyra's belly now. Was her ignorance a result of her age? Why did a name that seemed to dampen the spirit of every elf in Daro mean nothing to her?

Firas's brow furrowed. He glanced around at the few elves hurrying through the Court.

"Come on," he said. "Let's go somewhere else."

He led her to the Tower of Stars and ascended the stairs to the viaduct. Renyra's heart fluttered pleasantly as she stepped onto the tall bridge. Heights had always exhilarated her. Firas walked to the railing, and she followed him. He looked out over the bay, hair lifting gently in the breeze.

"Kaelo was Liera's son," he said. "Her only son as far as I am aware. I never knew him. It all happened in Tura, and I was young at the time, living in Morcanan, but the story spread to all the Great Cities." He paused, choosing his next words. "Kaelo was apparently a great metalworker, one of the best Tura has ever seen. The rest of his story I only know from rumor. He was wed, but another elf loved his wife." Firas sighed. "I know little of what truly happened, I do not think anyone does, but one day the three of them disappeared. When someone finally went to look for them, Kaelo was found standing on the sea cliffs outside Tura, his wife's body lying on the rocks below, and the elf who loved her lying at his feet with a hunting knife through his heart."

Renyra gasped. It was so appalling she could hardly fathom it. If Firas had been a child, this must have happened long before the Great War, so weapons would not even have existed among the elves except those used in hunting. There was no need for weapons.

"He killed them both? Because they loved each other?"

"As I said, I don't know. Kaelo would not speak a word afterward. He neither admitted to nor denied the crime, but given the circumstances, the evidence was overwhelming. Liera had no choice but to banish him."

"She banished her own son?" Renyra felt sick. No wonder Liera had blanched at Miyela's accusations.

No wonder she hardly smiles.

"She was the Lady of Tura then, as she is now. Son or not, Kaelo had committed a crime worse than anything witnessed in elven history, and it was her duty to carry out justice for her people. She disowned him and banished him from the Turi lands, telling the leaders of the other Kindoms what he had done. He was excluded from society after that, and was hardly seen for nearly a hundred years."

"A hundred years? What happened then?" Renyra was fascinated by the story despite her horror.

"After the elves began to make vierstone earrings, he returned to the gates of Tura demanding one for himself. Liera refused him, and he was forced back into exile." Firas shuddered. "A life of banishment without vierstone is a fate worse than death if you ask me."

Renyra went pale. "What you said about the rural elves ..."

Firas nodded, eyes full of sorrow. "Perhaps he found a hidden life near enough to a Great City to prevent it. Or maybe he wandered the wilds, devoid of feeling and connection. He may be dead for all I know

—killed in the chaos of the war, or lost the will to live. He has not been seen since."

"That's awful." Renyra hugged herself and looked toward the green cliffs. The vierstone shone in the sun, damp from ocean spray. She squinted. The cliff face arched in a half circle around the bay, and in the center of the arch of green was a dark stain.

A trickle of fear Renyra could not explain ran down her spine.

"What is that?" She pointed to the black mark.

Firas followed her finger and shaded his eyes. He frowned.

"I have no idea."

The luster of the green stone faded to matte where it darkened, and the center was black enough to make Renyra wonder if it was a fissure in the cliff itself.

"It looks ... dead." She expected Firas to berate her for her typical morbidity, but instead he nodded, looking worried.

"Do you think anyone knows?"she said. Surely news would have spread if anyone had discovered a threat to Daro's vierstone supply. She imagined many of the visiting elves had viewed the quarry upon their arrival, but if whatever had caused this was more recent, there was no reason anyone would have seen it before now.

"I doubt it," said Firas. "But they should."

They had to go to Dulon's personal rooms to find him. Renyra hadn't seen the Lord of Daro at all since the Council left and wondered if he had been shut up in his rooms all this time. His wife answered the door and went to fetch him. It was several minutes before Dulon came to meet them.

"Renyra! Firas!" he exclaimed with a ghost of his usual smile. Two buttons of his doublet were undone. Renyra wondered if he had been dressed when they called. "What can I do for you?"

"Something is wrong in the vierstone quarry," said Renyra. "We want to look at it more closely and thought you should see it."

The half-hearted smile remained on Dulon's face, but worry flickered in his eyes. "Of course! Let me get my keys."

They walked quickly through the Courts, Renyra almost jogging to keep up. As they entered the Tower of Stars, Dulon pulled out his key and opened the door leading to Quarry Bay.

The hair on Renyra's arms stood on end as they reached the bottom of the stairs. She had never been in the quarry and was beginning to get a better understanding of Firas's description of vierstone—of how it *felt*. She held onto Firas's sleeve as they traversed the narrow path around the cliff face.

Dulon stopped dead.

Firas almost ran into him and reached out to steady himself on the vierstone wall before inhaling sharply and snatching his hand away. Touching a large reservoir of vierstone would not hurt an elf, but the experience was unnerving and intense.

A string of curses issued from Dulon. Renyra followed his gaze and gasped. The wound was worse up close. A deep crack ran the height of the cliff face, and the vierstone extending to either side was a dull black. The black abruptly changed to green again in a jagged line, but the total affected area was wider than Renyra was tall.

Dulon reached out a hand, fingers stretching toward the cliff, but hesitated before touching it.

"Be careful," Firas said.

Dulon took a breath and let the tips of his fingers touch the black stone. He stiffened.

Renyra's heart jumped as an expression she had never seen on Dulon's face appeared—fear.

"What is it?" she asked.

Dulon let his hand fall to his side and shook his head, looking sick. He backed away from the wall and motioned her and Firas forward. Renyra stepped toward the crack, swallowed, and lay the palm of her hand against the stone.

Nothing.

Just weeks ago, Renyra had wondered at Firas's enigmatic description of vierstone's energy, but now she understood. Though she could not explain what she normally felt when she touched the stone, she knew there was *something* there, something almost alive. The blackened stone before her was still and cold. Lifeless.

Her eyes followed the crack. It was jagged like a fault line. Had an earthquake done this? But vierstone didn't break. Except it had. The Builders of Daro had melted vierstone into the city's foundations, yet the streets and buildings were breaking as easily as those in a human city might. But this was different. This was vierstone in its purest form, and it hadn't just broken, it had *died*. This was no natural geological process.

Whatever was causing all of this was a force with a will, one that could target individual elves, strike at will, and destroy a substance as old and vital as life itself.

Renyra made the sign of the star and stepped back from the wall. She looked at Dulon, the leader of her city, the engineer, the voice of hope and humor. His posture was slack. He stared into the depths of the fissure as though he could see his death at its heart.

A spark of fire ignited in Renyra's chest.

I will find the cause of this. Riu help me, I will stop the destruction of this city.

18

INTO THE VOID

Dulon stared into the black void. The rush of adrenaline and fear that had coursed through his body upon first touching the lifeless vierstone had faded into numbness. He had no feasible explanation for this. He had no solution.

But they will expect a solution. They all will. This will be your fault, and it will be on your head if it's not fixed.

Even this thought did not elicit any feeling in him.

"Dulon."

He heard the name, but it sounded far away.

"Dulon."

A hand touched his shoulder, and he started, coming back to himself with a jolt. Firas was watching him, his big eyes positively shimmering with worry, concern, sympathy. No. That was from the contact with his hand, from the proximity of vierstone. Dulon stepped back so Firas's hand fell away.

"Tell no one about this," Dulon said. His heart was racing. The rest of Daro couldn't find out. Not now. Word would spread to Faeran, and Daro would fall even further into infamy.

"What?" said Renyra.

"There is no need to cause panic."

"But ..." Renyra stammered, "but we can't just ignore this! Look ..."

Dulon interrupted her. "What, then, would you propose we do?"

Renyra opened her mouth, then closed it in frustration. "I don't know. But we can't keep this a secret."

Dulon chewed the inside of his mouth. He wanted to shout, to shake his fists at Riu.

What more could possibly happen? Our supply of vierstone threatened on the eve of war?

Then the thought struck him like a jolt of electricity: the war. A war that promised a new supply of vierstone, far from Daro, vierstone that so many elves had argued was naught but a source of greed, unneeded ... until now.

"You're right," Dulon said suddenly.

Renyra furrowed her forehead, taken aback by the change.

"We should not keep it a secret," Dulon continued, "but nor should we raise an alarm. We will consult the stone workers of the city, keep a close watch on the quarry, and tell the truth to anyone who asks." He would not broadcast the news, but he had no doubt it would spread through the city like wildfire. Dulon had always seen the wisdom of a backup supply of vierstone, but now the rest of the city would, too.

He took a deep breath and flashed a grin. "Thank you for showing me. Rest assured I will take this seriously and do all I can to protect the quarry. Now, I must return to the Domes." He slapped a hand on Firas's shoulder as he walked past. "Perhaps our heads will be a bit clearer and the worry less troublesome in lighter air."

Firas did his best to look reassured, though it was not particularly convincing. As Dulon made to follow him, he turned back to look at the black stain. Anxiety quelled his hope. This may be the answer to one of his problems, but how many more might it cause? He had never seen or heard of vierstone turning black and had certainly never felt a stone so ... dead. What did it mean? What could possibly cause so much destruction?

Dulon returned to the Domes, but had no intention of working. After the weeks of planning and paperwork during the Council, there was little he could do until Gellion returned. Trade agreements were set, and besides minor structural damage caused by the earthquakes, the city was in excellent repair. The elves of Daro were more than competent at running the ongoing tasks that kept the city functioning on a daily basis.

During the last months of preparation, Dulon had expected to take a well deserved reprieve following the Kindom Council. Visions of lying in bed with Maranyl until lunchtime, wandering the sunny cliffs outside the city, and making a serious dent in the city's supply of wine were only a few choice features of his envisioned vacation. Well, he could still achieve some aspects of his vision.

Dulon sat down by the window with his second glass of wine. The first had somehow disappeared during his walk from the kitchen to his chair. Maranyl was away. Had she said she had plans for the evening? He couldn't remember. A pleasant haze hung in his head, a veil over the events of the last week that made them easier to look upon without cringing. He took another gulp from his glass.

Evening light gave the room a golden tint. Dust motes hung in stripes where the sun's rays filtered through the window. Dulon let out a puff of breath and watched the motes scatter like startled birds.

Just like everyone in my life.

He took sadistic pleasure in the thought.

He had chosen not to think about last week's unfortunate parting. Each time his mind cautiously reached toward the memory, he withdrew as though scalded. He told himself it didn't matter. No elf apart from those already on the ship had followed Miyela's call to leave. No one had said anything since.

That's because they're whispering when your back is turned. Bowing their heads when you pass by.

His people didn't think him a competent leader.

The Morcani were prone to disapprove of him. Even in Morcanan, Dulon had always rebelled against the strict ways of his kin. Miyela had been chief of his naysayers each time he proposed an outlandish idea that did not conform to the perfect order of her world. So he had built his own. Yet the Council Members had made their opinion of him and his city more than clear over the month, and their thoughts had spread like poison through all of Daro, until his own people, the elves of Daro who had elected him with confidence all these years, doubted his aptitude to lead.

But were they wrong? Ambition and luck had landed Dulon in Daro when the site was founded, and his charisma had secured his position. Was there anything to back up his clever words and smiles? Had he fooled even himself into thinking he had adequate skill and wisdom to run a city?

From his pocket he withdrew a small string of beads: seven iron spheres, ending in a three-pointed star. He ran his fingers over their surface, the patterns etched into the metal rubbed smooth by centuries of use. He had not abandoned all of his Morcani roots. The familiar prayers came to his mind as he touched the beads, offering a small comfort, but his chest still burned and fluttered; his muscles tensed. He took a deep breath to dispel some of the tension and poured more wine.

What could he do? Gellion was in Tradira finalizing the alliance. There was no turning back from the path he had chosen.

Nor should we turn back.

He was losing control of this city in more ways than politics. How could he possibly stop the city from crumbling to pieces, the vierstone from dying? What if Daro became uninhabitable? The elves could use a new reservoir of vierstone to rebuild elsewhere, or to repair Daro if the earthquakes stopped. But first he had to prepare an army for battle, and the elves had not had an army for three hundred years. The elves born after the war had never even seen battle. He was suddenly grateful beyond measure for the success of the A'vaeri tournament. At least he had confidence the elves knew how to fight. Still, the logistics were overwhelming. They would need weapons, whether crafted new or brought from Faeran. But Dulon knew what the elves really needed was motivation. He had to inspire them to go to battle and convince them that their cause was just—or at least worth the sacrifice. How could he serve as a pillar of hope to his people if they thought him weak and self-serving?

Pain prickled behind Dulon's eyes, and he shook his head, biting his lip hard enough to draw blood in his anger at this further show of weakness. He washed away the metallic taste with more wine.

The next thing Dulon remembered was his head swinging from side to side. He squeezed his eyes and groaned, trying to still the movement, but it only became more persistent. He wrenched his eyes open and attempted to lift his head. Why was it so heavy? The swinging motion stopped, and he realized something had been shaking him. His vision focused to reveal Maranyl's face bent over him, eyes burning with such intensity that he felt he should have cowered, but instead he lifted an eyebrow and smiled.

Maranyl did not seem to like this. She shoved him backward so he was sitting upright in his chair. The world pitched wildly around him, and Dulon put his hands over his face to try and stop the spinning.

"What are you doing?" The words were clipped.

"Drinking wine," Dulon mumbled through his hands.

"I see that." There was a loud thump, and Dulon heard an empty bottle rolling across the floor. He moved his hands down his face and looked at his wife. She was glaring at him with her hands on her hips. He lowered his eyes.

"The first time I came home to this I let it go, but it's been a week. I love you, but you are acting pathetic."

Dulon flinched at the words and tried to dissolve into the back of the chair. With a fresh wave of vertigo, he almost felt as if he did.

"No!" Maranyl shouted. Dulon sucked in a breath as Maranyl lifted him none too gently by the armpits and pinned his shoulders to the chair back. She leaned forward so her eyes were level with his. "I said you were acting pathetic, not that you are pathetic. Drowning in self-pity, accepting criticism and insults as though you relish the pain, hiding from the city you claim to care more about than anything in this world —this is not you. It never has been, and so help me I will not let it become you. Do you understand me?" She shook his shoulders to force him to raise the eyes he had averted from her rage. "You are one of the most caring men I have ever known. You sustain hope in situations that crush others, and everyone around you has come to depend on that."

"Not anymore."

"I said stop it!" For a moment Dulon thought she would slap him, but instead she took a calming breath and continued. "What Miyela did was underhanded and wrong, but you always knew there would be elves who did not agree with the alliance. There still are in this city. But there are also a lot of elves who support you—or would if you held your head up again and gave them a chance to. You have to take responsibility for what you have chosen. You have nothing to be ashamed of, and if you show that to the rest of Daro, they will follow you."

Maranyl stood back from his chair and walked to the kitchen. "Drink this." She handed him a glass of water. "Go to bed, and wake up tomorrow the Lord of Daro, or someone else will."

She laid a hand on his cheek and gently kissed his forehead before walking into the bedroom and slamming the door.

19

THE DACIAN BALL

The Dacian mansion was no less elaborate at night than it was in the day. The windows glowed, and scores of lanterns lit the pathway to the front doors. Gellion leaned against a statue of an eagle. He wore a formal tunic and a pair of gloves. He had denied all offers of an escort to the ball and walked through the night alone, watching carriages bob through the streets toward the night's festivities like luminescent orbs on a river.

Now he watched the silhouettes of feathers and lace dancing over the heads of women filing up the pathway in front of him. A man brushed past him, his hand on the small of a woman's back. An earthy scent of spice lagged behind him.

Though far from looking forward to the ball, Gellion had decided it would behoove his cause to gain a better idea of the politics he was dealing with before meeting with the king. If Naval insisted on making him wait, Gellion would use the time in a productive manner. How different could a ball be from the feasts of Daro? He would remain subtle, shifting between groups and listening.

Gellion leaned forward as a group of eight climbed out of a carriage and began to weave toward the mansion. He stepped away from the statue as they passed and followed behind. They walked in pairs. All were chatting and laughing; some of the women were fanning them-selves. Gellion shook his head. His tunic and trousers were already growing damp; how could the women stand those layers of skirts?

No one noticed Gellion as his group approached the entrance of the Dacian Mansion, which stood wide open, filaments of music and the smell of roasted meat and bread wafting through the doors. A man stood at the door in the same red uniform as the servant from earlier in the day. He held a sheet of paper and a box wrapped in silk. As each attendee stepped forward to the servant, he looked at the paper, nodded, and held the box forward to accept ... something. Gellion bit his lip. It sounded like coins falling into the box. He had brought some Albaren money from Daro, but only enough for some meals at the market, and that was bundled safely in his pack in his rooms.

The last people in front of Gellion swept inside the mansion.

"Sir?" the servant said in a dispassionate monotone, not looking up from his list.

"Gellion," Gellion said with feigned confidence.

The servant scanned his list. "Your surname?"

Gellion paused. Everyone in Albarad had a surname. He did not want to draw attention.

"That is my surname."

"You are not on the list. Do you have a donation?" He shifted his box.

"I ..." Gellion looked into the mansion, hoping to see Dacian some-where in the crowds. "I did not know one was required."

The servant scowled and looked up at him for the first time. He peered at Gellion's face, and his eyes widened. He took a moment to find his voice again.

"A ... a donation is ... required from every guest." The man took a step back and glanced sideways, as though looking for a route of escape if Gellion became violent. Several guests had walked up behind Gellion and were watching the interaction with tense interest.

Gellion flashed a disarming smile.

"I'm sorry. I spoke with Marchon Dacian just this evening and he invited me. At such short notice, he must have forgotten to add my name. I would be happy to speak with him and sort out the matter."

The servant eyed him warily. "Even with an invitation, a donation is required."

Gellion bowed his head. "Again, I apologize for my ignorance. I am new to Tradira. Marchon Dacian failed to mention the donation. I am sure we can work something out if I could see him."

The servant's eyes darted in either direction. "Marchon Dacian is very busy with the ball. I cannot go and find him. Please step to the side."

Gellion allowed a flash of anger to show in his eyes.

The servant bit his lip and pressed himself into the doorframe. "I could find someone to search for him while you wait," he said quickly.

"Thank you." Gellion smiled again.

The man called over another servant and whispered into his ear, his eyes wandering to Gellion and then snapping back.

Again, Gellion found himself waiting on the competency of a frightened servant. He leaned against the doorframe and watched the guests filing through, smiling and nodding to them. His acknowledgement was met by whispers and giggles from the women, and narrowed eyes from the men. After a while, Gellion grew bored of his game and tried to see what was happening inside. Candlelit tables ringed the outskirts of a hall milling with people. Hoards of red clad servants dispersed through guests and chairs like liquid. Some tables bore cloths and large lanterns, the fanciest of which stood on the landing of the staircase in the center of the room. Several couples were dancing in the cleared space at the bottom of the stairs to a lyrical tune of strings. Gellion could not find the musicians from his restricted view.

"Gellion!"

Gellion looked up, startled to find Dacian standing next to him. The young Marchon clapped him on the shoulder. Gellion covered his surprise with a forced smile and leaned away slightly.

"I am so forgetful! You must forgive me. Please say you forgive me?" He turned to the door servant. "Orien you *must* let this man through. It is entirely my fault. This is Gellion." He gestured in a great sweep of one arm. "An elf come to visit with King Naval on important matters."

Dacian was speaking very loudly and looking at his guests both outside and inside the mansion. He gave Gellion a conspiratorial wink.

"He graciously agreed to attend my ball and requires no donation."

Gellion found himself being pulled into the mansion and looked down to see Dacian's fist around his sleeve. Gellion took a stride forward and shifted his body so that his arm slipped from Dacian's grip. Dacian, entirely unperturbed by Gellion's flat stare, began shouting at him over the din of the party.

"Come in! Mingle, dance! Dinner will be served shortly. You will sit at the highest tables with the most distinguished guests." Dacian's eyes swept the room. "Ah!"

Gellion clenched his teeth as Dacian once again took his arm and set off toward a group of men on the other side of the room.

"Marchon Cavalcont!" Dacian said as they neared the group. A man with iron grey hair slowly turned toward Dacian with a look of annoyance. Upon identifying the source of his interruption, the annoyance turned to disgust.

"Yes?" Cavalcont said.

Dacian pushed Gellion forward. "This is an elven emissary. He is in Tradira as a guest of the king."

Cavalcont shifted his gaze to Gellion. Unlike most of the men in Tradira, he did not have to look up. Gellion met the steely eyes, noting the wrinkles that spread like spiderwebs from their corners. Despite clear signs of age, Cavalcont stood upright and wore sleek garments. He offered a hand to Gellion, who took it with a firm grasp. Gellion gave Cavalcont a pained smile, attempting to convey his knowledge that he was acting as Dacian's trophy, and his lack of enthusiasm at the part. The corners of Cavalcont's mouth drew upward.

"A pleasant surprise," said Cavalcont. "Perhaps this ball will be worth my time after all." He exchanged a look with the men beside him, then spoke to Gellion. "We would be honored to have you at our table." He did not even glance at Dacian.

Even Gellion could sense the insinuation behind Cavalcont's words. The two men were clearly not friends, and Cavalcont was turning Dacian's boasting into an opportunity for himself. Gellion felt like a toy being tugged between two children.

Little as Gellion enjoyed Dacian's company, he had no desire to shame the man, and he turned an inquiring look on him rather than answering Cavalcont's offer directly.

Dacian's dauntless expression had faltered. He opened his mouth, but seemed unable to come up with a response. He was glaring at Cavalcont. Neither man spoke. Gellion watched, curious to see what would happen next.

"A generous offer Marchon," said Dacian. "And one that I am sure Gellion would be happy to accept, but I had intended that he sit at the highest tables tonight." Confidence was beginning to seep into Dacian's bearing again, but Cavalcont's smirk only deepened.

"As it happens Dacian, I passed by your family's cathedral the other day and noticed it could use some ..." Cavalcont paused, twirling his hand in the air and looking upward as though trying to grasp the right word. "Work. I have always been a charitable man and was quite generous with my donation this evening."

Dacian's jaw clenched. His eyes darted to the high tables and back as a flush began to creep up his face. Gellion suspected that to insult a family's cathedral was near blasphemy.

Cavalcont turned back to Gellion. "We were just about to take our seats. Would you join us?"

Gellion did not think Cavalcont's company was any improvement on Dacian's, but once again had no good reason to refuse. If he wanted to learn the political climate of Tradira, what better way than through a man with obvious political knowledge? He followed Cavalcont past the dance floor to the base of the stairs and began to climb, leaving Dacian standing alone among his chattering guests.

They were the first to take their seats, but within minutes, many of the ball attendees seemed to take their cue from Cavalcont and were finding their way to tables. Gellion noticed a fair number of guests remained standing, leaning against walls or continuing to dance.

Probably didn't pay a high enough donation.

A servant poured wine in Gellion's glass and sat a plate of savory pastries in the center of the table. Gellion thanked the man, who jumped and gave him a frightened look before hurrying to the next table.

"Have you been to Tradira before?" Cavalcont sipped his wine, grimaced, and pushed the glass away from him. He watched the people on the floor below.

"Several times."

"Recently?"

"Before you were born."

Still looking over the ball with a bored expression, Cavalcont gave a humorless snort. "It must be interesting, seeing generations of men. I expect each era cycles through the same selection of personalities." His gaze fixed on Dacian, who was moving from table to table, smiling and waving his arms as he spoke. With his outlandish wardrobe, he gave the impression of a flapping bird.

Gellion said nothing, waiting for Cavalcont to continue, but a group of people had begun to file into the remaining seats of their table. Cavalcont clearly knew them all and greeted each by their title. As the last couple ascended the stairs, Gellion did a double take of the woman, who was smiling at him with familiarity. It was not until she sat next to him that he remembered who she was. It was the woman in the black skirts he had seen in the Dom Regirium. Her hair was swept into a nest on top of her head tonight, and she wore a much fancier and much more revealing dress than she had the day before.

Cavalcont introduced Gellion to the table in a tone that suggested he was in the habit of having royal guests of a different race join him for dinner. Gellion was treated to another list of names that mostly bounced off his weary mind. Most of the guests did not seem thrilled with Gellion's presence. They eyed him sideways and shifted in their seats.

When Cavalcont began to introduce the woman beside Gellion, she interrupted him.

"Chiara Arceria," she said with a grin, offering Gellion her hand. From the stiffening of shoulders around the table, Gellion guessed Chiara had made a breach of feminine etiquette, but she kept her hand suspended confidently between them. Gellion took her fingers lightly in his. Cavalcont cleared his throat.

"Gellion is here as an *honored guest* of Marchon Dacian." His voice dripped with sarcasm, but the look he gave Gellion suggested the joke was on Dacian. The rest of the table chuckled, though many still watched Gellion with suspicion.

Gellion had wondered why a man who seemed to loathe Dacian had not only attended his ball, but given a donation substantial enough to seat him in the highest tables. That purpose was becoming clearer by the moment. This may be Dacian's ball, but Cavalcont sat at its head, undermining Dacian among the most prestigious and wealthy guests at the party.

Gellion tried to ignore the flare of heat in his chest. He had barely been in Tradira two days, and he already longed to return home. These were the people he had vowed to help? But then he remembered the children playing in the streets, the women hanging laundry on lines in front of humble houses. The people surrounding him now may represent Albarad, but they were not its core. They weren't the ones being harassed by raids on the borderlands, and they weren't the ones the elves were trying to help.

"I daresay you didn't have much choice coming to this ball did you?" Cavalcont asked Gellion with a cool smile. The rest of the table turned to Gellion, waiting to laugh maliciously at his answer.

"I thought attending a ball would allow me to mingle with the leaders of Tradira and form a better idea of the state of affairs," Gellion said in a measured tone. "I have lost touch with Albaren relations over the years."

"How prudent of you," said Cavalcont. "What states of affairs interest you?"

Gellion took a drink of his wine as he tried to think of the best tactic to lead the conversation toward Diernas.

His hand stopped halfway to the table as the liquid filled his mouth. He thought for a moment he had taken a mouthful of liquor before he realized the burning was from spices, not alcohol. He fought to swallow the wine without coughing, and his eyes watered. To either side of him, Cavalcont looked smug, and Chiara hid a giggle behind her hand.

Gellion looked around for water, but saw none on the table. Still fighting the urge to cough, he took a pastry and chewed as quickly as he could manage while retaining his composure, hoping his face wasn't turning red.

"Like the wine?" Cavalcont asked with a smirk. Gellion noticed the rest of the glasses on the table remained untouched.

He swallowed and took a deep breath as the burn of the spices lessened in his throat. "Do you commonly spice your wine?" His voice was only slightly hoarse.

"For special occasions, yes, but some have a heavier hand than others." Cavalcont rolled his eyes. "I prefer a subtle flavor for my own vintages."

"You make wine?"

"The Cavalconts have been making wine for centuries. Our wine is sold throughout the country and known for its quality."

A wine merchant. A rival of Dacian's business, no doubt.

"Do you sell your wine outside of Albarad?" Gellion asked.

Cavalcont scoffed. "Who would buy it? The Kayda think themselves above our extravagant beverages and the barbarians in Diernas prefer crudely made ales and fermented horse blood for all I know. We have no need to sell beyond our borders. The wealth of generations proves that."

Gellion nodded. "What do you trade with Diernas?"

"Spices and oil," said a man from across the table. His grey hair contrasted with the inky plait of the young woman next to him whom he had introduced as his wife. Gellion guessed she was half her husband's age. He strained to remember their names.

"Their lands are too cold to produce either, and they can't get enough of them," said the man. "Though they have a hard time coming up with enough trade of their own to pay with. Wish they could trade us water."

There was a chuckle of consent around the table, but Cavalcont looked annoyed.

"Marchon Abramo," he nodded to the man who had just spoken, "is a spice trader on the Isle of Sapor and faces many unique challenges." He cocked his head at Gellion. "Do the elves trade with Diernas?"

"No."

"Consider yourselves lucky."

Gellion felt a flutter of excitement in his chest. Might he finally get some answers? Just as he opened his mouth to inquire further, however, Cavalcont cut him off.

"Tell me, on what important matters does King Naval wish to deal with the elves?"

Gellion let out his breath and forced a smile. "Nothing I should discuss openly before meeting with him I'm afraid. But I'm sure he will tell you himself soon."

Cavalcont gave him a penetrating stare, then returned the smile.

"Yes, I'm sure he will."

With that, Cavalcont steered the conversation to other topics. The Marchons discussed their businesses and family drama while their wives sat silently and exchanged looks, often darting glances at Gellion. Chiara kept a steady watch on him throughout the meal. Gellion listened to the conversation, but gleaned no further information. He merely developed an ever decreasing opinion of those in his company.

After a while, the tables below began to thin out again, people dragging partners to the dance floor or joining other groups who hadn't sat at their table. Cavalcont rose and began to circulate from one table to the next, no doubt hoping to discuss the flaws in the dinner. Gellion felt a sudden presence beside him and heard a low voice in his ear.

"He does this every time Marchon Dacian hosts a ball. But Dacian has no choice but to invite him. Cavalcont's the head of one of the oldest Marchon families in Albarad."

Chiara had moved her chair closer to him. Gellion stiffened and glanced around. Her husband had his back to the table and was deep in conversation with two men.

"Why does he hate Marchon Dacian?" Gellion said.

Chiara's eyes shone with gossip. "The Dacians' is an upstart business. They have hardly been making wine long enough to have a vintage over thirty years, yet they obtained lands to produce enough grapes to sell at affordable prices. The Cavalconts have far superior wine of course, but who can compete with cheap wine?"

Gellion nodded. "Is land expensive in Albarad?"

"Oh yes—fertile land, that is. All that's left are dry patches for sheep grazing. As you venture from rivers and mountains, towns and agricultural land become sparse. Once every Marchon family was made by owning productive farmland, but the factories are starting to change that."

Chiara nodded to one of the men her husband was talking to.

"That is Elias Abramo. His family owns land on the Isle of Sapor, which is hotter and drier than any land in Albarad, but there is water *underground*." She raised her eyebrows at this shocking statement. "They use it to water the spice fields. I'd wager he's richer than the Dacians with the spices he sells. But he has his own rivalry." Her grin became wicked.

Gellion cocked an eyebrow. He was shocked by how much the wife of a Marchon knew about the inner workings of Albarad, but remained silent for fear of quenching the flood of information.

"Sergus Saprio manages the Isle of Sapor. His family found it hundreds and hundreds of years ago and has settled there ever since. But the Abramos live in Tradira. They hire servants to manage their spice estates and benefit from the island's wealth almost as much as the Saprios, but without lifting a finger." She rolled her eyes. "Not that most of the Marchon families actually lift a finger on their estates, but since the Saprios do, they turn their noses up at the Abramos."

"It sounds as though rivalries are common among the Marchon families."

"Of course. Wealth will spark rivalries in any circle, but the Marchons have the king's favor to fight over as well." Chiara laughed at Gellion's expression. "Are you surprised that I have thoughts that extend beyond my dress for the night and my husband's routine?"

Gellion shook his head. "Were you from my own people, I would not be surprised at all. At least half the elven leaders are women, and they are more than a match for us."

Chiara's eyes widened. Gellion continued.

"From what I've seen of the Albaren culture, however ..." He trailed off, reluctant to say anything offensive.

Chiara traced the rim of her wine glass with a fingertip.

"The men may hold all leadership in Albarad, but they do not hold all power. Though if you asked any one of them they would never consider otherwise." Her eyes moved to her husband's back. "I am treated as a lap dog, but one never thinks twice about discussing secrets in front of a lap dog do they?"

"I suppose not," Gellion said, though he did not know what sort of animal a 'lap' dog may be.

"What is the relationship between the Marchons and the king?" he asked, trying to sound casual.

Chiara raised her eyebrows. "Interesting question."

Not wanting to sound like a spy, Gellion retreated at once. "I'm sorry ..."

Chiara held up her hand and smiled. "An interesting question, and one you would get a vastly different answer to if you asked any person in this room." She leaned closer. "The Marchons hold a lot of power. The king can, and does, use that power, but would you want this many wealthy and influential people prospering under your rule?"

Gellion gave no answer. Why would a leader not want prosperity under his rule?

"With so many powerful families, disputes are bound to happen, but if you ask me, the king does precious little to *discourage* those disputes."

Gellion knit his brows. Chiara continued.

"If the Marchons are playing their power off *each other*, they're much less likely to test it against the king." She spoke slowly as though explaining to a child. "It's in the king's best interest to *let* that happen."

The fire in Gellion's chest simmered to life again. "You're saying the king encourages discord among his own people?"

"Sometimes scandals blossom out of nowhere." Chiara shrugged, eyeing him. "Scandals that make far too much sense with far too convenient consequences." She gave him a meaningful look. "Take the Camersio's for example—"

"*Ahem.*"

Chiara jumped. She leaned away from Gellion and turned to face her husband, who was glaring at Gellion.

"Marchon Arceria." A charming smile cleared Gellion's face of guilt. "Your wife was telling me about some of the other families in attendance."

The suspicion in Arceria's eyes only deepened. "Was she? Perhaps you should go speak with them yourself?"

Chiara bowed her head away from her husband, but the corners of her mouth twitched as she caught Gellion's eye.

"I would be happy to," Gellion said, rising from his seat. "Lady. Marchon." He bowed to each in turn and walked to the stairs, his mind reeling with the information he had just heard. Before he could descend to the ground floor and make his escape, however, Dacian appeared in front of him.

"Ah! Finally you are free again. Come!"

Once again, Gellion stumbled behind the man, fighting for possession of his own arm. Dacian stopped at the nearest group of people and began to introduce Gellion in a carrying shout. Several men and women nearby turned toward them; a few began to walk over.

Gellion clenched his teeth and fought to keep a neutral expression. This was going to be a long night.

20

OUTSIDE THE WALLS

A new determination possessed Renyra. Upon leaving the quarry, she had gone straight to the Archives, Firas in tow, and scrutinized his notes again and again, sending him to find any other books that could help them. To their preexisting list of books on geography, history, and weather, they added books on vierstone, trying to find some hint of what could cause what they had seen. There was nothing. No mention of lifeless vierstone, no mention of vierstone turning black, no mention of vierstone cracking, breaking, crumbling, or being compromised by any means, physically or otherwise.

"Earthquakes are caused by movement of the earth. They don't occur this often or usually this far from mountains. There is no volcano nearby." Renyra threw her hands in the air and looked at Firas in exasperation. "There is no possible explanation!"

Firas blinked slowly. "No explanation based on past experience."

"That's what I said!"

"No, it is not. Anything you read in these books was once unknown. We discover the reasoning behind things through experience and investigation."

"How can I investigate something I can't touch or see?"

"Study what you can touch and see." Firas shrugged. "Make observations. Make notes. Think."

Renyra did. She thought back to the cracks she had observed in the streets, to the vierstone quarry, to the dizzying split of reality, to Gellion.

"Paper." Renyra grabbed for a pen as Firas slid a sheet of paper in front of her. She wrote down every observation she had of the earthquakes. Together with Firas, she compiled a list of the approximate dates of each reported quake and the locations of any observed damage to the city.

There had been at least six earthquakes over the last month. Reported damages were scattered widely over the city, no instance close to another. This was strange. Wouldn't damage be concentrated in areas of weakness? Why would cracks in the ground or buildings never appear in the same area twice?

Every earthquake was accompanied by what she referred to as a 'disturbance,' yet neither this nor the shaking seemed to affect all areas of the city equally. Renyra had not even noticed the earthquake that had injured Gellion, yet other elves she knew in that part of the city reported strong effects. How could an earthquake be so centralized? Was every epicenter within the city? It didn't make sense. She thought of her hunting trip weeks before. She had seen no evidence of damage.

"I want to leave Daro."

Firas raised his eyebrows. "What?"

"I want to know if the earthquakes have affected any area outside the city."

"How would you do that?"

"I can look for rockslides, fallen trees." Renyra shook her head. "But to really find out I need to go to the nearest town."

Firas stared at her. "A human town?"

"Don't look at me like that. All I would need to do is ask one villager if they have experienced the ground shaking."

"Yes," said Firas slowly. "But you do not speak Albaren. And the human villagers are far more suspicious of elves than those in Tradira. You can't know how they will react to you."

"I only need to learn a few words of Albaren! I can ask Dulon. Write down the phrases I need to know. I'll be subtle."

Firas chewed his lip and nodded. "I suppose."

"We need answers. To get answers, we need more information, and there's only so much we can find looking at the fading evidence in Daro."

"Alright," Firas conceded, though he didn't look happy about it. "But I want to come with you."

"No. Two of us will be more intimidating to the villagers."

"I can wait outside the town."

"It will be faster if I go alone. I can ride. On horseback it will only take a couple of days."

Firas sighed in frustration. He had always been much more comfortable on a ship than on a horse.

"Fine," he said. "But be careful."

"I always am." Renyra batted her eyes at him with the most innocent face she could muster.

The next morning dragged on as Renyra waited for a suitable hour to go looking for Dulon. She knew what she was going to say and was not going to take no for an answer, though she did wonder how Dulon would react to her proposal. He hadn't been himself for weeks, and his behavior in the quarry troubled her deeply. It was almost as if he no longer cared about what was happening to his city, like his mind was always somewhere else.

That was why she had to do this. Dulon may be content to sit back and watch his city break while his people went to battle, but Renyra was not. Someone had to find out what was happening.

She waited until late morning to track down Dulon. The Domes of Rhelyon were quiet. The soft leather of Renyra's shoes whispered on the marble floors, but even that sound echoed eerily off the walls. Her eyes scanned every hall she passed, but Dulon was nowhere to be found. Reluctantly, she went to his rooms.

Renyra knocked on the door.

No answer.

She knocked louder, flinching at the echoes. The door didn't budge. No sounds emitted from behind it.

Was he asleep? Given his appearance yesterday, Renyra wouldn't be surprised if he was, despite the late hour of the morning. She sighed, thinking what to do next. She could keep searching the building, asking anyone she encountered if they had seen Dulon today. She could try to find Maranyl. Neither option gave her much hope of finding Dulon, but Renyra could think of nothing better to do.

She managed to find a few elves wandering the Domes, but no one had seen the Lord of Daro all morning. A search of the Courts and Dining Hall yielded no better results. Renyra ground her teeth in frustration. She wished she could just leave the city on her own. She didn't need Dulon's permission, but how would she ask any Albaren villagers about the earthquakes if she didn't speak their language? Other elves in Daro spoke some Albaren, but she didn't much want to go around asking for their help. Somehow it seemed best to keep her plan quiet. No. Renyra would walk through every public building and wander the city the whole day if she had to.

Fortunately it did not take the whole day. Gliding down the Rale path on Master's Street, Renyra caught sight of a fair head disappearing around a corner ahead of her. She leapt off her board and jogged to catch up, rounding the corner. It was Dulon, sure enough. His long strides had carried him halfway down the next road. Renyra called for him to stop.

Dulon turned, eyebrows raised. Renyra stopped in front of him and drew back in surprise when she looked at his face. Dulon's hair was immaculately combed and reflected the morning sunlight as though emitting light itself. His eyes were clear, and focused on her, amusement dancing in their depths with a familiarity that brought warmth to Renyra's chest.

"Why the hurry?" he asked.

Renyra, still taken aback by his appearance, didn't answer at once, and a flash of concern replaced the amusement in Dulon's eyes.

"Is anything wrong? Have you seen something?"

"Oh, no," Renyra said, regaining her composure. "Nothing like that. I just need to speak with you."

"I've just had a long meeting with some Builders and was on my way to the docks. Walk with me."

Renyra fell into stride with him. He slowed his pace to match hers.

"What can I do for you?" Dulon asked. His eyes scanned the streets and buildings around them as they walked.

Renyra hesitated. The request she had rehearsed was for a sulky and distant Dulon. In all honesty she had been looking forward to yelling at him, trying to break through the dark clouds that had descended on him and force him to see the gravity of their situation and the inadequacy of his reaction. Renyra's cheeks warmed with shame. She had intended to use his guilt to gain his help and his blessing for her journey.

But the Dulon walking next to her appeared to be the Dulon she knew and respected. What had happened in the last day? Perhaps yesterday had just been a bad day for him, and she had imagined the changes before, invented reasons for his supposed disappearance over the last week.

"We need to learn more about these earthquakes," she said, watching Dulon's face out of the corner of her eye to gauge any change in his demeanor. She detected none.

"I agree," he said easily, his eyes pausing on her before continuing their scan of the surroundings.

Renyra took a breath. "I want to travel to the nearest Albaren town and ask the villagers if they have experienced the same earthquakes we have."

Dulon's pace slowed to a stop, his brow creased in thought. "Why?"

"I think the earthquakes might only be happening in Daro. Even within the city, the intensity of their effects vary. If we could establish the range of the earthquakes, it would lead us closer to discovering their cause."

"Only happening in Daro?" Dulon's eyes narrowed, and he looked to the horizon. A warm breeze blew from the direction of the sea, playing with the strands of his hair. "Interesting."

Renyra shifted her feet. When Dulon said no more, she continued. "I would need to learn a few phrases of Albaren."

Dulon blinked, drawn from his thoughts, then began to nod.

"Yes. Yes, good." Suddenly his head whipped back to face her. "You should go. I can write the words you will need and teach you to pronounce them. The nearest Albaren town is called Lacrim. It is just on the other side of the Icemelt River. Two days' ride from here, maybe three. I can't imagine the earthquakes are only happening within the city, but if they are, we need to know. Come to my rooms tonight and I will get you what you need."

"Right." Renyra was surprised by his fervor, but was in no position to question it.

"I will see you then." He gave her a smile and tossed the hair from his eyes before setting off down the road again, feet clicking on the stones with purpose.

Dulon was as good as his word. He was waiting for Renyra when she came to his rooms that night and already had a list of words and phrases written in neat script on a piece of paper. He taught her the correct pronunciation, making notes by the words she had trouble with.

"Lacrim is a small village," Dulon explained as he traced a path for her on a map. "Even I have had almost no contact with the countryside of Albarad. You will need to be careful. Make yourself as normal to them as possible. I would suggest approaching a woman, or at least a man accompanied by a woman if you can't find one alone. Wear a Turi dress."

Renyra was bewildered by Dulon's suggestions, but after an explanation of the Albaren society that made her cheeks burn, she agreed to go along with them for the sake of accomplishing her goal.

That night she packed her bag, carefully folding a modest dress in the bottom and tucking her map and list of phrases into a back pocket. She would collect some food from the storehouses in the morning, but was confident in her ability to find wild plants and hunt if necessary. She would bring a javelin for the ride and hide a hunting knife in her boot when she approached the village. Firas had insisted on this, and Renyra agreed to it to set his mind at ease.

Renyra went to bed early, but lay awake until late in the night, picturing her route, practicing her Albaren, and trying to imagine what a village of humans would be like.

She felt a pang of guilt as Firas moved in the bed next to her. He, too, lay awake, but likely filled with thoughts very different from her own. She turned to face his back and laced her arm under his elbow. He pressed her hand to his chest and leaned into her. She kissed the smooth skin between his shoulder blades and sighed. Her ear warmed around her vierstone earring, and she felt the worry radiating off of Firas. She could almost feel it flowing into her and wished that she could take it from him as easily. Instead, she moved closer to him and tried to fall asleep.

The next morning passed with little fuss. Before the sun had fully risen, Renyra was almost ready to leave. Humid puffs of Nightjar's breath tickled her neck as she strapped her bag to the saddle.

"Wondering what I'm doing?" Renyra laughed, giving the horse's head a playful shove. Firas stood next to her, eyeing the animal with suspicion.

"All done!" Renyra patted Nightjar's rump, causing him to nicker and swish his tail. Firas took a step back. "Oh come on, there's nothing to be nervous about," Renyra teased. "He's a good horse. Aren't you?"

Nightjar continued to stare straight ahead with no visible change in expression.

"Just be careful," Firas sighed.

"So you've already advised. And so I will." Renyra stood on the tips of her toes, using Firas's shoulders for support, and kissed him on the mouth. He smiled, some of the anxiety melting from his face.

Renyra swung into the saddle, blew Firas a last kiss, and rode out the gaping gates of Daro.

The day was fine, and Nightjar was eager to stretch his legs. Renyra let him run for a short stretch, then pulled him to an easy lope. The motion was familiar to Renyra, and her body moved with the horse of its own accord, freeing her mind to focus on her surroundings. She couldn't let her enjoyment distract from her purpose.

There was only one main road connecting Daro to the rest of the continent, and it ran southwest down the coastline to Tradira. The road crossed the Icemelt over an arching bridge. Further down the river, where the water cascaded off the cliffs into the sea, a massive series of columns rose from the water, arcing like a huge bridge, and connected to a domed building of stone—the hydroelectric plant. Individual homes in the city used solar power to some extent, but the river supplied Daro with most of its power.

Just before the bridge, Renyra turned away from the road and set off southeast along the shores of the Icemelt. The banks of the river were sandy, and the water was grey-green. Further southeast, Dulon had said the waters spread and shallowed, giving way to fords that Renyra could easily cross on horseback. In the meantime, she planned to follow the river on the northern side, keeping an eye out for anything out of the ordinary.

By late afternoon, the sun was hot overhead. Renyra rubbed grit from her eyes and scanned the unbroken landscape with decreasing interest. The hills rolled before her unmarred. Saltbushes, sage, and heather grew in a patchwork over dry grass and rock outcrops. Blooming shrubs and orange sandstone provided splashes of color, and the Icemelt wove into the distance, an emerald brushstroke across the land. It was beautiful. The air hung heavy with the smell of herbs and soil, slightly metallic from the water and rocks.

Yet none of it helped Renyra. Just like her last hunting trip, she saw nothing unusual, no signs whatsoever of physical disturbance in the countryside. The further she rode from Daro, the more unlikely it seemed that she was missing something. There was nothing to see.

When the light grew dim, Renyra slid off of Nightjar, her legs unsteady after the day's ride. The horse snorted and pawed the ground, and Renyra unbuckled the saddle and lifted it from the animal's sweat-soaked back. He bobbed his head and trotted to the riverbank, sinking his nose into the water. Renyra followed his lead and dipped her canteen in next to him. Despite the heat of the day, the river ran cold, fed by the snowcapped Falspire Mountains to the east. Renyra could see the shadow of the mountains on the horizon. The elves knew little of the Falspires and had never ventured beneath their peaks. They had no reason to. Humans surely lived there, but they had never approached Daro, and the elves were perfectly content to leave them alone in turn.

Renyra cocked her head at the jagged purple line of peaks, growing difficult to distinguish in the darkening east. Did the people in the mountains experience earthquakes? Would they have an explanation for what was happening? There was so much the elves didn't know about this land. They only inhabited the smallest tip of Tala and dealt with only one group of humans. She wondered how far the scrublands stretched to the south, how far the mountain range ran before hitting another coast, if there even was another coast. The world before her suddenly seemed impossibly vast. Faeran was large, but the elves knew the land. They were a part of it. Here they were strangers.

The last wisps of color leached from the sky, stars emerging in their absence. Renyra spread her cloak on the ground like a fan and lay down in the center of it, taking comfort in the familiarity of the stars as she drifted to sleep.

The next day, clouds overtook the sky, throwing rain down in brief fits before blowing on their way. Renyra pulled the hood of her cloak up and rode on. She kept her eyes on the landscape, but had given up hope of finding any signs of earthquakes, especially with the rain. The day passed in swaying monotony atop Nightjar.

By late afternoon, the river was noticeably more shallow, and just before nightfall, Renyra led Nightjar across it, the water rising no higher than his knees. Lacrim would not be far now.

A ball of nervous excitement began to burn in Renyra's chest. She longed to ride through the night, to glimpse the glowing lights of the village before she went to sleep, but the ground was slick, and the night starless. She would have to wait until daylight.

At high noon on Renyra's third day of riding, the silhouettes of roofs appeared on the horizon. All weariness evaporated, Renyra hurried her horse forward, giving the town a wide arc until she found a cluster of gnarled trees that could shelter her well enough to pull on her dress. It had been difficult to find a dress 'normal' enough by Albaren standards to suit her purpose. She ran a scrutinizing eye down her front. The fabric was supple, but the cut was simple, and with the sashes and adornments removed, she could pass as an Albaren noblewoman at least, if not a country maid. She stuffed her riding clothes back into her bag and turned to Nightjar, who was eyeing her with an unreadable expression.

Renyra moved to mount him, then froze, looking down the long skirt. Cursing her own stupidity, she tied Nightjar to one of the trees and hid her pack, slipping the paper of Albaren words up her sleeve just in case her memory fled at an inopportune moment. She would have to walk the rest of the way.

Oh well, I suppose I will be more unassuming without a horse.

If things did take a turn for the worse, she had no doubt she could outrun any human in the village, so long as they didn't pursue her on horseback.

The ground was dry despite yesterday's rain, and Renyra lifted the hem of her dress as she walked to keep the worst of the dust off. As she neared the village, she was struck by how small it was. She counted hardly more than a dozen buildings, roofs shingled with reddish clay, and a central building of wood with a spire reaching to the sky. All were encircled by a wall. The Icemelt ran against the north side of the village and to the south, cropland stretched into the distance.

Smoke floated on the breeze above the houses, and two sharp barks of a dog rang through the air. Renyra tensed. There were wolves in Faeran, but the elves did not domesticate predators. Why should they? Horses, goats, sheep, and fowl served well enough as livestock for travel, food, and clothing. The elves needed no help hunting, and the thought of keeping an animal that served no purpose was absurd. Why waste resources on a potentially dangerous predator just so it could follow you around? Renyra said a silent prayer and hoped the creatures would stay well away.

The wall around the village was an obstacle Renyra had not foreseen. It was at least twice as tall as she was, but she easily found footholes in the stacked stones, though her dress made the climb unnecessarily difficult. With a leap, she landed on light feet inside the village, her skirt billowing around her.

The first thing she noticed was the smell. She wrinkled her nose at the stink of unwashed animals, feces, and urine. The tang of stagnant water drew her eyes to an algae-covered pond near the edge of the wall. Up close, the houses were water stained and had tiles missing from the roofs. Renyra stood still, listening and watching. She saw no one. Was the town deserted? But no, there was smoke, and the animals. Were the humans all in their shabby homes?

Renyra jumped violently as a cacophony of bells rang through the air. She shrank against the side of a house and looked toward the large building in the center of the village that she now noticed had bells suspended in the hollowed base of its spire. They were all swinging. The doors of the building opened, and what Renyra guessed were the inhabitants of the whole village filed out. Approaching a group of people this large would be a dangerous risk. She would have to wait until they dispersed. Most of the villagers began walking toward the open gate of the wall.

They must be returning to the fields. But why were they all in that building?

To Renyra's relief, some of the women and children began to walk the opposite direction, presumably back to their houses. She followed them, ready to break her cover the moment she caught a woman walking off on her own, but the women moved in a pack, each peeling off from the group to enter her home. Renyra's heart sank as the last two women disappeared behind a shabby wooden door. Should she approach one of the houses? Knock on the door?

Renyra was debating which method of approach would be less frightening to a human woman, when the sound of a voice behind her, or rather, below her, caused her to spin around.

It was a child. Renyra stiffened, wide-eyed and frozen to the spot like a mouse under a hawk's gaze. Never in her life had she seen a child. Never had she seen any person smaller than herself. She guessed it was a male child, though his black hair hung in thin tangles to his chin. He wore dusty pants and a ripped shirt. His dark eyes were round and curious.

"*Quina?*" the child repeated.

Panic clouded Renyra's mind, and she tried to remember something to say, anything to say.

"Hello," she said hesitantly in Albaren.

The boy held up a wooden dagger, but with the flat of the blade facing her. There was pride in his eyes. Renyra smiled and nodded.

"Yes," she said awkwardly. "I am from the coast west of Lacrim."

The boy stared at her, lowering his toy. Could he be a reliable source? If she could manage to ask him about the earthquakes, maybe she wouldn't need to approach one of the adults.

"I came to ask a question."

The boy cocked his head, then spouted off a stream of Albaren that Renyra could not hope to follow.

She continued as though he hadn't spoken.

"Have you had earthquakes? The ground shaking?" She motioned shaking ground with her arms.

The boy's mouth opened in shock. "Ground shake?" he said.

"Yes," Renyra said excitedly. "Does the ground shake here?"

His eyes widened and he shook his head.

"The ground here has not shaken?" she asked again, desperate that he understand her.

"No shake," he said uncertainly. He took a step back.

"It's alright," Renyra said, trying to make her expression comforting. Before she could say any more, however, a woman's voice rang behind her.

"Matteo!"

The boy's head snapped toward the house next door, a look of guilt on his face. Renyra turned to see a young woman walking toward them, carrying a basket of clothing. She looked to be no taller than Renyra, and though her skirts were threadbare and dusty, her tan skin was clean and her hair combed. She stopped in her tracks when she saw Renyra, fear and suspicion in her eyes. Renyra smiled at her and stepped away from what she assumed was the woman's son.

"Who are you?" The woman reached her hand out for Matteo, who darted to her side.

"Renyra, from the coast west of Lacrim," Renyra repeated. "I came for help, to ask a question."

The woman looked Renyra up and down. Renyra's heart pounded. Suddenly her dress did not seem as appropriate as it had back in the copse of trees. She had swept her hair over her ears, and Dulon had said the Albaren humans from the spice island had skin almost as dark as hers, but she knew she could never pass as an Albarad native.

The woman did not answer, but nor had she run, shouting for help. That was a good sign.

"We have had earthquakes—ground shaking. Has the ground shaken in Lacrim?" Renyra said in halting Albaren.

A dog barked from the house behind her, and Renyra fought to keep her composure.

The suspicion in the woman's eyes remained, but she said, "No."

And Renyra believed her.

The village was hardly in good repair, but there seemed to be no acute damage, just that of time and neglect. There had been no earthquakes here. There had been no earthquakes in the countryside.

Daro was alone.

21

SPREADING STAINS

Dulon's head spun, though he had not touched alcohol in days. His self-disgust had turned to anger, which he channeled into manic productivity. By the time Gellion returned, Daro would be pristine—every road smooth, every building mended, every statue shining. He had written to Liera this morning asking for a shipment of swords, spears, bows, daggers, and armor.

The elves had never intended to use the armories again, but it would have been a waste to empty them after the Great War. If nothing else, some of the weaponry and armor were works of art, crafted by metalworkers over dark and violent decades in which beauty had to be created, not found.

Daro's population was much smaller than Tura's. If he was lucky, Dulon would not need to waste any resources or time crafting new supplies for the coming battle, and with summer approaching, provisions would be plentiful. All Dulon truly needed to do in preparation for this battle was mobilize the elves—physically and mentally. If he could form a united army, he had little doubt they would hold their own against the humans with their bare hands. If he had learned anything during his time fraternizing with the Albaren, it was that the humans were a fragile race—clumsy and prone to injury and illness. Not to mention age.

The death of Dierna warriors may weigh on his conscience after this battle, but he would not let any of his own people fall.

Despite his newfound determination, however, Dulon's confidence was as precarious as a horse balancing on a barrel. He was careful to present his best face to the public, but it took all of his energy to do so, and the anxieties of his decisions and responsibilities threatened to drag him under every moment. Never before had he noticed uncertainty or suspicion in the looks of Daro's citizens as he passed by. Each glance was a stab in his chest.

There had only been one or two reports of earthquakes in the last ten days, but that hardly guaranteed the threat was at an end. Dulon could continue to repair damages to the city, but what of the vierstone quarry? He had kept himself busy with city logistics and battle preparations for days, but it could not wait any longer. He had to talk to Aryn. It had been Aryn who infused vierstone into Daro's foundations. The Builder knew vierstone as few elves did, and if anyone could shed light on what was happening in the quarry, it was her.

Aryn was in the Builders' quarter of Master's Street. Upon Dulon's arrival, she quickly stepped back from the city plans she had been scrutinizing and stood at attention. Dulon resisted the urge to say, "At ease, soldier," instead flashing her a disarming smile.

"Sorry to interrupt. I hoped to speak with you about something rather important."

"Of course, Lord Dulon."

Dulon sighed and continued. "Could we take a walk?"

For a moment, Aryn's composure faltered at this casual request, but she nodded and silently followed him to the door.

"I want you to see something in the vierstone quarry. Something concerning. I need the opinion of an expert."

Aryn looked down. "I have worked with the stone for centuries my lord, but none can claim to fully understand it."

"So I have heard. Still, you know more than I do."

When they reached the stone path leading to the quarry, Dulon let Aryn walk in front of him. He wanted to see her reaction, to gauge how bad this really was. The hairs of his arms stood on end as they neared the vierstone, and the anxiety and anticipation in his chest magnified. As the full arc of the quarry came into view, Aryn stopped. Her jaw dropped. And so did Dulon's.

The black stain had spread, now blotting out a quarter of the green cliffs.

It has only been three days. How can it have spread so far in three days? Or at all for that matter?

"What is it?" Dulon whispered, not trusting his voice.

Aryn shook her head in disbelief and took tentative steps toward the cliff face. She flattened her palm against the black stone.

"Dear Riu."

"Aryn?" Dulon could not keep the panic from his voice.

"I ... I don't ... what *happened*?"

"An earthquake? It must have been. But it wasn't this bad before. The black has spread." Dulon turned to Aryn in desperation. "Have you ever seen anything like it? Heard of anything like it?"

Aryn just continued to shake her head, mouth open. She ran her hand along the rock, her eyes distant.

"It is not vierstone. Not anymore. But it was ... it is ..."

"What does that mean?" Dulon tried to keep the exasperation out of his voice.

"I told you that none of us really understands vierstone, not the way we understand other elements. But when one works with it enough, they come to understand pieces of it. Vierstone does have a structure, a structure both like and unlike metal, stone, and glass that is unique to vierstone, and this," she indicated the black rock behind her, "does still have that structure, but there is more to vierstone than that. Apart from the atoms there is something *else*. It is something you can sense and feel, but not touch, not *see*. There is a ..." she paused, searching for the right word, "a *charge*, that runs through the stone. Only a skilled stone worker would be able to sense it in your earring," she pointed at the diamond stud in Dulon's ear, "but in a quarry like this, it is so strong you can almost feel it in the air."

Dulon's skin prickled. He did not like talking about this while surrounded by vierstone itself. He felt as though it were listening. Watching. Alive.

"But this does not have that." Aryn continued, turning back to the dead stone. "It is empty." She ran her hand along the cliff. When her hand met green vierstone again, she took a breath and removed her hand. "It returns here."

"What could be causing this? You break and melt vierstone all the time to work with it and this does not happen?"

"No."

A sudden thought came to Dulon that made his blood run cold.

"What if the whole quarry dies? What if this can spread *beyond* the quarry?"

"It couldn't possibly," said Aryn, though worry still clouded her eyes. "This is spreading through continuous rock. I cannot tell you what is causing this, but I can assure you it cannot spread through the air, like a disease." Aryn straightened and faced Dulon. "I will look deeply into this matter and report back as soon as possible. I need a piece of the black vierstone to study."

"Of course."

"I will do all that I can, my lord." Her brow creased in determination. She glared at him as though daring him to doubt her.

"Thank you, Aryn. I'm sure that you will." Dulon smiled at her, but couldn't muster the energy to summon more words of comfort or confidence.

Doing all that we can is all we can do. I hope it is enough.

There was little Dulon could do now but wait. His letter to Liera was on a Tura-bound ship that would not return for a week, Renyra was not due back for several days at least, and he would be no help to Aryn in her search for answers about vierstone.

The sun shone directly overhead, and Dulon's stomach growled. Once outside the viaduct, his feet turned automatically toward home, but he stopped. No. His main job now was to bolster the spirits of his people. He could not do that from the solitude of his rooms. He spun around and set off toward the Dining Hall, but as he reached the doors, he saw a sheen of familiar black hair crossing the Court. His hand paused on the door handle. He really was hungry, but he had been wondering about Kyna for days. Since seeing her on the docks at the ship parting—Dulon's stomach churned at the memory—he had caught no sight of her. Not that this was surprising. Dulon himself had been hiding until a few days ago. With a sigh, he dropped his hand from the promise of food and walked toward her.

"Kyna!" he called.

Kyna stiffened and turned, relaxing when she saw Dulon.

He grinned. "I thought I saw you stay behind."

"You saw right."

Dulon closed the distance between them in a few strides. Kyna held his gaze steadily, a corner of her mouth quirked upward. She really was a striking woman—nose straight, eyes slightly slanted. Her hair was like the pelt of a healthy animal. Dulon thought of the panthers that prowled the forests south of Morcanan and inwardly shuddered.

"Why did you?" he said.

"I stayed where the excitement was." Kyna shrugged. "I thought I would be of more use in Daro helping prepare for battle than lounging idly back in Tura."

Kyna did seem the type to be easily bored, but boredom was no reason to go to battle. Her nonchalance assured Dulon that she had not been born before the last war. That, or she had another reason to stay. Gellion's fiery hair flashed in Dulon's mind.

A reason indeed ...

At Dulon's appraising look, Kyna smirked. "Would you rather I say I remained behind because of my undying loyalty to the cause? My passion for human welfare and the future of vierstone?"

"That, in fact, would be nice to hear. But, I suppose I cannot be choosy among my help." He chuckled.

Kyna's eyes became more serious. "I do want to help, Dulon. Actually, I have been meaning to speak with you ever since the Council left."

"Have you?" Dulon was surprised. Through the weeks of the Council, he had taken Kyna to be more the passive observer.

Kyna lowered her voice. "I saw the way Miyela's talk spread through the city. If you want my opinion, we need to invoke a similar movement, but in favor of the alliance—in favor of you."

Dulon raised his eyebrows, taken aback. Kyna had been friendly toward him, but she owed him no loyalty. Why would she want to help him now?

"I like Daro," said Kyna, as though reading his mind. "It's unique among any cities I've ever seen. I could live in a place like this, but not if it crumbles beneath discord."

"You want to live here?"

"Maybe."

"And you want to help bolster the elves in support of the alliance?"

Kyna shrugged. "The decision is made. To oppose the alliance is to oppose order, to oppose you. Support brings unity. If this battle is to happen whether we will it or no, we may as well unite under the circumstances. The more elves leave the city under your command, the smaller the risk in battle. Besides, I agree that the elves should do all they can to consolidate vierstone in an accessible place. You never know what the future may bring." She spoke matter-of-factly, as though it were all simple—black and white. Just unite the elves. Just go to battle and get the vierstone. She almost made Dulon feel a fool, as though he had been overthinking things all along.

"Okay," said Dulon slowly, "what did you have in mind?"

"I may not be of much use planning alliances or battle tactics," she continued, "but I can talk. I can tell people who they should be following and why."

It was not a bad idea. Dulon needed to make a point of being visible and personally involved in Daro, but it would not hurt to have other sources of encouragement running through the city. He looked at Kyna. The sudden help was unexpected, but not unwelcome. Her expression was earnest, with no trace of a smile now. Dulon could think of worse people to have on his side.

"Alright, let's talk."

A corner of Kyna's mouth rose, and she followed him toward the Domes of Rhelyon.

It was the following evening before Dulon heard back from Aryn. He had passed the time frustrated and impatient, Kyna's underground support system adding to his list of things to wait on. If there was one thing about Dulon's role as Lord of Daro that had always rankled him, it was the delegation of tasks. He was constantly waiting on others to finish assignments before he could move forward with any project.

Kyna's task was simple in design, if not in execution. She would listen and she would talk—report what she heard and encourage support. Having been subject to them himself, Dulon had little doubt in Kyna's persuasive talents, and it would be useful to know the opinions of his opposers, as well as the general climate of the city.

It was not spying—Kyna would report no names or exact words—yet the plan left a residue of guilt in Dulon's mind, even as it brought him relief to know he was proactively easing the discord in Daro. He stoutly assured himself that this was not something Miyela would do. He was merely acting in the best interest of his citizens. He had no plans to act against those who continued to disagree with him.

The door across from Dulon swung forward without a sound, and Aryn walked forward. Anticipation began a slow burn in Dulon's chest. Aryn had approached him earlier that afternoon requesting an audience, and Dulon had suggested a meeting in the Domes after a scandalized refusal from Aryn to meet him in his personal rooms.

"My lord." Aryn inclined her head.

"Please sit." Dulon himself was perched on the end of an armchair, elbows resting on his knees and hands clasped. He watched her expectantly as she sat across from him.

"It is not good news, my lord."

Dulon's heart sank, and he felt a twinge of guilt as he looked more closely at Aryn's face. There were shadows under her eyes. She looked exhausted.

"I told you about the charge—the current—that runs through vierstone. I have been studying and comparing a piece of true vierstone with a piece of this black vierstone since yesterday. Though I can sense the charge in the green vierstone, I cannot see it or determine its source no matter how I try. I do not know what causes it, so I do not know what could have stopped it, but that is what has happened to this." She held up a jagged piece of black rock. "Something has stopped the current. I am sure that is why it turned black—why it died. I have read all that is in the Archives on vierstone, though that is precious little. There would be more literature on the subject in Tura, but I doubt it would help us." She held Dulon's gaze with frightening intensity. "This is something new, and something I cannot explain."

Dulon had been expecting it, but the blow was heavy nonetheless.

"I understand. Thank you for trying."

Dulon's calm acceptance seemed to incense Aryn.

"I have not succeeded yet," she said. "But I am not giving up." There was an almost crazed glint in her eye. "I will stay in the quarry and observe what is happening over time. If there is another earthquake, I will go to the source of any damage immediately. The foundations of this city should not be breaking any more than this vierstone should be black. I will find out why."

Dulon had to admire Aryn for her unflagging devotion to her job, but he couldn't have her spending nights in the quarry. What if there was another earthquake and more of the cliffs broke?

"Thank you, Aryn, but staying in the quarry really isn't—"

There was a light knock on the door. Dulon glanced at Aryn, then said, "Come in."

The door swung open to reveal Kyna. She looked between Dulon and Aryn.

"I'm sorry," she said to Dulon. "I was looking for you, and I heard your voice."

"That's alright," said Dulon. "I—"

"Could we have a word?"

Dulon hesitated, but there was little else to discuss with Aryn. He would speak with her later about her notion to camp in the quarry.

"Of course," Dulon said, looking to Aryn, who stood immediately.

"My lord." She bowed her head and marched out of the room. Kyna's eyes followed her.

"What can I do for you?" Dulon asked cheerfully.

Kyna pulled her gaze back to him. "I have begun to speak with citizens of the city and came to report what I've heard." She paused. She seemed to be debating her next words.

"I'm sorry," she said quickly, "but I couldn't help overhearing your conversation. Has something happened in the quarry?"

There was something behind the stoic curiosity in Kyna's face. Did she know something?

Dulon considered her before answering. "Yes," he said at last. "It has. Have you heard anything about it?" He kept his voice casual.

"I have heard there was a ... break. In the cliff."

So word had already spread to some degree at least. "Any details?"

"No more than that."

Dulon nodded. "Well, where the cliff broke, the vierstone has turned black. And the affected area is spreading."

Kyna's eyebrows rose. Did he sense worry behind those opaque eyes? He could never tell with Kyna.

"Turned black?" Kyna said.

"Turned black. Aryn is an expert with vierstone and says this blackened stone has stopped carrying the," Dulon paused over the description, "the charge that vierstone normally emits."

"How?" Kyna asked.

"I wish I knew. That is what Aryn is helping me discover. In fact, there is something else you can help me with."

***

Walking across the Court of Rhelyon in the fading light of evening, Dulon congratulated himself. Although he was no closer to discovering the source of the blackened vierstone, he had done well setting things in motion these last few days. He felt almost himself again. Aryn would continue to monitor the vierstone, Kyna would help him bolster support from his citizens, and now, with Kyna spreading word of the dying vierstone through the city, perhaps he would both find an elf who could explain the phenomenon and further garnish support for a battle that promised a new source of vierstone as a reward. His situation could be better, yes, but Dulon was handling things well. He thought of Maranyl and smiled, warmth permeating his chest. He would make her proud. He would get through this.

A chorus of shrill cries echoed from the bay. Dulon turned to see a flock of gulls winging frantically toward the heavens.

Probably startled by an eagle.

He watched their progress against the crimson sky, taking a deep breath of briny air. As he let it out, a queer sensation rippled over his skin. He looked around, alarmed, but saw nothing unusual. The feeling grew stronger, spreading up his body like a current. Something was wrong. He turned to go back to the Domes, but no sooner had he taken a step, there was an earsplitting crack like thunder and the ground pitched violently.

He fell hard on his side. Pain flared in his shoulder, and he was momentarily stunned as his head bounced off marble. Sharp cracks of splitting rock rent the air, and Dulon tried to stand, but the ground was still shaking, a deep rumble emitting from its depths like an angry animal. When at last he staggered to his feet, the air suddenly filled with a cloud of white dust, and Dulon coughed and spluttered. He threw his arms over his head and fell back to his knees. Amid the rumble of the earth, he heard a series of deafening snaps and the crunch of stone on stone, followed by splashing. He clapped his hands over his ears. Was the quake bringing waves against the cliffs? The zapping and buzz of released electricity exploded. Dulon huddled close to the ground, gripping the beads in his pocket.

Slowly, the resonant rolls of sound subsided, and the ground stilled. Silence descended.

Dulon dropped his arms and opened his eyes. The dust cloud still surrounded him, but between his knees, he could see the once white marble of the Court. A latticework of black spread through the stone like a spiderweb. Panic coursed through him.

It is the vierstone in the marble.

Dulon remembered the break in the street he had studied weeks before. He had seen the same black tendrils in the stone there, but had thought nothing of it. Whatever was happening in the quarry had begun in the city long before Renyra and Firas showed him the cliffside.

The air began to clear, and Dulon rose on shaking legs, straining his eyes to see through the settling dust. The first thing he saw was the

Domes of Rhelyon. The arching roof had split into three pieces. It had not collapsed, but he would have to evacuate the building immediately.

Then Dulon turned toward the quarry.

He dropped back to his knees.

Where the viaduct had been moments before, a gaping hole now extended into the Court, like a giant had taken a bite out of the cliffside. It was not waves he had heard, but a piece of his city falling into the sea. Dulon made the sign of the star.

The string lights in the Court had all gone out, and the Domes of Rhelyon stood still and dark. Flashes of light still emitted from broken power lines where they had fallen into the bay.

All he wanted was to sit here on the powdered stone until someone came for him, but that was not an option. He stood, brushed the debris from his shoulders, shook the dust from his hair, and ran to the Domes. He had to get everyone out.

22

THE ALLIANCE

A pair of liquid brown eyes stared at Gellion with adoration. He tried to ignore the gaze, letting his own eyes wander across the rows of retail shops across the street. Finely cut clothing, brass lamps, woven rugs, typewriters, religious relics, furniture—one could buy anything in the Central District of Tradira.

Even small animals.

A high-pitched whine emitted from the creature at his feet, and Gellion slowly dropped his eyes again. The thing was the size of his head, with airy wisps of liver and white hair floating around it like a cloud. It cocked its head and let its tongue loll out of its tiny mouth. Gellion shifted in his chair, moving his drink further from the edge of the table. The animal's owner must be having their lunch inside, leaving the dog to pester whomever happened to be nearest.

Just as Gellion resolved to abandon his drink and leave, the thing came at him. Gellion let out a surprised shout as the ball of fluff landed in his lap, wriggling like a worm. He brought a hand down to shield himself, but the creature began frantically licking it, and Gellion snatched his hand away, grimacing. He was absolutely sick of Albarad and all of its absurd culture. Even the utensil he had been using to eat his lunch was strange. Within the structure of the silvery metal, he had sensed an unknown element interlaced through the iron, an element that came from no rock. It seemed to be everywhere in the cursed city.

Half a week had passed since the Dacian Ball, and every day had brought a new excuse to keep Gellion from meeting with King Naval. He had done his best to spend the days alone, but still he found himself ferried between groups of people. At least he had managed to avoid any more balls.

At first, Gellion had avoided the outer circles of the city. Too many times before had he seen scenes that filled him with guilt and pity in the less affluent areas of Tradira. His curiosity had won out in the end— curiosity, a desire to escape the prying eyes of Naval's henchmen, and a sense of duty to see all of present-day Albarad before establishing an alliance with its inhabitants.

Gellion had slipped away from the Central District at midday, when most of Tradira's citizens were closed inside cathedrals, and few would question his wandering around the city. He had kept his hood up and wore his salt-stained traveling clothes.

He moved through the branches of streets, following the tributaries further and further from the river until the heights of the Central District were no longer visible. As he progressed, the streets cracked, and dirt encroached upon the stones.

By the time a chorus of bells clamored throughout the city, Gellion was well into the outer districts. In the distance, the bells were deep and resonant; here, they were tinny and clashing.

Gellion looked out from under his hood and watched the throngs of commoners flood from the cathedrals into the streets. None gave him a backward glance. They filed around him in groups, much like those Gellion had seen in the Central District—couples, families, friends. Their smiles to each other seemed more relaxed.

The crowds began to thin as people entered houses and shops. There were far more children in the outer rings of Tradira, and most ran without supervision. Few wore shoes.

Another block found Gellion standing at the doors of a cathedral. It was as lavish as the surrounding buildings were decrepit. Colored windows spanned every gap of wood, and a set of doors two stories tall opened onto a flagged entryway. Gellion glanced around, then entered the building.

It was cool inside—not by any electrical mechanism, but by thick stone and darkness. Benches filled the space from back to front, and statues lined the open sides. The front of the cathedral held a wooden sculpture that looked like a prickly mass of branches. Candles burned low around the heap of timber. Gellion walked closer, intrigued. No humans occupied the space, but the smell of candle smoke and sweat lingered in the air. It was comforting, somehow.

A flicker of movement caught Gellion's eye. Under the sculpture, a woman was kneeling before a set of candles. Gellion froze. What was she doing here alone? In the Central District, Gellion had never seen a woman unaccompanied.

Feeling an intruder on something private, Gellion started to retrace his steps, but was brought up short when the woman turned to look at him. Gellion still wore his hood and could only imagine how strange, if not alarming, his presence must seem in this empty hall. Bowing his head, he turned away.

"Wait."

Gellion was tempted to ignore the woman and flee the building, but the kindness in her voice made him pause.

The woman looked to be past middle age, with a web of lines around her mouth and eyes. She looked at Gellion's foreign clothes, worn and stained from travel, and smiled. The expression smoothed the years from her face.

"Where are you from?" she said.

"I—" Gellion bit his lip and shifted his feet. "A city far to the north."

"You are Kayda?"

Gellion hesitated. The word sounded familiar, but he could not place its meaning.

"No."

The woman nodded as though this was a satisfactory answer and stood, brushing her skirt with her palms.

Gellion started to back away again. "I'm sorry to disturb you, I was just looking."

"It is beautiful, isn't it?" She smiled and looked around the cathedral. "My husband cares for the building. He is a lucky man."

Gellion's urgency to leave was receding. "Do you live near here?" He reached for his hood and lowered it.

The woman's eyes widened when she saw Gellion's face, but she blinked away her surprise and nodded.

"Just a few blocks away, with my three daughters." Her smile returned. "They are grown now, and two have husbands of their own."

Gellion's mouth turned up.

"Do you have a place to stay?" the woman said.

"Oh," said Gellion. "Yes ... yes, I am staying—" Gellion thought of his luxuriant lodgings in the Dom Regirium. His face burned. "I have somewhere to stay."

"That is good." Her smile broadened. "If you need anything while you are here, you may come to this cathedral. Ask for my husband, Alessio. The family he works for is good to him. They own this building and make it beautiful for us. I am sure they would help you also."

Gellion looked away from her earnest gaze, his stomach tightening further.

"Thank you."

"It is always good to meet a visitor." The woman dipped her head to Gellion. She turned from him and walked out of the cathedral.

Gellion had stood in that dark building a long time, watching the woman's candle burn to its base.

The encounter had not been significant, really—only a few minutes' meaningless conversation—yet it had stuck in Gellion's mind like a burr. The woman's kindness had been a comforting warmth amid the cold politics of Tradira. Though the poverty of the outer districts grated on Gellion's conscience, it was good to know that the city contained more than conniving vipers like Dacian and Cavalcont.

Gellion took a deep breath and stood. The infernal dog slid from his lap and began spinning in circles on the ground, yapping.

Back to the vipers.

"There you are!" a voice called from behind Gellion.

Amadeo Benta was jogging down the street. His face was flushed and glistening with sweat beneath a top hat.

"I have been ... been looking everywhere for you!" Amadeo gasped for air and leaned over his knees for a moment before straightening. "The king has an opening for an audience."

"Now?" Gellion said.

"Yes! You must come with me at once!"

Gellion looked down at the long white hairs on his tunic and ran a hand through his hair, damp at the roots from the day's heat.

"Could I change ..."

"It does not matter, come on now."

Gellion once again found his arm being pulled in front of him. He snatched it back and squared his shoulders before following Amadeo at a measured pace, picking the dog hairs from his shirt and smoothing his own hair behind his ears. His hand brushed his vierstone earring and a wave of homesickness gripped his chest.

Soon. Just get through this meeting and you can leave at last.

The Dom Regirium was busy. Men walked briskly through the hallways carrying important looking stacks of paper with their noses pointed above the horizon. Amadeo led Gellion to the center of the building and opened the heavy doors Gellion had sat outside of a week ago.

The throne room was cavernous, lined on both sides with narrow windows and pillars that Gellion could not have wrapped his arms around. The floor reflected an intricately carved ceiling that arched in a crisscross pattern from the doors to the throne itself. A man sat on the throne, straight-backed with one ringed hand resting on its arm.

Amadeo tapped Gellion on the back to urge him forward and walked beside him with bouncing steps.

"My king," he said as they approached the throne, removing his hat. He bowed low. Gellion remained standing.

King Naval was more or less what Gellion had expected. A shrewd gaze shone from a face pointed with a salt-and-pepper goatee. Naval flexed his fingers, scraping his rings across the wood of his chair. A corner of his thin mouth turned upward.

"Welcome to Albarad." He had a tenor voice, smooth and controlled.

"Thank you."

"I have been most anxious to meet you."

I shudder to think how long I would have waited in your apathy.

"When I received your message that the elves would send a representative, I was delighted. You accept our offer then?"

"We accept your request," Gellion said.

Naval's shrewd eyes narrowed, but he smiled. "Very good. I expect Earl Benta explained our situation to you. My people live well in Tradira, but it is unfortunately not so further east. The Dierna have been a thorn in my family's side for centuries, and I will stop them from harassing my people once and for all. The mountain pass should be neutral territory, crossed only by trade caravans and licensed emissaries. Not that the Dierna have any proper titles," he said with derision. "You will see for yourself the barbarous living they lead. They are cruel and ignorant, try as we may to work with them."

"Why do they raid your villages?"

"Why?" He scoffed. "Do they need a reason? They revel in violence and conquest. It is sport to them. They multiply like rabbits and need more land to conquer, though they have land, soil, and water in plenty."

Gellion nodded slowly. It was time to get to the point.

"I understand your people are suffering, King Naval. My people have decided to help. But I warn you it is not without misgivings. The elves do not like bloodshed, nor do we wish to make any enemies in this land."

"The Albaren have no love of war and enemies, but alas, war and enemies exist, and they leave us with no option of parlay." He narrowed his eyes at Gellion. "We fight because we must, but with your help that fighting could be significantly less." He turned his palms upward. "You know our offer of recompense. Do you accept?"

Gellion knew he had no choice. Dulon had sent him here for this very purpose, and whatever his feelings on the matter, it was his duty to follow through. He could not bring himself to do it without asking one more question, however.

"Where is the stone?"

Naval cocked an eyebrow. "Down the coast," he said. "Near the southern end of the Kald Straight. I can send someone to take you there if you wish, but it is several days' journey and we hope to move toward Diernas soon."

Gellion hesitated. He was not here to argue, and he was desperate to get back to Daro. The elves had decided to trust the Albaren. Whether or not the humans deserved it, the elves would help them.

"We accept."

Naval nodded solemnly. "You will receive your reward when my people are safe."

Amadeo stood to the side, looking excitedly between Gellion and the king like a proud parent.

"Earl, take Gellion to Commander Vensure," Naval said, then turned back to Gellion. "He will inform you about our army and arrange the logistics of the assault."

A knock sounded on the doors to the throne room.

"Bring them in," King Naval said lazily, waving a hand to the door guards. He nodded once to Gellion, clearly dismissing him.

Startled by the brevity of their meeting, Gellion hesitated before returning the gesture and slowly turning to leave the throne room. On his way out, he passed a clean-shaven man carrying a stack of papers. A dog hair floated off of Gellion's sleeve as the doors closed behind him.

***

Gellion's meeting with Commander Vensure was not much longer than the meeting with King Naval. From Gellion's experience over the last week, he had expected the Albaren government and military to be inefficient and haphazard. He could not have been more wrong.

Commander Vensure stood when Gellion entered his austere office in the Academy. He was broad shouldered with cropped hair and fierce eyes. From one look, Gellion could guess the man rarely smiled and could likely wield a great-sword as easily as a knife. He looked Gellion up and down, appraisal and judgment clear in his face.

"You are the elven military commander?"

Gellion skirted the question. "I am here to discuss our battle arrangements."

Venture eyed Gellion for another moment before nodding once. He gestured to a table to one side of the room, where a map and neat stacks of paper sat in a grid.

"Are you familiar with the Dierna?"

"No. We have never had contact with them."

With a grunt, Vensure turned a map of Tala to face Gellion. He ran a finger down a series of inked ridges snaking down the center of the map.

"These are the Falspire Mountains. As they run south, they merge into the Sky Peaks. The mountain range serves as the border between Albarad and Diernas."

He pointed at a gap in the mountains two thirds up the length of the map.

"Restring Pass is the only gap in the mountains large enough for easy passage. This is how the Dierna are entering our territory. Just on our side of the pass is the Albaren village of Nescari. It has been badly hit by the Dierna and now hosts a military encampment outside its walls. That is where we will meet you. It is a four- to five-day journey southeast of your city." He pointed to where the Icemelt met the Semestrial Sea, then stood back and set his steely gaze on Gellion.

Gellion traced the map with his eyes. "Is there a road to Nescari from the north?"

"Yes. Follow the southern banks of the Icemelt until you hit it."

Gellion nodded.

Face devoid of emotion, Vensure proceeded to list Albarad's military statistics.

"We have an active army of three thousand men traveling to the pass. Our goal is to destroy all enemy camps within the pass and push them to Arvain." He indicated a dot on the southeast edge of the mountains. "That is the main city of the Elder Clan—the Dierna clan that has been causing the majority of our problems. Albaren outposts already exist along the border, but they need to be fortified and manned." He stood tall and looked up from the map. "We will fight until they surrender and submit to our terms."

He spoke in such a matter-of-fact tone that Gellion found himself nodding along to the plan. It seemed simple enough.

"How many elves do you have?" Vensure asked.

Surprised, Gellion realized no one had ever asked how many elves would come with their agreement. It seemed an important point to have missed.

"Around one thousand."

Vensure nodded, as though the number was what he had expected. Vensure proceeded to outline the Albaren army route from Tradira to Nescari, giving time estimates as to their arrival at each point. He outlined the route the elves should take and the day on which they should expect to arrive in Nescari. The elves were to provide their own armor, weapons, and provisions.

The plan seemed organized and well thought out. Gellion found himself gaining confidence in the elves' decision. The risks seemed less than he had feared.

In under an hour, Gellion's mission in Tradira was complete. His annoyance at the delay was trumped by his eagerness to return to his people and share this information with Dulon. The elf army would depart within the month. For better or for worse, their decision would be set in motion. Gellion was tired of waiting. He would leave in the morning.

<hr>

The grounds outside the Academy were filled with afternoon drills and training. In one quadrant, ranks of men in crisp cut uniforms stood at attention. In another, pairs lunged and parried with swords, emitting guttural shouts with each maneuver.

This is what the Albaren society was based on. Power. Skill. Death. Gellion wondered why a species with so limited a lifespan was so determined to spend their time risking their own lives and destroying those of others. They lived as though always preparing for something, eyes set forward so intently he could hardly imagine they even noticed the present. It made him weary. Sad. What was the point?

Gellion shook himself and walked faster. His mind often brought him to such dark and frightening places, but he had never learned to like them.

He focused on the buildings surrounding him as he crossed toward the city's center. Beyond the Academy and training grounds, the iron pillars of factories poked between the spiked roofs of public buildings. The same smokey haze hung in the air, gloomier now under dark clouds. Walking past him, people laughed, shouted, and moved their hands in outlandish gestures. Suddenly, one of the faces morphed into familiarity.

"Gellion!" Chiara Arceria extricated herself from a group of women. They stood back, staring at Gellion as Chiara approached him.

"Where have you been? I feared you had left Tradira! You have missed several balls, you know." Her eyes were teasing.

"I have been ... busy."

"Oh, I'm sure you have." She smiled. "Have you met with the king yet?"

Gellion glanced behind Chiara at the group of women.

"Yes."

"And?"

"Everything is settled."

Chiara rolled her eyes. "Oh come now. I have heard elusive talk before. Why can men never say things as they are?" She lowered her chin, looking up at him through thick lashes. "I shared plenty of gossip with you the other night. Surely you can tell me just a bit? I have nothing else to live for but thrilling information."

Gellion cocked an eyebrow.

Chiara sighed.

"How about a trade then?" she asked. "If you tell me why you are in Albarad and what you discussed with the king, I'll give you *more* gossip. My silly husband interrupted us before I could tell you about the Camersio scandal."

While Gellion had no interest in paltry court gossip, he could not deny that this woman knew far more than she ought about Albaren politics. He could not resist the prospect of learning more about the government with which he had just formed an alliance. Besides, the alliance was no secret as far as he knew. If the citizens of Tradira did not know about King Naval's agreement, they would soon enough.

Gellion gave Chiara a long look, then hid a smile as he asked, "Who are the Camersios?"

Chiara's eyes lit with excitement. "A wealthy trading family—they owned ships and were beginning to monopolize the coast. Tarcin Camersio, the head of the family, was making a powerful name for himself in Tradira. People liked him. He was wealthy, charismatic ..." She gave Gellion a significant look. "Making himself a bit too much of a threat if you ask me. Anyway, he had a younger brother, Durand. Durand was a bit of a dandy, always spending more money than he should and doing nothing of real use to his family, but he was harmless really. A dumb, innocent sweetheart." The fondness in her eyes made Gellion wonder how, exactly, she knew so much of this scandal.

"At the height of the Camersios' power, Durand was arrested for financial fraud. It all made perfect sense. There were witnesses, pristine evidence, and it fit with his gambling and lavish lifestyle. No one questioned the charge, and he was thrown in prison. A few weeks later they released him with a fine and a warning, pardoning him of the crime and sending him on his way. But by then the damage was done." She raised her eyebrows. "The scandal of the whole thing ruined the Camersio reputation. They eventually moved to a duchy. Lost stock in most of their ships."

"So," Gellion said slowly, "you do not think Durand Camersio committed the crime?"

"Oh I know he didn't," she said easily. "I was with him often the weeks before his arrest. I would have known if he was doing anything suspicious. And the night of his biggest supposed offense, he was assuredly not where they accused him of being." She winked.

Gellion tried to control the flush threatening to suffuse his face.

"Why did you allow his arrest?"

Chiara laughed. "The scandal caused by the truth would have been worse than the scandal he was accused of."

"I see."

Gellion regretted agreeing to Chiara's proposal. He wished he had not known about this further evidence of government corruption.

Naval and Vensure, though hardly warm, friendly people, had seemed honest enough, and interested in the well-being of their citizens. Was it possible this nastier aspect of Albaren society occurred without their knowledge? Did they simply ignore it in the interest of more important issues? But Chiara had accused Naval of encouraging discord among his Marchons. Gellion thought of the Marchons he had met. He would not want them in power either. Could Naval be guilty of Chiara's accusation, but still acting in the best interest of his people?

Chiara interrupted his thoughts with a polite cough. She was looking at him expectantly.

"Alright." Gellion raised his hands in surrender. He told her about the attacks on the Dierna border and the alliance between Naval and the elves, though he left out any mention of vierstone.

"I knew it." Chiara wore a triumphant grin. "The assault on the mountain pass and Arvain is public knowledge, but I have only heard rumors of the details. I knew there was something different, something the military was hiding."

"I expect the alliance will be public knowledge soon, now that it is official."

"Oh yes, I'm sure it will." Chiara's childish grin seemed to shout, "But I knew about it *first*!"

Despite himself, the corners of Gellion's mouth turned up. He looked around. Chiara's entourage was nowhere to be seen. They must have grown bored.

"I should return to my rooms," Gellion said. "I need to prepare for my journey tomorrow."

Panic flashed in Chiara's eyes. "You are leaving tomorrow?"

"I must return to the elves."

"Oh but you must come to the ball tonight!"

"I think I have had enough of balls," Gellion muttered, turning his feet toward the Dom Regirium.

"This one is different!" Chiara stopped him with a hand. "The Dacian Balls are lavish. Silly. This one is a true ball. You must come, at least for a while."

"Really, I—"

"You must eat dinner, yes? Just come for the food, have a glass of wine. Then you can leave." Her eyes were pleading. "It is such a nice change to have a source of real conversation."

Guilt burned in Gellion's chest. He longed to be done with Albaren society and its ridiculous parties, but he could sympathize with Chiara. Life for intelligent women in Tradira must hardly be satisfying, and though Chiara obviously made the most of her situation, Gellion suspected she was lonely.

"Where is the ball?" he asked with a sigh.

Chiara's face transformed. "The Arceria Mansion."

2 3

THE FALL

Chiara had been right about one thing. The Arceria Mansion was about as similar to the Dacian Mansion as a raven to a parrot. Where Marchon Dacian celebrated and displayed his wealth with statues, fountains, and color, money downright exuded from the grand simplicity of the Arcerias' Mansion. Every inch of wall and piece of furniture was of the highest quality: marble, gold, ebony wood, silk. Minimal adornment and open spaces focused one's attention on the intricate columns and ceiling, and made the space seem impossibly enormous.

Gellion laid down his fork and sipped a glass of smooth wine. The tastes of rich meat and spices lingered in his mouth.

"Tell me about your home," Chiara said.

Though dinner had been delectable, Gellion could not deny that Chiara's attentions were beginning to make him uncomfortable. With Nicabar Arceria, Chiara's husband, at the table, Gellion wished she would show more tact and subtlety in her infatuation with him. Her husband had been staring daggers at Gellion since he sat down, the glares increasing in their intensity with each glass of wine.

"It is a city of stone built into a cliffside several days' journey up the coast from Tradira."

Chiara rolled her eyes and smiled. "I did not mean the city you live in here. I've heard about that place. I mean where the elves come from."

Gellion stiffened. The elves did not speak of Faeran to humans. The two continents were too close for many elves' comfort, and it was best that the humans remained ignorant of that fact.

"The elves come from a land far from here, across the sea." He said vaguely, trying to immerse himself in a nearby conversation about proper tailoring.

"Did you live there?"

"Yes."

Chiara changed tactics.

"What do you do in your city here?"

"I am a metalworker."

"Oh!" She leaned toward him. "You must be amazing with so many years of practice. Will you show me something you have made?"

"I ... did not bring anything with me."

Across the table, the knuckles of Nicabar's hand turned white.

"I imagine the elves are wonderful at art. Are they? Do you have music and poetry and dance?"

"Yes."

Her eyes shone with imagination. "I should love to come see it one day. Your cathedrals must be incredible."

"Mmm."

To Gellion's relief, Chiara's onslaught of questions was cut short by the arrival of dessert. He coaxed the conversation back to Albarad after that, speaking as little as possible and planning to make his escape as soon as his plate was clear.

When at last servants cleared the table, Gellion stood and began to make his excuses, but before he could utter more than a few words, Chiara grabbed his arm and said, "Let's dance," whisking him toward the open space of the ballroom before he could muster the sense to protest.

It was all Gellion could do not to rip his arm from her grasp and shout at her. Nothing else seemed to affect the woman in the least.

"I want to leave." Gellion tried to keep his voice civil. "I need to pack." Gellion thought of his lone bag. "And I must leave at dawn tomorrow."

"One dance. You said the elves like to dance." Chiara placed one hand on his shoulder and grasped his own hand with the other. Amid the other couples moving around them, Gellion could hardly stand still to argue. He reluctantly moved his feet to the music, hating himself for enjoying it. He had always liked dancing. Though the style was different from anything he knew, rhythm and flow transcended culture.

Gellion blessed his height. With Chiara's head only reaching his chest, it was easy to stare above her and avoid both eye contact and conversation. After this dance he would insist upon leaving, and then he would be on his way to Daro by first light. He had half a mind to leave tonight, but a long trek through the rocky countryside did not sound appealing in the middle of the night.

The motion flowing around Gellion slowed to a stop as the music faded. Chiara pulled closer to him. He pushed her away as gently as he could and took a step back.

"Chiara, I really must leave now."

"Didn't you enjoy the dance?"

"I am sorry, but I should go. It was a lovely party."

She looked at her feet and nodded. "Can I walk you out?"

Every nerve in Gellion's body told him this was a bad idea. Nicabar Arceria was even now watching them, no doubt, waiting for Gellion to make a false move.

"I can find my way." He started to turn away from her.

"Have you seen the view from the balcony?" she asked desperately. "It is just off the ballroom. Please come, just for a moment. The lights are beautiful at night." She smiled, her pupils dilating as she closed the gap Gellion had forced between them. "I promise I will let you go after that."

Gellion clenched his jaw and sighed. "I will hold you to that."

"Agreed." She held out her hand.

Gellion sighed and indicated for her to lead the way.

Even in the heat of late spring, the night air was a cool relief after the ballroom. Gellion took a breath of the smoky air. In the distance, the moon reflected on the ocean like spilled paint. Lights shimmered below him, garishly bright in the Central District, fading to flickering pinpoints toward the outer rings of the city. He stared at the dark streets, and all of his energy seemed to drain away. He was tired of this city.

"Isn't it wonderful?" Chiara was watching him, her fingertips resting on the railing at her hips.

"It is a nice view."

"Don't you want to come closer?" She peered over the edge of the balcony and smiled back at him. "You can see the gardens below."

The doors of the balcony opened with a crash before Gellion could open his mouth to refuse. Chiara's eyes widened. Gellion spun around, and his heart leapt into his throat. Standing between the doors with his shirt collar undone was Nicabar Arceria. His face was red.

"You." He pointed a shaking finger at Gellion and took a step forward. His eyes shifted to Chiara and narrowed. "And you. You ungrateful little slut."

An ember of anger sparked to life in Gellion's chest.

"Do not speak to her that way," he said in a measured tone.

"You dare tell me how to speak to my wife?! *My* wife?!"

A stench of alcohol accosted Gellion's nose, and he clenched his fists.

"If this harlot would bear me as many children as men she beds," Nicabar said, "I would have the longest line of heirs ever known! Not that I would know if any of them were mine." He spat.

Gellion stepped forward, the ember in his chest now burning with a steady flame.

"Oh Nicabar." Chiara's voice dripped with sugar. She put a hand on Gellion's arm and drew him back. Nicabar blanched. "If you could father a son, it would have happened long before now, with your previous two wives. Remind me what happened to them?"

Nicabar was staring at her hand on Gellion's arm.

"Gellion has been most kind to me." To Gellion's horror, Chiara winked at him. "There is no need to be upset."

Nicabar seemed to be working exceptionally hard to piece together a retort, but all that came out was a slurred, "Demon! Incubus!"

To Gellion's shock, the man was pointing not at Chiara, but at him.

"What they say is true! You have all come here to corrupt us with your faery magic! To tempt us! Get away from my wife!"

"Nicabar, honestly." Chiara rolled her eyes, unfazed by her husband's behavior.

A flash of silver warned Gellion just before the man came at him. He ducked to the side, pushing Chiara away from him and out of the way of her husband's blade.

Fury exploded in Gellion's chest, sending burning adrenaline through his limbs until his skin was tingling with the force of it. He took one step toward Nicabar, flicking the knife out of the man's grasp with a fluid motion, grabbing the gaping collar of his shirt, and shoving him back toward the railing. Gellion's eyes blazed. Nicabar stared at him in terror, struggling away.

Then Gellion felt the man stumble and trip backward.

Gellion had too much momentum to stop and lunged with Nicabar against the railing. Nicabar flapped his arms, bellowing, then in one horrifying moment, he tipped backward. Gellion watched the man's shirt collar slip through his fingers.

Nicabar's yells receded in slow motion. After an eternity, a sickening slap rent the air. Then silence.

The anger coursing through Gellion's veins slowly turned to surreal horror. His ears felt full of cotton, and he swayed, gripping the railing for support. It took all of his will power to pull himself straight and look over the edge of the balcony.

Three stories below, a still body lay among a ring of rose bushes.

Chiara began to scream.

2 4

MONSTERS AMONG US

Froth dripped from Nightjar's lips when Renyra finally stopped for the night. She would reach Daro by noon tomorrow, she was sure. She removed the animal's bridle and led him to the Icemelt to drink. Guilt tugged at her as she watched him guzzle the cold water. She had tried not to overwork him, but her desire to return to Daro had pushed them both to speed. The novelty of her trip had long since worn away, and Renyra was desperate to see Firas, to tell Dulon what she had discovered.

After her halting conversation with the Albaren woman, Renyra had walked as confidently as she could out the front gate of the village, comforted by the thought that over two thirds of the population was absent. The moment she had cleared the gates, she ran—ran to Nightjar, hiked up her skirt, and rode away. She considered herself fortunate to have come through the town unscathed. Firas had been right. She had had no idea what she was walking into here, and the suspicion of the villagers could have turned nasty. At least she had not told them she was an elf. Given the young woman's reaction to Renyra's exotic appearance, Renyra could only imagine how she would have reacted to a nonhuman visitor.

None of it mattered now. Renyra had learned what she came for.

Whatever was affecting Daro stopped at the city walls. Renyra had expected as much, but the knowledge was disconcerting. What now? How could they combat a force they could not see or understand?

Renyra splashed water on her face and tried to focus on the spirits of Riu around her—the gentle hush of the river, the whisper of wind in the bushes, the solid soil beneath her knees. She took a deep breath. She needed sleep, and worrying now would not make tomorrow any easier.

When at last she fell asleep, curled in her cloak near the riverbank, it was to the chorus of frogs and the promise of seeing Firas on the morrow.

A rumbling sound woke Renyra long before morning light had suffused the sky. She opened her eyes, looking into the silver light cast by the moon, and listened. The sound came again. The hairs on Renyra's arms stood on end as an unreasonable fear spread through her veins. It had sounded like a growl, but by no beast she had ever encountered. It was like scratching nails.

Renyra reached for the dagger in her boot, intending to make slow movements until she could see the source of the sound, but a high-pitched scream from Nightjar sent her springing to her feet, dagger in hand.

The horse was rearing, eyes rolling, swinging his legs in panic at a shadow below him. The creature there was blacker than the night, but Renyra could see two glinting eyes reflecting scarlet in the moonlight. Another growl emitted from the monster, followed by a series of horrible barks. It lunged at Nightjar. Renyra threw her dagger, which embedded between the thing's shoulder and neck. It let out an unearthly scream and rounded on Renyra, teeth bared. It's teeth were as black as its coat, dripping saliva.

Renyra's eyes widened in horror. The nightmare sprung at her, and she leapt to the side just in time to avoid its snapping jaws. She wheeled around to face it. A weapon. She needed a weapon. Her eyes darted from her dagger, deep in the creature's flesh though clearly causing no serious damage, to her pack under Nightjar's pawing feet, next to her javelin. She ran toward it.

Thundering feet pursued her, accompanied by a growl that rose in pitch with each stride of the beast. As Renyra dove under him, Nightjar lost his head completely and snapped his rope, galloping away into the distance with a screech. Renyra grabbed her javelin and spun around with the point facing outward just as the monster fell on her. She stabbed up through its throat with all the strength she could muster, jerking its teeth away from her neck. She fought a gag as rotten breath and strings of saliva coated her face. The thing continued to fight, clawing at her as blood spluttered from its mouth. Renyra reached her free hand around its back and pulled her dagger free of its shoulder blades, stabbing the beast over and over in the back until it finally went limp.

She lay panting under the creature for a few moments, shock and adrenaline coursing through her limbs. Hot blood seeped into her shirt. She rolled the beast off of her and scrambled away from it. Gripping her javelin with two hands, she cautiously prodded the creature. It was dead.

Not trusting her legs, Renyra crawled to the river bank. The night was warm, but she shivered as she washed her face and arms in the cold water. Long scratches scored both of her arms, and her pants had tears running down the thighs, but the injuries were not serious and would heal in a few days.

No sounds broke the silence of the night. Even the frogs had ceased their chorus. Renyra signed the star over herself with a trembling hand and huddled in a ball next to the water. Nightjar was gone, and it was still hours before morning, judging by the moon. Renyra could not bear the thought of sleeping any more than she could walking alone through the dark brush, but sitting awake with nothing but moonlight was not much better. She should build a fire. Somehow even that seemed an impossible task. Her eyes kept moving to the heap of fur. What in all of Riure was it? Never in her life had she seen an animal like this. Never had she been so afraid.

Renyra had always thought herself brave. She easily performed stunning acrobatics thirty feet off the ground. She hunted animals capable of causing her serious harm with nothing but her javelins. She had always imagined that she would have fought well for the elves had she lived during the Great War.

Legs shaking, she rose and began to gather branches from nearby shrubs with leaden hands. It was as though she had lost all control of her limbs. Tears leaked from her eyes.

So many elves carried the burden of those centuries of war in their hearts. Renyra had always been envious of them. The Great War linked the elves in a way that only shared horrors can accomplish. It was a link Renyra did not share. She felt young and foolish by her accident of birth—a bright-eyed innocent with no real experience of pain. It was hardly her fault she had not suffered with the rest, and she knew it was pointless to feel guilty about her lack of misfortune, but she could not help the jealousy that gripped her heart at her exclusion, nor the anger she felt when elves treated her as naive for her lack of experience.

A part of her had almost longed for something to happen—not necessarily a war, but some trial she could help the elves face to prove herself. Now she would get her chance. A battle loomed on the horizon, but it was not excitement she felt.

Her gorge rose as a drop of blood not her own dripped down her arm. She had never been bothered by blood when hunting, but somehow this was different. This was blood brought by violence. Uncontrolled. Born of hate and fear rather than need and mercy. How could she hope to fight in a battle when fighting a single beast completely unhinged her?

Another tear ran down her face as she struggled to build a fire with numb hands. She put the river to her back, but still looked over her shoulder every few minutes.

She had not allowed herself to think about the impending battle. When the decision of the alliance was still unmade, she had told herself it was pointless to worry about what may never come to pass. Then the battle had seemed too distant to be real. Gellion was in negotiations, and Dulon had yet to secure weapons. But Renyra knew it was only a matter of time. The elves would go to battle. Would she go with them? Could she go with them? The thought of remaining behind was unbearable, but so was the thought of going.

Flames began to eat through the dry leaves Renyra had sprinkled on the branches. Five broken matches burned beneath the kindling.

Renyra took a shaking breath and tried again to focus on the spirits around her, but peace was lost in the shadows of the night. She stared into the flames until the embers died with the morning light.

Only when the sun had crested the horizon did Renyra have the courage to approach the beast. She stood over it and moved its body with her javelin until she could get a good look at it.

The closest thing it resembled was a dog—a huge dog. It had black hair that hung in matts and tatters from its body and a long, ratty tail. Its nose and ears were pointed like swords, and its claws were as long as Renyra's fingers. With a shaking hand, Renyra used the tip of her javelin to lift the beast's lips. She hadn't been imagining it. Its teeth were jet black and as wicked as its claws. Clouded red eyes stared blindly from its head.

Renyra was no expert on Albaren fauna, but this *thing* could not be a native animal; even the term 'animal' did not seem to fit it. In all her time hunting in the lands surrounding Daro, she had never seen anything like this. If Nightjar were still here, Renyra would have tried to take the beast back to Daro, but as it was, she could hardly lift the creature, let alone drag it for a full day of walking. She would have to leave it.

It was past time she set out for Daro. Renyra ate the last of her food, shouldered her pack, and started to walk.

By the time she finally reached Daro, the walls were washed in red from the setting sun. A thick layer of dust mixed with sweat and blood encrusted Renyra's skin and clothes, and her eyelids drooped with weariness. As she approached the city, a figure appeared in the gaping gate, then ran toward her.

"Renyra!"

It was Firas. What little color tinted his pale face drained away as his eyes swept over her.

"Sweet Riu, what happened?" He cupped a hand to her face, fingers lacing through her hair and eyes roving into the depths of her own as though searching for reassurance and answers.

"I'm alright. Just tired and sore."

"Your horse came back hours ago, still tacked. We had no idea what had happened. Dulon was going to send elves to search for you if you weren't back by tonight." Fear still clouded his eyes. Renyra's heart ached for him. She hadn't meant to cause him such anxiety and could hardly imagine how she would have felt if the situation were reversed.

"I am fine," she said again, holding his gaze and squeezing his elbows. "Really I am. I'm sorry I worried you. Nightjar spooked in the night and ran off without me. I didn't want to leave until morning, and it took me the whole day to walk here."

"But your arms ... and ..." He stepped away from her, gesturing to the rust-stained front of her shirt.

"The blood isn't mine. An animal attacked us and I killed it. That's why Nightjar ran off. I'll tell you all about it tonight, but right now I just want a bath and dinner."

Firas clearly did not want to wait that long for an explanation. Renyra smiled at him, trying to look reassuring.

"I promise, I'm not seriously hurt. Please can we go?"

The concern did not leave Firas's face, but at last he nodded his head and put an arm gingerly around her shoulders to lead her into the city.

After a lengthy trip to the bathhouse, Renyra curled up in a cushioned chair with a cup of steaming tea. It felt good to be back in her own home and even better to be clean and fed. The hot water of the baths had stung her cuts, but the wounds were already thinning and scabbing over. Within a week, they would be scars, and would likely fade to nothing in the coming months.

Now she just wanted to sleep, but she knew she had to recount her journey to Firas, and Dulon needed to know what she had found out. Firas walked out of the kitchen and sat across from her, expectancy in his eyes. Renyra sighed.

She told him about the untouched countryside, about Lacrim and the boy and the woman and what they had said.

"But last night I woke up to Nightjar's scream and a pair of gleaming eyes in the darkness. I don't know what it was, Firas. I've never seen anything like it. It was like a dog, but it had red eyes and black teeth and the *sounds* it made ..." Renyra shuddered. "It was as big as any wolf I've ever seen, and it reeked of rotting meat. I barely managed to kill it before it tore my throat out. I would have brought it back, but it was too big, and I was too far from the city."

Firas stared silently at the floor. The thoughts fleeting through his head were almost palpable in the stillness.

"The beast is concerning," he said, "but I cannot see how it fits with everything else, except by its strangeness. But the earthquakes ..." He shook his head. His eyes became distant and heavy with worry. "It is simply not possible. How can they only be affecting Daro? It is too small an area, and the earthquakes are too powerful. Unless ..."

Renyra waited for his answer. "Unless what?" she said sharply.

Firas continued to stare past her. "Unless they are not earthquakes."

Renyra raised her eyebrows, incredulous. "What do you mean 'not earthquakes?' The ground is *shaking*, what else could they be?"

"What I mean is, maybe they are not caused by the same thing as geological earthquakes. If movement in the earth was causing this, it would affect large areas of land. It must be something more shallow."

"Like what? Some sort of shockwave from an impact?"

"Maybe." Firas narrowed his eyes in thought. "But what could be causing it, I have no idea. Whatever it is, it is getting much worse. We have to find out."

"What do you mean getting worse?" Renyra said, cold spreading through her despite the steaming tea in her hands.

Firas looked up, wary. What did he know?

"You didn't feel it?" he said slowly.

"Feel what?"

"But of course, what you said, you wouldn't have would you? Not if ..."

"Not if what? What don't I know?" Renyra's knuckles were white around her cup.

Get to the point.

"Did you not feel the earthquake two days ago?"

"An earthquake? I—" Renyra thought hard, but recalled nothing. "No. I didn't feel anything. Was there another one in Daro?"

Unease passed across Firas's eyes. "I think you should come see for yourself."

———

Firas would say nothing more as he led Renyra toward the Court. Curiosity and apprehension warred within Renyra's chest. Had the Court been damaged? Was the quarry worse?

The Domes of Rhelyon came into view as they ascended the lift to the Court, a misshapen shadow against the city wall. The sun was well beyond the horizon now, but an oblong moon lent its luminosity to the Court. The fountain gurgled merrily, and for a moment Renyra could almost imagine it was the night of the fireworks again, the earthquakes and the impending alliance not yet real, but the strings of lights trailing from shrubs and trees were dark. Renyra frowned, straining her eyes. The illusion shattered instantly.

The dome was not misshapen from the darkness, it was caved in. To her left, the Court crumbled away into a gaping hole over the bay.

Renyra's fists clenched.

"Was anyone hurt?"

"I don't think so. Everyone was out by the time the dome caved in, and, as far as I know, no one was in the Court or the quarry. It was powerful though. I was home and didn't feel it as strongly, but those that were up here say it was like a giant was wrenching apart the cliff, and there was something like an electric current in the air and stones beforehand."

An electric current ... Renyra had never heard the sensation preceding the earthquakes described that way, but she could see how it fit.

"There's something else too." Firas's face was grave.

What more could there be? What could be worse than this?

"Look closely at the stone of the Court. It's laced with black. Dulon thinks it's the vierstone in the foundations turning black like in the quarry."

"What?" Renyra knelt down and scrutinized the ground. He was right. "But what does that mean?" Her voice was rising in pitch. "Did

Dulon ask the stoneworkers? What could cause this? Did the quarry crack again?"

"Dulon did ask, but no one knows. The quarry did not crack again, but—" He hesitated. Real panic was rising in Renyra's throat now. "It's completely black now. It's gone, Renyra."

"Gone?" she whispered.

This was beyond anything she could have imagined. Beyond her worst fears. She didn't know what to say. What was there to say? The city was crumbling and the vierstone was dying and no one knew how or why.

"What about the earrings? Crafted vierstone?"

"They are all fine. Only the streets and buildings affected by the earthquakes have turned black. And the quarry of course ..."

Renyra stared at the black tendrils in the stone. Localized earthquakes. Shallow earthquakes. Vierstone turning black. Firas was right. Whatever this was, it was from no geological origin. But what?

What?

Renyra wracked her brain, sure the answer must be obvious, but beyond her sight. Shifting within the ground caused earthquakes. But what caused shifting in the ground?

"Terra spirits."

Firas drew his brows together. "What?"

Excitement was beginning to build in Renyra's chest. "What if this is a terra spirit? A corrupted one? The earthquakes and the vierstone."

Firas stared at her.

"It could be!" Renyra said. "Corrupted terra spirits were the origin of earthquakes, how do we know they do not have a hand still in their daily occurrence?"

Incredulity was obvious in Firas's face. "The spirits cannot act so suddenly, nor so autonomously."

"How can we know that?"

"Alright, let us assume they can. Why would a terra spirit target Daro?"

"I don't know. Maybe it was ordered to ... by Olcon?"

Firas's voice was gentle. "I very much doubt that."

Renyra huffed. "It's only an idea."

"And a possible one. I am not discounting it."

"But even if this were a spirit, how would we stop it? The spirits cannot be killed as far as I know. They don't even have physical forms."

Firas glanced away.

Renyra narrowed her eyes at him. "Do they?"

"No." There was a hesitation before the word. Firas was one of the most honest elves Renyra had known, but he was rarely forthcoming with his information or opinions.

"Firas." She turned her eyes to the sky.

"The elves understand little of the spirits," said Firas. "I am only saying we should not discount any possibility based on our present assumptions."

Renyra worked her jaw. "I need to talk to Dulon. I have to tell him what I found out in Lacrim. I can't imagine how it will help, but he should know all the same. Maybe he will have other ideas." She hesitated as she looked at the crumbled dome. "Is he still living there?"

"No, everyone with rooms in the Domes moved to the guest quarters in the southern tower."

To the left of the central dome, the Tower of Stars had crumbled into the bay with the viaduct, but its twin still stood tall to the far right. Firas began walking toward it, and Renyra jogged behind him.

They found Dulon in a modest room with a bed, a couch, and a sink. It was meant for visiting elves staying only a few days or weeks. Renyra wondered if Dulon would try to repair the rooms of the central dome. There didn't seem to be much point if the earthquakes continued, and it would be dangerous work even without the threat of more earthquakes.

Relief flooded Dulon's eyes when he saw Renyra.

"Thank Riu you're back. What happened? Tell me everything."

Renyra launched into her story again, leaving out no detail. Dulon listened with a knit brow.

"The creature you describe is strange," he said when Renyra had spoken her fill. "I have travelled all over this area and never seen more than an angry fox. We will have to be more careful travelling, especially when we march into open territory to meet the Albaren. I am grateful nothing worse happened." He sighed. "I'm sorry. I should have sent you with more protection. I was distracted and eager for answers. But your instincts were right it would seem. I can't say what it means that the earthquakes are only in Daro, but it is valuable information all the same."

"We had another idea," Renyra said, exchanging a look with Firas. "What if these earthquakes—and the dying vierstone—are being caused by a terra spirit?"

Dulon raised an eyebrow and glanced at Firas. "A terra spirit?"

Annoyance flickered under Renyra's skin. Why were all of her ideas so far-fetched and ludicrous?

"Maybe," Dulon said slowly. He seemed about as convinced as Firas. "It is something to keep in mind, though if it turned out to be true I don't know how we would prove it, let alone stop it."

He had a point. How did one place blame or discipline on a thing without form or voice?

"What about the vierstone?" Renyra asked, letting her spirit idea pass for the time being. "What do you plan to do?"

Dulon smiled, but the weariness in his face remained.

"Aryn is still researching the matter. She is adamant. Hopefully she will find answers soon that may shed light on the rest of this unfortunate business. I'm afraid all we can do now is tread carefully and wait."

Renyra did not want to wait. The next day found her in the stoneworker quarter of Master's Street. She would ask Aryn herself what she had been researching and what hope she had of finding a real answer.

A thorough search of Master's Street yielded no results, however, and Renyra was forced to abandon her search to tend to the animals in the stables and eat lunch. It was past midday when she at last found Aryn in the Archives.

The woman was bent over a desk with ancient scrolls and tomes pushed to the edges and a small piece of vierstone in the center. She was holding the stone with her eyes closed, shaking her head.

"Aryn?" Renyra said tentatively, afraid of disturbing whatever the woman was doing.

Aryn jumped and wheeled around in her chair. Strands of fair hair stuck out from her ponytail, and her eyes were bloodshot. She did not look pleased at the interruption.

"I'm sorry to disturb you," said Renyra. "I've just been speaking with Dulon and wanted to ask about your vierstone research." The excuse sounded lame. "He wanted to know how you are getting on." It was not a lie. Dulon surely did want to know how Aryn's research was going.

Aryn took a breath. "I am starting to understand something—I think. I am close," she shot Renyra an annoyed look, "but not there just yet. I will let him know when I am." With that she spun back to her desk and picked up the vierstone again.

Disappointed, Renyra retraced her steps through the winding bookcases.

At least she thinks she may know something. Maybe by tomorrow this whole mystery will be solved.

In the meantime, Dulon was right. All Renyra could do was wait.

She had hardly walked down the street from the Archives, however, when she heard its doors bang open. She turned to see Aryn running toward her.

"Wait!" Aryn held up the piece of vierstone. It looked normal, but Aryn waved it vigorously. "I think I understand what must have happened. It is just beyond my grasp, but I can *see* it. There is only one piece missing." There was a crazed look in her eye. "But I don't know *who* ... I don't know who could have done it ..." She was looking at the ground now, as though talking to herself. "Or *why*."

She stared at her feet as though they may reveal the answers, then suddenly whipped her head back up.

"I have to go back to my workshop. I have to make sure. But I will go to Dulon as soon as I have. Tonight. Tell him."

With that, she leapt on the nearest levit board and sped toward the lift to Master's Street, leaving Renyra standing bewildered.

Not knowing what else to do, Renyra went to tell Dulon what Aryn had said.

"*Who* could have done it? You're sure that's what she said?" Dulon asked.

"Positive. But she seemed rather ... sleep deprived." Renyra did not say 'crazy.' "I don't know how much sense she was making."

Dulon frowned. "Perhaps we should go find her. I have been ... concerned about her obsession with this task."

Renyra's heart jumped. She had expected Dulon to say they should wait for Aryn to come to them. Would they know in just a few minutes what was destroying the vierstone—maybe even what was causing the earthquakes?

They hurried to Master's Street. The day was grey and few elves passed them in the road, but as they neared the stoneworker's quarter, a murmur of voices became evident on the breeze. Turning the bend in the road, they saw a group of elves gathered outside the stoneworker workshops. Dread began to creep through Renyra's body. The elves looked agitated, afraid, and they were pointing at the building in front of them.

Suddenly, Dulon sprang ahead of Renyra like a deer sensing danger. She followed on his heels.

In front of the gathered elves, between two buildings, was a pile of rubble. Several arches and beams remained, but the roof had caved in, and the walls had crumbled. It was one of the stoneworker workshops—Aryn's workshop.

Renyra looked around wildly, but saw no other signs of damage in the buildings next door or in the street.

Dulon was scrambling over the rubble. Renyra followed him.

"Wait!" an elf in the crowd shouted. "It's not safe!"

Renyra ignored him. She caught up with Dulon in the center of the collapsed building, where the edges of a workbench peaked out of the rubble. Dulon started clawing at the stone, ripping rocks away. He pulled a heavy shard out from under the pile, and an avalanche of stones cascaded off the bench in a cloud of white powder. He jumped back from the shards.

The dust cleared to reveal a section of Aryn's workbench.

A hand lay outstretched on its surface, a piece of black vierstone next to it.

2 5

WALLS OF WHITE

"She was killed instantly. A blow to the head most likely. There are many broken bones, but I cannot imagine she suffered. It would have been too fast."

Dulon stared with vacant eyes at the lump on the bed in front of him. A white sheet covered Aryn's body. Crisp. Untouched. He wanted to rip it off, throw it on the ground, punish it for its purity, its cruel irony.

"Perhaps you should sit down."

"No."

"There is nothing anyone could have done, Dulon."

She knew something.

"It was an accident," the elf continued.

No.

Dulon could feel Vayda's eyes on him, concern radiating from her bearing. The healer sat beside Aryn's bed, her hands folded in her lap. Dulon absently studied the intricate tattoos that snaked up her dark fingers.

Her concern made him sick. Whether or not he could have done anything to stop it, this had been no accident.

'Who' she said, 'who.'

But how could it be? No elf could cause earthquakes; no elf could destroy vierstone. Yet that seemed to be what Aryn had believed—had discovered? If it was a 'who,' the elf would not have wanted their secret revealed.

Renyra stepped forward, looking shaken.

"She's right, Dulon. There is nothing we could have done." She looked no more convinced than he felt. "And there's nothing we can do here now. We should leave." She caught his eye, giving him a significant look.

Dulon nodded curtly and stood. His hands were balled in fists as he turned away from the bed and followed Renyra down the whitewashed corridor of the House of Healing. In all his years in Daro, the building had seldom seen use. Elves did not catch diseases, and injuries from accidents were rare and often minor.

The House of Healing would be as little use to Aryn, but he had not known where else to bring her. She had lived above her workshop and had no family in Daro as far as he knew. Aryn had come from Morcanan, like him, at the founding of Daro. He wondered if Miyela had tried to convince her to return, to abandon the city she had helped build and the upstart leader she called 'lord.' If so, it had not worked. Dulon's chest tightened. It was weeks before any threat of battle, and he had already lost an elf. What if he had kept closer tabs on Aryn's progress? Arrived at her workshop sooner?

Then we would have been crushed too. Unless it was a direct hit. Unless an elf was behind the collapse and would have stayed his hand if others were present.

Dulon's mind was reeling. There were too many variables, too many unknowns and possibilities.

The sun was now peeking through the clouds, painting stripes of light on the pavement. A breeze had picked up and kept blowing Dulon's hair into his face. He ignored the silvery strands in his eyes and followed Renyra blindly, not caring where they went. He needed to think, to talk, to do something.

They were walking through a neighborhood now. Renyra stopped at a house backed against a cliff and stepped through an arched door with a teardrop window carved out at the top. Dulon walked into a simple living space. To one side stood a semi-circular kitchen, to the other, an array of couches, and in the center stood a table and chairs carved in Fieri style. Renyra gestured to one of the chairs and walked to the kitchen, where she began to pour water into a pot. Out of politeness, Dulon sat, though he itched to pace the room.

Renyra set the filled pot on the stove, and with a click, the metal saucer beneath it glowed red. She joined Dulon at the table. Neither spoke at once. Of all the thoughts racing through Dulon's mind, he could not seem to pluck one out and put it in verbal form.

"What exactly did she say to you earlier?" Dulon asked at last.

Renyra closed her eyes in concentration. "She said she was close to 'figuring it out,' but that she wanted to go to her workshop and be sure before coming to you." She squeezed her eyes tighter. "She said she could *see* something. Something in the stone I think? And that there was a piece missing. A piece of the mystery? A piece of the vierstone? I don't know. Then she said she didn't know who could have done it or why." Renyra opened her eyes and looked at him. "That's all. Like I said, she wasn't making sense. It was as though she were talking to herself, not to me. What did she tell you when she first saw the blackened vierstone?"

"That vierstone had a kind of charge running through it, and that the black vierstone did not. Something had stopped it somehow. But she couldn't figure out how it could have happened."

"And then she came to the conclusion that some*one* had stopped it?"

Dulon shook his head.

"That seems to make the most sense out of her words, but we can never be sure now."

Renyra's eyes lowered to the table. Tears welled and suspended on her lower lids, but she blinked them back.

"I didn't know her, but it's just so terrible. Unimaginable. I've never seen—" She trailed away.

Dulon started to raise a hand, but stopped himself, unsure what to do.

"Could ... could an *elf* have been responsible for this?" Renyra looked horrified at the thought.

Dulon sighed. "I don't know, but if an elf truly is responsible for the dying vierstone and earthquakes, he or she would not have wanted Aryn's discovery known." He shook his head. "It's too much coincidence for my liking. The buildings around Aryn's workshop were not even cracked. It was an attack, which means we are dealing with something sentient. But I cannot imagine a terra spirit having the intelligence, let alone the drive to attack an elf based upon her knowledge."

Frustration coursed through Dulon and he slammed a fist on the table, causing Renyra to jump.

"But it is impossible! The vierstone is one thing, but no elf can move the earth!"

"Could the two be separate?"

"The blackened vierstone seems to be a direct effect of the earthquakes. Unless someone is cleverly using the quakes as a cover, I cannot see how the two are unrelated."

A whistling from the kitchen paused their conversation. Renyra leaped from her chair, returning a few moments later with the steaming pot and two cups. She sprinkled a handful of dried flowers into each cup. They sizzled as hot water engulfed them, and a heady aroma rose with the steam and filled the air. Warmth suffused Dulon's hands as he brought a cup to his chest. The scent and heat were calming.

"This is no longer a matter of cracked streets and natural phenomena," said Dulon. "These earthquakes have now caused serious destruction and taken a life. The vierstone quarry is gone, and even the vierstone in the city's foundations is dying. If an elf is causing this, we have to find them."

"How?" Renyra's voice was uncertain, but her eyes were full of determination.

Dulon wanted to throw his hands in the air and say, "I don't know," but he bit back the words.

"I will have to think about it. We must be careful. If this is an elf, we do not want them to know we are on their trail. Tell no one what we suspect."

Renyra nodded.

"In the meantime, we need to focus on the battle. Even if we catch the monster behind this and stop the earthquakes, we have to get that vierstone from the Albaren. Repairing Daro would be useless without it."

Back in his rooms, Dulon thought hard. The news of Aryn's death was bound to spread through the city by morning, and he already had Kyna circulating the news of the quarry. He would have to address the city as a whole, and soon, but first he needed to know how his citizens were reacting to all they heard—fact and rumor. He needed to talk to Kyna.

She was not difficult to find. Dulon had hardly stepped outside when he saw her striding across the Court. She caught sight of him and quickened her pace.

"I was hoping to find you," she said. "I just heard about Aryn. What happened?"

"Come with me."

He led her back inside, walked to the nearest meeting lounge, and closed the door behind them.

"Aryn had found out something about the vierstone," he said in a hushed voice. "I was just going to find her when the earthquake hit and collapsed her workshop." He pushed down a fresh wave of grief and continued. "I think she had discovered what was happening to the vierstone."

He paused. The fewer elves that knew about his search for a potential murderer the better, but Kyna had been talking to the elves of the city for a week and was in a better position than him to conduct a discrete search. He had to trust someone.

"Before I was able to meet with her, she—" He considered his words. "She implied that an elf might be responsible for the dying vierstone—possibly even the earthquakes, though she did not know who, or why."

Kyna's eyebrows rose. "An elf? But how?"

"I have no idea. Aryn seemed to barely understand it, and no other elf in Daro knows vierstone the way she did. But consider it—after she discovered this information, her workshop mysteriously caves in from an earthquake that affected no other parts of the street, let alone the city? It is too neat."

"So you think an elf killed her? And destroyed the vierstone quarry and is causing all of these earthquakes?"

"I have no other explanation, and despite the impossibility of it, it does make sense with the rest of the evidence." He shook his head. "But why would an elf want to destroy vierstone and the city?"

He had been agonizing over the question since his conversation with Renyra. The only explanation he could conceive was too terrible to consider.

"Tell me what you have been hearing among the elves," he said.

"Before I spread news of the quarry, the elves were wary, but mostly indifferent to the decision to support the alliance, if not in full support. I sensed little animosity toward you directly, and most elves would at least grudgingly admit to the need for vierstone. But the news of the black vierstone frightens them. Some think going to battle amid such uncertainty is madness, but most seem to be receptive to your push for securing more vierstone." She leaned forward. "You have support, Dulon. It is not universal, but it is enough. I will keep talking, but I think you should address them now."

"I had planned to. Tonight. But first I want to know what you've noticed about the Morcani. Are there still elves loyal to Miyela in the city? Have you seen anything suspicious or heard whispers?"

"Not specifically," Kyna said slowly, her brows knit. "I would say the Morcani make up more than half of those still wary of the alliance, but I have not seen any evidence of mutiny." Her almond eyes locked on Dulon with a penetrating gaze. "Do you suspect they might be behind this? The vierstone and—" She shook her head. "But Aryn was Morcani."

"I know." Such treachery was unthinkable, but Dulon could not banish the thought from his mind. "But I can think of no other motive for this mindless destruction besides undermining Daro and all it represents. It is no secret that Miyela disapproves of Daro. She did before the Kindom Council, and she certainly does now. What better way to punish a city built on wasted vierstone than to destroy that for which it was founded?"

Kyna didn't answer. She just looked at him, deep in thought.

Dulon sat up straighter and took a deep breath. "Thank you for all you have done. I have one more thing to ask of you."

Kyna looked at him impassively.

"Watch," Dulon said. "Listen. Do not speak a word of what you know, but use it to inform what you see and hear. We must find the elf responsible for this, if it is indeed an elf. Come to me with any suspicions, any information you find. I hope I am wrong about Miyela's involvement, but take special care with the Morcani." He stood. "I will call a city meeting tonight."

Dulon walked through the streets handing out slips of paper with details of the city meeting and encouraging all he encountered to spread word to everyone they knew. By the evening, he was confident that all of Daro knew about the meeting, whether or not they decided to show up. He had decided to host the gathering in the Dining Hall. The space was big enough to hold everyone in the city and was more conducive to discussion than the auditorium-style seating in the Performance Hall rooms.

He sat discreetly at a table near the wall and watched elves slowly file in to join those already seated from dinner. Voices were hushed, the mood subdued. Dulon had planned his speech carefully. The elves needed explanations, they needed rallying, they needed hope. He would do all in his power to give it to them, and as he did so, he would watch. Between himself, Renyra, and Kyna, he hoped to catch any suspicious reactions or whispers among the elves.

When most of the room was full, Dulon rose and walked to the front of the tables. Silence fell.

Dulon stood with his head high. He let his eyes drag across the room, withholding his characteristic smile.

"Much has changed since I last stood here." His words rang and faded in the stillness. "We have been witness to treachery and to cruel words. We have seen our city break from earthquakes we do not understand. We have watched in terror and confusion as the stone that gives this city—gives *us*—life and longevity, fades and dies before our eyes. And." He paused and took a breath. "We have lost a valued member of our community. A skilled Builder. A kinswoman and a friend." Eyes turned down, heads bowed, elves traced the star over their breasts.

"I know that some of you still have misgivings about the wisdom of the alliance. I understand. Why should we spend time, energy, and resources on a risky crusade while our own home threatens to crumble beneath our feet? But will closing our gates to the world do anything to save our city? If, *when*, we do discover the source of these catastrophes, how will we rebuild without vierstone?" He let the question sit.

"Now it is more important than ever to remain united. If we turn on one another, we will fall as surely as this city will fall." Dulon looked from one face to another. Green eyes of every shade shone back at him, betraying nothing.

Dulon straightened and relaxed his shoulders.

"Now." He allowed a grin to begin climbing up his face. "Let's work together." Several elves seemed to break out of a trance, startled by his change in demeanor. He started to pace.

"Here's what we know. The earthquakes have occurred in a seemingly random pattern across the city, though never in the same place twice. The source of the earthquakes, whatever that is, is *within* the walls of Daro—the earthquakes do not extend beyond the city. Something, likely the same source as the earthquakes, is destroying vierstone, turning it black following damage from the quakes." He clapped his hands together and looked up through his lashes. "Among us we have over a thousand pairs of eyes and ears. Surely one of them has seen or heard something significant. If you are the owner of such an appendage, please speak now."

No one spoke. Elves glanced around, waiting for someone else to break the silence.

A cleared throat caused a rippling of heads toward the center of the hall.

"I do not have any observations to share, but how is the vierstone turning black? What is happening to it?"

It was Veldon. He asked the question politely, as though he were an apprentice inquiring of his craft mentor. It was not a question Dulon wanted to answer.

"I don't know. Aryn had been researching the blackened vierstone before her—accident."

Veldon flushed and dropped his eyes. "Oh."

A sudden hope welled up in Dulon. Of course. Why hadn't he thought of it before? Veldon could work vierstone. Could he have spoken with Aryn prior to her death? Could he himself find out what was happening to the vierstone?

"Did she mention her research to you?" Dulon tried to keep his voice casual.

Veldon shook his head. "No. I never had the chance to work with her."

Dulon's heart fell, but he kept his composure. He would have to consult Veldon in private regarding his knowledge of vierstone. Dulon did not want a repeat of Aryn.

"What did Aryn find?" called a voice from the back of the room.

Dulon did his best to repeat Aryn's description of vierstone's properties and what may have happened to the destroyed vierstone.

"But how can we save it?" someone shouted. "Is the vierstone in Faeran safe?"

"As far as I know," said Dulon. "But I will ask the elves of Tura as soon as I am able."

"It shouldn't be breaking in the first place!" a Morcani said. "Morcanan has endured at least as many earthquakes as this in the last decade, and it has never sustained any damage."

A chorus of agreement met this, but no one had an explanation, Dulon least of all.

"How can earthquakes be contained to a single city? Are we sure they even *are* earthquakes?"

"Two elves have now been directly hit! How can we stay safe?"

The meeting dragged on, degenerating into voiced fears and complaints with many questions and few answers. Dulon shared all that he knew, with the careful exception that the source of their fears was likely a some*one* rather than a some*thing*. No one knew any more about vierstone than Aryn had, and suggestions of explanations were becoming increasingly far-fetched.

"A volcano is forming beneath the city!"

"It is an electric current from a far-off storm cell striking like lightning!"

"It is Riu's judgment come to pass!"

It was not until the suggestion of a dark creature from the depths of the earth tunneling and sapping vierstone of its vitality that anything of interest came up.

"I do not know about a great tunneling monster from hell, but I have seen some strange things the last week along the shoreline," said Carden, a fisherman. "Twice in the last few days, I have pulled long, black-mottled fish from my catch. They have bulbous eyes and fanged teeth and their fins are more like arms, with grasping fingers. They put up a hell of a fight, lashing out at me as well as the other fish. I have never seen anything of the like."

Dulon perked up in interest. "Has anyone else noticed ... disconcerting creatures around?"

Torron, a Fieri elf, stood. "I have been on gate duty this week. A few nights ago—that was the night after the big quake that broke the viaduct—I saw shadows moving on the edge of the light cast by the city as I closed the gates for the night. They moved in no natural way, and I thought I was imagining things. I even thought I saw pinpricks of light that might have been eyes. Tonight I saw a similar thing. I closed the gates just before I came here."

A chorus of muttering broke out. Unease prickled Dulon's skin. These stories sparked memories of days long past, memories he had not thought of for centuries and had no desire to remember. Renyra's account of the demonic dog had disturbed him more than he let on, but he had seen the same apprehension in Firas's eyes as she had described the beast. Now there were more of them? But it couldn't be happening again—

The surrounding mutters were punctuated by *shush*ing as another voice spoke up.

"I went hunting beyond the city earlier this week." Renyra stood, though she hardly topped the heads of many an elf sitting down. "I was attacked by a monstrous dog with shaggy fur, black teeth, and crimson eyes. It was a horrible creature." She showed the fading claw marks on her arms. Several elves gasped.

Dulon could feel fear spreading through the room. He needed to step in. But what could all of this mean? How could creatures from nightmares have anything to do with the earthquakes and vierstone? What was happening to the world? Dulon suppressed a shudder as he thought of the earlier accusation that all of this was judgment from Riu.

Don't be ridiculous. There is an explanation for all of this, you just can't see it yet.

Dulon held up a hand. The room slowly became quiet again.

"Thank you to everyone who shared their experiences and insight. There is no reason to panic. There is an explanation for what is happening, and we will find it." He spoke with a light confidence, his posture relaxed and expression calm.

"I want a watch set at the gate every night." Dulon raised his voice. "I will send an armed party beyond the city to investigate the countryside. As for those of us in the city, I want anything out of the ordinary reported directly to me. Anything. All earthquakes will be reported to me, no matter the degree of shaking or damage caused. Gellion should return any day now with details of our alliance with the Albaren. I expect a shipment of weapons and armor from Liera within the week."

He stood tall and brushed his hair out of his eyes. "I need you to be with me on this. We will find answers, and we will find solutions. We will fight the Albaren's battle and come through it having liberated a struggling nation *and* with the vierstone we need to rebuild the city we have saved. We will emerge from this fire stronger than before—just as the elves always have."

Dulon smiled. Thousands of eyes glinted back at him, fiery with pride and determination. Among them, Maranyl wore a smug grin.

AN AUDIENCE OF MEN

There were no prisons in Faeran, so Gellion did not have any standard by which to compare the quality of his cell. He did know that the cells he had passed to get to the upper floors of the prison had been in much worse condition than his, with multiple people per cell and no windows. He was alone, at least, and a high window lined with bars let in feeble rays of sunshine to one corner. He stared at the stripes, studying the way they bent at the intersection of floor and wall. Twice he had watched their cycle from floor to ceiling, fading to darkness in between.

Anger, indignation, fear, guilt—Gellion had felt them all and labelled each as useless in his present situation. Mostly he was bored. The A'vaeri kept him reasonably sane during the long hours of solitude. He ran through the familiar motions both in his head and with his hands and feet, but even this practice could not keep his thoughts fully occupied.

Servants brought him food. While the meals paled in comparison to his dinner at the Arceria Mansion, the fare was passable. He tried to question the servants each time they came, but they remained silent. He had no idea what was happening outside the prison and no idea what was going to happen to him. He was not particularly afraid for his fate. The worst case scenario, he imagined, was being sentenced to death, but the possibility seemed small, and he could probably find a way to escape if it came to it.

What really worried Gellion was the potential damage he had done to the alliance. Dulon had sent him to Albarad as an emissary to secure an agreement between the elves and the humans, and instead he had publicly caused the death of a prominent political figure at a party. He remembered the looks of terror, even of hatred on the faces he had passed as the guards led him through the mansion. He had been too shocked to protest.

Gellion buried his face in his hands and constricted his fingers until the nails bit into his skin.

It was not my fault, he repeated to himself over and over. *He was trying to kill me. I defended myself. He fell. I did not push him.*

An accident. That's all it had been. A terrible, horrifying accident.

The man's death should not bother him so much. The world was better off without the lecherous old man. Gellion had done nothing wrong, nothing to be ashamed of. Not to mention Gellion was about to go to battle. Causing death was something he had accepted with that decision. Gellion clasped his hands to stop the shaking.

It was not my fault.

Over the last two days, the man's screams had plagued Gellion's mind, but so too had the terrifying power of his own anger. After nearly a millennia of life, Gellion had become all too acquainted with his temper, but he had always managed to keep it in check, at least to the point that he had never caused physical harm. Nicabar's death had been an accident, but in that moment, he would have killed the man. He had wanted to hurt him.

What if that same anger had possessed him while in the company of an elf? What if instead of a party full of Albaren aristocracy, his own kin had run upon a scene of him staring over the railing at a body he had put there? What if it had been a cliff—Gellion shuddered to think of the power of circumstance, the power of his own anger.

Creaking metal drew Gellion back to his surroundings. The door of his cell swung forward on rusty hinges, and a man stepped through. He wore a soft cotton robe cinched around his ample waist with a cord. His hair was shaved to the skin, and watery black eyes shone beneath a deep-set brow.

"Good afternoon, sir. I am Father Alban, cleric of the Central District of Tradira." He bowed his head and smiled at Gellion.

Gellion made no response.

"I am sorry it has taken so long for me to come," said Father Alban. "The King did not hear about your arrest until this morning, I am afraid, and it took until after noonmass for his servants to find me."

He looked at Gellion as though expecting a pardon for his tardiness and thanks for his eventual arrival. Gellion gave him neither. The cleric sighed, closed the cell door behind him, and pulled a chair from a corner to face Gellion. The wood creaked as he lowered his bulk onto it.

"I will come to the point, then. Nicabar Arceria fell to a premature death two nights ago, and numerous witnesses claim you pushed him over the ledge."

"I did not push him," Gellion said calmly, his heart racing. The patronizing smile Father Alban gave him set his teeth on edge, but Gellion kept his peace.

"Now, now. Denial is no way to come to terms with our mistakes. I do not think you planned the murder of Marchon Arceria, but you did kill him."

Gellion clenched his teeth and took a deep breath. "He attacked me. I pushed him away, but he tripped and fell over the balcony. I did not push him over the edge, nor did I intend to kill him."

"Why would Marchon Arceria attack you?"

"I danced with his wife at the ball. He was drunk."

"Ah," Father Alban said in an all too knowing tone. Gellion wanted to scrub the condescending smile from the man's face.

"I did nothing but dance with her."

"Of course. Of course." Alban leaned his elbows on his knees, looking Gellion in the eye. "I am not asking for explanations. I am asking for you to confess. The Almighty forgives those who admit their sins and show remorse."

Anger pricked at Gellion's skin. "What exactly are you asking me to confess to?"

Father Alban raised his eyebrows. "Why, to murdering Marchon Arceria."

"I did not murder him! His death was an accident."

"The citizens of the Central District do not see it that way, I am afraid. They call for justice, and rightly so. Confess and we can publicly pardon you. Show your repentance, and the people will allow us to release you." He smiled. "Though I would not remain in Tradira long, if I were you."

Anger was burning in Gellion's chest again. "You ask me to stand before a crowd, say that I intentionally killed Marchon Arceria, and plea for forgiveness?"

"I ask that you admit your transgression and repent of your actions so that the public can see your sincerity."

"I thought it was the Almighty's forgiveness I sought."

Anger flashed in the cleric's beady eyes. "You will confess and repent, or you will remain in prison." He stood. "It is your choice."

Gellion glared at him, the absurdity of it all beyond his ability to form a retort.

"If you decide to do the right thing, tell the servant who brings your dinner tonight," said Father Alban. "They will get the message to me. I will come for you in the morning, if you agree, and you can be on your way out of the city by afternoon. Good day to you, sir."

He left the room without a backward glance.

Gellion sat for a long time, simmering in rage. All things considered, it was not so bad, what they were asking him to do. Bend the truth, suffer a few minutes of shame, and he could be on his way. It was not as though Gellion gave a damn what any of the Albaren thought of him. Were it only his own feelings on the line, he would stand before all of Tradira and say anything they wanted without batting an eye. But how would this confession affect the relations between the humans and elves? He supposed that a confession was better than sitting in prison in the country with which he was meant to negotiate. He had no choice. Either he confessed, he remained in prison, or he escaped, and the last two would almost assuredly dissolve any terms of friendship between the two races.

Gellion could not grasp how confessing to a crime would redeem him in the eyes of the Albaren. Divine forgiveness was not something granted by the approval of men, to be exclaimed before an audience. How had his reputation become reliant on admitting to murder? The entire thing was ridiculous. Gellion slammed his fist into his mattress. A cloud of dust exploded from the fabric and floated upward in slow motion.

He would have to swallow his pride and his anger and do this, however counterproductive it seemed, for the sake of the elves. It was his responsibility to account for his mistake. He hoped it would be enough.

He desperately wished he had just gone home after dinner that night. It had seemed such a small decision to step onto that balcony for a few moments. The memory of his anger washed over him again, and with it, the face of his old mentor flashed before his eyes. Gellion squeezed them shut. The gifted metalworker had been reserved and slow to anger, but in him Gellion had sensed the same penchant for deep emotion as in himself. Gellion had never seen the man lose his temper, but he had sensed the power of it boiling under his skin, seen the effort it took for him to control it.

But he did not control it. It escaped him once, and it destroyed his life.

Had Gellion made the same mistake? Was Gellion following in Kaelo's footsteps?

That night, Gellion spoke with the servant bearing his dinner.

The next morning, he lay in wait for Father Alban's arrival.

Father Alban met him with a smug smile and two guards. Each sported a sword at his waist. Gellion wondered if they would return his dagger after this was over. He doubted it.

They led him down through the levels of the prison and into the sunlit street outside. Gellion squinted in the light, eyes watering. Passersby stared open-mouthed as the guards led him toward the court of the Central District. Father Alban walked in front of him in a stately manner, as though the head of a formal procession.

When the court came into view, Gellion felt a jolt in his chest. It was filled with people, all facing the bridges that joined the Dom Regirium to the Dom Creda. On the lower bridge stood King Naval.

The guards walked Gellion into the Dom Regirium, ascended the central stairs, and led him down a corridor that ended in a glass door. As the sun's glare shifted, Gellion could see Naval through the glass. His expression was grave.

A torrent of voices reached the bridge when Gellion took his place beside the king. Among whispers and excited chattering came angry shouts. Naval gave Gellion an appraising look, then raised a hand, muting the crowd.

"My citizens." Naval's voice carried through the court, echoing off of the buildings. "Marchons, earls, clerics, and tradesmen. I stand here before you with an elf from the city of Daro. He came here at my behest, to seal an alliance between the elves and men." Murmurs rose. Men and women turned to each other, sharing their reactions to this piece of news. "We requested the aid of Daro in our war against the Dierna. They have accepted." Naval paused and waited until silence once again engulfed the court.

"Gellion has been our guest here for nearly a fortnight, and three nights ago, attended a ball at the Arceria Mansion. Marchon Nicabar Arceria, head of the Arceria family, fell to his death from a balcony on which Gellion was found with the Marchon's wife." He turned to Gellion with a blank stare. "None witnessed what happened save Marchess Chiara Arceria."

A ripple of heads in the crowd led to a woman standing near the base of the bridge.

"Marchess Arceria claims that Gellion pushed her husband over the balcony in a fit of rage."

Naval raised a hand again to halt the angry cries building from the masses, but Gellion was no longer paying attention to the crowd. He was staring at Chiara. She met his gaze with a look of unmistakable satisfaction.

"Now, now," Naval said. "Gellion was not unprovoked, I am sure, but he has come here today to address the Central District."

Naval nodded to Gellion. It took Gellion a few moments to regain his composure and remember what he was supposed to be saying. He pushed down the anger simmering under his skin and dragged his eyes away from Chiara. He raised his head and took a deep breath.

"Heathen!" a voice barked.

"Murderer!" cried another.

Gellion ignored them.

"People of Tradira." His voice filled the court, silencing any further protests. "As your king has said, I came to this city to form bonds of trust and friendship between our races. For generations, I have watched your people grow, expand, and increase in wealth. Over the last week, I have come to know many of your society better than I could have imagined in such a short time."

A corner of his mouth drew up in a grimace that could have been mistaken for a regretful smile. He let his gaze fall on Chiara. Though he kept his voice carefully under control, he did not hide the fury burning behind his gaze.

"The fault for Marchon Arceria's death is mine to bear. I did not intend for it to happen. Marchon Arceria's death was an accident born of a moment's dispute. A moment I wish I could take back."

Chiara shifted under the weight of his accusing stare. He raised his eyes to address the full court.

"I ask for your grace and for your forgiveness." The words nearly caught in his throat, so loath was he to utter them. Taking a breath, he swallowed the last of his pride and continued. "I ask that you do not judge my people on the rashness of my own behavior and a moment's weakness. I ask for your mercy."

Stillness settled on the court. Hostility was still evident from the audience, and many faces retained their anger, but others bore expressions of hesitation and confusion.

King Naval gave Gellion a lingering look, then faced the court.

"Gellion has confessed and asked to be absolved of his crime. I hereby publicly pardon him for the death of Marchon Nicabar Arceria. May we all show mercy as the Almighty commands us."

No one protested. Naval placed a hand on Gellion's shoulder and turned him toward the Dom Regirium. Gellion clenched his jaw and let the king lead him off the bridge. He should be relieved, he knew. He had saved the alliance and was free to return to his people, to forget any of this nightmare had ever happened. Yet anger still gripped his insides, tinged by a guilt that had nothing to do with the people he had just addressed.

As he walked through the glass door at the end of the bridge, Gellion looked out the corner of his eyes to see Chiara standing with her arms crossed, watching him.

<hr>

Gellion's departure from Tradira was uneventful. A servant brought him his bag, filled with all his possessions—except his dagger. As soon as Gellion left the Central District, his reception was no more hostile than at his arrival. He doubted the rest of the city knew anything of what happened in the Central District. He doubted they cared.

He sighed as he began the arduous trek up the brittle hills north of the city. Dust coated his boots, sweat slicked his back, and thoughts clouded his mind. Chiara had betrayed him. He was sure of it. Had she merely been playing games and then turned on him when things turned serious? Or had she planned this from the beginning? She could not possibly have known Nicabar would attack him on a balcony.

But she may have known he would attack me, and set up the most convenient location for the confrontation.

The sweat on Gellion's back turned to ice. Nicabar had tripped before he fell. Gellion had thought the man just turned his ankle as he stepped back, but Chiara had been on the ground near him—

She wouldn't kill him. She wouldn't frame me.

Gellion berated himself for his own naiveté. He hardly knew the woman, and from what he did know, sentiment did not seem a priority in her life. He had been an idiot and risked everything he had come here for.

But if Chiara orchestrated the whole thing, the man's death was not truly my fault.

He had nothing to feel guilty about.

Gellion kicked a gorse bush, the thorns breaking on his thick boots. He ran up the rest of the hill and looked down on the cove where he had anchored his boat. It bobbed just offshore. At least he would not have to wait for low tide again.

The day was good for sailing, and Gellion felt some of his anxiety ease as he skidded over the waves away from Tradira. He knew the source of the weight in his chest, and knew too that it would not go away until he acknowledged it. Whether or not Chiara had planned Nicabar's death, Gellion had still lost his temper and held some measure of responsibility for the accident. Nicabar had been a greedy drunk who treated his wife poorly, but he had been a man. It was not Gellion's place to decide his fate.

Gellion bowed his head into the wind and wiped the water from his eyes.

"Forgive me," he whispered to the air.

No storms darkened the horizons of Gellion's journey, and with favorable winds, he saw the spires of Daro reaching above the cliffs within two days. The joy he had not allowed himself to feel welled in his throat as the prospect of home drew near. He thought of Valder and Veldon and smiled. He even missed Dulon, the lovable fop.

He had barely been gone two weeks, yet it seemed years since the infamous parting of the Council. He wondered how things had gone since then. How had Dulon handled Miyela's betrayal? Were battle preparations in full motion by now or were the elves waiting on word from him? He had not expected his trip to take so long.

The glittering wharf of Daro formed the center of a pendulum as the tip of Gellion's boat swung from side to side. He grinned broadly as specks became bodies, and one of them lifted a hand in greeting. From the glint of fair hair and the elf's lanky posture, Gellion recognized Firas. He must be working on one of the ships. Gellion wondered if Valder was with him and squinted to get a closer look.

A vibration rent the water.

Gellion stiffened and looked around him. Waves chopped at the sides of his boat, but he saw nothing unusual.

The vibration came again, stronger this time.

Gellion's heart beat faster. Was this another earthquake? Gellion returned his attention to the wharf, but none of the elves seemed to have noticed anything.

A whale?

A third vibration was accompanied by a resonant growling from beneath the water. Gellion had never heard a whale make that noise. He saw Firas standing alert now, a hand shading his eyes.

One moment the water was still, the day bright.

Then everything was a thrashing mass of spray and canvas, a bone-chilling shriek filling the air.

Gellion yelled as he flew into the air and landed in a writhing mass of waves and glistening skin.

Sound muted as he went underwater. Time slowed as he rose to the surface.

He gasped for air and spun in the water, trying to get his bearings. He could hear the frantic shouts of elves in one direction and splashing in the other. He turned toward the splashing. His blood ran cold.

The sailboat was a twisted mass of metal, its canvas wrapped around the sinuous body of a creature Gellion could not have thought up in his worst nightmares. It was larger than a whale, but its body was tubular, tapering to nothing at one end. Jagged spines tore through inky flesh along its back and belly. Its front flippers bent and elongated to resemble arms, and in its head, giant orbs sat where eyes should have been. The thing tore at the boat's sail with row upon row of razor teeth as it continued to screech and writhe.

Transfixed by the horrible scene, Gellion took several moments to register the screams of the elves on the wharf.

"Gellion!"

He turned to see Firas paddling toward him in a row boat.

"No!" Gellion mouthed, trying not to splash as he waved an arm at Firas. "Go back!"

With a glance at the creature behind him, he slipped beneath the water, swimming as fast as he could just beneath the surface. Ahead, he could see the hull of Firas's boat below the water. He headed straight for it.

Hands grasped his shirt and pulled him up. He rolled into the boat, half flooding it with water.

"Are you alright?" Firas's eyes were huge.

"Fine," Gellion gasped. "Go!"

Firas's head whipped toward the open sea. Gellion would not have thought it possible for Firas's eyes to get bigger, but they did. Gellion pushed himself up and saw the wreckage of his sailboat floating in the water, the creature nowhere to be seen. Firas plunged his oar into the sea, rowing frantically, his eyes set on the wharf a ship-length away. Gellion saw Valder standing at the end of the closest dock, waving for them to hurry.

His brother's hands grabbed Gellion under the arms as the rowboat slammed into the side of the dock, and he scrambled backward onto the slippery wood. Just as they pulled Firas out of the boat, it exploded into the air. Gellion saw a black shape coming at him and lunged away, dragging Valder with him and hitting the ground hard.

He heard a crunch as the end of the dock fell into the water.

"To the shore!" he bellowed, scrambling to his feet. He pulled Firas up by the collar and shoved both him and Valder ahead of him. The three elves sprinted up the dock, not daring to look behind them. Another shriek rent the air as they leapt from wood onto solid rock. Valder staggered as he landed, and Firas and Gellion bowled into him. All three landed in a sodden heap.

More splashes, more splinters, then silence. Gellion untangled himself from his brother and sat up. The dock on which they had stood moments before was gone. In its place, a hideous head hovered above the water. Its bulbous eyes stared unblinking, its teeth bared, then it slipped beneath the water.

"What—was it?" Gellion took in great lungfuls of air. He could hear the pounding of feet on the docks—elves drawn by the ruckus.

"A monster," Firas said. "And not the first we have seen in your absence."

Gellion looked at his friend. Firas's eyes were shadowed with worry.

"You have missed a lot, brother." The same worry showed in

Valder's eyes, though it was much more out of place on the usually cheery face.

A sense of foreboding spread through Gellion's bones. Water dripped down his nose as he looked out to the now still sea.

What had he returned to?

PART III

KNIFE IN THE NIGHT

A loud silence filled the room as Dulon pushed through the door. He looked around, then bit his lip to prevent it quirking into a smile. Gellion sat straight-backed, his gaze concentrated on Dulon in a way that suggested he was pointedly not looking at something else. Next to him, Kyna leaned back in her chair, toying with a pen.

"Morning," Dulon said cheerily, dropping into a chair opposite the two. This time he could not hide the grin that spread over his face. Gellion cocked an eyebrow as though berating him for unprofessional conduct.

"Shall we start?" Gellion asked.

"Of course." Dulon cleared his throat and sat straighter. He would tease Gellion later.

In the two weeks since Gellion's return, Dulon had not extracted a word from him about the frequency of his outings with Kyna, but it was not for lack of trying.

"The last of the supplies arrived from Tura two days ago," Dulon said. "We have sufficient armor and weapons to outfit an army of one thousand—most of Daro. Some elves should stay behind to man the city in any case, and I am gathering a list of volunteers to remain."

Dulon placed a list on the table in front of him. It had not been difficult to fill.

"Now," he continued, "do you have the reports from this week?"

Gellion nodded and produced a roll of parchment. "The guards at the wharf and the city gates report continued disturbances and several attempted breaches of the city by 'unnatural'," he spoke the word in quotations, "beings. No reported casualties from any encounter. Another hunting expedition left this morning, led by Renyra, and is scouting north and east of the city."

He took a deep breath.

"Power outages in the northern neighborhoods and continued problems in the buildings nearest the Court, though power is restored in the guest quarters. A section of the Rale path is down through the housing district. "

He scanned down the paper. "Three more earthquakes. One near the wharf, one in the orchard across from the greenhouses, and one in the east neighborhoods. Damage was average, with split ground and cracked buildings, but no collapses." He looked up. "I do not think elves should go into the greenhouses until the glass is repaired."

Dulon sighed and nodded. He was adding stars to his map of Daro. The new locations fit perfectly in the grid forming across the map. If he had doubted this was the work of a sentient being before, he could not deny the probability now. He couldn't imagine why the earthquakes were filling in a grid of the city, but the order could not be a coincidence.

"That just about fills it." Dulon shook his head. "We may have missed a location from the first few weeks, but these are the only gaps— near the front gate, the Archives, and the central portion of Master's Street." He pointed at each empty space in turn.

"What then?" Kyna's eyes were roving over the map. "What happens when the grid is complete?"

"Our punishment is complete?" Dulon gave a half-hearted smile.

Gellion snorted. "Punishment from whom? And what would be the purpose of causing earthquakes evenly spread over the entire city, then stopping?"

"Obsessive perfectionism?"

Gellion glared at him.

"Oh, I don't know." Dulon sighed in exasperation. "If all of this is happening to make Daro weak, to undermine everything we have done and all we stand for, a thorough destruction is better than a haphazard one."

"You still think this is coming from Miyela?" asked Gellion. "You have not found a spec of proof, Dulon."

"There is no proof yet." Dulon looked to Kyna expectantly.

"I have no evidence," Kyna said. "But I have heard whispers. Disquiet simmers among the Morcani like a quiet current, one that I can sense but not pinpoint. They still do not want to fight. That much is obvious. Some resent Daro." She cast a sideways glance at Dulon. He knew 'Daro' meant 'Daro's leaders.' "We do not know all that Miyela said or did before she left. She could very well have left some devoted followers behind."

"You mean spies?" Gellion let out a sharp laugh. "This is ridiculous. Why would Miyela spend so much time and energy on a city worlds away from her and her people? Yes she was against the alliance and wanted her people to have no part of it, but that does not mean she vowed to destroy the city, let alone discovered how to create earthquakes and destroy vierstone!"

"You heard what she said on the docks," Dulon said, "*Who will remain behind to watch their city crumble*?"

"That does not mean she is causing it."

"How many of the volunteers remaining in Daro are Morcani?" Kyna asked.

Dulon stared at her. "I ... I don't know." He grabbed the list and scanned it. Dread weighed in his chest as he progressed down the names. "At least two thirds of them."

Kyna shrugged a shoulder and raised her eyebrows.

Gellion threw his arms in the air. "How is that suspicious?! The Morcani that stayed behind may be loyal to Daro, but they do not agree with going to battle, so they are electing to remain behind. That is their right."

"Or an opportunity," said Kyna.

"To do what may I ask?" Gellion narrowed his eyes at her.

"To finish what they started."

"And what is that?"

"That is what we have not yet discovered."

Fire blazed in Gellion's eyes, but he took a deep breath. "May I remind you of one important detail? The first earthquake was the night of the welcome feast—before we had even announced the prospect of a battle, let alone agreed to it."

Dulon opened his mouth, then closed it. Gellion was right. Miyela would have had to come to Daro with the predisposed notion to destroy the city. Had she? She had known Dulon was the Lord of Daro long before her arrival, and her dislike of him had been no secret for centuries. Could she have come to the Council with the purpose of destroying Daro, or at least its reputation? Even for Miyela, it seemed extreme, but it was not impossible.

"Not to mention," Gellion continued, "the Morcani put more stock in tangible spirituality than any other Kindom." He gave Dulon a significant look. "You should be well aware of that. Vierstone is a sacred substance. Can you really imagine Miyela would desecrate an entire city's worth of lifestone to prove a point? That is assuming she could even discover how to destroy it, and since Aryn, a vierstone master *and* a Morcani might I add, could hardly understand how to do it, I find that highly unlikely."

Dulon frowned. He had no counterargument to that. No matter the extremities of Miyela's beliefs and ambition, she was devoted to Riu, and he could not imagine her deliberately causing the death of an elf, let alone one of her own Kindom. But what if Aryn's death really had been an accident? Or caused by another Morcani who had gone too far?

"You make valid points," Dulon said with resignation, "but I still think Miyela could be behind parts of this, if not all of it. Who is to say the very devotion you speak of could not drive her to extremes for the greater good?"

Gellion shook his head, clearly not convinced. "Speculation and spying have their place, but I think the best way to discover the source of all of this is to catch the culprit in the act. We should stake out the remaining three locations day and night."

Dulon nodded, reluctant to leave behind their discussion of Miyela.

"Not a bad idea, but we would need to be discreet, and we should observe from a distance."

The elves of Daro would depart the city in a week to meet the Albaren. Dulon would need to recruit quite a few trusted elves for a watch for that long, but he was determined to solve this mystery before leaving the city.

And if the Morcani are somehow responsible, I do not want to give them free reign of Daro while we are gone.

"I will speak with the gate guards to keep a watch on the entry courtyard," said Dulon. "Gellion, you take Master's Street. Kyna the Archives. Recruit elves you trust completely to help."

Gellion and Kyna nodded. Dulon felt the corners of his mouth rising with their confidence. His eyes sparkled.

"I know it can be difficult to keep your head when one of these earthquakes happens, but if we keep our distance and know what we are looking for, we might have a chance of seeing something."

They saw nothing. Two nights passed with no earthquakes, and Dulon was growing impatient.

All those earthquakes when I would have done anything to stop them, and now Daro is still.

Dulon paced the top of the wall. The sloping gates of Daro stood just to his right, sealed against the night. Sweat beaded on Dulon's brow, and each breath of air hung thick in his lungs. He could hear the hum of insects, and the distant rush of the tide struggled through the soupy air. He stopped his pacing and turned his back to Torron, who stood with his hands on the parapet, gazing into the hazy darkness beyond the city.

Dulon had decided to accompany the watch himself tonight, and for as many nights as it took for a chance at witnessing the earthquake he knew would strike soon. There was no reason for the culprit to be suspicious. For all any elf knew, Dulon was simply keeping watch outside the gates, guarding against dark monsters. His focus, however, was turned to the other side of the wall. His eyes scanned the deserted courtyard below him. No elves. No movement.

The moon was just past its highest point, and it was growing harder to concentrate. Weariness tugged at Dulon's eyelids and dragged his mind away from his task. In less than five days, he would be leading a thousand elves out of the city—taking them to battle for the first time in over three hundred years. Suddenly it all seemed absurd. What had he been thinking?

What if Miyela was right?

He clenched his fists. No. The Albaren needed help, and the elves needed vierstone. If all went to plan, they would only need to fight a single battle. He would not let it become a war of months or years.

Still, the minor fiasco that had been Gellion's diplomatic trip to Albarad concerned him. Dulon had expected Gellion to return within a week of his departure with details of the alliance and reports of meetings and councils with Albaren officials and military leaders. Instead, Gellion had been gone two weeks, passed among foppish aristocracy, and put on trial for murder. Hardly the promising start to a fruitful alliance.

Dulon had cautioned Gellion to keep the details of his trip quiet from most of Daro. The elves needed no further reason to balk against the upcoming battle. But Gellion's experience concerned Dulon for other reasons. From Gellion's account of the Albaren Marchons, human perception of the elves was a mixed bag to say the least, wrought with suspicion and fear. How would an army of human soldiers react to marching into battle with a thousand elves? Why did King Naval trust the elves so thoroughly when his people viewed them as unnatural heathens?

King Naval had seemed unconcerned according to Gellion, confident and matter-of-fact about the alliance, and Dulon took solace from the confidence with which Commander Vensure had outlined the battle plans. And, as Gellion had pointed out, the humans they sought to help were not the conceited popinjays of the Central District of Tradira, they were the innocent residents of the villages along the Albaren border. So long as the elves could work with the commanders of the Albaren army, the suspicion of the soldiers should be of little concern, let alone the attitude of the Marchons on a distant coastline.

A high whinny cut through the stillness, and Dulon jumped, his head jerking toward the stables, but the sound died away in the heavy air. Nothing else stirred.

"It does get to you." Torron's voice rumbled from the outer parapet.

Dulon turned to see him still facing the scrubby hills.

"What?"

"Watching for demons night after night. *Seeing* demons night after night—you start to see eyes in every shadow, movement in every breeze." Torron sighed. "Why are they here?"

The question expected no answer, and Dulon had none to give.

"I have heard the reports of the hunting parties," Torron continued. "I have watched outside the walls with my own eyes. Creatures that look as though they crawled from the depths of the earth. And they are converging on Daro."

Of all the problems facing his city, this was the one Dulon had done his best to ignore—at first. Believing that the earthquakes and dying vierstone were the work of an elf was hard enough, but there was no conceivable way an elf could create an epidemic of demon animals. Only one thing had ever accomplished that feat, and it was an explanation so utterly impossible that it was not worth considering. So, the phenomenon had sat as a disturbing enigma in Dulon's mind beneath the importance of earthquakes and vierstone—until Gellion's near miss with the sea serpent. It was one thing to guard the walls at night and hunt in parties, but the sea was essential to Daro's prosperity. Anything that threatened the elves' ships threatened the city's livelihood.

"We will fight them." Dulon put as much confidence into the words as he could muster. "Daro will not fall—not from earthquakes and not from monsters."

Or from battles.

He ran his hands over his face. He had begun to wonder if it would not be better for the elves to return to Faeran for a time after this battle was finished—return to Daro when whatever was afflicting it had passed. But the thought of giving up and fleeing to Tura, or, he shuddered, to Morcanan, was unbearable. He would not admit defeat unless he had no other option. All was not yet lost.

A low hiss from Torron caught Dulon's attention. The dark elf motioned to Dulon with a hand, though his eyes remained focused beyond the wall. Dulon strode silently to his side, following his gaze into the scrub hills.

At first he saw nothing, then his eyes fixed on a glint of light. Just beyond the glow of the city, the shadows shifted and moved in a pattern indicative of an animal, though Dulon could not make out an outline. Two pinpoints of red appeared amid the shifting mass, then four more sets behind them, like candles sparking to life. A shiver ran down Dulon's spine. They were only eyes, yet he could feel the hair on his arms standing on end. There was something *wrong* about those eyes, though for the life of him, Dulon could not describe what it was.

"Have you seen them before?" Dulon whispered.

"Yes. And others like them. But I have never seen them in full view out of the shadows. They hover at the edge of darkness, watching and waiting. They do not like the lights of the gates."

"What about the rest of the wall?"

"I do not think they can scale it. They move on four legs."

"Have you tried to shoot one?"

"Yes. They vanish like smoke as soon as I release the string."

As though they had heard Torron's words, the eyes blinked out of view.

Dulon knew he should turn back to his watch of the inner courtyard, but some instinct kept him from turning his back on whatever was in those shadows.

Don't be ridiculous. You are on top of a three-story wall.

Another whinny rose shrilly in the air, accompanied this time by several bleats from the paddock outside the stables. Dulon leapt back to the inside parapet. Nothing stirred in the streets below, but after a few moments, he heard a deep rumble, and the stone beneath his hands vibrated. He looked around wildly. A sharp crack reverberated through the courtyard, and he saw a cloud of dust spew from the walls of the Archives.

Kyna.

Dulon ran along the wall and down the spiral staircase next to the gate. Torron called his name, but Dulon ignored him. He skipped the last few steps to land in the courtyard. In the distance, another goat bleated, followed by a very elven scream.

Panic tore through Dulon. He sprinted to the nearest levit board, slammed his heel down, and sped past the stables, the Archives looming before him. Should he call Kyna's name? He opened his mouth, but bit back his voice. It seemed foolish to draw attention to himself. What if she had found the elf responsible for all of this? What if they had attacked her? Surprise would give Dulon an advantage. He slowed his momentum when he had passed the Archives, but he did not see Kyna anywhere. The night was again silent.

Indecision and frustration battled within Dulon.

"Kyna!" he shouted, his voice bouncing off the buildings around him. There was no answer.

Dulon jumped to the ground and turned in a circle, scanning the dark streets. Had she gone down Master's Street or toward the Court? He let out a forceful breath, then turned his feet toward Master's Street.

After two steps, his feet stuttered to a halt. A flash of silver had caught his eye along the outer walls of the Performance Hall. Dulon glanced down Master's Street, then turned toward the gleaming object. It was a dagger. The blade was embedded in the mortar between the stones of the wall, its hilt curving back in a graceful arc.

"What—" Dulon whispered under his breath. He grasped the smooth metal of the hilt and wrenched the blade from the wall with two hands. He stared at the dagger in bewilderment. Had someone thrown it? Tried to stab another elf and missed? Dulon doubted the knife had been lodged in the wall for safekeeping. He had to find Kyna.

He spun back toward Master's Street and took off at a run down the stairs leading from Court Road.

A shape hurtled at him from the bottom of the stairs. Dulon shouted in surprise and threw himself sideways, landing with his feet separated by two steps and the dagger raised in front of him. The other elf had hurtled past him and was poised on the top step. They, too, had a knife.

"Identify yourself!" Dulon held his stance, trying to make out the features of the elf's face in the shadows.

The knife pointed between Dulon's eyes lowered. "Dulon?"

Dulon recognized the voice and lowered his own dagger.

"Kyna." He sighed. "What happened? Are you alright? I heard a scream." He ascended the stairs as he talked. Kyna stepped back and sheathed her dagger.

"I'm fine." She was breathless, but her eyes shone with adrenaline. "I was watching the Archives from the paddock. There was an earthquake. I saw movement between the Archives and the Performance Hall, so I jumped the paddock fence and ran toward it. The elf must have seen me coming. When I rounded the corner, a knife came at my face. I swerved just in time and it hit the wall behind me."

That must have been when she screamed.

"Did you see them?" Dulon asked excitedly.

His heart sank as she shook her head.

"No. They wore a hood. After the dagger missed, the elf fled down Master's Street. I followed them as far as I could, but they disappeared. We could still look if you want, but I expect the elf is long gone by now."

Dulon tried to restrain his disappointment.

"It's alright. I'm just glad you weren't hurt." He brushed the hair back from his face and attempted a smile, though he feared it came out as a grimace. "Now we *know* we're dealing with an elf, but we've lost the element of surprise."

"I know." Kyna slumped back against the wall, then the dagger in Dulon's hands caught her eye. "Is that the dagger they threw at me?"

"Yes." Dulon turned the weapon over in his hands. It was a beautiful thing, expertly crafted with a narrow blade and intricate engravings.

A corner of Kyna's mouth curved into a smile. "We can use it to track them."

"My thoughts exactly," Dulon said as he scrutinized the blade, looking for an etching of craftsmanship. Elves almost always left their mark on a piece of work, especially one this impressive.

"Aha!" Dulon's face split in a grin. He had spotted thin etch marks near the base of the blade, but they were difficult to make out in the dim light.

"Come with me." Dulon strode back down Court Road to the Performance Hall, Kyna following on his heels. Once inside, he flipped a switch, and lamps illuminated along the walls, casting a steady glow on the blade. Dulon tilted the knife and squinted at the fine etching near the hilt. His grin faded.

"What is it?" Kyna asked. "Do you recognize the symbol?"

"Yes," Dulon said slowly. He drew his brows together, and he stood straight.

"And?" Kyna prodded after a pause.

"We should return to Master's Street." Dulon held the blade for Kyna to see. "This is Gellion's mark."

They did not find Gellion anywhere along Master's Street. Dulon suspected he would be well hidden if he were keeping watch on the area, but surely he would have emerged when he saw Dulon and Kyna walking the streets?

Dulon was doing his best to keep a rational head. It was easy to submit to wild suspicions in the late hours of the night, and he refused to give them any credit. Gellion loved this city. He had served Daro faithfully for nearly two centuries, and Dulon trusted him with his life. Gellion had crafted scores of daggers, and any number of elves in the city may own one, especially given the impending battle.

Besides, plenty of earthquakes happened while Gellion was away from the city.

The thought gave Dulon too much relief. Was he truly so paranoid as to suspect one of his closest allies?

The more likely fear was that Gellion would have no idea to whom he had given this particular dagger. Then they would be back at square one in their search, only without their previous secrecy.

After Dulon and Kyna had walked Master's Street twice, whispering Gellion's name and watching the rooftops, Dulon was ready to give up and seek Gellion at his house. Before he could voice this suggestion, however, he heard the scuff of boots behind him.

Dulon whirled on the spot, knife held aloft. Beside him, Kyna mimicked his motions.

"It's me!" An elf presented a set of empty hands before stepping closer. His colorless shadow of hair turned red as he neared.

Dulon let out a breath. "Where were you?" he demanded, his heart racing. "We've been looking for you nearly half an hour!"

"Where have *I* been? I was looking for you! I heard a scream." Gellion looked at Kyna, eyes blazing.

"I'm fine," she said.

Gellion's nostrils flared. "I tried to come to you at the Archives, but I heard running footsteps as I neared. I followed the sound for two blocks, but no matter how close I got, I did not see anyone running." Uncertainty colored his eyes. He looked between Kyna and Dulon. "It was not either of you?"

"No," said Kyna. "It was the elf we have been looking for. I was chasing them."

Gellion's eyes widened. "What happened? Did you see them?"

"There was an earthquake near the Archives, and I saw an elf just around the corner," said Kyna. "They threw a knife at me when I tried to sneak up on them, and I followed them, but they got away."

"They threw a knife at you?" Gellion looked horrified. "Did you see—"

Kyna was already shaking her head. "No. I did not see their face."

"But we might have a lead," said Dulon, holding the dagger out to Gellion and watching his face carefully.

At first Gellion looked at the weapon with simple curiosity, but the moment he wrapped his palm around the hilt, his face changed.

"This is one of mine," he whispered.

Dulon said nothing.

"But how?" Gellion knit his brows, seeming as baffled as they were at finding one of his daggers at a crime scene.

"To whom did you give that dagger?" Kyna's voice was smooth and light, but her eyes belied her casual tone.

Gellion brought the knife closer to his face, eyes scanning every inch of it. He shook his head.

"No one. This is one of the daggers I keep on display in my workshop. I've never given it to anyone."

"Clever."

Gellion and Dulon turned to Kyna.

"They knew not to incriminate themselves. Use a display dagger straight from the shop and no one can trace it to them." Kyna cocked an eyebrow. "This elf is no fool, and now they know we are on their trail."

A SPAR OF TWO

"Try again," Gellion said.

Kyna let out a puff of air. "This is pointless. I don't fight with a staff."

"The A'vaeri can be translated to any weapon—or no weapon at all."

"Perfect, no weapon at all suits me just fine."

Gellion sighed, summoning what little patience remained to him. "You did agree to this, you know. No one is forcing you to learn it."

"I know," Kyna snapped. She chewed her lip. "Fine. Show me again."

Gellion resumed his wide stance, his hands spread across his staff with his lead hand matching his lead foot. As slowly as he could manage, he brought his back foot forward, jumping off the ground and spinning to land in the same stance on the other side before pivoting and lunging forward with his staff.

"The hand movements are the same with a weapon in each hand." Gellion had decided that knives better suited Kyna's build and had given her two short rods to practice with. "You just stab with the front blade. You could also bring both hands forward like this." He flourished his staff in a figure eight before pushing it forward with both hands stretched in front of him.

"Show off," Kyna muttered.

Gellion smirked.

The moves he was showing Kyna were meant to be fast and powerful. If he was forced to perform them in slow motion, he would add his own fun. Gellion had never tried to teach an elf A'vaeri before. He had been shocked to learn that Kyna not only did not practice A'vaeri in any form, but knew nothing of its origins, philosophy, or basic motions. Not all elves incorporated A'vaeri into their lives, but as Kyna had expressed her intention to follow the elves of Daro to battle, learning some of the art's basics would do her no harm.

Gellion's expression sobered. He still bristled at the thought of Kyna going into battle, but knew better than to try to persuade her out of her decision.

"Come on now, try again," Gellion said.

Kyna rolled her eyes and assumed the same stance as Gellion, then mimicked his motions as best she could. Her footing was hesitant, and she landed facing the wrong way with her hands reversed.

Gellion laughed.

It felt good to laugh. If Gellion's trip to Tradira had not gone according to plan, Daro had not fared much better in his absence. He had returned to an attack by a sea demon and a walk through a city crumbling from the outside in and devoid of vierstone.

In the weeks since his return, no elf had made any headway on discovering the secret behind the dying vierstone. Gellion himself had tried, but his talents had always lain in metalworking. Concentrating too completely on vierstone flared his emotions in ways that left him anxious and volatile. He would leave its study to elves better suited to the task. Elves like Veldon. Still, the blackened and lifeless stone disturbed Gellion deeply. That an elf may be causing all of this was more disturbing still.

Images of the figure in the mist plagued his thoughts more than ever before. Gellion had not told anyone about what he had seen the evening before the Council left when the ground had split beneath him. He had probably imagined the figure, but even if he hadn't, the experience shed no light on who the elf was. As for what had happened in Tradira—Gellion did his best to forget that completely. The task was easier when Kyna was around.

Kyna cursed at Gellion's laughter.

"I'm sorry, I'm sorry," Gellion said, raising his hands and trying to stifle his amusement. "You really aren't bad."

"You're a terrible teacher."

"So I have been told."

"You could have warned me of that before offering to teach me."

"But then we wouldn't be having so much fun."

Kyna glared at him.

"Close your eyes," Gellion said.

"Excuse me?"

"Close them."

Kyna held her glare for a moment longer, then shut her eyes.

"Imagine you are a flame spirit—bear with me—keep your eyes closed." He placed his hands on her shoulders, his heart racing at the contact. He felt Kyna stiffen in surprise, then slowly lower her shoulders again under his touch. "Think of how fire moves—how it dances, jumps, sparks, flares, and whips. It is hot and fast, consuming all in its wake. This is how you want to move—strike fast, with force and deadly blows. Draw on your own energy. Your breath."

"You sound ridiculous."

"And you look ridiculous when you fight."

Kyna's eyes flew open, burning with an anger Gellion had begun to think she did not possess.

Good.

"There, you are starting to feel something. But anger is a poor source of energy. It is unpredictable and difficult to control." He let go of Kyna's shoulders and picked up his staff again, then began to spin the weapon and move through a few poses on the balls of his feet. "Channel the anger into something more productive. A forest fire is powerful, but you cannot use it for a tool." Well did Gellion know the truth of this, but knowing something and practicing it were very different things. Maybe if he said the words enough, he would start to take the advice.

"Come on." Gellion halted his staff and gestured for Kyna to come at him. "Try that move again but toward me."

Kyna's knuckles were white around her rods. She took a breath, then moved one foot forward. Gellion made to prod at her side with his staff, but she spun away, her feet leaving the ground for a moment before planting with the right foot forward. She lunged with both rods in front of her, stopping a hand width from Gellion's chest.

Her eyes locked on his. There was still anger there, but also triumph. They shone with a brightness Gellion had never seen in them. Strands of dark hair, dislodged from exertion, framed Kyna's face like willow leaves, and a sheen of sweat made her skin glow in the sunlight.

Gellion stared at her, his chest seeming to rise into his throat as longing welled within him.

Kyna had made a grand entrance back into Gellion's life the same day he had returned from Tradira. He could still hear the squeaking of the stones beneath his sopping boots as he had almost fallen over at the sight of her. For several moments he had stood there, dripping wet, mouth gaping like a fish.

That crooked smile had spread over Kyna's face as she took in his appearance.

"Welcome home," she had said, and her voice had spoken music.

Ever since, their confusing relationship had resumed, if one could call anything with Kyna a relationship. One moment they would be having a meaningful conversation, the next, Kyna would change the subject with a snide remark, or else her eyes would drift to her surroundings, and Gellion may as well be talking to stone. Her tongue was sharp and her eyes mocking, yet something about her drew Gellion beyond his ability to resist. He longed for her company when they were apart, but hated the way her presence could unnerve him. Like now.

"Better?" Kyna arched an eyebrow.

Gellion cleared his throat and nodded, not trusting his voice.

Spending time alone with Kyna was like taking a sailboard into the sea. It filled Gellion with exhilaration at the possibilities, but the risk of being crushed by a wave was always a step away. Much safer was a boat and shipmate. That was where Dulon came in. Despite the Lord of Daro's constant looks and teasing, Gellion enjoyed working with him and Kyna. It was easier to spend time with Kyna in the presence of another with a task set before them, even if that task was discovering the identity of the potential murderer who was destroying their city.

"A'vaeri's not so hard." Kyna said. The burning look in her eyes had faded back to her usual mask of stoic irony.

Gellion relaxed. "Well, you have one move down—passably. Shall we go through the next few hundred?"

Kyna's smug grin fell. Gellion smiled.

The afternoon fell away in a glorious dance of training and raillery that left Gellion in high spirits. For a few hours, the name Arceria did not even enter Gellion's mind, Daro seemed whole and safe, and the purpose of the A'vaeri training was not to prepare for a battle but to be close to Kyna.

His eyes followed her movement as though in a trance, and his skin prickled whenever she drew close. Only the methods of the A'vaeri itself kept Gellion's mind tied to his task, and when evening fell, it was all he could do to bid Kyna good night and watch her stride back toward the guest rooms alone.

Something within Gellion compelled him to reach out to her, to turn her around and take her in his arms. The thought brought a violent heat to his skin, and his chest seemed to explode in excitement, a fireball of emotion ripping through his middle and overwhelming his senses. He shied away from it as though scalded.

Leaning against the wall of the arena, he balled his fists and took slow breaths. This was why he could not give in. No emotion this powerful could bring about any good. He had told himself this dozens of times, yet he could not seem to stop himself from pursuing as much time with Kyna as he could manage. A successful outing with her was a thrill, something to be proud of, like an encounter with a wild panther where he had come through unscathed. And yet their time together calmed him. The upcoming battle seemed easier to face when he was next to her, and the phantoms of his past further away.

Gellion ran a hand through his hair and started to walk back to Master's Street.

His mood darkened when he reached his workshop, the pleasant haze in his mind clearing to reveal his problems in stark relief. Ever since

Dulon had found Gellion's knife at a crime scene, Gellion had become paranoid about the contents of his shop. That was two of his possessions now taken straight from his private space. Was he so unlucky, or could it have been the same elf? He drew out a key to unlock his door.

Why would an elf bent on destroying the city sabotage your chances in a craftsman competition?

The thought made Gellion pause with his hand on the door handle.

Unless it was, as Dulon suggested, a political statement.

Gellion had brushed Dulon's comment off as paranoia at the time, but could the man have been onto something? Gellion may not be the Lord of Daro, but he was the next highest authority in the city, and he had been as responsible as Dulon, if not more so, for the decision to accept the alliance. Could this thief be an elf so against the principles and existence of Daro, they would not only sabotage and frame the city's representatives, but break its very foundations? The form in the mist came to Gellion's mind again. Could it have been an elf? Someone trailing Gellion and waiting to take their chance? The encounter had been the night before the ship's departure. Could an elf have been trying to make a final statement before the visiting elves left Daro?

The lamps of Gellion's workshop illuminated with a click as he pushed through the door. A quick walkthrough affirmed that all of his possessions were present, including his repossessed dagger.

Part of Gellion was glad he had been in Tradira at the time of Aryn's death. The thought seemed callous, but otherwise suspicion could very well have fallen on him for all of this. He had been on Master's Street, closest to Kyna, when the earthquake at the Archives hit. His knife had been embedded in the wall. But why would he sabotage the city he had spent centuries building? Why would anyone?

It was a question Gellion could think of no rational explanation for, and one that the elves were running out of time to answer.

WRITHING RIVER

A luminous haze on the horizon told Renyra that Daro was within an hour's ride. She sighed with relief and patted Nightjar's neck, her hand coming away damp and stuck with little hairs.

"We're close," she told the elves riding at her flank. "Keep a wary eye."

Her hunting party straightened in their saddles. Hands strayed to bows and dagger hilts, making sure they were ready if needed. The weight of Renyra's javelins on her back reassured her. The weapons had served her well in the last few days. The hunting expedition had attacked two small packs of the same gruesome canine Renyra had faced weeks ago, along with a sinuous brush panther and two lizard-like beasts that had sprayed a stinging chemical from their mouths.

Despite the monstrosity of the animals, the most disconcerting experiences of the expedition had been those from which the elves had no bodies to take back—wisps of light appearing and disappearing in the brush. Chill breezes through the muggy nights that almost seemed to have shape. Renyra had thought she was going mad until Baelik, a broad shouldered Remsgri accustomed to hunting in the jungles of Riverseep, had finally voiced his concerns to the consensual agreement of the hunting party.

As the elves had moved further from Daro, the attacks and strange sightings had grown fewer, and eventually stopped altogether

Just like the earthquakes.

Renyra could not understand it. It was as though the monsters were drawn to whatever was happening in the city.

As Dulon had requested, the party had kept a specimen of each animal to bring back to Daro. Renyra could hardly imagine how inspecting the monsters would shed any light on their origin, but Dulon had insisted, saying that any information could be valuable.

A bead of sweat dislodged from the base of Renyra's hair and crawled down her neck. The promise of a bath and clean sheets was even more welcome now than after her trip to Lacrim. She was exhausted. The expedition had been traveling by night and sleeping by day. Most of the targets of their search melted into whatever holes in the earth they had crawled from when the sun rose, but the lizards had attacked them in broad daylight as they slept. Renyra had been keeping watch when it happened.

The black reptiles were nearly the size of swordfish, with sleek sides and wickedly sharp spines along their backs. Their eyes had seemed to absorb the sun without reflecting any light, and crimson frills had fanned from their cheeks when the great lizards sprayed venom. A bandage bound Renyra's left hand where the foul liquid had touched her skin.

One of the lizards was strapped behind Renyra's saddle. Nightjar had refused to have the dogs or panthers near him, even dead.

"Ho!"

All five horses halted at the command. Rhien, an elf not much taller than Renyra with skin a shade darker, held up a hand.

Renyra had formed the hunting party of two Fieri, a Remsgri, and a Morcani, those Kindoms most experienced at hunting. With little access to fish and long winters limiting their crop production, the Morcani hunted most of the food they did not trade for. Their skill was not limited to hunting meat, however. Firas had told Renyra of the Wildwood just outside the walls of Morcanan, and the strange creatures that sometimes strayed from its depths. While the Morcani only ventured into the outskirts of the forest, to travel without weapons was dangerous.

Renyra's own skill came from hunting the ambling beasts of the grasslands, though that was not without its own risk. Still, vicious as they could be when threatened, the great cats and wild dogs of the grasslands fought only to defend their territory and prey. The creatures she hunted now were different. They did not hunt to eat, but to kill, and they attacked mounted and armed elves unprovoked.

Renyra had not wanted to lead this hunting party, but to refuse Dulon would have cast her as weak and afraid. How could she explain to him the terror that seized her when she fought these animals, or how this was so different than the hunts she led for Daro's food supply? She was in a constant state of nerves and dreaded each encounter with cold fear.

"Where?" Renyra asked softly, watching Rhien.

"The river."

Renyra pressed her reins to Nightjar's neck and pulled a javelin over her shoulder as she turned toward the Icemelt. At first she saw nothing unusual. The water rippled as it flowed over stones and branches, shining silver and black in the moonlight. But as Renyra's eyes followed the water downstream, she saw that the pattern changed. The colors and reflections were similar, but the movement was wrong. Renyra squinted, Nightjar's mane tickling her nose as she leaned forward. Her stomach turned over.

The water was *writhing*. It looked like a mass of eels, but the bodies were as thick as the great snakes of Riverseep.

Renyra wanted nothing more than to wheel her horse around and gallop to Daro. These creatures were in the river after all, they could pose no direct threat to the city. But Dulon's instructions had been to kill and bring back any unusual creatures they came across. This definitely counted as unusual.

"Be cautious." Renyra waved the others forward.

Nightjar's nostrils flared as they neared the water. He tried to step backward, but Renyra urged him on, muttering words of comfort as she drew her javelin back.

"Ho," she whispered. The horses stopped.

As one, the rest of the elves drew their arrows, pointing into the thrashing water.

Then all at once, a horse snorted, and a dozen glistening bodies lunged from the water.

"Shoot!" Renyra cried, hurling her javelin as Nightjar reared.

She landed on her back, and her other two javelins clattered around her. Gasping for air, Renyra sat up to see a flat head with bulbous eyes coming toward her, mouth agape. Two front legs dragged the thing's trailing body across the ground. Its skin was smooth and rippled with muscle.

A lindworm.

Renyra could hardly believe her eyes. Lindworms were the stuff of legend, seen last during the Siege of Mathtier emerging from the corrupted waters of the Scalding Springs. She had not seen them, of course, but she had heard stories.

Renyra's hand grasped for a javelin. She shuffled backward and staggered to her feet, drawing the weapon and throwing it straight between the worm's eyes. It made a sickening squelch, and the worm shook its head from side to side, trying to dislodge the shaft. Renyra drew a long dagger from her belt and sliced through its thick neck.

Black liquid the consistency of honey oozed onto the ground, and Renyra leapt over the thing's body, grabbing her javelin and biting her lip to keep from gagging.

The scene before her was chaos. Two elves remained on horseback, but were having difficulty controlling their mounts well enough to shoot any arrows. Rhien and the other Fieri elf dodged between the worms on foot, stabbing with daggers and arrows. Nothing seemed to permanently incapacitate the worms.

"Cut off their heads!" Renyra shouted, throwing two javelins into the fray to slow the monsters down. She wished she had a bow. There were too many worms at once, and retrieving her throws was becoming dangerous.

A shrill scream echoed through the night. Two lindworms had wound themselves around the legs of one of the horses. There was a terrible splintering sound, and the horse fell to the ground shrieking in terror and agony. Bile rose in Renyra's throat, and cold spread over her skin. The lindworms had broken its legs.

Baelik jumped from the poor creature's back and slit its throat, leaping on the worms with a cry of rage. As he fought one, the other latched its mouth onto the horse's neck.

While Renyra stared in horror, a heavy weight crashed into her legs, and she yelped as her feet were swept out from under her. She landed on top of a worm and felt the end of its tail curling around her ankles. Panic overwhelming her senses, Renyra twisted in the worm's grip and hacked at its eyes with her dagger. It loosened its grip enough for Renyra to draw back her feet and kick away.

She rolled sideways, but before she could get back to her feet, another tail wrapped around her arm. She tried to stand, but the thing pulled her back to the ground, using its weight to drag her toward it as its tail made more loops up her arm. She sliced at its slimy skin with her other hand, but the angle was awkward, and she was afraid of cutting her own arm in the darkness.

The muscles in the worm's tail began to constrict. Renyra gasped in pain, tears streaming down her face, and renewed her efforts to cut the worm's tail. She finally managed to slice through a segment, cutting herself in the process, but the worm just wound the rest of its tail further up her arm, continuing to squeeze.

"Help!" Fear and pain clouded Renyra's mind.

The worm's body twisted, and Renyra heard a loud *crack*.

Renyra screamed. White spots burst before her eyes as waves of sickening pain spread like hot metal through her arm and up her shoulder. She tried to reach the worm's neck with her knife, but the movement caused her vision to black out for a few seconds, and the renewed pain made her head spin.

The worm's tail was crawling up her shoulder now. Soon it would reach her neck, and there was nothing she could do. She drew a breath, trying to shout for help one more time, but suddenly the pressure released.

She scrambled backward, crying out in pain as her arm slid through the thick coils of worm. Baelik stood over the lindworm's head, black goo dripping from his dagger. He took a step toward her, but Renyra was falling away from him through a black sky. She felt the world close around her, then nothing.

Renyra woke to whitewashed walls and the smell of calendula blossoms. She blinked slowly, waiting for the ceiling to stop drifting and come into focus. There was a pleasant fuzz surrounding her head, and she smiled as she took a breath of the sweet air. Then she moved.

It felt like her arm was full of splinters, each one attempting to break through the skin. Renyra gasped in pain and looked down. Linen strips bound her arm to a metal splint, and a sling tucked her wrist to her ribs.

The memory of the lindworm attack flooded into her mind with sudden and terrible detail.

A hand came to rest on her uninjured arm, and she jerked away from the touch, memories of slimy tails flashing before her eyes. The movement sent a fresh spike of pain through her arm, and she yelped.

"I'm sorry," said a hurried voice. "It's alright, it's only me. Lie still."

The rapid beat of Renyra's heart slowed at the familiar voice. She turned her head on her pillow to see Firas sitting beside her, his forearms resting on his long legs.

"Good morning." He gave her a smile, but its corners were tempered with concern.

She was in the House of Healing. Had the attack been only last night? She closed her eyes at the thought, but it just brought the images into clearer focus.

"What happened to the others?" she said.

Firas placed his hand back on her good arm. Renyra's pulse steadied at the touch.

"There were some injuries, but no one was killed. Apart from the horse that is." A shadow passed over his face. "Baelik told me what happened, and I saw the bodies." He said the word as though it left a bad taste in his mouth. "All of them. Those creatures weigh my mind with worry, Renyra. There is evil in their hearts and in their making."

A faraway look glazed his eyes.

"Have you seen creatures like them before?"

"I recognized only the lindworms, but all manner of monstrosities similar to the other beasts walked the earth during the Great War."

The Great War again.

The thought gave Renyra pause. First the earthquakes, and now demons walking the earth.

"Firas," she said tentatively. "Please tell me. I know speaking of the war pains you, but it may be important to whatever this is—the earthquakes, the monsters."

Firas's eyes dropped to study a fold in the bedsheets near his knee.

"Do you think I have not thought on this?" His voice was barely above a whisper.

"I—yes. I am sure that you have. I didn't—" Renyra lowered her own eyes and took a breath. "I only think that any information we can gather is valuable, and the more elves who know that information, the more likely one of them may see a solution."

Firas did not speak at first. Renyra glanced up to see his eyes still fixed on the sheets, his shoulders rising and falling in a long sigh. He raised his eyes to meet hers.

"The phoenix did not fight the elves alone. As part of its army, it formed legions of monstrous creatures—animals, most likely possessed and morphed by corrupted spirits."

Renyra could feel the blood draining from her face. She looked at her unbandaged arm, her eyes tracing the flowing tattoos of earth, water, ether, and fire. The spirits were life formed by Riu, just as the elves were. Through them he had shaped the earth, and through them he maintained the earth. Renyra knew there were corrupted spirits: earth spirits that caused poison and disease among animals, water spirits that created floods and toxic water, flame spirits that delighted in destructive fire and volcanoes, and ether spirits that made violent storms. But to possess and alter a living thing? She had never heard of spirits doing such a thing.

"The phoenix corrupted wolves, panthers, bears—all manner of creatures. Then there were the kelpies, lindworms," he nodded to her broken arm, "lake serpents, and flame salamanders. They all fought with the phoenix's armies, infiltrating every Kindom territory in Faeran. The creatures were not the worst of his army," Firas closed his eyes as though in pain, "but they were vicious, and difficult to keep behind walls."

Renyra shuddered, wondering what could possibly be worse, but too afraid to ask.

"Outside the battles, other creatures became more numerous. Creatures that looked like they had crawled from the depths of the earth, summoned by the evil spreading through the land. So far as I know, sightings of those creatures did not extend to the southern reaches of Faeran. I suspect the beasts originated in the mountains, closest to where the phoenix and its armies kept their stronghold. Others emerged from the depths of the Wildwood. Morcanan was caught between the two, and we were forced to fight like cornered beasts, even amid the battles raging over the years. It became commonplace. One did not leave the city walls without weapons and companions. After the war ended, the savage creatures slowly disappeared. By the time I left Morcanan, unusual sightings were again confined to the Wildwood, and occasionally its outskirts."

Renyra had been listening with wide eyes. "You think a similar evil is in Daro?"

"Maybe, but if it is, it is masked from my sight."

"The source of the earthquakes," Renyra said quickly. "What if it is evil, and these creatures are drawn to its power?"

"It could be." Firas wrinkled his brow in thought. "I do not think we need fear another Great War. If nothing else, I think we have proven the earthquakes are not the result of a volcano."

"Proven? What do you mean?"

Firas's eyes lit as though suddenly remembering something. He glanced around the room, then lowered his voice.

"Dulon came to me earlier this morning. He says he will come speak with you later, but an elf was spotted at the site of an earthquake. They got away, but they all but incriminated themself through their behavior."

"Dulon saw the elf? But surely he saw something to narrow the search! Their build, their hair, their clothes?"

Firas was shaking his head. "I do not think Dulon saw the elf himself. Whoever did said they wore a hooded cloak."

Renyra opened her mouth to ask more questions, but Firas held up a hand.

"I know no more. You will have to ask Dulon for details. But if the methods by which this elf is destroying vierstone go against what is natural, which I daresay they must, it could explain the convergence of these creatures."

Hope blossomed in Renyra's chest. "If we stop them, we may stop all of this."

Firas nodded, but his big eyes remained morose.

"What is it?" Renyra asked.

"We leave for battle in three days. The city will have little protection for weeks."

"The gates have kept the creatures at bay this far. I'm sure—"

"My concern is not for the creatures." Firas looked at her earnestly. "If whoever is causing the earthquakes and the dying vierstone is not caught by the time we leave, they will either accompany an army into battle, or remain here with a barely populated city. I do not know which would be worse."

Renyra deflated into her pillows. He was right. They still did not know the elf's motivation, but whatever it was, the elf was clearly capable of causing serious harm, and the upcoming battle would provide ample opportunity for sabotage. Not to mention, if the elf knew Dulon was on their trail, catching them had just become infinitely harder.

"What can we do?" she asked.

Firas's smile was sad. He stroked his thumb over her arm.

"I do not think there is much we can do but wait, watch, and keep our wits. What *you* can do is rest."

A surge of anger and frustration rippled through Renyra's body.

"I do not need to rest." Her voice came out louder than she had anticipated, and she took a breath. "I broke my arm, not my legs." Pushing herself up with her good arm, she swung her legs off the bed.

Firas did not try to stop her. He sat back in his chair as Renyra stood over him, her eyes just above his. Firas's mouth curved up at her look of defiance. He raised his palms to her.

"My love, there is little in this world I think you could not do if you put your mind to it." His eyes traveled to her arm. "But even for you it would be foolish to go to battle with a broken arm."

Renyra froze. She had not even been thinking of the battle to come. Of course she could not go with a broken arm. A relief as shameful as it was powerful washed through her, followed by disgust and regret. Once again she would keep her innocent safety while others risked their lives. She would stand apart from the bonds forged by trial and pain. And she would have to wait while Firas fought. Her insides went cold. That was a fear as powerful as her fear of battle itself, yet it was out of her control now. She would have to stay behind.

"I can stay with you," Firas said. His voice was sincere, but he did not meet her eyes.

Renyra knew how he loathed fighting; she knew he did not want to go to battle any more than she did, but she also knew the sense of duty that ran through the blood of every Morcani elf she had ever met. No cause mattered as much as loyalty, no personal preference as much as the good of all. Firas would not be able to bear staying behind while his city went to battle.

"Go with the army," Renyra said. "They need you, and I will be fine here." She smiled. "It could be for the best. Someone who knows the truth of what is happening here needs to stay behind."

Firas tilted his head back and met her gaze. His kind eyes seemed to see into her soul, and their depths revealed a love and confidence that suffused Renyra's face with heat. He smiled.

"Daro could not ask for a better guardian."

A PILLAR OF STONE

Gellion could see Veldon coming at him out the corner of his eye. He glanced the other way, but Valder was advancing on that side. No way out. He remained perfectly still, then, just as he could see the whites of Veldon's eyes, he ducked down, lunging one foot forward and bringing his staff in a swooping arch just over the ground. Veldon sprang from the stones, tucking his knees to his chest and brandishing two sticks, which he brought downward in fists toward Gellion's back. Arching his back, Gellion spun sideways and landed crouched, just in time to block an attack from Valder, who had leapt over Veldon.

The maneuvers continued, the brothers periodically switching allegiance, sometimes in the middle of an attack. None could touch the others. As their shadows lengthened, and the light took on a golden hue, Gellion collapsed on the ground next to Valder, an unspoken consent of exhaustion understood between the three brothers.

He rested his staff on his knees, the metal warm in his hands.

"You are growing slow, brother." Valder grinned and nudged Gellion with a foot. "You used to pin me to the ground any time I raised so much as a stone against you."

Gellion scoffed. "You were half a child the last time we sparred. But if we threw away these sticks, I could still pin you to the ground in moments."

Valder raised his brows, a mischievous glint in his eyes. "Is that so?"

Gellion's staff hit the ground with a clang as Valder lunged at him. The two landed in a struggling mass of bunching muscles and kicking feet. Valder had surprise on his side and gained the upper ground first, holding one of Gellion's wrists between his shoulder blades and sitting on the small of his back, but Gellion's size won out quickly. He bucked backward, loosening Valder's grip, and slipped his free hand around the back of Valder's knee. Pulling forward, he raised his torso off the ground and tipped Valder onto his side, then to his back.

Within half a minute, Gellion had Valder fully restrained, his face smashed against the stone.

"Okay!" The word came out muffled.

"What was that?" Gellion asked in a polite voice.

Valder growled.

Grinning, Gellion looked up to see Veldon, who was sitting with folded legs and an expression of judgmental amusement.

"He did attack me," Gellion said.

Veldon looked to the sky, but a smile played about his lips.

Gellion laughed and climbed off his brother. He sat beside Veldon. Valder glared at him, brushing himself off with dignity.

"I did warn you." Gellion shrugged, his face perfectly straight.

Valder muttered several words unfit for public conversation and dropped down on the other side of Veldon.

"Have you made any progress with the vierstone?" Gellion asked Veldon.

Dulon had approached Veldon shortly after Gellion's return, asking him to make an attempt at the mysterious black stone, but to do so quietly.

Veldon's face sobered. "No. I have only truly worked with vierstone for a few years, and I can sense nothing from the blackened stone. I do not know what to look for, or even rwhat Aryn was looking for."

Gellion was disappointed, but not surprised. The vierstone masters had been working with lifestone since its discovery before the Great War. Even in all that time, their discoveries of the mysterious substance had been incomplete and contradictory. Many of those elves who had devoted the most years to the study had died in the Great War, including Gellion's father. Those that remained were scattered throughout Faeran. Aryn had been the only master in Daro. For Veldon to come upon her discovery in a matter of days or weeks was expecting far too much of chance.

They had run out of time. The elves would leave the city for Nescari the following day, and they were as close to reviving the vierstone as they were to catching the elf responsible.

A chill passed over Gellion. If an elf destroying vierstone was disturbing, an elf committing murder to keep the secret was unthinkable. Yet from the depths of his horror, guilt rose like a floating corpse. Was he not guilty of the same crime? He had not planned to murder Arceria, but the man's death had been the result of his temper. Could he judge the perpetrator in Daro so harshly with a man's life on his own conscience?

I did not murder him. It was an accident.

A shove from Veldon brought Gellion's focus back to the Court. His brother's eyes were fixed toward the guest quarters. A smile tugged at his lips.

"Over there," he whispered.

Gellion followed Veldon's gaze, then stiffened. Kyna had just emerged from the guest quarters.

She began crossing the Court. Her hair flowed behind her with each stride, a glorious sheet of ebony.

Gellion felt a flush creeping up his neck.

Valder gripped Veldon's arm and leaned forward, ogling in mock disbelief at Gellion.

"Do mine eyes deceive me? Is that my *older* brother blushing?"

Gellion shot him a look fit to wither a soul.

Veldon smiled and shrugged Valder off.

"Leave him alone." He lifted a brow at Gellion. "Though you have been keeping her company more often than I think you let on."

Gellion passed a hand through his hair and straightened.

"We are both working with Dulon," he said. "Of course we spend time together."

"Kyna showed no interest in working with Dulon before," said Valder, smirking.

"She was only here for the Kindom Council before, and there was nothing to help with."

"Ah, of course." Valder drew his brows together and nodded seriously. His eyes tracked Kyna for a moment. "Not my type, but you could do worse."

Gellion shrugged, as though none of it concerned him. In truth, Gellion had been as perplexed by Kyna's continued presence in Daro as any other. He had asked her why she had stayed, but her answers had been as enigmatic and vague as anything else the woman said. Gellion could not help hoping that he had been a part of her decision to stay, though the mere existence of that thought shamed him.

"Don't you want to go see what she's up to?" Valder said, grinning.

Gellion kept a straight face as he held his brother's gaze.

"I think I will."

Valder's leer faltered. Gellion stood, turned on his heel, and set off toward Kyna.

Kyna stopped when she caught sight of Gellion approaching. She turned her sharp eyes on him and raised an eyebrow.

"Care for a stroll?" said Gellion, conscious of his brothers' staring eyes behind his back. "It is a beautiful day."

"It is a hot day."

Gellion shrugged. "A bit warm, but hardly sweltering. You must be used to the heat by now."

"I do not make a habit of getting used to unpleasant things. I avoid them."

"A sad life you lead."

"A comfortable one."

"It is good to stray from one's comfort zone."

Kyna rolled her eyes, then glanced down the stairs. "I was on my way to the storehouses to sort the last of the city's rations for the journey. You can help."

"Sounds thrilling."

Kyna's eyes strayed past him. "Would your brothers like to join?"

Gellion jerked his head over his shoulder to see Veldon and Valder peering from around the fountain in the middle of the Court. They quickly dropped their heads to scrutinize the sparring sticks in their hands.

Gellion rolled his eyes. Kyna smiled.

"Come on," he said, walking straight for a line of waiting levit boards near the lift to the second tier. The storehouses were on the first tier, and the Rale would be faster and much less sweat-inducing than walking.

Kyna pulled back as they approached the boards.

"What?" Gellion said.

Kyna was eyeing the levit boards. "I would prefer to walk."

Gellion raised an eyebrow.

"You asked to go for a stroll, not a ride," said Kyna.

"That was before we had a task to accomplish across the city. I thought you hated the heat? This will be much cooler than walking."

Kyna seemed to be struggling to come up with a response. A rarity. Gellion cocked his head and began to smile.

"You're not afraid of levit boards are you?"

"Of course not." Kyna tossed her hair back with dignity. "I would just rather walk. Most of the path to the storehouses is shaded anyway."

"Uh-huh."

"I'm not afraid of them," Kyna said. "Besides, they're hardly faster than walking."

"You've clearly never used them correctly," Gellion said, fond memories of races against Valder flashing through his mind.

Kyna looked at him blankly, then made to turn toward the stairs.

"Fine, fine," he said, hardly keeping the laugh out of his voice. "Come on then." He held out his arm to Kyna and was gratified by the merest hint of surprise behind her usually steady gaze. She looked at his arm as though it were a strange creature she was not sure she should approach, but after a moment she placed her hand upon it. Goosebumps trailed past Gellion's elbow, and his skin seemed to almost vibrate.

Kyna looked him in the face, her eyes impassive again.

"Lead on."

Gellion did a poor job hiding his grin as he walked through the streets with Kyna on his arm. Trees rustled in the breeze and cast shadows on the path. He and Kyna passed the brewhouses and the city tavern, a faint din of conversation emitting from its open windows. Gellion could almost imagine that all in the world was normal, that he was on a simple walk with Kyna on a warm, sunlit afternoon with centuries of peace and certainty before them.

But over the top of the tavern's roof, the crumbling pillars of the viaduct stood, sentinels to disaster. Below his feet, he could see black lacing through the pavement. He blinked hard to erase the images from his mind and looked at Kyna.

"Have you been practicing A'vaeri?"

Kyna shrugged. "Some."

"You really were good, you know. For a beginner."

"Your flattery knows no bounds."

Gellion grinned. "So why did you never learn it? Were you—" He paused. Most elves did not like discussing the Great War, including himself, but Kyna was an enigma he could not interpret, and he longed to know more about her. "Did you not fight in the war?"

"No," she said. "I was born after the war."

So she was young. Somehow this surprised Gellion. He supposed it was Kyna's confidence that masked her age.

Kyna did not elaborate on her answer, and Gellion let silence follow them down the last set of stairs that led to the storehouse. They walked into a cool blast of air as the storehouse doors opened. Gellion sighed. He could not deny that it was much more pleasant in here than on the streets, especially after a sweat soaked afternoon of sparring.

The air in the storehouse was dry and sweet. Shelves lined the walls and made a labyrinth of pathways through the center of the room. Gellion followed Kyna past stocks of grain and seeds into the next room, where a central table stood surrounded by bags, jars, and bins on one side, and cloth packs on the other. On the table, Gellion saw a sheet of paper outlining what each pack should contain—enough food for one elf for several weeks of travel. He expected hunters would supplement the rations with fresh game and gather fruits and nuts along the way.

Gellion grabbed a limp bag and began to fill it with dried fish and nuts.

"You fought in the war."

Gellion's hands froze. He glanced at Kyna. She had stopped a distance from the table and was watching him.

"Yes," he said. He grabbed a stack of oatcakes and shoved them into his bag, berating himself for bringing up the war.

"The whole thing?"

Gellion nodded. He slid an empty bag toward Kyna, hoping the work would distract her.

Kyna took the bag, but her eyes lingered on him as she began packing it with food.

"What was it like?"

Gellion's hands tightened around a block of cheese. He could feel the color draining from his face. How was he supposed to answer a question like that? Even if words could describe the horror of those battles, there were not enough of them to encompass two centuries of terror.

"Worse than whatever you are imagining," Gellion said softly.

"You only fought monsters, didn't you? Animals."

Gellion closed his eyes. Anyone who had seen those creatures would not discount them as 'only animals.' They had been vicious, nightmarish demons bent on death, but they had not been the worst of the phoenix's army. Not by half.

"No," Gellion said. "Not just animals." He paused, loath to go on. "There were wights in the armies. Dead elves animated by corrupted spirits."

Kyna stared at him, a flicker of surprise in her eyes.

Gellion looked away. The elves were reluctant to speak of the war; they never spoke of the wights.

"Did any living elves fight for the phoenix?" Kyna said after a heavy silence.

Gellion nodded.

Kyna raised her eyebrows.

"But they were hardly recognizable by the time they fought in battle," Gellion said.

"What do you mean?"

"The phoenix turned them into demons."

He put his pack down as his pulse began to quicken. Images of glowing eyes beneath fanged helmets flashed inside his mind.

"Their bodies still bore the same shape," he said. "But their eyes reflected a cold gleam, and they felt nothing but hate for their past Kindoms. There were not many of them, but they commanded armies."

"So they killed their own people?" Kyna's eyes were turned down, a line between her brows. "For what cause?"

"Most say they had no choice, that the phoenix took them and corrupted them until they were no longer themselves."

A prickle of sweat began creeping down Gellion's neck. He could feel memories of the war looming from the depths of his mind, depths he did his best to leave untouched. The air in the storehouse seemed suddenly thinner. He struggled to keep his breath even. The betrayal of his body sparked a flame of anger in his chest.

"Has no one ever told you this?" The words came out harsher than he intended.

"Not really. Elves usually get upset when I ask." Kyna raised an eyebrow.

The anger melted out of Gellion as quickly as it had come.

"Sorry."

Kyna started packing food again. "Did any of the elves survive?"

"What?"

"The elves who fought against their kin."

"I don't think so. If they did, they fled to places so dark no elf ever saw them again."

"It would seem elves have killed more than most like to let on."

Gellion stiffened. "What do you mean?"

"They say only one elf ever committed murder. And the elves curse his name as though he were Olcon himself."

It was with great effort that Gellion kept his expression under control. He could feel a flush of cold spreading over his skin.

"But these elves killed thousands with their armies," Kyna continued.

"They were no longer elves," Gellion said.

"No?" Kyna cocked her head.

Gellion did not want to talk about this. Many elves had disappeared in the first century of the war. Some had undoubtedly been killed by the phoenix, or used for its own evil purposes, but Gellion was sure some had sought the phoenix of their own volition.

The phoenix had woven tales of a recreated world which the elves could help create—could own and take pride in. It had offered freedom and power. Most of the elves could see behind the glamor. What the phoenix offered would have been given only under its own control. The elves would have become slaves.

Still, not all elves had been opposed to the power the phoenix offered. Had some of them chosen to betray their kin? The phoenix's commanders had been imbued with terrible spirits, possessing powers that made them hardly recognizable as elves. It was a cruel fate that the families of those elves would never know whether their kin had chosen their fate, or had it forced upon them. To believe the former would be to admit to previously unthinkable corruption within their own race. It was a possibility that most elves adamantly refused to entertain. Elves did not kill. Elves did not murder.

Gellion's hands were starting to shake. He did not know what made him say it, but before he could catch the words, they flew from his lips.

"I may have killed a man."

Kyna's eyebrows rose. It was the only change in her expression.

"May have?" she said.

"A human. When I was in Tradira. It was an accident. He fell to his death, but I had lost my temper. I grabbed him as he was lunging at me with a knife, and he lost his balance. I didn't mean for it to happen." Gellion took a steadying breath. "I don't think it was my fault. His wife ... his wife may have orchestrated it from the beginning. But—" He picked up a jar of honey, twisting its stopper absently.

Kyna was watching him thoughtfully. She was remarkably calm, almost annoyingly so.

"If the fault lay with this woman, why do you feel guilty?"

"Because I would have done it anyway." He could not meet her eyes.

She shrugged. "You don't know that."

"I do."

"Anyone can lose their temper."

"But how many kill because of it?" Gellion's eyes blazed as his head snapped up. "One, as you say. And that elf lost worse than his life for it. I do not want that."

Kyna held his gaze. She seemed to be trying to read something behind his eyes, though her own expression was as inscrutable as ever.

"No," she said at last. "No elf would want that."

After a moment, she dropped her eyes back to her work and started packing her bag again.

Gellion stared at her. He did not know what reaction he had been expecting of Kyna, but this complete lack of reaction was somehow worse than if she had started shouting about his eternal damnation. Suddenly, Gellion did not want his confession met with calm acceptance, or even the attempted comfort his brothers had given. He wanted someone to understand the gravity of his actions and the reality of his fears.

What could he do to make Kyna understand? What could he say? Just once he wanted to know what she was really thinking, to see what she was feeling—that she *could* feel.

"Did you hear what I said?" Gellion said. "I killed a man—a living soul—and you act as though I have done nothing but admit to a petty theft."

Kyna closed her pack and moved it to the side. She looked up at him.

"What would you like me to say? Do you want me to agree that what you did was unforgivable?" She shrugged a shoulder. "I don't think that."

Gellion struggled to find words. "I—No. I just—" He shook his head. "I can't understand you! Nothing phases you. Nothing upsets you."

"That is not true."

"No? I have never seen it. Nor has anyone else, I imagine." He threw the words at her. "No anger, no pain, even your laughs are shadowed in mirth."

The tiniest flicker of something stirred behind Kyna's eyes, but it was replaced by a cold stare.

"Perhaps I am just more accomplished at controlling my emotions, rather than throwing them about for all to see," she said.

"So accomplished you could fool Riu himself!" Gellion shouted. "Do you actually care about anything? Anyone?"

He slammed the honey jar on the table. It smashed. Glass shards scattered, and the viscous contents oozed over his fingers. He watched its slow progress, and his anger seemed to seep away with the honey.

Neither of them spoke. Gellion slowly looked up.

There was a line between Kyna's brows. She looked down and picked a small piece of glass off of her hand. It left behind a smudge of amber residue.

Shame prickled across Gellion's skin. He ran his clean hand through his hair and turned away from the table, slumping back against it. He stared at the floor and sighed.

"He was my mentor," he said quietly.

He had to tell someone. It had been eating away at him for weeks. Not even Valder and Veldon knew.

There was a long silence.

"Who was your mentor?" Kyna said.

"Kaelo."

For once, Gellion saw genuine shock in Kyna's eyes. It was only slightly gratifying.

"Everyone hated him for what he did," Gellion said. "I didn't understand at the time. I was hardly more than a child when he was banished. He was a good mentor. Few of words, but patient, and skilled beyond any metalworker in Tura. I wanted to be like him in every way." He grimaced. "Now I fear my wish may come true."

Gellion looked down in silence. After a time, he turned to clear away the honey and glass.

"You are not like him," Kyna said quietly, in as serious a tone as Gellion had ever heard from her.

He closed his eyes and tried to believe the words. There was no way

Kyna could know an elf born and banished centuries before her time, but the promise meant the world to Gellion all the same.

Kyna walked to a nearby shelf and brought him a rag.

"Thank you," he said, and started to sweep the glass shards into a sack.

———

Gellion retired to his workshop in the evening. He had watch duty the first half of the night on Master's Street. He both hoped and dreaded that something would happen. It was the last night before most of the city's population left for weeks. If the elf responsible for the earthquakes wanted an audience, this was their last chance; if they wanted a deserted city, they were about to get their chance.

Gellion walked to the knives on display at the back of his workshop and examined them. All in place. Each blade gleamed silver in the glow of the lamps. Gellion selected two short knives and slipped them into the scabbards at his waist. If his target for the night was still armed, Gellion would not be caught defenseless. If only he had his tunic. A familiar clenching of his chest caused Gellion to turn his back on the empty stand in the back corner of the room. What he wouldn't give to go unseen tonight.

With a sigh, Gellion shut off the lights and stepped into the falling darkness. The wind was picking up, and the stars were obscured. He locked the door behind him and turned down the alley beside his workshop. His fingers felt for wedges and cracks in the stone wall, and with the aid of window ledges, he scaled the side of his workshop, pulling himself onto the slanting roof with one fluid movement.

He paused, listening to the sounds of the night.

Nothing stirred.

On his belly, he edged himself toward the street until he could just see over the lip of the roof onto the smooth path below. It was still early enough that elves were walking home from dinner, checking in on their shops before turning in for the night.

A couple walking down the street paused in front of the shop across from Gellion. One elf lifted his hand to his partner's face, and the two touched foreheads, exchanging words lost to the night. Heat spread over Gellion's skin, and he looked away. Standing watch at the front gates would have been much less awkward.

The hours passed.

Gellion found himself alone with his thoughts for the first time since his afternoon with Kyna. His stomach still twisted into knots at the memory. He was ashamed of his outburst, and grateful for the small comfort Kyna had given him, but his frustration with her was not entirely gone. His mother's words from weeks before plagued his thoughts. *'He judges you based upon his own understanding of the world, just as we all do.'* Was Gellion no better than Tornac, blaming Kyna for her apparent lack of emotions when he struggled so hard to control his own?

It started to rain. The drops were small, but quickly threatened to soak Gellion as they whipped back and forth in sheets. At least the weather brought his mind back to the present, miserable though it was. Veldon would relieve him of his shift in just over an hour, but that was a long time to remain lying on a roof unprotected in the rain. It would only take a few minutes to climb down and get a cloak from his workshop.

After a sweeping glance of the street, Gellion inched backward until he was out of sight from the ground below. He leaned back on his heels and moved in a crouch to the side of the roof overhanging the alleyway.

He paused at the edge, peering over to ensure that a window was below him. He began to lower himself, gripping the roof with both hands and feeling for a purchase of rock with the toes of his boots.

I should have taken off my shoes.

The slick leather of his boots kept slipping on the marble.

Finally, he dangled from the roof with straight arms, and his feet found the top of a window. He dropped onto its lip, then started spidering down the wall beneath it.

Just before he reached the ground, a wave of vertigo spun his head, and a grating current flowed over his skin.

Gellion's hands froze on the rock. He could feel the hairs on his arms standing on end despite the water slicking his skin.

No, not now.

Gellion flung himself to the ground, intending to sprint to the road before the earthquake hit, but after one leap, his feet careened sideways as the snap of rock rent the air.

Adrenaline coursed through his veins. He twisted in the air and managed to land on both feet. He sprang from one foot to the other, correcting for the shaking ground in midair with each stride.

The wall of the building next to his workshop crumbled, powder and debris mingling with the rain. Gellion dodged sideways and skidded to a halt on Master's Street, looking around wildly for any sign of an elf.

He saw nothing.

The ground bucked again. Gellion spun around as the buildings to either side of his workshop collapsed as though an invisible foot had stepped on them. The crash was deafening, and debris filled the air. Gellion shielded his face with his arms as the wind whipped pieces of wet rock toward him.

Then everything was still. The shaking stopped as suddenly as it had started.

Gellion stood before his workshop. It sat untouched amid a sea of rubble.

The slightest flicker of movement through the rain caught Gellion's eye, and he wheeled around to face the alleyway across from his shop. The movement came again, but even staring directly at its source, Gellion could not make out more than the outline of a head and shoulders seeming to appear and disappear with each gust of wind.

He did not wait.

Drawing his knives from his belt, he lunged toward the figure. He saw it retreat, but his mind could not make sense of its shape or movements. He shook his head. He ran.

The figure fled before him, and though Gellion's eyes strained to see in the dark rain, his ears picked up the perfectly normal scuff of boots on stone. Following the sound with his eyes, Gellion almost tripped when he saw a pair of boots, clear as anything could be on a night like this. Only above the elf's calves did their shape become blurred.

My tunic.

Gellion's breath caught in his chest. His prize creation had been taken by the elf causing the earthquakes, destroying the vierstone. Was this why the thief had taken it? To perform his foul deeds with less risk of notice?

Gellion clenched his fists and let out a snarl as he followed the elf through the scattered houses of the northern neighborhoods. The elf scaled a stone wall into the orchards, and Gellion scrambled up after them, but when he landed on the other side, his quarry was almost to the greenhouses and heading toward the wharf. Gellion put on a burst of speed. If he lost sight of the elf, he would never pick up the trail again. This was his last chance. This could be Daro's last chance.

Gellion threw one of his knives, aiming for the elf's legs. Just before the blade could hit its mark, the elf leapt sideways, and the knife went skidding over the ground with a loud 'clack.' Gellion cursed and ran harder.

Without warning, the figure slid to a stop, turning to face Gellion.

Caught off guard, Gellion slowed his pace momentarily, then charged forward.

The figure crouched down, and Gellion saw a pale hand spread its fingers over the stones.

"No!" Gellion threw his other knife, not caring where it struck this time, but his target shifted sideways, and the blade glanced off his metal tunic, falling harmlessly to the ground.

The hood of the elf's tunic reflected the dark colors of the street and trees, but within its depths, Gellion saw the line of a nose and a flash of eyes. Then the ground split in front of him, and he felt himself thrown backward.

He hit the ground hard and lay stunned for a few moments. By the time he pushed himself to sit, he was alone in the street. Gentle raindrops pattered on the outjut of stone in front of him that had pitched him into the air.

He stared at the pillar of rock. Cold prickled over his skin. No elf could do that. No elf could move stone with a touch and command it to do their bidding. Of course, no elf could destroy vierstone either. Yet this elf had.

They were watching me. Waiting until I left the roof to make their move.

Gellion's nails bit into his palms. Why had he abandoned his post?

He couldn't have waited an hour longer? But he had no doubt the elf would have made their move anyway, likely when Veldon came to relieve him. What Gellion did not understand was why the elf had left Gellion and his workshop untouched. Why would an elf who had shown no hesitation disposing of Aryn deliberately spare him?

Unease prickled under Gellion's skin. The elf's bearing, their eyes, even the brief flash of their nose had sparked a hint of familiarity in Gellion's mind, but he could not place it. Had he seen the elf in Daro? Even spoken to them? Whoever they were, there was no point searching for them now. There never had been. Clearly the culprit had been aware of their pursuit from the beginning and was more than adept at hiding and defending themself.

Gellion pushed himself to his feet. He ran a hand through his sodden hair and swept a final glance toward the wharf and through the orchards. Wind and mist buffeted the leaves of the trees, but all else was still. His knives lay strewn on the pavement. He picked them up and slid them into his belt, then turned toward home. There was no point going back to his watch. There was nothing to watch for now. He would tell Veldon to stay in bed for the night.

The greenhouses were dark, their glass glimmering in the rain. Gellion passed them and started to turn into the southern neighborhoods. The slap of footsteps brought him up short. He reached for his knives and spun to face the sound.

It was not a cloaked figure running toward him, but Dulon. Gellion lowered his knives.

"Thank Riu I've found you!" said Dulon. "I came to your workshop, but half the street was destroyed. I feared the worst."

Gellion felt oddly touched by the concern in Dulon's eyes.

"I'm fine," he said. "But I saw them, Dulon, the elf who is behind all of this. They are undoubtedly an elf. They have my tunic." He saw Dulon's confusion. "My entry for the craft competition," he explained quickly. "It was a tunic of woven metal that reflects light to render its wearer virtually invisible. That's how they have remained unseen and disappeared under chase. And they can—they can *move* stone. I caught up to them, and they just put their hand on the street, and it cracked and reshaped in an instant."

Dulon's eyes were wide. A line creased his brow, and he shook his head.

"I no longer care how they are doing it. I care that we stop them doing it."

"How?" Gellion said. "We can't catch them in the act, or capture them on foot. We have no leads as to their identity."

"Did you catch no glimpse of their face? Even a scrap of clothing or impression of their height? Were they male or female?"

Gellion shook his head. "It is hard to be sure. I would hazard a guess at male judging from the height of their outline and shape of their nose. They were pale of skin—Morcani or Turi then. Maybe if we can find the tunic it would lead us to them?"

Dulon shook his head slowly. "We don't have time. Tomorrow we leave the city, and there is no way to postpone the departure."

"Then what do we do?" Gellion was tired of making decisions.

A muscle was working in Dulon's jaw. Rain dripped down his nose, and his eyes bore into the ground. Then he raised his gaze to Gellion.

"We march to battle. We fulfill our promise to the Albaren, and we fight for their peace and our hope of vierstone. We stay on our guard, but continue to move forward. There is nothing else we can do."

Sometimes it was easy for Gellion to forget that Dulon had fought in wars and commanded cities and armies. Looking at him now—his leader, his friend—with squared shoulders and flames in his eyes, Gellion felt the relief of confidence. A soldier to his commander.

"No," said Gellion. "I suppose there isn't." He held out his hand. "And I will be beside you when we do."

Dulon's face split into a grin, and he clasped Gellion's hand.

"I would have it no other way." He kept his hold on Gellion's hand, an idea forming behind his eyes. "And there might be one last way to identify our elf."

THROUGH THE GATES

Dulon rose from his bed early, though he had hardly slept in it. Maranyl turned over fitfully, then stilled again. A soft smile spread over Dulon's face. He almost crawled back under the blankets. Much as he wished it to be, however, this was not a day of leisure. This was the day he had been anticipating and dreading since the last Council meeting, the day he was to lead a thousand armed elves across Albarad to the first battle he'd seen in what seemed an eternity. It felt like one of the monsters assaulting Daro was trying to claw its way out of Dulon's stomach. He grimaced and tiptoed out of the bedroom.

After some last minute packing and a forced breakfast, Dulon stepped outside and looked on the Court of Daro. Dew still frosted every surface, reflecting and bending the weak light of early dawn. It brought Dulon comfort. Dew was such a normal thing.

There was plenty to do before the elves departed late morning, but before beginning battle preparations, Dulon had one more engagement to keep. A last breath of morning air, and he returned to the guest quarters, walking through halls of rooms until he found the one he wanted. The door he tapped on reminded him of a flustered Gellion weeks before, awkwardly asking after one Kyna that he needed to 'ask a question.' Dulon's mouth twitched. The two had been circling each other ever since, neither one willing to open up to the other. He hoped one of them would find the courage after this was over.

The door opened to a fully dressed and groomed Kyna, who showed no surprise at Dulon's early call.

"Come with me?" he asked.

Kyna nodded without a word, closing the door behind her and locking it. Dulon led her to a meeting room on the floor below, glancing down the hallway before shutting the door behind them.

Kyna stopped in surprise. Gellion sat on a couch, waiting for them.

"Morning," he said.

"Morning." Kyna quickly recovered and sat across from Gellion.

"We are waiting on one more," said Dulon.

Gellion nodded, but Kyna cocked an eyebrow.

A few minutes later, the door opened slowly, and Firas walked in. If he was confused by the company of the room, he didn't show it. He calmly walked to a chair and lowered himself into it.

Dulon nodded to him.

"We are here this morning," he said, "to make a final stab at the identity of the elf who has caused every earthquake since the first night of the Kindom Council and destroyed our entire supply of vierstone. These, along with Aryn's possible murder, are no small crimes, and the individual responsible must answer for them. Personally, I do not want such an individual alone in an abandoned Daro, nor armed at my back in battle." He turned his attention to Gellion. "Gellion saw the elf in question last night."

Kyna turned her head sharply to Gellion. Firas's eyes widened.

"They had pale skin," said Gellion. "That narrows it to a Morcani or a Turi. I also suspect they were male, though I cannot confirm it." He sighed. "Firas has not been party to our speculations thus far, so we should fill him in."

Firas turned to Dulon, waiting patiently with the slightest line of confusion between his eyes. Dulon had not yet told him why he was here.

"We—" Dulon hesitated. "*I* have suspicions that Miyela is behind all of this."

Firas's eyebrows moved toward his hairline, but he made no comment. Dulon continued.

"I simply cannot think of any other elf with plausible motivation for these acts."

"What motivation is that?" Firas asked.

"Miyela made it no secret that she opposed the building of Daro. She is of the opinion that we—that is, I—should not have built a city using the resource we came here to mine. She has never approved of my ideas or leadership, and I expect the very diversity of Daro insults her. Then of course, was her response to the alliance with Albarad. I know there is no clear evidence against her or any other Morcani at this point, and that it would be nearly unthinkable to attribute any of these crimes to our," Dulon had to force out the word, "Kindom Leader, but it is the best lead I have, and I must ask you Firas, for the sake of all the elves in Daro, if you know anything about this, or if you know an elf who might."

Firas was a long time responding. He stared straight ahead, deep in thought.

"I disagree," he said. "I understand the reasoning behind your suspicions, and I cannot say whether or not the elf responsible is Morcani, but if they are, I do not think their orders come from Miyela."

"Why?" Dulon asked, uncomfortably aware of his desire for Miyela's guilt.

Firas shifted in his seat. "I did attend a few—meetings, when Miyela was here, rallying the Morcani against you." He looked apologetic. "I did not know the extent of her plans until just before the parting feast. But there was never a mention of earthquakes or vierstone. It was all about the alliance. If Miyela was planning this from the beginning, she did not let the Morcani at large know of her plans."

"It would make sense to keep the full plot quiet," said Dulon. "The more elves who knew, the more likely her plans would be discovered. Do you know if any Morcani visitors remained in Daro after Miyela left?"

"Not that I know of."

"What if her grand exit was a cover-up?" Dulon said. "Make all the elves believe the Morcani have removed themselves from the situation, then leave behind an elf in secret to finish her plans."

Firas's look was somber. "Miyela may be many things, Dulon, but I cannot see her as a traitor. I am sorry, but I have told you all I know, and that is my opinion."

Dulon swallowed his disappointment.

"Alright. Thank you Firas, you may return to your home to prepare for the day."

Firas bowed his head and left.

Dulon turned to Kyna in a last desperate attempt.

"Have you learned anything else? Seen anything else?"

Kyna shook her head. "Whoever they are, they cover their trail well. I can find no evidence."

"And you are absolutely sure you saw nothing of their face when they attacked you? Even a strand of hair?"

"No."

Gellion was looking at Kyna with his brows drawn together.

"You said they wore a hood," he said slowly. "Was it—an ordinary cloak?"

Kyna looked at Gellion with calculating eyes, then glanced at Dulon and looked down.

"No," she said. "It was your tunic."

A muscle worked in Gellion's jaw. "Why didn't you tell us before?"

Kyna hesitated.

Dulon watched her, his own brow creasing. He had not considered it, but it did seem a significant detail to leave out—a tunic that made her attacker nearly invisible as she chased them. Why wouldn't she have said anything?

Finally Kyna spoke. "I did not want to put you under further suspicion."

Dulon looked between Kyna and Gellion, an awkward silence stretching the passing seconds.

"It doesn't matter," Dulon said at last. "We know Gellion is not responsible, and knowing about the tunic would not have made it any easier to see or catch the elf." He let out a long breath. "We've run out of time. We must mobilize the elves to leave before noon. Whoever our criminal is, they will either accompany us to battle or stay here. We will all be careful. Renyra, at least, will remain behind with full knowledge of what we are up against. Hopefully it will be enough."

A chill crawled along Dulon's skin as he looked over the ranks of elves lined before the gates of Daro. He had hoped never to see such a scene again, yet it held an unnerving beauty. The metal tips of spears, bows, and halberds shone with sunlight over a sea of black, brown, yellow, silver, and red. All of these elves stood waiting for Dulon's instruction. They were here because of him. With a word, he could send them back to their homes, or order them to march to battle. Dulon wished he had a choice.

At the head of the procession stood Gellion, his brothers beside him and Kyna just behind. All wore the thin, strong armor Liera had supplied for them. The metal conformed to their bodies and smoothly followed their movements. It was limned in colors that glinted in the light. Dulon wore the same armor himself and marveled at the technology that had created it. He remembered still the thick armor he had strapped to himself at the beginning of the Great War, how it had weighed him down and slowed his movements. So, too, did he remember the iron sword he had carried. Now, he hardly felt the presence of the streamlined spear at his back. He reached behind him and disengaged the weapon from his armor with a soft *click*, bringing it over his shoulder. The spear was smooth and silver from base to tip, an uninterrupted piece of metal. Etchings decorated the shaft, and intricate patterns cut through the blade, leaving only its razor edge fully intact. Dulon held the spear above his head, and silence descended upon the elves.

"Elves of Daro." Dulon lowered his spear as his voice echoed off the city's wall. "Ages, it seems, since the ships bearing our kin arrived at these harbors to mark the beginning of the Kindom Council. Since that day, everything has changed. We have seen our city break, we have seen our vierstone disappear, we have seen a friend die."

Every eye turned down. Only the distant crash of waves penetrated the still air.

"Daro is a city of no single Kindom," Dulon said. "It is a community of elves made stronger by the gifts of all. We have created something beautiful, and we have created something strong—stronger than anything yet seen in Faeran. We have suffered terrible loss these last weeks, but we will not allow it to weaken our bonds of kinship. We will not be cowed, and we will not be diverted from the task we have promised to see through."

"The Albaren have also suffered. They have watched their villages pillaged and burned. They have watched their kin slain and assaulted. But theirs is an enemy they can see. An enemy we can confront."

Several cries of agreement issued from the army. Some elves drove the shafts of their weapons into the ground to show their support. Dulon raised his chin, eyes blazing.

"Now, more than ever, we must remain united as one kin. We must fight both to rebuild our people and to give the Albaren a chance to rebuild theirs. Through this battle we will bring freedom to our neighbors and renewed life to this city," he gestured to the gates of Daro, "and the elves that inhabit it."

Dulon planted the butt of his spear in the ground and squared his shoulders.

"Do we stand together, Kindom of Daro?"

A synchronized chorus of thuds met Dulon's ears as his army struck the ground with spears, halberds, and javelins, and struck their armor with the flats of their blades.

"Then let us go."

Dulon turned, setting the gates of Daro over his shoulder. He tossed the hair from his eyes and set his steps southward toward the Icemelt, toward Albarad, toward battle. Behind him, he heard the music of two thousand boots on stone.

32

UNDER THE HOOD

Renyra picked at the threads of her bandage. It had been a week since the lindworm attack, and she no longer needed the sling, but it would be another week before she could remove the oppressive fabric binding her limb. Her mind was growing restless with boredom. Even the occupation of the greenhouses was denied her.

More than the well being of the plants, it was Renyra's own sanity that caused her worry. Ever since her injury, she had lain or sat, or walked from one stationary activity to the next with grim monotony. Dulon had courteously updated her on the happenings of the city, but she was not to strain herself by participating.

She rolled her eyes.

Now they were gone. There was no elf to restrain her activities now, but nor was there anything to do.

Renyra swung her legs over the side of the wall and looked over the tops of tiered buildings. The silence that lay over the city was palpable. As the sun's rays tilted across the ground, few lights illuminated the windows of Daro. Renyra had seen little of the elves that had remained behind. The taverns and shops were closed. Even the Dining Hall and Archives stood dark and empty.

Despite the eerie vacancy of the city, it looked peaceful, almost normal, from the top of the gates. Gulls cried in the distance, waves lapped at the docks, leaves rustled in the briny breeze. But if Renyra looked closely, she saw gaps where buildings had collapsed and dark lines tracing roofs. The viaduct was conspicuously missing, and one less pier extended into the sea. A lump formed in Renyra's throat. She loved Daro. She loved all it stood for and all it had become for her. To see it lying battered and devoid of life at her feet struck her to the core.

Looking away from the dark city, her thoughts drifted to Firas. Three days he had been gone. Had the army reached the Albaren? Had they encountered trouble in the wild hills? A company of a thousand elves was surely too great a foe for the small bands of creatures roaming the outskirts of Daro. Besides, each day, the elves passed further from the city, further from danger. And into another type of danger entirely.

Renyra wrung her hands and stretched the anxiety from her muscles. There was nothing she could do for Firas or any of the elves with him. Her job was to watch the city and ensure her friends and family had something to come back to when all of this was over.

In just a few weeks, the elves of Daro would come home triumphant, free of the burden of battle and equipped with a new supply of vierstone. They would repair the city and build it up greater than before. The perpetrator would surely be caught and dealt with in due course, and all of this would be a nightmare of the past.

With a deep breath, Renyra forced her shoulders to relax and watched the sun's descent toward the watery horizon. Even amid turmoil, the beauties of the world went on, unaware and unhindered. Renyra closed her eyes and focused on the warmth soaking into her skin, the tang of the air, the rumble of the waves.

Her eyes flew open.

No wave had caused that sound. Her heart fluttered as she stood and took a step back from the parapet. She had not felt any shaking. Her eyes scanned the water, but her view of the wharf was obscured by the buildings on the lower tiers.

Boom.

A tremor. The accompanying sound was muffled, but seemed to permeate the air like faraway thunder.

Boom. Boom.

Goosebumps spread over Renyra's skin. Even from this distance she could see ripples forming in the water. Was it another sea monster? Renyra began to step sideways toward the stairs that led to the street, keeping her eyes focused on the lower tiers of the city. In the time it would take to get to the docks, whatever was happening may be over, and she would have lost her vantage point, but she could do no good standing back and watching.

Renyra jumped as a series of crackling snaps echoed through the city. Clouds of dust erupted below the first tier in a rapid line of succession from west to east, accompanied by deep *plunks* of splashing.

Panic clawed at Renyra. This was not another earthquake. This was something more. This was what they had all feared.

And what I promised to stop by remaining behind.

Sweat moistened her palms. How was she supposed to stop the elf? Would she have to kill the culprit? Her hand strayed to the javelin at her back. She never went without a weapon now.

Boom.

Clenching her fists, Renyra sprang to the staircase. There was no time for hesitation. She would have to make her plans on the spot when she had seen what she was up against.

Her heart pounded with the rhythm of her steps. At the bottom of the stairs, she leapt onto a levit board and leaned forward, willing it to go as fast as it could.

Off the board. Down the lift. Onto another board.

She crouched for balance as she soared at frightening speed along the Rale path of the second tier. Ahead she could see the bathhouse. To her right, houses stretched into the distance. Several elves had emerged from their homes and were looking around with anxious expressions.

Another series of sharp cracks sounded, and the ground trembled. It was a strange sensation, hovering above the Rale path as the world moved around her. In the midst of the noise came a cry of fear. More splashes, then silence.

Renyra leaned further forward, threatening to fall off the front of the board in her desperation for more speed. She passed the greenhouses and the orchards. She was almost to the first tier. The lift and the top of the stairs grew closer.

She squinted. Something was wrong.

With a gasp and a scream, Renyra stopped her board so suddenly she almost pitched forward, and winced in pain as she was forced to windmill her arms for balance. She grasped the structure of the lift with her good hand and leaned over a dizzying drop that took all the breath from her lungs. The bottom of the stairs crumbled to nothing. Sea spray hung in the air where once the stone expanse of the first tier had been. It was gone.

Foaming water coursed and splashed among the submerged remains of rock and roofing. Sparks of electricity snapped and flashed throughout the rubble. The docks lay beyond, splintered but still standing, and ships bobbed in the restless water.

Renyra's blood turned to ice. Had there been any elves on this tier when it fell? There had been storehouses, market stalls. It was possible. And she had heard a scream. A shudder passed through her.

Boom. Boom.

Renyra spun around. The sound was still distant, but she could feel its resonance in her feet. Would the second tier fall next? She eyed the levit board hovering next to her, glancing with apprehension at the crackling power lines in the sea. It was probably best she go on foot from now on. Huffing in frustration, Renyra turned back up the street and started to run toward the neighborhoods. She had no time to knock on doors, to try and reach every elf still inside their homes. She had to hope that the disturbance had roused all from their houses.

"To the upper tier! Go to the upper tier!" Her voice cracked with the strain of sudden use. Several astonished eyes turned to her. A few elves began to run, and others took up her cry, turning down streets.

Renyra left the neighborhoods behind her, hoping that every elf would escape. There were less than a hundred remaining in the city. It could be done.

As she careened onto Master's Street, the sound of snapping stone rent the air once more, and an explosion of light and crackling smoke rose with grey clouds of dust near Quarry Bay. Renyra's feet seemed to stop of their own accord. She stared with wide eyes at the destruction.

She had to try to stop the elf causing this, but how could she succeed where Gellion and Kyna had failed? More likely, she would fall to her death with the collapsing cliffs. Was her time better spent ensuring the safety of Daro's citizens rather than the city itself?

Another boom. More snaps.

Renyra heard the fissure splitting through Master's Street before she saw it.

All thoughts of catching the perpetrator forgotten, she turned on her toes and sprinted toward the third tier, her toes barely touching the ground in her haste. A jagged crack split through the stone of the street, forking and turning like lightning. She leapt sideways away from the deepest opening and moved her feet between the thinner lines as she kept running. To either side of the road, sparks set off in quick succession along the power lines. The Rale path would be no use now. She could hear the rumble of collapsing stone further behind her. She ran harder, legs burning.

As she neared the stairs that climbed between the Archives and the Performance Hall, she saw elves running from the eastern neighborhoods. She came up behind a group of them.

"Hurry!"

The elves did not turn to her voice, but obeyed. Renyra followed at their heels, taking the steps two at a time toward the third tier.

"Get out of the city!" she cried.

There was no reason to think the elf would stop at the lower tiers.

Renyra could hardly fathom the beauty that was being destroyed, the memories, the work of centuries. But there was no time to think about that now. Grief was an indulgence that would have to wait until the immediate danger of its cause was behind her.

Renyra watched elves running toward the gates. Good. She had done all she could to raise the alarm. Now it was up to each elf to get out. She took a deep breath. She had to at least try to find whoever was causing this.

She looked around frantically for a vantage point. She needed to see the progression of the destruction to find its source. Normally she would have sidled up the side of the Archives, but she was not a confident enough climber to scale any building with one arm.

A stone wall ran the length of the third tier, separating it from the lower tiers. Where the wall met the stairs, it cascaded toward the ground, mimicking falling water.

Or steps.

Renyra pulled herself onto the lowest section of the wall with her good arm, then scrambled up the sloping stone to the flat top of the wall. A cry of anguish fell from her lips. To her right, the earth lay in jagged fragments, pieces jutting into the air. Rock and soil were exposed to the air, and pieces of road and grass strung between them. Any buildings still standing were morphed and twisted, with chunks of wall or roof missing. The dark surface of the Rale path wove among the rubble.

A fiery rage was burning in Renyra's chest. The terror that an elf *could* do this was dwarfed by the fact that they had *wanted* to. No vendetta against Daro, against Dulon, against a battle with humans could inspire this kind of merciless destruction. This was centuries of work, love, and craftsmanship, all falling to pieces in a single night.

The western half of the second tier still stood, but the whole city shook with a ceaseless vibration now. Renyra could feel it in her teeth.

More snaps crackled through the air. Stone exploded to powder in the western neighborhoods. A few startled shouts rose with the dust clouds. From the wall, Renyra could hear the slap of shoes on stone as elves fled through the houses.

The elf must be there—in the neighborhoods on the side nearest the greenhouses.

Renyra thought hard. It would be difficult and dangerous to try to find the elf amid buildings that might fall at any moment. The elf would eventually have to come to the third tier, and they had cut themself off from the other two staircases. The stairs at the west end of the city were the only way out of the destruction the elf had wrought.

Renyra ran across the wall, keeping her arms extended to her sides and praying that no sudden shakes would send her flying to either side. She almost laughed at the sight she must present, colorful wraps flowing behind her outstretched arms as she ran a story above the ground. She did her best to ignore the crashing and crumbling to her right. So, too, did she ignore the wild panic that seemed to be trying to burst out of her chest. She focused on her breath, on her feet.

Sweet Riu protect me. Sweet Riu protect me.

At last, she reached the western stairs. She crouched, bracing her shaking hands on the stone of the wall and muttering prayers and curses under her breath. Two elves scrambled up the stairs and rushed to the gates. Renyra hoped they were the last. She swiveled on her toes to face the greenhouse. The building still stood, towering glass reaching for the sun beyond the bathhouse. The western neighborhoods now resembled the crumbled remains in the east, and in the orchard beyond, trees lay on their sides with their roots in the air.

Renyra took a deep breath, waiting for the inevitable.

Boom.

The glass of the greenhouses turned suddenly opaque, millions upon millions of tiny shards momentarily bound together by the memory of their past union. Then they fell.

The sound was ethereal—a shimmering of the air, louder than any crack of thunder. The glass turned to shards of light in the dying sun, casting glittering beams across the city. Renyra sank her teeth into her lip, willing away the ridiculous tears that blurred her vision. It didn't matter. All that mattered was saving the elves of Daro and preventing whoever had done this from ever doing it again.

After the last tinkling of glass subsided, a terrible silence filled the city. Only the hungry rush of the ocean disturbed the still air. Renyra held her breath, every muscle in her body taut.

Movement disturbed the settling dust on the street below her. Renyra sucked in a breath, keeping perfectly still. She thought she could make out the vaguest outline of an elf, slowly approaching the stairs. Adrenaline coursed through Renyra's limbs. She did not want to be caught perched on a wall, as clear a target as a bird on a fence. She slid off the wall as quietly as she could, landing on the balls of her feet. In a crouch, she ran to a nearby tree, just off the road leading to the gates, and peered around it to the stairs.

Rays of sunlight slanted through the hanging motes of rubble. From the backlit haze, a figure emerged. Renyra's fingers tightened on the bark of the tree. She squinted into the light. The elven outline was amorphous, its edges scintillating. Renyra's throat tightened. Images of corrupted ether spirits, ghosts, and demons filled her mind. Yet as the figure came nearer, she heard the faint fall of footsteps, and a pair of feet materialized out of the haze. Gellion had warned her about the tunic, but seeing it in person took her breath away. It reflected and bent light in ways her eyes could not comprehend.

As slowly as she could, Renyra reached behind her and unfastened the javelin from her back. She wrapped her fingers around its smooth shaft and poised it over her shoulder. Her heart was pounding. Surely the elf could hear it?

Still in a crouch, Renyra took two careful steps backward, bracing one foot in front of the other and reaching the javelin back behind her ear. She focused on the center of what she perceived to be the elf based on the placement of their feet and hands, and waited as they drew closer. She wanted a clear shot. There was no room for mistakes.

The footsteps grew louder. A shadow formed on the street. Unlike the elf themself, their shadow's outline was clear. As the distance between them closed, Renyra could just make out the shape of a hood and shoulders. Fear held Renyra's muscles. The javelin sat poised and unmoving above her shoulder. She took a breath, closed her eyes, and focused on the ground beneath her feet.

They are just another monster.

With a deep breath, Renyra opened her eyes, aimed below and between the elf's shoulders, drew her hand further back, and threw her weapon with all her might.

The javelin soared in a straight line, charging through the air toward its target with deadly speed.

Then it stopped in midair.

A hand had wrapped around the javelin. Renyra's heart dropped into her stomach. The elf had caught the javelin as though it were a caesir ball someone had tossed.

Renyra tried to shrink back behind the tree, but the elf was too close now. They knew the direction from whence the javelin had come.

Their feet slowly turned toward Renyra. She crouched, frozen with terror.

Run. Run for the gate.

But her legs did not obey. Given the elf's power, she doubted she would have made it there anyway.

From the depths of the hood, she could feel the piercing stare of eyes. Pale fingers flexed around the javelin. Renyra flinched, but the elf did not raise the weapon. Instead, they brought their other hand to its shaft and began to pull downward. The metal bent. Renyra's eyes widened. The elf released their grip, and the useless weapon fell to the ground. A hand raised to the elf's hood, brushing it back to fall over their shoulders.

He was Turi, there was no doubt about that, but Renyra had never seen the elf before. She stared transfixed into his eyes, so dark they were almost black. There was triumph in his face, almost joy, yet it was tainted by the malice in his eyes. A corner of his mouth rose.

Renyra stood on shaking legs, stepping out from behind the tree. She took a steadying breath and raised her chin.

The elf's eyes wandered over her, amusement and disdain in their depths.

Then he walked past her.

He did not even spare her a backward glance as he strode to the center of the main street. Renyra stared. Heat stained her cheeks even as relief spread through her limbs. She could hardly make sense of the emotions battling in her mind, but chief among them was confusion. She took a few steps forward, then stopped. What was she supposed to do now? She had no other weapons, nor did it seem they would have helped her if she had. The elf stood head and shoulders above her, so stopping him by force was no use.

The elf stood with his back to her, facing away from Daro's gates toward the distant Court. He knew Renyra was no threat to him. He had not even thought it necessary to restrain her. Renyra could feel her pulse picking up, but it was not out of fear this time. She could do nothing to stop the elf now, but she had seen his face and what he had done. She would tell Firas, Dulon, anyone who would listen, and she would find him. He would answer for his crimes.

But first she had to get out of the city. She had to get to the rest of the elves and warn them—warn them of what?

The question vanished from her mind as every hair on her body stood on end. She tensed, looking around wildly. The elf was crouched with his palms on the stone, head bowed in concentration. A strange vibration traveled up Renyra's legs at a much faster frequency than the usual quakes. Every cell in her body rebelled against it. Terror seized Renyra, clearing her mind of all rational thought. This was *wrong*. Whatever was happening should not exist. She felt it to the core of her being.

A resonant hum rose from the ground, so deep in pitch it was hardly audible. Then a series of ear splitting cracks tore through the air, each further away than the last, as though following a straight line. There was a deep rumbling that seemed to come from the center of the earth itself, and the vibrations turned to violent shakes.

In horror, Renyra saw the Archives and the Performance Hall collapse into rubble. Beyond, she could just see the top of what remained of the Domes of Rhelyon. It, too, fell in shattered pieces.

The loud snapping of stone came again, this time traveling north toward the second tier.

And she understood.

Every earthquake had been laying a latticework of cracks through the foundation of the city. Each seemingly minor attack had been weakening the armor, waiting patiently for the killing blow until victory was not only assured, but simple. All the elf had to do now was link the fissures together, and the city would fall.

A high whinny sounded through the chaos, quickly accompanied by others.

The stables.

She had to get out of Daro. She had to ride to the army. This elf must have wanted an empty city to complete his work. He had turned aside Renyra's attacks with ease, but over a thousand elves together could have stopped him.

But it did not make enough sense. The earthquakes had begun before Dulon had even announced the Albaren's plea for aid. How could the elf have known that the city would be abandoned, that the elves would agree to go to battle?

There was no time to theorize. This whole thing was wrong. The earthquakes, the monstrous creatures, the alliance. Renyra did not know what linked them all, but she knew that it was somehow significant, and that Dulon—that all the elves in Tala—needed to know as soon as possible.

Breaking out of her horrified trance, Renyra bounded across the trembling street to the stables. She did not care if the elf saw her. He could stop her with the twitch of a finger if we wanted. He could have killed her before, but he had not. All she could do now was focus on getting to the army by any means possible.

An uproar of screams and snorts met her ears as she swung open the stable doors. The lights had gone out, and only by the dying glow of the sunset through the windows did she manage to unlatch the stalls. She leapt backward as the panicked beasts thundered past her toward the stable doors.

At last she got to Nightjar's stall. His eyes were wild, showing whites, and his hot breath blew on Renyra's face.

"It's alright." She tried to keep her voice calm, to reassure him so he would not bolt the moment she opened his stall. "It's me."

She lay a hand on the animal's face, stroking his short fur as she entwined her fingers in his halter and fastened a rope to it. She unlatched the stall door and slid through it. Wrapping the lead rope around the animal's thick neck, she pulled herself onto his back and urged him forward.

Nightjar snorted and tossed his head, dancing sideways at being asked to walk into a door, but finally nudged it enough to swing it open. With a scrabble of hooves on stone, the horse turned to the doors and set off at a brisk trot into the street.

The elf was no longer there. It took all of Renyra's strength to rein in Nightjar long enough to take in the sight before her. The streets around her still shook. The wall separating the third tier from the second looked like it was tipping backward.

Then, a crash beyond any she had yet heard echoed through the city. With a deep groaning, the wall fell. There was a booming splash that seemed to never end. The second tier had joined the first into the sea.

She could no longer restrain Nightjar. With a screech, he wheeled around and bolted for the gates of the city. He stumbled twice, stepping over cracks and jumping where the stone of the street jutted up or caved in. Renyra hung onto his neck for dear life.

They were out.

A large group of elves huddled on the far side of the Icemelt. Renyra thundered past them, trying to pull up on Nightjar enough to shout to those nearest.

"Stay here! I will go to the army!"

Then she was galloping down the road. The ground gave a final shudder, and Renyra heard more crashing behind her.

It was done. Daro lay in the sea.

A splendor of the elves, the city that tied them to this continent, the reason a thousand of her friends and kin were marching to battle. Her home. Lost.

33

NESCARI

Kyna sat perched on a rock, one leg extended in front of her. A slender knife was in one hand, a sharpener in the other. The blade passed through the stone groove with a metallic ring. Gellion's eyes followed the knife's motions, occasionally glancing up to watch Kyna's face as she worked. The fluttering in his chest was annoying and constant when he was with her, but not unpleasant. He was growing used to it.

Five days the elves had been on the road, and during the long hours, Gellion's relationship with Kyna had followed its usual sarcastic lightness, but with a new undercurrent that Gellion could only identify as embarrassed trust. He was almost comfortable around her now, and felt small leaps of adrenaline each time she walked next to him in their monotonous march.

Pleasant as the journey was at times, the metal sliding over Gellion's limbs and the halberd at his back served as constant reminders of his true task.

With thoughts of the Albaren came a nagging anxiety, not just for the battle to come, but in anticipation of meeting with those who knew of his transgressions in Tradira. King Naval would not be accompanying his army, nor did Gellion need to worry about Chiara's presence, but his nails bit into his palms every time he thought of Commander Vensure's smug face.

With each hour, the elves had neared their destination, time dragging in the moment, yet somehow rushing toward that which they dreaded. They had met no trouble by creatures or humans along the way, and the ground had remained dry under their feet. Where the road passed Albaren settlements and villages, humans stopped and stared or ran inside.

Nescari was the largest city north of Tradira. It sat just on the Albaren side of Restring Pass, a day or two's journey from the Dierna city of Arvain. Gellion could see Nescari's buildings rising against the horizon south of the army camp. The human soldiers' tents rose by the thousands, a mountain range of canvas. It had only been a few hours since the elves arrived.

"Three thousand."

Gellion blinked and turned to see Dulon standing behind him, scrutinizing the human encampment before them.

"Four thousand with the elves," he said. "That is the final count according to Commander Vensure."

"About what we expected," Gellion said.

Dulon nodded. "A man of little humor." He indicated the commander's pavilion with a jerk of the head and a wry smile.

Gellion snorted.

Dulon came to collapse next to Gellion like a marionette with its strings cut.

"Well, we're here. It's actually going to happen. We will make history these next few days, for better or for worse."

"I suppose we will," said Gellion.

There was a strange light in Dulon's eyes.

"I still fear this is all a mistake," he said. "That everything would have turned out better if I had swallowed my pride and listened to Miyela. Maybe she was right. Maybe I was only hungry to prove myself the competent leader of Daro at any cost—greedy for vierstone to make up for my mistakes."

"No," said Gellion. "It was not just your decision, Dulon. Every elf had their opinion. We made the best choice we could." He shrugged. "That is all we can hope to do."

Dulon inclined his head, his eyes distant. Then he let out a breath and stood.

"I need to make rounds of the camp," he said. "Give instructions for our departure in the morning."

He offered a hand to Gellion, who rose to his feet.

"Would you see that the evening's preparations are in order?" Dulon said. "Food and shelter and all that?" He waved a hand dismissively, and Gellion was relieved to see a touch of amusement return to his face.

"I will."

"I'm meeting with Commander Vensure again after dinner to discuss the details of tomorrow's plan. I would like you to come with me."

Gellion's stomach clenched. He had hoped to keep a low profile among the humans, to get through this battle with his head down and return to Daro with no elf the wiser to his mistakes in Tradira. That the elves were now camped beside the Albaren army showed that he had not compromised the alliance too badly, but he hoped the eventual exchange of vierstone would not be affected by his actions.

"I think," Gellion said slowly, "it would be best if I remained in the background until we return to Daro."

Realization dawned in Dulon's eyes. "Ah. Of course." He looked away. "I wasn't thinking."

Silence stretched between them.

"Well." Dulon straightened, forcing a grin. "I will find you later this evening, and we will take our own council. I expect the elf army will move separately from the human army, and I still want you as a leader of our forces." He raised an eyebrow in question.

Gellion nodded. "Of course."

"Excellent!" Dulon slapped him on the back.

Gellion watched him walk through the camp, bending and talking to every group of elves he passed. There was a weight to his movements, the usual bounce of step, toss of hair, and airiness of manner lessened somehow, but he was putting all he had into maintaining the morale of the elves. His effort gave Gellion hope.

After checking on the food and supplies, Gellion sat to a few games of spyre with his brothers. Valder was his usual self, but Veldon was quiet and slow to smile. Gellion watched him with both pride and apprehension. Veldon was under no obligation to be here. He bore no loyalty to Daro, and had hated fighting in the war as much as Gellion, though both Veldon and Valder had been too young to fight until its final years. Now, a wife and a home awaited Veldon's return in Faeran. He was risking a lot to stand with his brothers, and Gellion loved him for it. He could only hope that the risks did not become sacrifice.

With a shake of his head and a hard blink, Gellion threw his turn and watched the colors spin across the board. There was no good thinking of these things, yet still his mind strayed to his brothers next to him, to Dulon, probably meeting with Vensure now, and to Kyna. His throat constricted. It had been so long since he had to worry for the lives of his friends and family. It was not something he had missed.

Valder and Veldon leaned back as a shadow fell over the board. Gellion looked up to see Dulon standing above them. Backlit from the glow of the lamps, silver shone at the edges of his hair and laced through the fabric of his jacket.

Dulon nodded to Valder and Veldon before turning his gaze to Gellion.

"Come with me?"

Gellion stood and stepped over the game board. He could feel his brothers watching him as he followed Dulon to the edge of the encampment.

"Here." Dulon turned his back to the ring of lights. His expression was serious. "We could all use a good night's sleep tonight, so I'll get straight to the point. Vensure's tactic is simple. Most of the Dierna attacks have been from raiding parties based out of Restring Pass, presumably from the city of Arvain controlled by the Elder Clan. There are five clans of Dierna, but they fight among themselves more often than not. It's possible another clan holds some responsibility for the raids against the Albaren, but it is unlikely the clans are working together."

"Our goal is to eradicate all Dierna outposts within Restring Pass and encroach upon the Elder territory as far as needed to drive them back. Then we will approach Arvain. Vensure suspects the city will surrender quickly with the combined might of our armies. Once we have regained the pass, driven the Dierna threat back from the border, and negotiated terms, the Albaren will build their own outposts and a wall along the pass to regulate trade interactions and deter deleterious border crossings."

A line drew between Gellion's brows.

"How long does Vensure expect this to take?"

"A few days at most, unless it comes to a siege outside the city."

"Only a few days?" Gellion's eyebrows shot up. "Do the Dierna know about the threat?"

"No. The Albaren have kept their plans quiet."

Unease crawled along Gellion's skin. An unsuspected attack seemed underhanded.

"Do the Dierna even have an army?"

"Depends on your definition of army. They have warriors that come together to fight the other clans, and the raiding parties seem to come from a single source."

"Do they have a leader?"

"Yes. Vensure will offer to deal with him at Arvain, but he does not expect the man will accept without an attempted fight. He hopes the threat and a demonstration of our armies' power will be enough to prevent further attacks in the future." Dulon rolled his eyes. "Vensure says the Dierna 'routinely forget the might of the Albaren since their border is so far from the heart of the Albaren power, and they must be reminded of its presence.'" Dulon mimicked a surprisingly good Albaren accent with a pompous posture.

"That sums up the Albaren mindset, alright," said Gellion, hiding a smile despite himself.

"Yes," said Dulon. "I am getting that impression for myself, though I admit I had hoped your descriptions were exaggerated."

"Would that they were," Gellion muttered. "What of our army then? How will we organize?"

"We will sit between the split Albaren forces as we march. The tactic is not very elegant. With the disorganized outposts and cities of the Dierna, there is not much wit needed to launch an attack. We will surround any outposts to attack and approach Arvain from the front. It sits on a lake, so it has three sides open to forces. Vensure seems to think the Dierna will either rashly storm the field and quickly be overrun, or else stand a siege for a few hours until the city is breached. Once the city is breached, he is confident we can reach the clan leader and end the battle."

"Vensure seems confident of many things," said Gellion.

"I know. We must hope he can predict the Dierna as well as he thinks he can."

Gellion sighed. "So the tactic, essentially, is to follow the Albaren and attack en masse at Vensure's orders?"

"Essentially, yes."

"And the Albaren accuse the Dierna of barbarism," he muttered.

Gellion ran a hand through his hair.

Just a few days. A few more days, and this will be over.

Relief could not follow this thought, however. They would not return to a welcoming Daro. Rebuilding would take years, and they still had a traitor among them. The mysterious elf's nose and glittering eyes flashed in Gellion's mind. He could see the crouch, the bearing of the elf. Familiarity prickled at the edges of his memory again. For a moment, he thought he would grasp it, then the memory slipped through his fingers like water.

"It is only a few days." Dulon echoed Gellion's former thoughts. "Then we can forget this ever happened. If any other Amadeos come knocking on our gates, we will politely throw them into the sea."

Gellion couldn't sleep. He tossed in his bedroll for hours before giving up the fight, rising to his feet and moving soundlessly through the camp. From the rustling and sighs around him, Gellion guessed he was not the only one plagued with a restless mind. The calls of night insects formed an eerie chorus that echoed through the starlit hills. Looking toward the moon, Gellion saw a familiar shadow outlined against the edge of the camp. He went to the elf on silent feet.

"Can't sleep?" he said.

Kyna turned to him without surprise. Her face glowed silver in the moonlight, etched in sharp relief where the shadow of night obscured her features. The effect was beautiful and disconcerting. Gellion's skin prickled.

"I have always liked the night." Kyna's eyes returned to the shapeless hills.

"You have never admitted to liking anything," Gellion chuckled, stepping next to her.

Kyna smirked. "The night is the only time one can truly feel alone, reside solely in one's mind without light to distract, reveal—" She trailed off. "It is a different sort of life."

Gellion looked at her curiously, his eyes following the angles and curves of her profile. For a just a moment, he could almost *see* her, the moonlight reflected in the depths of her eyes; he could almost sense her, that inexplicable barrier that encased her thin to the point of touch.

Hardly conscious of what he was doing, Gellion slowly extended his fingers until they brushed Kyna's.

The veil between them lifted. It was only for a moment, but in that moment, Gellion caught a glimpse of her—a true, unmasked glimpse. He saw her contentment in the night, he felt her exhilaration at his touch. Her triumph. Her confusion. Her fear.

Kyna snapped her hand away, turning toward him with a sharp intake of breath. They stood face to face, Kyna's chin tilted up, Gellion's tilted down. His heart was pounding. Kyna looked into his eyes, searching their depths, a rare string of emotion laid bare in her own. There was an energy between them, a current. It pulled Gellion toward her. He leaned forward. She held still.

Then the opacity returned to Kyna's eyes; the veil dropped back in place. She stepped away from him.

Gellion felt as though he had been leaning against a wall that suddenly vanished, leaving him scrambling for his bearings.

"We should try to get what sleep we can," Kyna said, a barely perceptible quaver to her voice. "The sun will rise in a few hours."

Gellion stared at her, at a complete loss for words. After all these years, all these centuries, he would have finally let himself give in. He would have opened to her—he *had* opened to her—yet she had turned away. She, who felt the same pull to him—he had seen it, had *felt* it— had still turned away from him. Heat suffused his face.

"I saw it." His voice was barely a whisper. "You feel. Through whatever walls you keep, I saw you beyond them, and you cannot tell me you don't feel as I do."

Kyna just looked at him. Gellion thought he could detect the slightest color of fear to her gaze, but his perception was once again separated by an unseen barrier.

"Why?" Gellion had to fight to keep his voice down, conscious of the sleeping elves a stone's throw away. "Why do you do this? Why can't you just *let* yourself feel something? I asked before if you cared about anything, and you do. You do. But you're too afraid to do anything about it."

"I'm not afraid," she said. He could barely make out her words above the hum of insects.

"Then what?"

She set her jaw. Her eyes stared blankly just beyond Gellion. Each moment was agony.

"Say something," he hissed.

Slowly, Kyna's eyes moved to Gellion's, two pools of black in the moonlight, their depths imperceivable.

"I can't," she said.

A hint of pain flitted across her face before she turned away.

Gellion watched her walk back through the camp, her form blending with the shadows until she disappeared.

34

A THIRSTY RIDE

Heat hung on the air, distorting the horizon and drawing sweat from Renyra's forehead. Nightjar's feet plodded one after the other, clopping on the road in rhythm with his swaying body. Renyra closed her mind against the images of pooling water that cycled on a continuous loop in her head. She had seen the last of the Icemelt this morning, when the road had forced her to turn south into the dry scrubland that stretched all the way to Restring Pass. She would have to stop at a village for water, but it was hours yet to sunset, and she did not want to risk being caught. Time was too precious.

After their flight from Daro, Nightjar had run until the last light left the sky. Renyra had forced him to slow his pace then, afraid he would break a leg in the darkness.

Then had followed the longest night in Renyra's memory. Weaponless and with no supplies, Renyra had clung to Nightjar's neck, straining her eyes into the shadows for signs of glinting eyes or movement. By Riu's mercy, luck, or the simple alert presence of her moving horse, no creature had attacked her, but she had seen flitting shapes all around her and heard rustlings and eerie cries until morning.

Since the first light of day, she had urged Nightjar to a canter as often as she could, but was painfully aware of the limits of his body. She did not dare push him too far, or she would never reach the elves before the battle began. So too was she aware of the limits of her own body. Her arm ached in its bandages, and her eyelids were heavy with exhaustion.

In the dragging hours of the journey, Renyra thought. She still did not know what she would tell Dulon, or what she hoped would happen after she delivered the news. Would the elves leave their battle to return to a destroyed city? What good would that do? Now more than ever they needed vierstone, though with Daro gone there was no reason to stay in Tala.

Waves of grief wracked Renyra's body. Already her life in Daro seemed a fairy tale of the distant past. The elves would have to return to Faeran. Would Firas insist they go to Morcanan? She shuddered at the thought of frozen winters and the eternal condemnation of judgmental stares. The face of a silver-haired elf swam before her eyes, mouthing 'Tathé.'

Renyra shook her head and drew her thoughts back to the problem at hand. The elves needed to know what had happened. They needed to return to what had once been Daro as soon as possible and find the elf responsible for all of this. They needed to warn the elves back in Faeran. No one knew the unknown elf's motivation for what he had done. What if he didn't stop with Daro? Who *was* he? Renyra had seen his face, but would any elf know him based on her description?

There were still so many unknowns. On top of everything, Renyra could not shake the feeling that something about the Albaren alliance was wrong. It was too convenient that the elves had left Daro just when the city was most vulnerable to destruction. Had the elf merely used circumstance as opportunity presented itself, or had he had something to do with the alliance from the beginning? If he had, would that make the Albaren's cause any less genuine? The battle any more dangerous?

Renyra squeezed her hands in frustration. Nightjar snorted and pranced.

"Ready to go again?" She pressed her heels to the horse's sides, and he dropped into a lope.

Within half an hour, a jagged outline on the horizon promised a village in the distance. Renyra licked her lips with a dry tongue and urged Nightjar faster. A quick stop to steal some water and food, then another night of riding.

Whether or not her fears about the alliance were well-founded, her fears for Daro and for her kin back in Faeran were real, and the sooner the elves acted, the better.

RESTRING PASS

The morning broke grey and heavy. Dulon wandered through his army, watching elves don armor and pack belongings. He held his shoulders square. He lifted his face and set an expression of quiet confidence upon it. His heart raced, galloped, pounded—he could not decide which described it better. It was not fear of losing the battle that plagued him. It was not even fear of dying. Neither seemed a likely outcome of the coming days. Was it fear of anticipation? Fear of killing? Or was it fear that even a single elf would die, and the burden of their soul would rest on his shoulders all his life?

A hand touched his own, and Dulon started. He realized he was no longer walking and wondered vaguely how long he had been standing still, staring into the distance. Maranyl stood at his shoulder. Her eyes were large and knowing.

"You got up early this morning."

"Yes," said Dulon.

"Couldn't sleep?"

"Could you?"

"Well enough, though the elf tossing and turning at my back tried very hard to prevent it."

"Sorry," he muttered.

A smile touched Maranyl's lips, and her grip on his hand tightened. "How are you?" she asked.

"Brilliant."

When Maranyl did not answer, Dulon met her gaze. There was sympathy in her eyes. "It is a heavy burden, but one you have born well. The elves trust you. They will follow you without question."

"That's what I'm afraid of."

Maranyl sighed. "My dear, you think too much. Accept the circumstances you have been dealt, embrace the decisions you have made, and carry them out with conviction."

Dulon grunted.

"I will stand beside you." She gave him a teasing smile, as though this should solve all his problems.

Maybe it did.

Dulon's own smile broke through his reserves, and some of the tension bled from his muscles. Keeping Maranyl's hand in his, he continued his walk through the camp. Elves bundled their sleeping rolls into packs and fastened weapons to their armor.

Dulon glanced toward the human camp and saw half the tents still standing. Impatience itched at Dulon's feet. He wanted to leave. This waiting was worse than anything ahead could be.

"It looks like we may be leaving a fair bit past dawn." Dulon motioned toward the Albaren. "Still, I think I will start forming ranks, give the day's instructions."

Maranyl let go of his hand, but remained with him as he moved through the elves. He gave directions to those he had chosen to lead ranks, and within half an hour, the elves stood in neat lines facing Restring Pass. Gellion stood at the head of the second block of elves. He nodded to Dulon as he passed. There were shadows under his eyes.

Toward the back blocks, Dulon saw Kyna standing slightly off the line of elves next to her, one foot slack and a distracted expression on her face. He walked over to her.

"Having fun?" he said.

Kyna twirled a knife in her hand. "Immensely."

Dulon searched her eyes for any trace of fear, but found none. He lowered his voice.

"Thank you for helping me bring the elves this far. Whatever reason you stayed behind in Daro, I am grateful for it."

Kyna looked away. "You would have done it on your own," she said, shrugging.

"All the same. I appreciate your support."

Vensure's voice rang through the air, shouting angry orders. Dulon could see the humans starting to gather in groups on either side of the elves.

"We should be leaving soon," he said. "I need to return to the front."

Kyna nodded absently and began twirling her knife again, her gaze wandering.

Dulon strode back to the first block of elves and forced himself to stand still. His eyes moved to those most veteran fighters he had placed in the first block in hopes that their grim confidence would inspire and instruct those behind them. There was nothing left to do but wait.

The sun was fully past the horizon by the time the armies finally began to move.

No horns announced their send-off. Dulon watched the backs of the human soldiers in front of him. Those within sight held themselves stiffly and kept casting nervous glances behind them as though afraid the elves would attack or cast unnatural spells on them at any moment. Dulon made a point to bestow a grin on any who looked his way. This seemed to frighten them more.

The morning passed without sight or sound of any Dierna. With surprising rapidity, the dry shrubbery of the Albaren plains melded into soft grasses and dark soil. Trees from the surrounding mountains encroached into Dulon's field of view, and to the north and south, the Falspires rose to the skies. Restring Pass carved a flat expanse, a bite out of the mountain range, and to the east Dulon could just make out the swell of tall hills on the horizon.

That must be Diernas.

As the sun crested the sky and began to sink again to the west,

Dulon stepped out of the lines to find Vensure. The commander gave Dulon a shrewd look as he approached. Dulon fell into step next to him.

"No signs of an outpost yet," Vensure said. "But that is not entirely surprising. The Dierna would be fools to make their camps so close to the Albaren border. If we continue at this pace, we will reach Arvain by noon tomorrow. We should encounter at least a few outposts before this evening, and we must let no Dierna escape to warn the city of our arrival."

"What if there are spies hidden in the pass?" Dulon asked.

Commander Vensure scoffed. "They have no reason to scout the pass. We have made no moves to defend it until now. Besides, I have outriders and spies of my own. They will find any lurking Dierna long before they see us. I will send someone to alert you of any changes."

Vensure's face read dismissal, and Dulon's hackles rose. The man acted as though Dulon were a subordinate, not the commander of an army graciously offering aid in their time of need. Dulon held hard eye contact with Vensure for several moments before smiling and nodding politely. Then he walked back to his place among the elves.

With each passing hour, Dulon's confusion increased. He scanned what he could see of the horizon for outposts, but aside from the beaten path the army followed, the land was wild. He saw no fences, no walls, no buildings, no sign of human habitation anywhere. Surely they should have seen the Dierna by now, or at least an abandoned outpost or camp?

The sun sank below the hills, casting an early evening over the land. Finally, the armies stopped to make camp. Dulon waited for no orders, but went to find Vensure once more.

"There is no sign of the Dierna anywhere," Dulon said without preamble when he found the commander.

Vensure turned slowly to face him. He seemed to be considering his words.

"I know," he said at last, profoundly unhelpful.

"You seemed sure there would be."

"I know," the man said again. "I expected to come across them by now."

"Have you seen these outposts before?"

"We have reports of them."

"From whom?"

"Inside sources."

"Could they have been wrong?"

"No," Vensure said firmly. "I do not know why the pass is so quiet, but my spies are not wrong. We must be on our guard tonight. Tomorrow we will face the Dierna whether or not we find their outposts. Tomorrow we march on Arvain. Make your camp for the night and set guards. Be ready to leave by dawn."

Dulon sighed and nodded, thinking of their start this morning. He wondered what the commander meant by 'dawn.'

Dawn was, in fact, dawn. Commander Vensure seemed anxious to leave the next morning and whipped his soldiers into a frenzy taking down camp before the sun was free of the horizon.

The armies packed everything. They still had several hours' hike to the end of the pass, where it made more sense to deposit their weightier possessions before approaching Arvain. Dulon wondered if they would return for their things that very evening, making camp after a day of victory and returning to Daro on the morrow.

The sun raced between clouds, casting shifting shadows over the mountains as the armies resumed their march. A cool breeze blew down from their peaks, contrasting sweetly with the warmth of the morning. Dulon drew a deep breath of the earthy air. Daro was beautiful. He had come to love the salty tang of the air, the twisted shrubs and trees, the heat and the orange soil. Yet despite the enmity he held for Morcanan, Dulon's heart sometimes longed for the cool forests and shadowed passes of his old home. He missed soft ground and gurgling streams. He missed cool mornings and mist. He thought of evenings spent curled by a fire deep in the halls of Morcanan, Maranyl by his side as a blizzard raged outside the mountain. Dulon knew he would never return to Morcanan, but he would not let its oppression taint the memories he held in fondness.

He looked beside him and watched Maranyl. She walked with

straight shoulders and her chin tipped upward. Catching his eye, she raised a brow. Dulon grinned and she laughed, a sweet sound.

He held the melody of her voice in his heart as the sun rose and the land spread in front of them. To either side, the mountains had begun to melt into tall hills that seemed to flatten further with each hour. Still the armies encountered no outposts, no Dierna, no sign of life. Unease nagged at Dulon's mind. How could Vensure have been so mistaken? Where were the Dierna?

Vensure halted the procession just before the wide expanse of the Dierna hills. Soon they would be free of the pass—visible for miles.

They piled their possessions under the sparse trees south of the road. Dulon dropped his pack, keeping only his spear and a thin canister of water attached to his hip. Nerves were beginning to take root in Dulon's middle. They were close now. Just an hour's walk from Arvain according to Vensure.

For the final stretch of the march, the elves would walk beside the first block of Albaren soldiers so Dulon could hear the commander's orders and relay them to his people.

It took a quarter of an hour to reorganize, but soon Dulon found himself walking again, this time with his view unimpeded by human soldiers. As far as the eye could see, the land sloped in great swells and valleys, smaller hills rippling across their surface. Yellow-green grass swayed in the wind. With the moving shadows from the clouds, the effect was mesmerizing, like looking at a sea of amber seaweed, or a golden field reflected in the waters of a rolling ocean.

"It's beautiful." Dulon hardly noticed he had said the words aloud until Vensure's patronizing voice responded.

"It is pastureland. Cropland. Water. Infinite opportunity wasted on the Dierna."

The thought of destroying all of this for crops and houses broke Dulon's heart, though he knew the need for these things as well as any.

Grass brushed Dulon's knees as they progressed into the hills. In the distance he saw glimpses of houses and fences, but the hills obscured any clear views.

"Arvain is just around there." Vensure pointed past a large hill to their right. "When we emerge on the other side of the hill, the Dierna will be able to see us, but it is a short distance to the city from there. They will have little time to respond before we reach their gates."

They began to turn around the base of the hill. The edges of a lake came into view, its waters dark and choppy from the wind, stretching into the distance with no visible far shore. Dulon's view of the lake expanded with each step, until he could see the beginnings of a city wall in front of it.

They marched further.

The hill was falling away to their right now. With a few more steps the city would be in full view. Dulon took a breath of anticipation.

Two more steps, one more.

Dulon's heart sank into his stomach.

Commander Vensure stopped dead, muttering a curse.

Arvain sat proudly on the shore of the lake, tall buildings rising from its center in rectangular steps. Patches of sunlight reflected off of wooden walls and shingled roofs. A large gate stood at the center of the encircling wall of the city. It was closed.

In front of the gate stood an army.

Dulon could hardly hazard a guess at the number of Dierna that stood armored and armed before them, but he was reasonably confident it was almost as many as the men and elves at his back.

The Dierna had known of this attack all along, and they had been waiting.

A horn blared from the city, and the Dierna charged into the fields of grass.

SOLDIERS HIDDEN

Renyra sighed as cool water ran down her neck. Her knees sank into spongy earth and the shade of a tree held the sun's heat at bay. To her right, Nightjar drank deeply from a stream.

The urgency of Renyra's errand had not abandoned her, but a few minutes' refreshment was well worth the cost. She had ridden for four days, finally giving in to sleep the last two nights. She had entered Restring Pass the day before, and the hills of Diernas were clear on the western horizon. The trampled grass around the road told Renyra the armies had already come this way. Had the armies already arrived at Arvain? Could they be fighting even now? What would she do if they were?

With a sigh, she grabbed her small satchel of stolen goods—mostly hard bread and dried fish—and swung back onto Nightjar's back. Her hand strayed to her hip to ensure the kitchen knife still hung at her belt, then she urged Nightjar toward the hills.

The army's trail led to the southern edge of the pass, then on to a collection of taller hills trailing from the mountains. If Renyra climbed to the top of one, she would be able to see for miles, and an army of thousands was sure to be easy to spot. With a click of her tongue, she urged Nightjar up the sloping grass.

The horizon sank lower and lower, the hills seeming to flatten, until the land curved into haze in the distance. Renyra saw clusters of dwellings, but nothing resembling a city. Arvain must lie directly to the south.

The crest of the hill was in sight now.

Renyra pulled back on Nightjar's halter. She strained her ears.

Strange sounds rode the breeze, twisted and clashing in its grip. Voices. Shouting voices.

Nightjar jumped forward with a snort as Renyra pressed in her heels, heart suddenly pounding. The ground flattened, and a sudden burst of wind tore past her, the sounds of battle now a flood through the air.

Renyra gasped.

On the flat expanse of ground before a city on a lake, thousands of bodies writhed in a shifting mass. Flares of light flashed like fireflies over the field as the sun caught in the metal of weapons. Renyra stared in stunned fascination. She had never seen so many people, elves or humans, together in one place. How could they know who to fight in that chaos?

Her hands clenched in Nightjar's mane. Firas was down there. Dulon, Caerlyn, Gellion. Even if she could will herself to enter the battle, Renyra would never find them among the thousands that shifted in constant motion. Even if she could find them, what good would it do? The elves could hardly pull out of the fight now, and at the moment, a distant enemy of unknown identity was sure to seem unimportant compared to scores of angry humans trying to skewer them.

Nightjar pranced on the spot, unnerved by Renyra's change in mood and by the sounds wafting up the hill.

Sweet Riu, what do I do now?

She crossed the star over herself and put her face in her hands. She had no weapon, no armor, and her arm was still sore. She was exhausted and she was terrified. Joining the battle would do nothing but risk her life, yet how could she just stand here and watch?

Raising her head, she looked around frantically, as though the answer would appear written on the hills.

And it did.

Renyra's eyes widened. In a valley between the hills north of the city, an unnatural shadow spread across the grass.

More soldiers.

Were they Albaren reinforcements? Somehow it did not seem to fit. Her knowledge of battle tactics was lacking to say the least, but why hide half your troops behind you in an open fight?

A jolt of adrenaline coursed through Renyra's limbs. If those were enemy soldiers, she was standing alone on top of a hill in clear view of them.

No alarm had sounded. Maybe they had not seen her.

She rode Nightjar down and through the sloping hills once more, making steady progress toward the area where she had seen the hidden soldiers. Her view was obscured by the swells of land now, and she feared she would come upon the army before she was ready, revealing herself and guaranteeing capture or worse.

At the bottom of what she hoped was the hill concealing the soldiers, she slid off Nightjar's back and wound his lead rope around some tall grass, hoping it would encourage him to stay in one place long enough for her return.

Crouching so the grass tickled her nose, Renyra made her way up the slope. As the ground began to straighten and curve downward, she flattened herself on her belly, wincing as she moved with her knees and her good forearm. She heard no sound, but if the soldiers were in hiding, that was not surprising. Cautiously, Renyra arched her back and rose on one hand until she could see over the tips of the grass.

She looked down on helmeted heads. There were hundreds of them, and she could only guess how many continued beyond her vision. The faces beneath the helmets were pale. Cropped beards lined the jaws of some, but others were smooth and angular. Most of the soldiers wore leather to the wrists, with silvery metal strapped to their chests and shoulders. Curved swords hung at their hips.

Renyra had seen few Albaren, but she knew none of these humans resembled Count Amadeo Benta. These were Dierna troops.

She had to warn the elves.

The terror of the battle beyond her vision froze her blood, but if the Dierna's second army stormed the field, all those she loved would be in danger. The Albaren and the elves would be sandwiched between their enemy.

Renyra had to find any elves she could and tell them to spread the warning. If she found Dulon, all the better, but if not, she would have to hope that the message reached him.

Dropping back to the ground, Renyra sidled backward until she could stand without revealing herself, then ran to Nightjar, who looked up at her with a mouth full of grass.

"I'm sorry," she said as she threw his rope over his neck and sprung onto his back. "Get me to the elves and your job is done, I promise." The horse swished his tail and shook his head, but moved forward at a lope.

The sounds of battle grew louder. The land flattened as it approached the lake on the other side of Arvain, and Renyra stopped Nightjar at the edge of the field. She would be in full view of the armies now. At least the army with its back to her was on her side, but the soldiers did not know that. She would simply have to ride across the open ground and hope no one attacked her. The distance would take less than a minute to cover.

She patted Nightjar's neck, took a shaking breath, and pressed her heels to his flank. Nightjar surged forward, leaving the safety of the hills behind them.

THE HORN

Damp strands of hair distorted Gellion's vision. He raked them away with one hand as his other wielded a halberd in a swooping arc. He felt the impact of two men crumpling away from the blow and steeled himself not to be sick. Everything was happening too fast for him to think about what he was doing, but he could feel a dull panic sitting just beneath his skin, waiting to overcome him at the slightest weakness. He would not let it. He could not.

His concentration shifted among the humans moving toward him. He tried not to see their faces, but their gleaming eyes invariably drew his attention. He saw fury in their faces, but also fear. Most held swords. Some were women.

Gellion moved his feet forward, sideways, forward again. He stepped over fallen weapons and bodies, doing his best to ignore the tang of sweat and blood and worse filling his nostrils. The air was stagnant and humid. All the while he stabbed forward with his halberd, using it as shield, weapon, and crowd control all at once. It was easy. His body remembered everything and flowed through the A'vaeri's dance as though he were alone in the arena. Keeping his enemies out of arm's reach was a simple task requiring little thought.

The harder task was keeping his brothers in sight. He could only hope they were trying to stay near him as well, and that the elven forces would remain close.

Marchon Arceria's likeness swam among the features of each face Gellion passed. Gellion channeled his frustration through his halberd. What was the Marchon among the dozens he now slaughtered? It didn't matter.

Why did it still matter?

He blinked hard and shook his head, trying to focus.

"Gellion!"

Gellion wheeled around, but saw only indistinct soldiers.

"Here!"

Veldon leapt over a fallen body and landed lightly on his feet beside Gellion. He pressed his shoulder to Gellion's while his eyes darted around, scanning for enemies.

"Gellion," he repeated. "There are more troops lying in wait behind us." Veldon slashed at a soldier who had come upon his right side. "Dierna soldiers—" he stepped sideways into Gellion, moving them both out of the arc of a spear.

Gellion nearly dropped his halberd.

"What?" he shouted above the noise. "How do you know this?"

"Word is spreading through the elves," Veldon panted. "Someone saw them—we must pull back."

Even as Veldon spoke the words, Gellion could see the mass of elves around him beginning to move backward. Before he could respond, Veldon had moved past him and positioned himself next to Valder. Gellion backed away from the forces bearing down on them.

Surprise reinforcements? How had the Dierna been so prepared for this attack? The army before the gates of Arvain had been shock enough, but Gellion had been confident they could overcome the Dierna. Even now the enemy's numbers were dwindling. They were skilled fighters, but the elves were better, and with the Albaren, the Dierna couldn't hope to win the day.

Fighting off another army from behind shook Gellion's confidence severely. They would be hard pressed to escape and turn tail, let alone win the battle. How could Vensure have been so wrong? He should have known that something was off when they encountered no Dierna soldiers in the pass. He should have sent more scouts ahead. He should have turned back.

This was all the Albaren's fault. Gellion had thought Vensure a competent commander, if not an agreeable person, but to make a mistake of this magnitude demonstrated his arrogance. He had underestimated his enemy. He had overestimated his secrecy. The Dierna had been forewarned against this attack. There was no other explanation, and it seemed they had brought in forces from far beyond Arvain.

Fury boiled in Gellion's blood. The elves had placed too much trust in the abilities and judgment of the Albaren. Gellion had placed too much trust in the elves. How could he have let the opinions of Daro overpower his judgment? The best the elves could hope for now was to escape with their lives and reassess the situation. Was vierstone worth this?

"Retreat!" he shouted. "Fall back! It's a trap!"

Gellion looked around frantically. He needed to find Dulon.

All offense abandoned, he ran back through the elves, calling Dulon's name and spreading word of the Dierna reinforcements as he went. Still, humans broke through the elves' retreating ranks, and Gellion was forced to fend off more than one attack in his search.

The panic beneath Gellion's skin was spreading through his body and rising up his throat now. He fought for control.

"Back! Get back!" a familiar voice called.

Gellion spun and saw a flash of Dulon's hair. Gellion shoved and maneuvered his way toward him.

Dulon's eyes burned. Authority seemed to radiate from him as he held his spear aloft and shouted orders. His hard expression melted into relief when he saw Gellion.

"You know the situation?" he asked, pulling Gellion with him in the quickening pace of the retreat.

"Yes."

"I don't know if the Albaren know. We have to find their commanders—Vensure if we can. He can't be far, he was beside me when we charged. He must see the madness of remaining in this fight when the Dierna numbers could double any moment. We have to return to the pass."

Gellion nodded and opened his mouth to respond, but found himself shoved into Dulon instead. He staggered backward, unsure of what had just happened, but was forced back against Dulon by the elves at his back.

"What's going on?" he shouted.

"I don't know." Dulon's voice was muffled in the press of bodies. He craned his neck upward. "I think the Albaren behind us don't understand what's happening. They've stopped our retreat."

"Do you see Vensure?"

"Not yet, let me through!" he yelled, squeezing through the elves around him and pulling Gellion with him.

Together they pushed through a mixture of elves and men until they spotted the plumed helm of Commander Vensure.

"Commander!"

The man turned, narrowing his eyes when he saw Dulon.

"What is the meaning of this?" he snapped. "Why do your elves retreat?"

"There are more Dierna troops waiting in the hills to attack," Dulon shouted. "They will smash our armies between both forces. We have to return to the pass. If we can't escape, we can at least make a stand with our enemies on one side."

"You do not command these armies, elf." The suspicion deepened in Vensure's eyes. "How can you know this?"

"Someone saw them."

"By someone you mean an elf? How did they see an army hidden in the hills in the midst of a battle half a mile away?"

"I don't know who saw them or how. Why does it matter?" Dulon's voice was hard as stone. "This is no trick. If the Dierna have reinforcements, this is a fight we do not want to continue."

"If? If?! I will not retreat from these barbarians on the whim of a possibility that there are more of them than we thought!"

"They knew we were coming," said Dulon. "We did not prepare to fight a full army warned of our presence!"

"And how did they know?" A mad gleam sparked in Vensure's eyes. "How did the Dierna know that we were coming? I assure you my men are faithful."

Gellion's hackles rose at the accusation in the man's voice.

"Why would we betray this alliance?!" His fury exploded through his panic. "You are the ones who came into this battle ill prepared, dragging our people down with you! We are trying to salvage what we can of a situation *you* put us in."

Vensure's gaze locked on Gellion. A strange expression settled over his features, and something like satisfaction shone in his eyes.

"I did underestimate you," Vensure said. "I didn't expect you to betray the alliance. Oh, I am not so naive as to think that you care about the fate of the Albaren. This has always been an alliance of bribery. Benta told us you refused our offer outright until he claimed to possess the stone that you covet."

Gellion could feel Dulon's form stiffen beside him. Gellion felt a cold dread begin to creep through his veins. 'Claimed' to possess?

"But I thought your greed would outweigh your treachery," Vensure said.

"We didn't betray you," Gellion said through his teeth.

Vensure ignored him. "It does not matter now. The outcome will be the same."

Gellion tried to make sense of Vensure's words. His dread grew. The sounds of battle seemed to grow distant.

"Our last kings were fools to trust you," Vensure continued. "King Naval knows better. You sit content in your city, hoarding your technology and strength, but you disdain us. You trade with us now, but as soon as we are no longer convenient, you will turn on us. You are an unnatural presence in this world. We serve the Almighty faithfully, and his creation will benefit from your absence."

"Our absence?" Dulon's face was red. "How do you intend to be rid of us? We could cut you down where you stand now, and your armies would scatter like chaff in the wind."

"Oh I don't think so," Vensure said. "All of the Albaren know you for what you are. They fear you—hate you. They know of your treachery and of your heathenism and want your blood quite as much as the king."

"What treachery?" Dulon growled. His face was as terrible as Gellion had ever seen it.

A spark of satisfaction shone in Vensure's eye.

"The treachery they have seen. Gellion here showed the elves' true nature when he so kindly visited our capitol."

All the blood drained from Gellion's face. His anger cooled to a cold numbness. Chiara's face swam before his eyes.

"You put her up to it," he said softly. "It was all meant to happen. The trial—"

A corner of Vensure's mouth twitched.

"You played your part well."

Rage and shame warred in Gellion like fire and ice. The king had never wanted him to 'repent of his sins.' It had all been a show to disparage the elves, to justify the Albaren's betrayal of a murderous and unnatural race. 'Demon' Arceria had called him—an incubus possessed of faery magic. How could Gellion have been so blind? How could they all have been—

Vensure reached behind him and drew a curved horn from his belt.

"You were right about one thing," he said. "Your elves will be caught between enemies, and the odds will not be in your favor."

He raised the horn to his lips. Dulon lunged at him, but four guards leapt from behind Vensure and reigned an onslaught of blows upon Dulon, forcing him backward.

"Stop him!" Dulon shouted.

But it was too late. Vensure's horn sounded in a sonorous blast, cutting through the battle like a ship through waves.

There was a moment of stillness as the echo died.

Gellion turned his head, watching the gaze of the Albaren soldiers shift to the elves among them.

Then the Albaren let out a cry both joyous and vengeful, and chaos burst forth once more, holding a new terror. Gellion raised his halberd as a sea of swords converged upon him.

A smile twisted across Vensure's face.

3 8

SWORDS ON ALL SIDES

Renyra was running. She was trying to lead the elves away from the battle, trying to find Firas, but neither was going as she had planned.

Her chest had swelled with relief as the elves began to move backward, away from the battle, but now they were caught in a standstill, and she did not know why. She ran sideways, trying to move past the unseen barrier that blocked their progress. Her eyes scanned the face of every elf she passed. None were Firas.

"To the side—" she called, but her voice faltered, and her feet skidded to a stop as the deep braying of a horn rose and fell in the air.

For a moment, Renyra could hear her breath—the beat of her heart —in the sudden silence.

Then the sounds of battle resumed.

What had the horn meant? Were the Dierna reinforcements attacking?

"To the side!" she shouted again, renewing her attempts to bring the elves toward the hills.

Cries of terror rose behind her, and she paused. Her hand tightened around the trampled sword in her grip. Though the weapon was unfamiliar, it gave her some comfort and a measure of protection.

The shouts rose in pitch, laced with fear, but also anger. Renyra looked around wildly, but all she saw was more fighting. Elves fighting humans, humans fighting—

Renyra watched more closely. Those humans did not look like the soldiers she had seen in the hills, and they were coming from the wrong direction.

A pair of blazing eyes locked on her. Renyra's breath caught in her throat as a thick man barreled toward her, sword aloft. He was Albaren. She was sure of it. Surely he did not mistake her for a Dierna soldier?

She spun out of the way at the last moment of his attack, sending him stumbling forward with the force of his sword. Holding her injured arm to her chest, Renyra crouched and swung her sword in a frantic arc, cutting into the back of the man's knees. He bellowed in pain and fury.

Renyra scrambled backward. No more was she shielded from the forefront of battle by ranks of her own people. Elves and humans were on all sides, locked in desperate combat.

The meaning of the horn's blast sank into Renyra like molten lead. They had been betrayed. But why? The elves had come here to help the Albaren.

Renyra could not make sense of it, but there was no time to scrutinize the mystery. From a glance, Renyra knew the elves were superior fighters, but the humans kept coming, and she could already see Dierna soldiers pressing back into the fray.

Mind racing, Renyra began to run again. There were enemies on two sides, but there were four sides to this fight. If the elves could escape to the west, they might be able to flee north into the hills. But how could she communicate this to an entire army? In growing panic, Renyra could see the elves spreading thinner and thinner as they moved in all directions, driven apart by the growing numbers of humans infiltrating their forces.

Two more men charged her. Renyra ducked around their blades, trying to stab her sword behind their defenses, but they were large and strong, and Renyra was one-handed.

Using his weight against him, she tripped one man from behind, and he crashed to the ground in a heap of armor. Leaping backward, she glanced away a blow from the second man, but he advanced on her with a grim smile. He raised his sword as Renyra backed away. Her eyes darted to either side of the man. She could outrun him if she could dodge his sword. She would have to choose her moment carefully.

The man stopped mid stride with his sword poised over his head. An arrow protruded from between his eyes. Renyra stared with mingled relief and horror as the man slowly toppled backward, the weight of his sword pulling him to the ground.

Behind the fallen soldier stood a willowy elf, lowering a small bow and running toward Renyra.

Relief washed through every nerve in Renyra's body, stronger than her terror, more real than her pain. She ran forward and allowed Firas's arms to envelop her. It was only a moment, they had no more time than that, but for that moment none of it mattered—Daro's destruction, Albarad's betrayal, even the battle engulfing them.

"We have to run to the side," Renyra said at last. Pulling away from Firas was like stepping back from a fire into a freezing night.

Firas stared at her. His eyes darted up and around, and understanding dawned in his face.

He shook his head. "But ... but how? How are you here? Did you follow us all the way?"

"No." Renyra picked up her sword. "No Firas, Daro is gone. It's destroyed. It's in the sea. But there's no time to explain now. None of it matters if we can't get out of this."

He stared at her a moment longer, a thousand questions in his eyes, but he nodded.

"Ok. How can I help?"

"Shout. Get the elves to follow us."

Firas did not hesitate. He raised his chin, and his clear voice rang over the heads of armies.

"To the side! Elves! Run to the west! The hills!"

"Good. Now keep shouting."

Together they ran through the battle, dodging attacks and shouting encouragement as more and more elves joined their flight.

The field seemed endless. In the chaos and terror, Renyra wondered if they weren't somehow running in circles.

At long last, a gap became visible where the soldiers thinned and the hills began. Hope blossomed in Renyra's chest. The elves could outrun the humans. They just needed to get to the hills.

"Go!" she shouted, and Firas took up her cry. But as the gap grew closer, a surge of movement caught Renyra's eye.

No.

The hope in her chest sank through her stomach.

The rear of the Albaren army was charging around from behind. The gap was closing quickly, and even if she, Firas, and those elves behind them made it through, the majority of the elves would not.

"Stop!" Fury and frustration cracked Renyra's voice.

The elves slowed as half the Albaren force clashed with the Dierna, and the other half flooded through what had once been the elves' only escape. The soldiers charged toward the center of the battle.

The elves were surrounded.

Riu help us all.

Renyra traced the star over her body and tightened her hand around her sword.

39

TO SAVE A CITY

Dulon could no longer tell where his arm ended and his spear began, though he did not know if it was due to his prowess, or the jellylike numbness of his limbs. He swung the weapon without thinking, registering only whether those in front of him were human or elf. A rage such as he had never known burned within him, fueled by shame.

He had done everything he thought was right. He had tried so hard. He had failed.

The alliance had been a trick from the beginning. Had the Dierna even attacked the Albaren villages, or had that been a lie, too? But why take the fight all the way to Arvain if so? Vensure was clearly an accomplished actor, but his confusion at the lack of Dierna outposts in the pass had seemed genuine.

No, Dulon decided, the Albaren's revenge upon the Dierna was real enough. They had merely brought the elves along to intimidate and weaken the Dierna until their meager forces were manageable, then planned to turn on the elves when victory was assured. What better way to defeat two enemies than by pitting them against each other in a battle as much a surprise to one as the other?

But it wasn't a surprise to the Dierna. They were not the meager force of barbarians Vensure anticipated. The commander clearly didn't have infallible loyalty among his troops. The thought gave Dulon little satisfaction.

Cries of terror and dying elves surrounded him. Each individual left a black mark on Dulon's soul. He had earned the trust of his people and brought them unwittingly to a slaughter.

The moment Vensure had mentioned vierstone, Dulon knew that the Albaren quarry had never existed. How the Albaren had known of the stone and its importance to the elves, he could not guess, but from the beginning it had been nothing but a feigned bargaining chip. And it had worked splendidly.

Dulon shouted in frustration as he sliced and stabbed. He watched his enemies fall through his sodden locks of hair. Beside him, Gellion's halberd whooshed through the air, a graceful blur on the edge of Dulon's vision.

He did not know where Maranyl was. He could not think of her, or he would lose the little control he still possessed. She was an able fighter. He could only hope that she would make her way to the forefront of the fighting and find him.

The Albaren were thinning, spreading their forces to surround the elves on three sides with the Dierna at their backs. The only course of escape was directly through the Albaren, and he intended to lead the way through or die trying.

Gellion leapt forward, leaving two men in the dirt under his feet. Dulon twisted away from his own opponent, catching him in the ribs with a backhand blow and pushing further toward the hills. Ahead, he could see the dancing plume of Commander Vensure. The man stood encased in the shields of three guards, shouting orders.

Dulon's fury burned white-hot.

"Ahead!" Dulon yelled.

Gellion's eyes locked on the commander like a hunting wolf. He bared his teeth. His eyes looked black in the shadow of his hair, yet burned with a ferocity frightening to behold.

Together, the two of them carved their way toward the shields. Dulon could feel a group of elves moving in behind them, fighting from the sides while he and Gellion pushed forward. Vensure's plume grew ever nearer.

"There you are," said a breathless voice from Dulon's side.

Dulon's head jerked toward the voice. His instinct was to bring his spear crashing into its source, but at the last moment, recognition dawned in his mind, and he stayed his hand with a frightening force of will.

Muscles relaxing and eyes softening, Dulon felt a smile twitch at his lips.

"Some turn of events," Maranyl said with a grin.

Dulon felt the absurd urge to laugh. He spun his spear at the head of an Albaren with only a slight glance away from Maranyl.

"I must admit this is not how I envisioned today going."

"You seem to be doing an admirable job getting us out of it."

A surge of gratitude swelled in Dulon. Looking forward, the distance to the hills seemed shorter. If he could only get to Vensure.

The man was close now. Dulon could feel the eyes of his guards boring into him, waiting for his next move.

"Lead some elves to the side, there," Dulon said to Maranyl, pointing to the left of the commander's guards. "Gellion and I will go for Vensure."

Maranyl nodded, giving his arm a squeeze before running behind him and shouting off rapid orders to a group of elves.

Dulon watched them move forward, clearing a wider path to his left. Maranyl fought at the forefront of the party, wielding a short sword in each hand. Even with a battle raging around him, Dulon could not keep the smile from his face as he watched her move with the grace and precision of a dancer.

Breaking his trance, Dulon turned to give his orders to Gellion, but his eye caught Vensure's on the way. He froze. Vensure was staring at him with a look of supreme satisfaction. A wicked smile curved up his face, and he spoke in the ear of one of his guards.

Disconcerted, Dulon stared back at Vensure with a look of defiance. He would show no fear to the man.

"Gellion," Dulon said in a loud, calm voice. "Vensure's guards.

Together." He glanced to the side and received a hard nod of acknowledgement from Gellion.

"I'll go right," Gellion said, "and—" but he cut his speech short as a man took a swing at his neck. Gellion ducked sideways and turned his halberd on the inconvenient attacker with a look of exasperation.

Dulon looked back at the guards to plan the best approach for attack.

There were only two.

Vensure still bore the same smug expression, but his eyes were fixed at a point to Dulon's left. Dulon followed his gaze.

The battle around him slowed to meaningless motion. Cotton filled his ears, muffling the sounds to a distant monotony.

Maranyl stood at the forefront of the elves, facing into the bulk of the Albaren army. She parried and stabbed and swung, all the while trusting her back to the gap that the elves behind her were pushing forward. Yet she had gone too far. It was not elves at her back, but Vensure's third guard.

Dulon opened his mouth to shout and raised his spear to throw, but both were too late. The guard thrust his sword forward, and the blade disappeared between the plates of Maranyl's armor.

Dulon's cry died in his throat. No sound could embody the mind-numbing horror that hit every nerve of his body in a single instant.

He stood as though in a nightmare.

Maranyl jerked forward, then slowly looked down at the red blade below her breast. The guard drew back his sword with a violence that turned Dulon's vision red, and he watched his wife crumple to the ground.

The muffled sounds in Dulon's ears turned to a roar. A strength he had never known he possessed spread like fire through his muscles. He forgot about Gellion. He forgot about the elves behind him. He forgot about everything in the world that was not Maranyl and those who had taken her from his world.

Dulon closed the gap between himself and Vensure in two strides. The guards were ready, shields aloft and swords drawn, but Dulon sent the first shield crashing to the ground with a single blow of his spear. The guard cried out in pain and tried to swing his sword up toward

Dulon, but Dulon hewed the man's hand at the wrist and sent both hand and sword to the dirt. As the guard stared in horror at his limb, Dulon thrust his spear into his neck.

The satisfaction in Vensure's eyes wavered, and he stepped backward, calling for more soldiers.

Dulon slashed the next guard's shins beneath his shield and brought the tip of his spear up underneath it, feeling a crunch as it broke through metal and bone.

There were four more soldiers between him and Vensure now, but Dulon did not care. There was no doubt in his mind he would kill the commander, even if he had to take down half his army first.

Dulon rushed into the soldiers with an eagerness borne of revenge and a wild desire for pain. His spear moved in ceaseless arcs and thrusts, clanging against the metal of swords, shields, and armor, and cutting through fabric and flesh.

Tears coursed down Dulon's face and seemed to boil against his skin.

Men fell around him, forming a gruesome path to mark his progress. More soldiers converged upon him. Flashes of pain flared all over Dulon's body. A sword bit into his shoulder, a shield smashed into his leg. He ignored them all. No pain could be greater than that which burned at the center of his being.

He had brought the elves here. He had brought her here. He had told her to lead the elves forward. He had shown Vensure his attachment to her.

Dulon gripped his spear with two hands. The men continued to fall around him.

The distant part of Dulon's mind that still formed rational thought saw that open ground and the hills beyond were close now. He took two leaping bounds forward, swinging his spear in a wide circle to scatter the last few soldiers that lay between him and Vensure.

The commander looked around, saw that he was alone, and faced Dulon at last, raising his sword with grim acceptance in his eyes.

Dulon thrust his spear toward the man's face. Vensure met the blow with his sword and dodged sideways, stabbing at Dulon's ribs and glancing the edge of his blade off his wrist.

Dulon twisted away, ignoring the searing pain throughout his body at the movement. He swung at Vensure's head; he thrust at Vensure's chest. Each time, he struck the man, but not hard enough for a killing blow.

Vensure was good, but as the duel progressed, he repeated the same patterns. He was clearly not accustomed to fights lasting longer than a few moves. He feigned too often and had the slightest pause before each one. Dulon waited for the next pause. Just one more time. There.

Dulon pretended to fall for the feint, then stabbed his spear the other direction. Vensure had no time to compensate. He fell against Dulon's spear, the tip driving straight through his body. But as Vensure lurched forward, he drew a curved dagger from his belt and thrust upward with the last of his strength.

Ice cold pain spread through Dulon's core. He saw the last remnants of smugness leave Vensure's eyes as they glassed over.

Dulon let go of his spear and stumbled backward.

The roaring in his ears was fading, but in the distance, a chorus of horns echoed off the hills.

40

—

SHADOWS OF THE PAST

All of the breath left Gellion's body as he watched Dulon fall to the ground. He had tried to reach him, to help him, but it had all happened too fast. Soldiers had surrounded Dulon before Gellion realized what was happening.

Now Gellion stood in a sea of bodies. Even those still living stood motionless as horn blasts continued to echo from the city walls and across the battlefield. Gellion did not care what they meant.

Dulon was dead.

Gellion took deep breaths, trying to control the waves of grief, rage, and panic clouding his mind. This was not the time. The Albaren were now leaderless, but so were the elves, and Gellion had brought them here as surely as Dulon. It was up to him to get them back.

The way to the hills now stood open before him. The Albaren to either side stood dumbly, shocked into stillness by their commander's death, the horns, or both. Gellion could not hesitate any longer.

"Through the gap!" he called at the top of his lungs. "To the hills! Go!"

The elves around him began to run. Gellion continued to shout orders and encouragement, watching with a thundering heart as scores of elves made it through the Albaren soldiers to open ground. They just might get out of this.

Then an answering horn blast echoed from the hills.

A distant rumble of voices, feet, and hooves underlay the sound, and grew louder with each moment.

Gellion's stomach dropped as an army charged over the hills, flooding toward the battlefield.

The rumor had been true. The Dierna reinforcements had arrived.

If the battle to this point had been chaos, Gellion did not know what to call the madness that now spread like flames across the field. The Albaren scattered, running for the hills and Restring Pass alongside the elves, all past grievances seemingly forgotten in the haste of their terror.

"The west! The mountains!" Gellion's voice cracked with the strain. The elves could not be here when the armies converged. They had to get out. The Dierna had horses and could ride down the elves on flat terrain. The mountains were their only hope now.

Gellion ran, dodging past elves and humans, leaping over bodies and fallen weapons. Behind him, he could hear the shouts of the Dierna, jubilant at the flight of their enemies and the charge of their comrades.

There was no point yelling orders now. The elves were scattered and panicked, and he could only trust that each had the good sense to run in the right direction. They would have to regroup as best they could once they were in the mountains.

As he ran, Gellion searched desperately for his brothers, but to no avail. His lungs burned, and sweat stung his eyes. He could hardly tell elves from humans anymore.

Then he heard his name, faintly at first, so that he wondered if he had imagined it, but then again, closer and louder.

"Gellion!"

He slowed his pace and turned sideways, to see none other than Renyra running toward him, Firas loping behind her. Firas had a long cut along his hairline, but otherwise both elves appeared unharmed.

Gellion stared at Renyra. "How did you get here?" he shouted above the din of noise surrounding them.

Renyra did not stop, but ran along beside Gellion.

"I rode from Daro. Gellion, the city—" She broke off as she was forced to leap around the other side of a lumbering Albaren.

"What about the city?" Gellion's voice came out high. What could have happened in Daro that would send Renyra across Albarad to the midst of a battle?

"It's destroyed." Her voice cracked on the word. "It's gone."

Gellion felt his feet dig into the ground, his legs bracing the impact of their own accord. Renyra ran two more steps, then doubled back, alarm in her eyes.

"We have to keep going!" she said desperately.

"What do you mean destroyed?" Gellion demanded.

"It's in the sea—the whole cliffside." She glanced toward the hills.

The Dierna were nearly on the battlefield.

"In the sea?"

The chaos around Gellion seemed to fade in the force of his despair.

Gone. Completely gone. His city.

"We have to get back," Renyra said. "Most of the elves got out, but I don't know what happened after that."

"How?" Gellion still stood in place, elves and men running past him on either side.

"I will explain as we go. Gellion, we have to keep moving!

Renyra took his wrist and began to drag him forward. Gellion followed in a haze.

Dulon gone. Daro gone. What was there to go back to? Why run at all?

He shook himself out of his grief as questions flooded his mind.

"What happened?" he said. "How did it happen? Did you see who did it?"

"The earthquakes across the city—they were weakening the city's structure, the cliff's structure, like a latticework of cracks in the ground just waiting to be linked together. He just walked through the city, connecting them, and everything broke apart."

"Who is he? Did you see him?" The image of the hooded elf came to

Gellion's mind, the edges not quite clear. He remembered the flash of eyes, the sharp line of a nose. Again, familiarity came to him, but retreated before he could grasp it.

"Yes," Renyra said, "but I didn't know him. I've never seen him before. He was Turi."

A surge of adrenaline rushed through Gellion's body, though at first he did not know why. Then, in an instant, the unnamed familiarity took shape.

Turi. Yes, he had been Turi. Renyra wouldn't have seen him before. Few in Daro would have.

"He had black hair," Renyra said. "Eyes so dark they were almost black. Gellion, he could bend metal at a touch, crack stone with the palm of his hand."

The face that had haunted Gellion for months suddenly solidified, clear in his mind. He saw its likeness beneath the hood of his own tunic, the tunic Kaelo had taught him to make. Naturally, the man would have known what it was when he saw it, and what better way to move about a city unseen?

"He saw me," Renyra continued. "He stood right in front of me and broke my javelin, but he just walked past me, like I was no threat."

Why should an elf who could destroy vierstone and collapse cliff sides be intimidated by a lone elf? Yet Kaelo had seemed to deliberately spare Gellion more than once. Did he remember? Did he recognize the boy who had once admired him beyond any other?

"Where is Dulon?" Renyra said. "I haven't been able to find him. He might know who the elf was."

The present situation crashed into Gellion's thoughts. Kaelo's face, ever serious, melted into the laughing visage of Dulon. Gellion hadn't been expecting it, and the fresh wave of pain wracked his body and nearly stopped him in his tracks again.

Gellion was saved answering by a loud clashing sound behind them.

The Dierna had joined their forces.

The ground seemed to vibrate from the thunder of feet and hooves and the impact of bodies and weapons. Yells of anger, terror, pain, and triumph permeated the air. Gellion ran faster.

"Listen," Gellion panted, his voice cracking. "Dulon, he's ... he's gone. But I know who the elf was."

Renyra opened her mouth to respond, shock and confusion in her eyes, but Gellion shook his head and cut her off.

"There isn't time. You need to know." He glanced behind him to see the progress of the Dierna soldiers.

"It's Kaelo. I don't know how, and I have no idea why, but it was him."

Renyra stared at him. Beside her, Gellion saw Firas's face set in grim thought as his long legs carried him along with their pace.

"Kaelo?" Renyra said incredulously. "But—I thought he disappeared—centuries ago. Why would he be in Tala? Why would he destroy Daro?"

"I said I don't know!" Gellion replied in frustration. There was no time to think about it now. "But however he came by these powers and whatever his purpose, it can spell no good for the elves in Faeran." A sudden thought occurred to him. "Are there any ships remaining? You said most of the elves got out of the city—are they still there?"

"The ships anchored in the bay should be fine—they were far enough from the cliffs. There weren't many of them though, and for all I know the elves who stayed behind in the city may have taken them across the sea by now."

Gellion was furious with himself. He should have recognized Kaelo that night. He should have known, somehow, who was behind everything—his missing tunic, his dagger, the shadow trailing him around the city, the *power* behind the attacks. He had been too distracted by the Albaren, too stubborn and loath to allow the memories of his mentor back into his life, even after all these centuries.

But it still didn't make sense. Kaelo had been a truly gifted metalworker, yes, but to discover how to destroy vierstone and fell a city with the touch of a hand? How could he have come across such power? And what was the point? Why target Daro—a city the elves had built centuries after his banishment?

The thundering of the ground grew louder. Gellion careened sideways as a horse galloped past him, its rider swinging his sword at soldiers to either side. The hills leading to the mountains were close now. Just a bit further and they would be able to use the terrain to their advantage, find places to hide until the battle subsided.

Another horse ran past. The Dierna were catching up.

The panic among the fleeing elves and Albaren doubled. Soldiers ran in all directions, smashing into each other in their attempt to run from the horses and find the nearest way out of the fray. Gellion found himself buffeted back and forth. He kept his eyes on the peaks of the Falspires.

Renyra was no longer beside him. Even Firas evaded Gellion's view now. He scanned those around him but saw no sign of his friends. He kept running.

A dark head of hair bobbing ahead of him caught his eye. Squinting, Gellion made toward the elf, weaving, dodging, and ducking between soldiers and horses.

"Brother!" he shouted as he drew nearer. The elf's head turned sideways, but he apparently decided he had imagined the voice and continued forward.

"Veldon!" Gellion was sure it was him now.

Veldon spun around. Relief suffused his face when he saw Gellion, and he waited for him to catch up before turning back toward the mountains.

"Thank Riu!" Veldon said. "I feared the worst. I saw you at the front of the fighting before the Dierna charged from the hills. Are you hurt?" His eyes scanned Gellion as they ran.

"I'm fine. Have you seen Valder?"

"I lost him just a few moments ago. He was alright then. It's impossible to keep together in this mess."

"We're almost out of it. They won't follow us into the mountains."

"Hopefully." Veldon looked worried.

Gellion didn't hear the horse until it was right behind him. He turned to see flared nostrils in front of his face.

Before he could reach toward Veldon, before he could even shout a warning, pain exploded in the back of Gellion's head, and his vision flashed white, then black. He felt himself falling. Falling away from the pain, the noise, and the edges of the mountains just out of reach.

41

A FLEET OF SHIPS

Renyra sat on a pillow of vegetation, her knees drawn to her chest. She stared blankly at the darkening sky. The beginning flickers of stars winked in and out of existence as wispy clouds drifted past on the cooling night breeze.

She huddled close to the warm assurance of Firas. He was the only thing that was certain now. His presence anchored her to the present when her mind insisted on analyzing the past and imagining the future.

Other elves dotted the forested slope, huddled under trees and against rocks. Some nursed injuries, some shed silent tears of grief, others sat motionless, lost in their own thoughts and imaginings. Renyra knew few of the elves around her beyond casual recognition. Soran knelt beside another elf, talking to them in a low voice as they sipped at a canteen of water. The dark haired woman Renyra had so often seen with Gellion sat a few paces away with her legs crossed, staring at the ground and holding her knives absently to her sides.

The elves were without a leader, a home, or any idea of their remaining numbers. Renyra estimated a few hundred elves had gathered to this place throughout the evening. Was this all that remained? Were others still wandering the hills and mountainside, or even now making their way back to Daro? Did any elves lie alive on the battlefield, too injured to join their kin?

Renyra shuddered at the thought. Firas tightened his grip around her shoulders. There was nothing any of them could do if that was the case. Returning to the gates of Arvain would be suicide.

For what seemed the hundredth time, Renyra ran over the list of names in her head. Firas and Caerlyn were safe, but no elf had seen Gellion, Valder, or Veldon since the Dierna forces broke through the fleeing elves. Were they together? Were they in the mountains? Or would she never see any of them again?

Dulon was dead. Other elves had confirmed the terrible news and the circumstances in which it had happened. Renyra signed the star on her breast once again. Dulon had been a brave leader with a good heart and had died fighting for his people. Surely he would meet Riu with joy beyond this life? Tears rolled down her cheek as she thought of his grinning face.

She no longer had the energy to be angry. The Albaren had betrayed them. Kaelo, the infamous elf whom she alone had never heard of until weeks before, had destroyed Daro, and no one knew why or how. These were just facts. Facts that she had to accept. Facts she saw no point in questioning just now.

What was relevant now was deciding what to do next. The simple course of action was obvious—return to the ruins of Daro and pray there were still ships that could take them back to Faeran. They would dock in Tura and bring news of all that had happened since the Kindom Council.

It was a comforting thought. Responsibility would transfer to the Council Members of Faeran. Renyra would relay Gellion's words along with her own account, and then she and Firas would be free to build their life anew. Perhaps they would go to Telem Fier.

But the humid breeze of the mountains dragged Renyra back to reality. The elves were exhausted, afraid, without supplies, and surrounded by wilderness and enemies. Returning to Daro would be a long and difficult journey. They could not travel through Albarad. They would have to cross Restring Pass south to north, and go through the Falspires until they met the Icemelt River.

With Dulon gone and Gellion dead or missing, who remained to lead the journey? Renyra closed her eyes. She was the one who had brought the news of Daro. No elf knew the paths of the Falspires, but she knew the lands between the mountains and Daro better than most.

She just wanted to follow, to stop thinking and making decisions. She wanted to sleep.

No sooner had the thought entered her head, Renyra felt her eyelids grow heavy. The mental and physical demands of the last week settled over her like a heavy blanket. Her job was not done, but for the moment, the elves were as safe as they could hope. She allowed sleep to swallow her, falling into its soft embrace with relief.

The next day dawned bright and breezy, oblivious to the pain and fear of the elves. Warmth suffused the land within hours of the sun's rising, and birds wove their melodies through the rustling trees.

There was little preparation to do before beginning their journey. The elves had no supplies to pack. Renyra spread the word to gather among the trees.

By now, news of Daro's fate had spread, but Renyra announced it again, giving a short account of all she had seen. The elves listened with grim stares. Some eyes burned in anger, but most just bore deep sadness. Renyra outlined her course of action—to return to the ships of Daro and sail to Faeran. No one questioned her. There were no other options to propose. The elves could not wait in the mountains any longer. They would have to hope that any lost elves joined them along the journey or met them in Daro.

With no further preamble, the elves began to walk north.

The journey back took nearly two weeks. The Falspires proved a steep and rocky labyrinth difficult to traverse. More than once, the elves lost their sense of direction and had to double back after several hours' walking. The relief was palpable when they reached the mouth of the Icemelt and saw familiar scrubby hills in the distance.

As the elves neared Daro, malicious cries and glowing eyes began to plague the nights again. The creatures seemed even more numerous than before. With everything that had happened, Renyra had nearly forgotten about that particular problem. The elves set watches each night and surrounded their camp with fires.

Somehow, Renyra had hoped that when the elves finally reached Daro, it would still be there, standing strong on its cliffside awaiting their return—that the evening of destruction had been a terrible nightmare, and she had travelled through Albarad for nothing. She knew it was a false hope, yet when the elves at last reached the end of the Icemelt and saw the road break off at the edge of a jagged precipice, she mourned anew for her lost city.

More elves had joined the company along the journey, but their numbers were barely more than half what they had been when they left the gates of Daro three weeks before. Gellion and his brothers had never shown up.

The elves approached the cliffside in silence. What seemed like miles below, a crumbling heap of earth, rock, and rubble sloped into the lapping tide. There was no sign of the elves who had remained behind, but Renyra had not expected them to wait. It had been weeks since the fall of the city. They would have returned to Faeran by now.

She looked to the harbor, hoping to see a few ships remaining beyond the shattered docks, but what she saw instead brought hope to her aching heart. A fleet of ships sat anchored in the sea, sails of Tura flying on their masts.

The stranded elves had gone back to Faeran after all, but they had returned for their kin.

EPILOGUE

Gellion's head spun. He tried to focus on his surroundings, but the lamplight kept bending and stretching around the walls. He was sitting on a hard floor, as far as he could tell, with an equally hard wall behind him. Memories slowly trickled back into his mind. Horns. Horses. Running. Lots of running.

He groaned as he sat up straighter. Everything hurt.

A rustling sound broke through the fuzz of his brain and he started, wincing in pain. A figure lay on his back an arm's length away. Gellion blinked several times, and the form of Veldon clarified. His hands were behind his head and he was looking at Gellion.

"Good morning. I thought you would never wake properly."

It took a few moments for Gellion to make sense of the words.

"Properly?"

"You've been moaning and muttering. When they bandaged you, you tried to slap their hands away."

Gellion looked down at himself. He was still wearing his stained and torn clothes from the battle, but his armor was gone, and fresh bandages encased his left arm and his ribs.

"How long have we been here?" he asked. "Where is here?"

"A couple of days I think. They knocked me out too, so I'm not entirely sure." He sighed. "As for where we are, I assume in Arvain, though I do not speak human, and they show as little interest in speaking elvish."

Gellion rested his aching head against the stone wall behind him. What he wouldn't give to have a bit of Kaelo's power now. He would break out of this cell and bring the whole cursed city down on his way out. He shook his head in disgust. Two human prisons in as many months.

Now that his mind was clearing, anxiety began to fill it. What had happened to the rest of the elves? Had they escaped to the mountains? Were any others imprisoned? The anxiety deepened as he thought of Valder.

And what of Kyna?

He tried not to think of any of them.

The reality of Dulon's death hit him afresh, and he nearly gasped from the blow that seemed to have crashed into his stomach. He could feel panic starting to rise through the grief.

No.

None of these thoughts would help him get out of his current predicament. He needed to think.

They were in a Dierna prison. The rest of the elves were either dead or on their way back to the ruins of Daro, where they would take ships to Faeran.

A cold fear sparked in his chest. The other elves would think he and Veldon were dead. They would have no way of knowing they were imprisoned. If the elves took the last ships to Faeran, there would be no reason for them to return to the shores of Tala. Ever.

Gellion stood, swaying dangerously at the sudden movement.

"Hey now," Veldon said, scrambling to his feet to keep Gellion from toppling over.

Gellion ignored him and staggered to the narrow window of their cell. They had to get to Faeran. He had to warn the elves about Kaelo. What if Renyra hadn't made it out of the battle? No one would know what had happened in Daro or who had been responsible.

He raked his hands through his hair, letting out a snort of frustration.

None of them knew what Kaelo was capable of. And he had no idea what his old mentor's goal was. Whatever Kaelo's purpose, Gellion had no doubt it would not end at Daro. If Kaelo had gotten to Tala once, he would get back to Faeran, and when he did, he would be a threat to every elf of every Kindom.

Gellion clenched his jaw. He berated himself again. He should have known it was Kaelo. He should have stopped this before it began.

He hadn't.

But he would stop it now. He would get out of this. He would sail back to Faeran. And he would confront Kaelo as he should have done centuries before.

CHARACTER LIST

ELVES

Fieri

- Auralia (uh-rah-lee-uh): Fieri Council Member, Lady of Rone
- Caerlyn (kair-lihn): Sira performer, friend of Renyra and Firas
- Cuvan (koo-vahn): Fieri Council Member, Lord of Telem Fier
- Rhien (ree-ehn): hunter in patrol parties
- Renyra (reh-neer-uh): Sira performer, hunter, greenhouse worker, Firas's wife
- Soran (sor-an): greenhouse worker
- Torron (tor-on): gate guard
- Vayda (vay-duh): healer in the House of Healing

Morcani

- Aryn (ahr-ihn): builder and vierstone master
- Carvell (cahr-vel): Morcani conspirator
- Corron (cor-on): Morcani conspirator
- Dulon (doo-lon): Lord of Daro, host of the Kindom Council, Maranyl's husband
- Firas (feer-ahss): Renyra's husband, shipwright, Sira performer
- Lia (lee-uh): Morcani conspirator

- Lythin (lith-ihn): Miyela's assistant
- Maranyl (mahr-uh-nihl): Dulon's wife, engineer, musician
- Miyela (mee-yel-uh): Morcani Council Member, Lady of Morcanan

Remsgri

- Aiken (eye-kehn): electrician, craftsman competition entrant
- Baelik (bay-lik): hunter in patrol parties
- Rhosti (rah-stee): Remsgri Council Member, Lord of Remsgraen

Turi

- Carden (cahr-den): fisherman
- Eldian (ehl-dee-an): Lord of Maramor, father of Gellion, deceased
- Farra (fair-uh): Veldon's wife, lives in Maramor
- Gellion (gehl-ee-un): Daro Council Member, metalworker
- Kaelo (kay-lo): metalworker exiled by the Turi before the Great War
- Kyna (kihn-uh): visiting elf of the Kindom Council
- Liera (lirr-uh): Turi Council Member, Lady of Tura
- Malo (mal-oh): Sira performer, craftsman competition entrant
- Tenille (tehn-ihl): Turi Council Member, Lady of Maramor, Gellion's mother
- Tornac (tor-nak): Gellion's older brother, lives in Maramor
- Valder (vahl-durr): Gellion's younger brother, shipwright
- Veldon (vehl-duhn): Gellion's youngest brother, stoneworker, visitor from Maramor
- Vyra (veer-uh): Tornac's wife, deceased

Albaren

- Abramo, Elias: spice merchant on the Isle of Sapor, Marchon
- Arceria, Chiara: wife of Marchon Arceria
- Arceria, Nicabar: head of a wealthy trading family, Marchon
- Benta, Amadeo: Earl, messenger of King Naval
- Camersio, Durand: younger brother of Tarcin Camersio
- Camersio, Tarcin: head of a wealthy trading family, Marchon
- Cavalcont, Javan: wine merchant, Marchon
- Dacian, Nero: wine merchant, Marchon
- Father Alban: cleric in Tradira
- Naval, Danelo: King of Albarad
- Orien: servant at the Dacian Ball
- Saprio, Sergus: Duke of Sapor, spice merchant
- Sartor, Arturo: head of a steam engine empire, Marchon
- Vensure, Justus: military commander of Tradira
- Vespa, Solan: financial advisor to the king, one of the Heads of the Bank

If you enjoyed

ESSENCE OF STONE

Look out for Book II of the Lifestone Trilogy:

Sneak peak of chapter one follows...

ASHES OF STONE PREVIEW

1. A TRAITOR

The doors before Gellion were simple, yet somehow elegant. Crisp paint lined a border that wandered over the top and sides of each panel. The doors were clean. Proud. At the prison guard's touch, they swung forward on silent hinges.

Gellion took a deep breath and let it out in a controlled stream. This was not the first time he had stood before a human leader to defend himself, nor was it the first time the safety and livelihood of the elves depended upon his amicable release from prison. How did this keep happening?

He limped slightly as he crossed polished wood to the man standing at the room's head. Aside from this man, the hall was empty. Wide windows lined the back wall, looking over a lake that could have passed for the sea. Its surface, ruffled with waves, stretched to a distant haze.

Gellion's head and ribs still ached from the battle. Had it been only a few days since Gellion's world crashed around him? It could have been a week as far as he knew. Both Gellion and his brother had woken in their cell to the monotonous passing of the sun on an unknown day, and their human guards had not deigned to enlighten them on the happenings of the outside world. Part of Gellion didn't want to know. He didn't want to know if Valder were dead—or Firas, or Kyna, or any of the rest of his friends, family, or kin. For all Gellion knew, they were all back to Daro by now. Gellion's breath caught in his throat.

What was once Daro.

He blinked hard. No. He could not think about that now.

With a massive effort of will, Gellion anchored himself to the present. None of the rest of it mattered if he couldn't get out of this city, if he couldn't get back to Faeran before it was too late.

Gellion stopped several paces away from who he assumed was the leader of Arvain. The man stood with both feet firmly planted on the floor; there were no chairs in the room. His face was lined, and his hair was a matte of silver streaked with grey, but his eyes were bright and intelligent. They held Gellion's gaze.

"Your name?" He spoke in lightly accented Albaren, the trade language of the humans.

"Gellion."

The man nodded slowly. "I am Eurig."

Silence followed. Gellion shifted his weight, concentrating on keeping eye contact with Eurig. Was he supposed to acknowledge the man somehow? He inclined his head.

Eurig only looked at him.

"You are the—king?" Gellion said.

Eurig let out a puff of air. "We do not have kings. I am the head of the Elder Clan. The Lawgiver." His eyes continued to bore into Gellion, as though trying to read his soul. At last he spoke again. "Why did the elves ally with the Albaren?"

Gellion almost flinched. It was a question he had been expecting, and one that had haunted his waking hours for days. Why had the elves allied with the Albaren? If Gellion had voted 'no' that day—what now seemed years ago—would he be standing in Daro now? Would Daro itself still stand? Would Dulon—

No. Don't think about it.

"The elves are no friends of the Albaren," Gellion said.

"Yet you accompanied their army to our doorstep."

Gellion hesitated. "Yes."

Eurig raised his eyebrows.

"The elves have traded with the Albaren for centuries," Gellion said, "but we have had little contact with them otherwise. King Naval came to us, asking for our aid, claiming that the Dierna were raiding their villages, killing innocents, cheating them in trade, and encroaching upon their borders."

Eurig's face remained calm, but a fire burned deep in his eyes.

"Did he, now?" he said softly.

"We agreed to help the Albaren based upon their word." Gellion's nails bit into his palms. "Then they betrayed us."

Eurig's brows twitched upward again. He remained silent.

"They turned on us in the middle of the battle."

"Any who trust the Albaren are fools," Eurig said. "Yet ignorance is no excuse for your actions. The Dierna expected an army of two thousand Albaren. Instead we met nearly three thousand in addition to an army of elves. Still, we took the day because we planned for treachery, and we were not disappointed."

A shudder rippled down Gellion's spine. He could still hear the braying of horns just before the Dierna reinforcements had charged from the hills, scattering both the elves and the Albaren like a school of fish among sharks. Yet that memory alone was not what made his blood run cold. As the horns reverberated in his mind, a painfully sharp image of Dulon's face followed, blood streaked and staring, his easy smile lost to Riu forever.

"All the same," Eurig continued. "I lost a quarter of my army in that battle. Men, women. Members of my clan and of Ash Clan. Fathers. Mothers. Sons. Daughters."

Gellion's heart was thudding against his chest. The Dierna had been the enemy. They had raided innocent villages. The elves had fought for what was right. They had fought for vierstone.

A vierstone quarry that never existed.

Gellion took a steadying breath. Not now. Not in front of the clan leader. He could not show weakness.

"The elves pose no further threat to the Dierna," Gellion said. "What remains of the army you saw is gone—returning to our lands. I am sorry for the death we have caused. Please—" Gellion paused, swallowing his anger and pride and guilt in a dry throat. "I humbly ask that you would allow us—my brother and me—to return to our people. We will bring no further harm to your clan."

Eurig raised an eyebrow. His eyes were an icy grey, somehow more disconcerting than the muddy depths of the Albaren's. With a last considering look, Eurig's gaze wandered to the side, sliding out of focus.

"The elves." He spoke as though to himself. "We have heard of the elves, though until recently, none of us had seen them. The Albaren traders wove tales—wild and colorful. Tales of the elves of the north—the faeries, the creatures whose faces do not grow old and whose powers transcend the will of the Almighty."

Gellion stiffened. How long had the humans brooded on these fanciful legends of the elves? His people had never paid much heed to the humans, content to politely ignore them in all matters beyond trade, yet somehow that passivity had bred tales of mystery, hostility, and fear. Gellion had been shocked by the attitude and accusations of the Albaren. The elves were not heathens or demons.

Eurig turned his head sharply back to Gellion. "Who are the elves? Where do you come from and what do you want in this land?"

Gellion did not answer at once, taken aback by the sudden change in Eurig's tactic.

"The elves come from a land far from here," he said slowly, choosing his words with care. "We built a city on the northern coast of Albarad for purposes of our own, but that purpose is now—"

That purpose is now destroyed.

"Now—fulfilled," he said. "The elves are leaving this land, never to return."

Eurig narrowed his eyes, clearly not appeased by Gellion's enigmatic answer.

"Why should I believe that? You come here with an army and no explanation, then claim that the elves are truly a peaceful folk, homebound, never to bother us again?"

Heat crept up Gellion's neck. "I told you, the Albaren—"

Eurig held up a hand to stop him. "I know what you told me." His eyes bored into Gellion. "Do you know why the Dierna were prepared for your attack?"

Gellion opened his mouth to answer, then closed it. The elves and the Albaren had emerged from the hills before the gates of Arvain to see a full army waiting for their surprise attack. Gellion had briefly wondered who had betrayed the Albaren, but the question had become lost in the midst of much more pressing matters.

Eurig scrutinized Gellion's face, as though watching for his reaction. "Well?" he said.

"I—" Gellion shook his head. "I assumed it was an Albaren traitor, or a Dierna spy."

Eurig's eyes narrowed further. "It was neither."

Gellion looked at Eurig, trying to understand what the man was getting at.

"It was no Albaren, and it was no Dierna," Eurig repeated. "It was an elf."

Gellion stood stunned.

Every nerve in his body reacted to the word. A chill spread over his skin.

An elf? But why? *How?* In the two centuries of their time in Tala, the elves had never made contact with the Dierna. What possible motivation would have driven one of Gellion's own people to warn the Dierna of an Albaren attack? An attack that the elves were a part of? It had been no secret that many of the elves in Daro did not approve of the alliance with Albarad, but to sabotage a battle in which their own kin's lives were at stake?

Eurig watched him. "An elf comes to my people, warning us of an impending Albaren attack and passing us inside information, then an army of elves shows up on our doorstep standing beside the very enemy they had betrayed. An enemy you now claim betrayed you." A corner of his mouth twitched upward. "You see, then, why I am reluctant to believe the plausibility of your story."

At last Gellion found his voice, plucking a single question from the tangle in his mind.

"Who was the elf?"

"You claim that you did not know of this?"

"I didn't," Gellion growled, fighting to control the rising heat in his chest. "Who were they? When did they contact you? How did they contact you?"

"Enough." Eurig's voice echoed through the empty hall. The guards standing back from Gellion straightened, strengthening their grip on their swords.

"I did not bring you here to ask me questions," said Eurig. "How am I to trust the word of a race pleading innocence by ignorance and victimization by deceit when one of that race warned me of an attack they failed to mention they were a part of?" He chuckled without humor. "I cannot even phrase it in a way that does not sound ridiculous. What game are the elves playing?"

"I knew nothing of this. *We* knew nothing of this. I swear to you—I don't know who the elf was who contacted you, but they spoke with no authority for Daro. All that I told you is true. The elves acted as we thought was right. We placed our trust in the wrong people. Please. You must release us. Our people are in danger. We have to return to our home."

"Release you?" It was as close as Eurig had come to shouting. He took a breath and lowered his shoulders. "You give me no satisfactory answers and you expect me to trust your word that the elves are no threat to Diernas? I ask again. Where do you come from and why are you here?"

Gellion's head pounded, and a restless energy born of anger and fear clawed at his skin. He could not tell Eurig the truth. This entire disaster had sprung from a single human king learning about vierstone. To explain the elves' secrets to an equally powerful human leader would be madness.

But Gellion had to get back to Faeran.

Kaelo's face flashed before his eyes. Was the mentor of Gellion's youth still in Tala? Had he already secured passage to Faeran in whatever way he had come to this continent in the first place? Or was his revenge —or whatever motivation fueled his actions—complete at the destruction of Daro and its beloved vierstone?

"I cannot tell you," Gellion said. "I'm sorry, but I must protect my people."

Eurig's face was a mask of stoicism. "And I must protect mine," he said shortly. "I will not release traitors and secret keepers who threaten the safety and livelihood of the Dierna."

By unspoken order, the guards to either side of Gellion stepped forward and turned him back toward the entrance to the hall.

"Listen to me!" Gellion shouted, resisting the guards and facing Eurig again. "You have to let us go! You have to believe me! If we stay here even a week it will be too late!"

Eurig made no answer. The guards forcibly turned Gellion's shoulders and pushed him in front of them as they walked.

Gellion's heart beat to the time of his steps. Fighting would get him nowhere, but neither would sitting in a locked cell. He would find a way to get out of this city. He had to.

The prison was a short walk down the street. The road was wide and cobbled, with people and horses passing purposefully up and down its surface. Gellion watched them. Most wore plain clothes of simple wool or linen. All stared as he passed.

The guards stopped in front of a wide door with iron locks. At a hefty pull, the door swung outward with a groan.

Stale air hung like a moth ridden blanket inside the prison entrance. Within, sunlight faded, and the merry sounds of livelihood from the street muted to a distant memory. The guards pushed Gellion ahead of them and marched him through two gates of iron that separated the main doors from the prison halls beyond. Gellion glanced into a large common room to the left of the main entrance. Bars of sunlight striped across couches and game tables, and a great fireplace blazed on the far wall. Several men in crisp uniform lounged about the space and blew smoke from pipes.

"You are not here to sightsee," one of Gellion's guards said gruffly, pushing him past the common room and toward the stairs at the end of the hallway.

Veldon's eyes flicked up as Gellion slipped through the door to their cell. A clang and catch behind him sealed their captivity. Gellion paced to the high window across from the door and huffed in frustration.

"Went well, did it?" Veldon said. He was leaning against a wall, fiddling with an earring of green stone between his fingers.

Gellion said nothing. The silhouette of a bird passed over the slice of sky beyond the window, letting out a joyful caw. Gellion thought of the soaring seabirds of Daro. His fists clenched.

"Well, what did he say?"

"We aren't going anywhere." Gellion sighed. "The clan leader fears the elves are a threat to Diernas and wants information on Faeran and the elves as a whole. I gave him nothing, and he did not like it."

Veldon nodded. "Fair enough."

Gellion rounded on Veldon. "Fair enough!?"

"What would you say if a mysterious nation of humans came to Faeran under banners of war, then ran back across the sea, pleading that they never meant any harm?"

"That's not what we did."

"It's a bit of what we did."

Gellion's stare was murderous.

"I'm not saying you should have told him anything more," Veldon said quickly. "I'm merely pointing out that his reaction is rational given his understanding of the circumstances."

"I told him what happened. I told him about King Naval's accusations against the Dierna, of the alliance, of their betrayal. We were greater victims of this fight than the Dierna!"

"Did he believe you?"

"I don't know." Gellion ran a hand through his hair. "There was more to it than that."

Veldon's brows drew together. "What do you mean?"

"Eurig—that's the clan leader—says that someone gave the Dierna inside information about this Albaren attack, and it was no Albaren or Dierna."

Veldon's eyes widened. They were almost greener than the vierstone in his hand and matched their brother Valder's with shocking precision. Gellion turned away, pressing down the well of anxiety threatening to rise into his throat. If Valder was dead, it would be his fault. His mother would never forgive him. He would never forgive himself.

"An elf?" Veldon's voice was barely a whisper.

Gellion nodded.

"But who?"

"I don't know. Eurig would give no details."

Veldon shook his head. "I don't understand. Why would an elf betray the attack? And judging from the size of the Dierna army, they must have known weeks, maybe even months in advance. Do you think the elf may have tipped them off before we even accepted the alliance with Albarad?"

"Why? As an anonymous benefactor to a nation they had never even seen?"

Veldon rolled his vierstone earring between his fingers. Looking down at it, he said, "Could it have been the same elf who caused the earthquakes and destroyed Daro?"

Gellion stiffened. He himself had not known of Daro's destruction until just before the end of the battle days before. Renyra, a Fieri elf and the wife of one of Gellion's closest friends, had stayed behind in the city with a broken arm while most of the elves marched to battle. Mere days after their departure, the elf responsible for the last month of inexplicable earthquakes and dying vierstone had sent the city crumbling into the sea. Renyra had ridden across all of Albarad to bring the news of Daro's destruction to Gellion and Dulon, but she had arrived in the midst of battle. Gellion had told Veldon of Daro's fate, but had left out the detail that he knew who had caused all of it.

As soon as Renyra had described the man who sent Daro into the sea, Gellion had known who it was. He knew who had somehow acquired the ability to break stone and metal at a touch, render vierstone black and lifeless, and tear a city apart at its foundations. He should have realized it long before. The shocking reappearance of Gellion's past mentor still made his head spin and tied his stomach in knots. Kaelo had been banished centuries before the Great War for the unthinkable crime of murder, and had not been seen for over six hundred years.

"It could have been the same elf," Gellion said vaguely.

"I have been thinking about the elf. He must have known the city would be deserted. Maybe he had something to do with the alliance."

"The Albaren proposed that alliance to weaken the Dierna and to rid Tala of the elves in one fell swoop. It was entirely for their own purposes."

"But they knew about vierstone." Veldon held up his earring as illustration. "You said yourself that neither you nor Dulon ever told the Albaren about vierstone, yet they knew to use it as a bargaining chip. Only an elf could have told them that, and if it was neither of you, it must have been someone else."

Gellion frowned. Could Kaelo have told the Albaren about vierstone—orchestrated the battle just to empty Daro? The alliance had done more than present an abandoned city. The decision to join the alliance had caused a rift through the elves like Gellion had not seen since the Great War.

"But why would the same elf warn the Dierna of the alliance he had endorsed?" Gellion said.

"A penchant for mischief?" Veldon smiled weakly. "Alright, I don't know," he said to Gellion's sour expression.

Gellion put his back to the wall and slid down next to Veldon. The susurrus of conversation from the streets below carried through the thick glass of the window. Veldon tilted his head down and refastened his earring, then leaned back and stared at the ceiling.

"Do you think any of it was true?" he asked softly.

"Any of what?"

"The raids. The murder and the rape and everything else the Albaren accused the Dierna of committing."

"I don't know."

"The Dierna have not presented themselves as a barbarous race so far."

"No, they haven't. But they were no merciful servants of Riu in battle either. Vensure—" Gellion paused, a flare of hatred catching the name in his throat. He had never liked the Albaren commander, but now he hoped the man's soul would rot in hell for what he had done to Dulon.

"Vensure expected to see Dierna outposts in Restring Pass. He was a treacherous viper, but I don't think he fabricated the Albaren's grievances against the Dierna. The Albaren would have fought that battle without the elves, I'd wager. They just would have been denied the double victory they hoped for." He slammed a fist into the floor. "I really don't care a whit what the Dierna or Albaren have or haven't done or why they did it. I care about being free of them both and crossing the

Semestral Sea before Kae ..." he caught himself, "before the elf works the same devilry in Faeran as he did in Daro. Before the last elven ships in Tala leave us here for lost."

Veldon hugged his knees to his chest. "They must think us dead." He turned his eyes on Gellion, pain and pleading in their depths. "What must Valder think? What if the elves send word to mother and Tornac when they get to Tura?"

Gellion's face softened. His brother's blind faith that Valder was still alive, mourning them for dead, wrenched his heart.

"All the more reason to get back to them soon."

Veldon did not look comforted. "When do you think the elves will leave Tala?"

"It took us about six days to get here from Daro on foot. But the elves won't be able to take the road back through Albarad, and some of them may be hurt. All the same, I expect they will set sail as soon as they get to Daro, so long as there are still ships in the harbor. In that case, we would have to travel fast to catch them now."

"And if it's too late?"

"We find another way." Gellion spoke the words with as much confidence as he could muster, but he had no idea what that other way would be. They needed to leave now. They needed to catch the elves before they took the last ships across the sea. Riu knew how long it would be before he and Veldon could find alternate passage, and come autumn, the Semestrial Sea would be impassible for half a year.

"Is there any reasoning with Eurig?" Veldon asked.

"Not without telling him everything about the elves and threatening the safety of Faeran further. Even then, I don't think he would release us in the next few days. He's sharp—shrewd. It will take some serious convincing to depart Arvain on amicable terms."

Veldon took a deep breath, releasing his knees and turning to face Gellion. A smile played at the corners of his mouth.

"Then we will have to escape."

ACKNOWLEDGMENTS

Writing a book is the most amazing and frustrating and wonderful thing. While most of the long hours are spent in solitude, it is astounding how many people it takes to turn an idea and some words into a novel.

There were those who helped shape the book itself—the words, the art, and the story. Equally important were those who supported me through the years of creating—the writing, the editing, the laughing and crying and fist shaking and celebrating. Thank you all. I couldn't have done it without you.

To Pamela, thank you for supporting this project and every project I have ever endeavored to pursue. To David, thank you for sharing your love of literature with me the last twenty-eight years and for being my first reader and reviser when my story was still a mess to behold.

Thank you Emma, for your words of encouragement each time I realized anew how hard writing a book was. You are an inspiration and a true friend.

Thank you Jake, for everything. For sharing me with my characters and my computer screen and supporting me in everything I do with undeserved confidence.

To my editor, Al, thank you for your hours of work and attention to detail, and your ability to see the art beyond grammar. To Grace, thank you for your beautiful illustrations that captured the world in my head more perfectly than I could have imagined.

Last, but certainly dear to my heart, I want to thank the authors of every fantasy book I have ever read for showing me the beauty, magic, and power of stories. There are too many to name, but your influence shaped my world.

ABOUT THE AUTHOR

Haley Rylander is an author and a book lover, as well as an aerial circus artist, scientist, and slightly obsessive dog owner. It is her goal to write inspiring stories set in other worlds that reflect our own world in ways that can only be achieved through the magic and power of words. Haley lives in upstate New York with her husband. This is her first novel.

haleyrylander.com

facebook.com/AuthorHaley

www.ingramcontent.com/pod-product-compliance
Lightning Source LLC
Chambersburg PA
CBHW022018300726
48970CB00003B/941